To Andi[illegible]

best wishes

Zoe Simps

“She had been forced into prudence in her youth,
she learned romance as she grew older.”
Anne Elliott, in Austen, J. (1818). Persuasion.

“Experience is the name everyone gives to their mistakes.”
Wilde, O. (1892). Lady Windermere’s Fan.

“There are hopes of her being forgiven in time.”
Frederick Wentworth, in Austen, J. (1818). Persuasion.

"What fun to find some serious psychology of behavior change within a novel of a baby boomer returning to the University, facing life-transforming experiences inside and outside of the classroom." James O Prochaska.

A MATTER OF DEGREE

a novel
by

ZOE SIMPSON

First published 2008 by Fossil-Imprints
PO Box 366, Southampton, SO32 1WP

ISBN 978-0-9558404-0-1 (UK)

A CIP catalogue record for this book is available from the British Library.

Words from *I know him so well* quoted by kind permission of
Sir Tim Rice and Heartaches Limited.
Words from *Can't get you out of my mind* written by Matt Hales and Ben Hales, performed by Aqualung and published by Warner Chappell, 2002.
The *Journal of Happiness Studies* is published by Springer Science and Business Media.
Cover photograph by kind permission of Calshot Activities Centre.

Typeset by Fossil-Imprints, Southampton
Printed and bound in Great Britain by
RPM print & design Ltd., Chichester, West Sussex
on paper from sources managed to FSC rules.

To Lynette, who said: 'Never say never.'

To Kathy, who said: 'You'll do it somehow.'

To Dr James O Prochaska, who showed me how.

And to all baby-boomers who grew up with St Ignatius Loyola's prayer worming into our subconscious. All together now:

"... *To give and not to count the cost;*
To fight and not to heed the wounds;
To toil and not to seek for rest;
To labour and not to ask for any reward,
save that of knowing that we do Thy will."

CONTENTS

PART ONE
Introduction
1.1

'You OK?' I couldn't read Xiu's unlined face, but her soapy hand brushing against my forearm was comforting.

'Yeah, fine thanks.' I turned back to stowing wine glasses and swallowed.

My body was laced into its annual Mother Christmas outfit. You know, the one which rides through Christmas with a container load of tension sunk within a calm sea of capability. I couldn't open the container, just yet.

'Any more washing-up, Nessie?'

'No, everything's just about done, thanks.' The three Chinese students kissed me damply, before leaving me to pick their way up the pontoon and back to the International Hostel.

It didn't take long to collapse back down the rest of a Christmas conjured from a small space on Mum's narrow boat. I put away the washed dishes. I knotted a black bin liner messy with disposable plates, mince pie wrappers and chestnut shells ready to take up to the Marina's refuse area. I added an ASDA Cava bottle for the recycling bin.

What with the condensation on the barge's portlights, the three Blu-tacked gold chains had half-masted themselves. I dumped them in the recycling bag over scrunched-up wrapping paper, party-popper nests and fractured cracker bodies. And that was me, done. I couldn't bear to dump £6.99's worth of potted, frosted mini-tree. Not yet, anyway.

Outside, stars didn't shine through the nebula of the city as I plodded up through the marina. Downstream, hardly any houses showed coloured lights. It wasn't the sort of neighbourhood to host flashing Santa Claus and reindeer competitions. Even the two waterfront pubs were dark, tonight. Only the tallest crane in the city shone out above the Three Kings pub, holding a tiny, lit tree aloft.

Around ten-thirty, left with confetti-ed paper and the odd dab of Xmas pud mashed into the carpet, I'd had enough. Nutrasweet programmes with glitter might have distracted me, but I didn't have a television on board. I lay on the saloon berth, staring at my Christmas letter.

My three young Chinese friends had read the draft, asking about my family, giggling even more than usual after two glasses of wine and several liqueur chocs.

> *'Leah finished Uni with a first and is travelling in South America. She is currently working in a monkey sanctuary in Guatemala.*
> *Benjie returned safely from gapping in Africa. He scraped into medical school in London. He has joined every club going, but left the tuba at home (unfortunately). This Christmas sees him on a rugby tour of South Africa.*
> *Ella (Mother) is still going strong. She sold her house to live on a canal barge in the City marina (when she's not flitting round India).'*

Mum, Benjie, and then Leah pierced the day with excited phone calls. From the sound of their exotic Christmas Days, none of them echoed my emptiness.

I'd concocted a jolly English day for my guests, with a thrifty tin-foil turkey breast and all-the-trimmings. Now my chattering surrogate family's warmth had faded into utter stillness in the cabin. Even the road across the dock sounded subdued.

I'd left my husband out of the reckoning all day.

'Paul lost his job in April after eighteen years, when production moved to China.
Thanks to the redundancy payment, he is enjoying a few months pottering round the do-it-yourself jobs in the house. He is taking his time, looking for the right opportunity.'

Well, what else could I write in my Christmas letter? The truth? My husband is a depressed control freak intent on decimating our house and marriage? Of course not. Doesn't everyone write spin?

He hadn't phoned me. I hadn't phoned him. I'd doodled that skinny Christmas tree in the margin last week. I highlighted its boxes and baubles in fluorescent pink and lemon and swallowed a bolus of despair. The Paul situation would have to be faced at some stage. Not now.

'As for me, I've started an MSc in Exercise Science at the university. It's interesting and fun, if a little scarey.'

A tad understated. Bare survival, more like. I seemed to be two people these days. One was the traditional letter-writing mum, anchor-point for a family free-ranging over the planet. Another me drifted, a dithery shade, temporarily released to live in the City marina as a student.

I wasn't making much of a job of post-modern womanhood. One C grade and a gamut of embarrassingly dyspraxic incidents stretched across my first term. And as for the assumptions I'd made about Nick … My toes curled up my hut socks like beleaguered hedgehogs. Even so, as a vision … independence was … enticing. I promised to sort

myself out, toughen up and try a lot harder come January 1st.
Then I howled into the dregs of my merry Christmas.

1.2

1st October

I loaded my new student rucksack. Reversed out between our semi-det and the hawthorn hedge and turned down a mist-streaked lane.

This is it. I am a new woman, at last. I took a calming, confident swallow, then double-checked:

Sandwiches, water? Yes.

Cigarettes? Yes.

Paper, pens? Yes.

Everything, yes?

No.

I faltered two miles towards the motorway, doubt snitching in under my bra. Radio 4 cut in with the eight o'clock pips.

My internally panic-fired, central-heating boiler ignited. Whoomph.

Where the bloody hell's my purse?

My brain switched itself into automatic flustered mode, a place where nothing worked properly for days on end. 'Please God … not today.'

I shunted round in a fourteen-point turn. Back at the driveway, my newly-washed Smart car skidded through the gravel.

'Paul, have you seen my purse anywhere?'

My husband of thirty years glanced up calmly from toast and *The Building Regulations, 2000*. 'I thought you'd gone. No, sorry.' He lowered the thinning grey patch on top back to vertical.

Panic blocked my windpipe. 'Student Card, credit cards, money. Mobile. Disappeared off the face of the earth.'

'I don't think you should go without them. When did you last have ...?'

Truisms were the last thing I needed. 'I don't know!' I snapped. 'If I knew that, I'd have everything in my hand right now.'

'Have you looked ...?' He put down his triangle of toast, a neat mousehole bitten from the middle. 'Oh ... let me look. You really should be more careful, love.'

I followed his pill-spotted working fleece into the dank utility cupboard. The cat froze, tongue extended, leg vertically stretched.

'Manx! Get off the dirty washing.' Bums up, we tunnelled in from either end.

'They do exist. They must be here somewhere.'

'Bollocks!'

Paul excavated methodically through yesterday's jeans. 'Here's your mobile but not your purse, I'm afraid.'

Skeins of icy heat tingled round my heart and down my fingers. 'Shit, Paul, what do I do now? I should've left at eight.'

'Hang on.' The kitchen reverberated as he leapt the stairs, two at a time. The stairs creaked as he thumped singly down in his woolly socks. 'Here, take this tenner.'

'Thanks, darling.' I breathed again, zipping the note inside my Gardener's World waterproof jacket, next to the fag packet.

'Calm down, Nessie.' A workmanlike hand reached out for my hair.

I ducked away. 'Not my ... ninety pounds' worth!'

'Ninety pounds! We can't afford that sort of ...'

'Cheapest I could find ... Do I look OK?'

He squeezed my arm. 'Of course. You'd better get a move on. The motorway will be bad. Are you sure you're alright? …'

We notched habitual mouths.

'… Phone me with any problems … You *have* got credit on your mobile?'

'Yeah, don't worry … I'm fine now, thanks.'

At eight twenty-one I departed, redolent of menopause.

***

The city emerged from an indentation in the hills. In the distance, pearly skyscrapers balanced on the mist like shining Oxford spires, waiting for me.

Nine-fourteen. The traffic snailed down the approach road. I lit a cigarette and breathed a mite easier: maybe I could still make ten o'clock. This time, I wasn't delivering Leah or Benjie to university, car loaded with student jetsam. Somehow, I'd coaxed the money from our bank account to be a student for myself.

Thirty minutes later and three fags later, I inched left to a multi-storey car park. Navigating narrow ramps and parking weren't my strongest points. I left Smartie askew in a miniscule bay between two Chelsea tractors. That'll do, I thought, flinging down four flights of echoing concrete stairwell. At the bottom, the ticket machine read four minutes to ten.

'Eighteen pounds for twenty-four hours!' Oh my God, it would have to do until lunchtime. Map in one hand and rucksack on my shoulder, I fled back to the jumble of shops and cafés and panted uphill to the university.

The newly-built sports centre jostled with students. Without my card, I couldn't swipe into the Department. No smoking. Still puffing, I queued. Sweat trickled down my chest under my new Penn State U look-alike sweater. I fidgeted my hair five minutes round the minimalist clock, more like a boiler about to blow than an embryonic academic. Wherever had the confident new woman gone?

'Here's the lecture theatre,' the receptionist smirked. She held open an inconspicuous door for me to tiptoe through. There wasn't time to take a deep breath or square my shoulders. The world glanced over, then looked away politely, which told me all I needed to know about my appearance.

I shoehorned into a stifling, sloping room, crammed with students. Half a dozen late arrivals propped against light walls. Two girls bent over mobiles. Could this really be the vast lecture theatre I'd seen on their open day? A God-like male voice, somewhere in the blur of people down the front, dropped nuggets into a tinnitus hum of air conditioning.

Bit by bit, I deflated, until my ears switched into listening mode. '... the busiest year of your life. As well as completing six modules and assignments, you will need to programme time for a research proposal, data gathering and analysis, plus writing a twenty thousand word dissertation.'

In a moment, the Voice sabotaged my dreams of a civilized, scholastic life of quiet, diligent endeavour. My vision wobbled; my kneecaps twitched uncontrollably.

'A Department of Exercise and Health Science is an exciting academic environment. Live, breathe, and eat it. Sleep later. I'm sure you will enjoy your MSc year with us ...'

***

A forty-ish woman perched on the café stool next to me. I eased my sweatshirt over my brown polyester trousers.

'Who was that?'

'Ron Rawlins. Professor.'

'Ah. Yes.' I sipped my first carton of filter coffee. 'I missed some of his talk. How do we know where to go next?'

'It's all up on the website.' Hers was decaff.

'Website?'

'Yes, preliminary reading, details of the modules, deadlines, exam …' The outside corner of her eyelid twitched as she talked, that first day. '…everything you need to know. Haven't you seen the website?'

'The university website?' The morning had already whirled itself from my grasp.

'No, the student section of the Department's ... oh, I'll show you later. You can use a computer, can't you?'

'Oh, of course.' I glimpsed my worn brown trainers, next to her crisp black pumps, perched on the bar stool's chrome frame. 'So that's why I wasn't sent a reading list. What else did I miss first thing, er, Cathy?'

'Oh. Just safety stuff. You know, the usual unlikely scenarios. What to do if there's a bomb threat from Animal Rights activists. Exit and muster points, if there's a fire.' She smiled at me from her knowledgeable height. 'Just follow everyone else. What are you thinking of doing for your dissertation?'

'D .. d .. dis…?' Dissertation plans on her first day? Had I heard her properly?

'My BSc dissertation was about self-efficacy for competitive women's games,' she ploughed on. The three other mature students' voices scrambled in my other ear. I had to concentrate to hear. She smoothed back a glossy chestnut mane with a competent, well-kept hand. 'Of course, I only got a 2:1 for it, just missed a First. My participants were too good. There wasn't enough range.'

I shoved despairing lowlights behind my ear. 'Self-efficacy? What's that?'

'Oh, don't you know? You're not a psychologist then?'

By this time I was a free-fall sky diver. 'I'm not anything at the moment. Well, other than an ex-PE teacher, that is.'

'Is that why you came on the course?'

'Yeah, I'm …' My er, practical fingers combed the other side of my hair. Could I really say I'd suddenly envied my daughter on her graduation day? 'I'm looking for a new start, now my kids have left home.' I still couldn't squash down the fuzzy hammer that thumped my chest when I remembered. *Kids have left home.*

'Well, self-efficacy is your self-confidence, your belief in your ability to do something. Bandura, 1986. Very famous theory. You're not pulling my leg, are you?'

'No, 'fraid not. It's thirty-five years since I last read a psychology text book.' I hoped my smile was casual.

'Really?' Her dark red lips pursed. 'Oh … I finished my degree two years ago, in Birmingham.'

'Perhaps you could bring me up to date on … everything else that's changed, then,' I said weakly, my unlabelled parcel of self-efficacy already lost in transit.

***

My random access memory clogged by lunchtime. I loped off to rescue Smartie. Half an hour of enforced Scout's pace back to the Sports Centre re-hydrated my morning sweat. Students milled around, but none I recognized. Still trotting, I found an IT classroom, like a converted nuclear bunker beneath a row of Victorian houses, half a mile down the road.

Jonathan Griffiths, the lecturer, clicked the door behind me. 'Here we are. Very last copy of our handbook on the network and e-mail system.'

I trudged into page one of thirty-two.

'You need … log on first,' whispered a young Chinese voice from the next computer.

I squinted at the screen, where tiny icons blurred and collapsed on me. For some time, I'd held school books further and further away as I read. Now it came home, that if I was to read grown-up print, I'd have to acquire reading glasses, urgently.

I probed the depths of my rucksack, searching for my notebook. My new tin cascaded with a tinny clang. A Retro pen from Benjie and seven-fifty's worth of change spilled over the carpet. My missing purse revealed itself from the rucksack's front netting. Eyes peered round computer screens. Jonathan's shaved head bobbed resignedly.

What a dolt. 'Err, sorry everyone.'

Burning-faced, I scrabbled for my errant belongings. I fumbled my student card back in the purse, avoiding the eyes of the startled rabbit in the photograph. Shopping list, Nessie. I scribbled down *Boots*. By the time I'd read how to log on, Xiu, the Chinese girl, had finished Jonathan's tasks and was activating her Athens password.

Afterwards, I trailed Cathy's nipped-in waist back to a windowless MSc workroom, secreted in the hushed, open-plan.

'Cathy, I can log on!' I navigated to the Department's web-site, an e-scholar at last. Cathy answered her e-mails and searched Web of Knowledge for her first set of research articles.

Ten minutes later, she stood up, slipping a skinny notebook in her handbag. 'Are you alright, now?'

'Great, thanks. I'm on to compiling the e-mail list.' Suddenly the instructions made sense. In slow-motion and squinting, maybe, but I was rolling.

'I have to get into town before the shops close. I'll leave you to it, then.'

'Thanks for all your help. See you tomorrow.'

The web site provided e-mail addresses for the lecturers. I'll use those, I decided, typing in the first name, Scott Woodhouse.

Suddenly, it flooded through, too urgent to ignore. I'd already missed six or seven cigarettes. A dull ache infiltrated my brain. Every body fibre tensed, craving nicotine. My mouth salivated for the dry touch of the paper; my tongue lusted for the round perfection of a cigarette.

Why not? The room's empty, I reasoned. The corridor outside's quiet. I can use one hand to type. Still concentrating on the screen, I groped in my jacket pocket for fags, then sat back for a moment to light up. The first drag of smoke soothed my throat. In five seconds, it permeated through the rest of my being. That's better. Turning back to the keyboard, I entered the names with two fingers from my left hand.

A thin wail pin-pricked my concentration. They're testing the alarms, I thought idly, pondering a name for the e-mail group. Just like school. The sound reverberated into a barracking.

'My God, it's a real fire!' Whatever had Cathy said?

Flustered, I stubbed my half-smoked cigarette into the packet, picked up my rucksack and leapt for the exit.

The door stuck shut.

'Keep calm!' I imagined Paul damping my panic. Turning back, I okayed the e-mail list and shut down all eight computers.

'There must be a key.' My mouth boiled dry as I searched the room. No key. Two heart-thumping minutes of searching later, a discreet notice suddenly popped up near the door: *Press to open.*

Relieved, I poked my head into a deserted open plan. No smoke. The alarm wailed on. Breathe, Nessie. Which way is out? Like Theseus, but without the knitting wool, I retraced my steps to the outside world.

1.3

Adrenaline winded me. I froze, although I couldn't smell smoke or see any buildings on fire. Outside the Sports Centre, a hundred amused people chatted together, their daily motion arrested in mid-flow. Some relaxed with drinks from the café, extending coffee breaks. A few carried laptops. The more nerdy ones perched on the low brick walls, working on battery power.

I had nothing to swallow. My feet shivered a salsa step behind a usefully-placed litter bin as I looked around.

Girls in skimpy lycra hugged their arms, looking decidedly chilly. Half a dozen barefooted females, hot from the showers, protected their untanned bits from the autumnal breeze with inadequate towels. Just then, a fire engine swept up, blue lights flashing and siren blaring and stopped in front of my building.

I shut my eyes. The incendiary of panic in my chest could explode at any moment. Oh God, no, did I start this?

Burly fire persons in full kit threw down hoses to hitch up to the hydrant. Black Lego figures leapt out and sprinted round the building.

A second appliance screamed in as an officious-looking little man in a dark suit buttonholed the head fireman. Two police cars swooped in from the other end of the street. The Chief ignored the man, put his ear to the radio and gesticulated. Fully-kitted fire-fighters, axes at the ready, galumphed past my litter bin and disappeared inside the Sports Centre.

Barriers and cones magicked themselves into the plaza. Protective policemen ushered several young women, now wrapped in silver foil, into patrol cars. Space-blanketed males huddled together. The short official strode towards the entrance door behind me; a policewoman held him back.

'Hmmph, I'm the Dean. Let me into my building.'

'Sorry, sir, Fire and Rescue are sweeping through at the moment.'

'I must secure the computer network.'

'I'm afraid we'll have to wait for their permission. The incident must be assessed before anyone can re-enter.'

'Hmmph. But this is vital. Data could be irretrievably lost.' He puffed up his chest, and his blue Oxbridge tie flapped in the breeze.

'Excuse me,' I waved my hand in the air. 'Excuse me, sir, I've turned the computers off in the IT workroom.'

The Dean looked through me.

'I'm sure they won't take long, sir,' said the policewoman. 'There's no smoke, it's probably a false alarm.'

'False alarm? I'll kill the joker who ...' The Dean reached for his mobile phone, jabbed buttons and jabbered furiously.

'I've warned IT what's going on.' He glanced up to the building opposite. Interested faces hung out of the IT Department's open windows. 'Hmmph! Where's the damned Sports Centre Manager when you need him. Are Security here yet?'

'Not yet, sir.'

Just then, two fire fighters led a couple through the foyer. The firepeople strode back to the engines. As they hurried over to the Dean, I recognized the woman lecturer's burning bush of hair from the morning's introductions.

'We've searched the Department. It's all clear.'

'Nick Smallwood! Where on earth have you been, all this time?'

So, the high-rise hunk with the frizzy blonde hairs on his rugby-player's calves and the dregs of a tropical tan, was the famously-sexy Sports Centre Manager.

'I erm, found Kirsty in her office.' Nick looked red-faced, as if he'd been working out in the gym.

'All clear,' the Chief said to the police officer. Then, 'Are you in charge here, sir?'

'Yes. I'm Dean of Faculty. Alan Rathbone.' The Dean held out a small, academic hand.

'I'm On-scene Commander.' The Chief pulled out a large, workman's hand. 'OK, sir, there's no fire. It was a smoke alarm.'

'You're sure it's not the electrical wiring to the computers?'

'Negative. It's usually an illicit smoker.'

'I don't allow any smoking in my computer … hmmph … salons.'

'Well, you seem to have one.' I stopped breathing. Time for me to edge away. 'I'll need to see your test records, just to confirm the smoke alarms and emergency lighting were checked within the last week.'

'I'm a very busy man.' The Dean bristled. 'I am only here liaising with one of my Departments. You'll have to contact the Maintenance Unit for that.'

'Nessie! What is that … happens?' The Chinese gang of three from the course eyeballed me. Xui spoke the most fluent English.

'I … there's been a false alarm. A fire drill.' My voice tailed away. Please girls, no more.

'False? How you spell that?' Laboriously, Xui tapped the word into her mobile, and showed the rest her resulting display. 'Then?'

'Alarm. A, L, A, R, M.' Confusion spread through the group. I peered at Chinese characters on the display.

'You have … found … false arm?'

'No, no, it was a FIRE.'

'Fire? How you spell that, please?'

'F .. I .. R .. E.' I remembered to speak very slowly and clearly.

'Fire?' She looked at the translation. 'Ah, there has been fire.' Staccato Chinese poured out to the rest of the group. They gasped in concern. Excited words ping-ponged backwards and forwards.

'Where fire started?' asked Xui eventually.

My head pounded. I was 90% sweat. I needed a fag. At that point, I melted away.

***

By the time I'd retrieved the car, the evening rush hour was regurgitating homeward. Some optimistic left turns put me out near the motorway. Around seven o'clock, my mobile rang. I pulled in to the Service Area to return the call.

'Vanessa.' It was Ella.

'Hi, Mum.'

'How did you get on today, dear?'

I took a calming breath of nicotine. 'I'm still on the motorway.'

'Yes, I thought so, I tried at home. Paul said you'd rung, but I thought I'd make sure you're alright.'

'Yes, I'm fine thanks, Mum, just a bit tired. Very interesting day.'

'I thought you might have dropped into the Marina to see me this afternoon.'

'I've been a bit busy. Shall I come down tomorrow afternoon, when I've finished in the Library?'

'Well, I'm out at my Third Age meeting until two. Come then. I've got some exciting news!'

'Oh yes?'

'I'll tell you about it tomorrow!'

Whatever was Mum up to now?

***

It was almost dark when I stopped for cigarettes. Anwar's corner shop-cum-Post Office was still open.

'Hi, Nessie. Big day today, huh?'

'Big culture shock. I'm really tired.'

'Paul's done well, too,' nodded my neighbour, Edward-from-the-posh-house-next-door.

'Oh,' I said absently. 'That's great.' I wondered if Paul would have supper ready. Last night's mince, plus a tin of tomatoes and a dash of dried herbs, was ripe for bolognaising.

My emergency stop in the driveway skidded Smartie across the shingle. A giant orange giraffe of a Kubota digger stood next to the front door, blocking the garage space.

'Paul?'

I looked over the front garden, where giant tractor marks scored the grass like some prehistoric monster on the prowl. By the side of the garage, a goodish-sized hole subsided into the space where I usually parked. I opened the front door into a cool, empty smell that meant no supper on the go, yet. From upstairs a dying whale sounded.

'Paul?'

The whale died abruptly. He appeared at the top of the stairs clasping Benji's tuba.

'What on earth's going on?'

'I thought I'd pick this up and start learning to play it, now Benji's at uni. I've found his Grade 1 music book.'

'No, I didn't mean that.' I sank onto the oak settle from Mum's house. 'What's going on outside?'

'Ah, the garage, do you mean?'

'Well, the hole by the side of the garage would do for starters.'

He rumbled downstairs in his slippers. 'The digging's gone well today, hasn't it? I've only just finished and showered. I was thinking of getting some supper ready.'

'Paul, what are you talking about?' Mahogany-brown eyes side-stepped mine.

'The garage extension, of course. Have you forgotten? The Planning Permission runs out in November. If I don't make a start on it, we'll have to apply all over again.'

'But …'

'It will add value to the house and give me something to do until I get more work.' His dark circles glared out at me.

'Yeah, well I can see that, but Paul … we haven't even discussed it!'

'I'm sorry, Nessie darling, but three years ago we did agree it needed doing.'

'Don't darling me,' I spat. I was exhausted, dehydrated and stinking of stale sweat. 'How much will it cost?'

'Sorry.' Paul gave me his Mr Reasonable look. 'Let's go and have a cup of tea and I'll show you the budget. I've tried to talk to you before, but you're always too busy with something else. What's for supper?'

I opened the new pack of ciggies. At least my Mum had remembered it was my first day at school.

1.4

A Japanese girl next door peered through a pair of sunglasses at her screen. She fished a chewing gum-sized packet from her miniscule leather bag and fixed it into her Library computer.

'What on earth's that?'

'Memory stick,' she hissed back.

'What do you use it for?'

'Save things.' Her text bleeper went off, just as her Hotmail messages appeared on screen.

My own e-mails welcomed me to the Epidemiology of Health and Illness module, asked me to confirm my module choices, signed me into Library Services and invited me to three Student Union events and a Faculty Post-graduate reception. By eleven o'clock, I felt I'd done a day's work.

I leaned back, trying to relax in the thicket of Library computers. No smoking, of course. Why hadn't anyone mentioned books, yesterday? Last time round, in the Seventies, it was pistols at dawn over set books.

Upstairs, I borrowed one of five resting copies of Bandura's epic *Self-Efficacy* and straggled back down to search for journal articles and a photocopy card. A single article later, I discovered the Reserved Collection, grabbed the only book from the reading list and opened up. *Twenty-four hour loan.* Buggar. I settled to reading.

At twelve-fifteen, I whirled into the Department's packed workroom.

'Nessie, what's up? You look frazzled.'

'Hi … I've only got three quarters of an hour left out of a whole day. Oh Cathy, I can only find one article in the Library.'

'Well, most articles are accessed from e-journals, these days.' Cathy returned to her e-erudition.

'E-journals?' On the floor, my rucksack collapsed. 'What? Howev …?'

'Sit down. Now …' Cathy steered me through the virtual portal. The e-Library offered one journal from my wish list of ten.

My teeth clenched. 'Well, I suppose the preliminaries are half the battle. Err, Cathy, sorry, but do you know about the printer, please?'

I trailed back to the Library to hunt another machine, selling print tokens. Thirty-five minutes later, the Departmental printer flung out a single copy.

At this rate, it would take all year to access the materials to start my assignment. Steaming not-so-gently, I smoked two fags as I route marched to the car and retreated to Mum's canal boat-home.

***

Smartie's black and silver body vibrated across the cobbles like a tin can kicking round the small, dusty industrial estate.

Mum didn't answer her phone. I leant against the security gate, wondering how to get through. Above the marina, an old dry dock provided gritty hard-standing for several dozen boats. Below, a hundred assorted vessels jostled and sang in the fresh breeze. An unkempt fishing trawler sprawled along most of one wall, gear piled on deck.

A young woman stepped from the shower block in a pink dressing gown, towel turbanned round her hair. Her large Alsatian followed as she approached.

'Hi, I'm visiting my Mum's boat, *Iris*. May I ...?' Sheering away from the dog, I tail-gated her onto the pontoons.

'Jason! Heel.' I clomped down the gangway like Billy Goat Gruff.

'I don't think we've met before. I'm Ella's daughter, Nessie.' A chunky French fishing smack, red sails furled, moored next to a narrow boat. A rain-shower of geranium petals splashed the barge's black coachroof.

'Hello, I'm Delia.'

Down each pontoon spine, narrow boats formed ribs to the Marina. All except *Iris*. She wasn't in her usual berth towards the far end.

'Have you any idea where Ella's gone?' We passed three small motorboats.

'No ... oh, wait a minute, what did she say in the loos this morning?'

'She told me her meeting finished at four.'

'Ah, no, I remember. She's taken *Iris* up to the Pump Out berth.'

'Not on her own?' The dog's claws scratched on the wooden decking as he trotted beside her. His black and tan halo of fur bristled in a passing gust of wind.

'Oh no, two of the lads from the yard went with her, to handle the ropes.'

'Thank goodness for that! She's never taken the boat out on her own.'

'Oh ... She's new to narrow boating, then?'

'Yeah. She only bought *Iris* in March.'

'Brave, at her age. She must be in her seventies.'

I laughed. 'Eighties!'

'Really? She doesn't look it.'

'Do you know her friend, Phyllida? With the boat moored up in town?' Delia shook her head. 'Well, Phyllida persuaded her into it. Mum was quite depressed for a couple of years, you see, after Dad died.'

'Oh dear …'

'We thought she'd find it much too difficult, coping with life afloat. But actually, it's done her the world of good.'

A pocket-size yacht cowered under a plastic cover. 'Hi, Derek.' Delia circumnavigated the scruffy owner, jig-sawing a plywood sheet on the pontoon. 'They're all very friendly here.'

'Mum talks to anyone.' In the afternoon sunlight the original stone of the basin shone soft and grey, lacy with bright pink weeds. The wind muted the rising traffic noise from the other side of the basin. Only random raw clangs disturbed the historic industrial peace. 'I can see why she likes it here.'

We stopped by Mum's empty space. 'Do you know when they're due back?'

'They should be here any minute.' She smiled. 'I must get back before my hair dries. See you later.'

Delia nipped into a floating caravan, berthed on the other side of the pontoon. Jason lay down outside her door, ears erect, watching me suspiciously.

Next door to the marina, the University Rowing Club arrived by minibus. In two minutes, a tribe of students wheeled five boats down the concrete slip to the water. I smiled, spotting freshers a mile off.

Gingerly, they climbed into a quad, which rocked wildly when they tried to ship the oars. Just then, the coach appeared, perched on a tiny catamaran, like a decrepit pedalo with an outboard motor.

'Now then everyone, five minutes to the first buoy, rest one minute, five minutes to the second one. Wait there.' He looked round his rowers. 'I'll stay with *Lightning*.' The other boats accelerated smoothly away and off up the river in practised co-operation.

Clouds scudded along overhead. The crew of *Lightning* fought to get underway against choppy little waves.

'Tell them, left blades,' the Coach bossed the novice cox. The catamaran's outboard sputtered off towards the main river.

'Left blades.'

Slowly, the bow of the boat graunched on the concrete slip.

'Too slow! Both blades, tell them both blades,' shouted the coach through his loudhailer, booming it round the marina basin. 'Reverse scull.'

'Reverse scull,' mimicked the cox. Pairs of oars paused in disarray.

A gang of workmen from the tea bar joined the dog-walking spectators.

The four novices dipped their sculls haphazardly into the water, smacking concrete.

'Pull her round, then!' bellowed the coach, turning his pedalo back towards the slip. The cox, a small, skinny lad in a pristine rugby shirt, stared at the coach. Then he vaulted out of the boat, and up to his waist in yellowy-brown waves. He waded forward and grabbed the bow, tugging it round to face the wind.

'OK, pull,' bellowed the coach through the loudhailer, buzzing the pedalo round in a tight circle to avoid their line of fire. *Lightning* shot off out into the river, minus her cox, just as I spotted the stumpy black bow of *Iris*, buffeting down the outside of the Marina. Anticipating the next frame, I rushed towards the end of the pontoons. Jason pursued me, growling.

'Mum!'

Ella looked over to me and waved happily from the tiller.

'Vanessa.'

'Watch for the – BOAT!'

There wasn't time for any more. As the narrow boat swung into the marina, the skiff glanced obliquely off her hefty black topside. The coach turned his pedalo hard to starboard to avoid *Iris*, in a swirl of golden suds. I heard the thwack and dodged along the last pontoon. The rowers cannoned into the coach's outboard motor, before capsizing into the river, only nine or ten metres from the safety of the slip.

Something had happened to the pedalo's steering. It accelerated away in a circle to starboard, narrowly missing the yacht moored next to me. The second circle was tighter. Third time round, the pedalo cleared downwind of the yacht's red ensign. The coach seemed to be trying to inch back to the outboard, but his movements rocked the little craft. Slowly and deliberately, one sponson flipped up. Gracefully, he slid into ten or twelve feet of dirty dock water. Blobs of broken-off polystyrene icebergs drifted off towards infinity and beyond.

I glanced round at *Iris*. She was safely back in her berth. The lads from the yard had tied the lines and left. Jason was edging me towards the water with small I-mean-it growls. I stood my ground for a moment, assessing the emergency.

The coach had a lifejacket bulging up round his head, but he spluttered and splashed like a weak swimmer as he tried to hold onto the stern of the pedalo. The pedalo was about to sink. I was the nearest person, far closer than the onlookers on the walls. It was My Shout.

Grabbing the lifebuoy from the yacht alongside, I slid into the water. Jason followed. I'd never attempted an open water rescue before. My track pants grabbed my legs and my shirt billowed out in clouds of air round my shoulders and upper arms. Foetid water slapped my face as I kicked towards the casualty in the water. Breaststroke, of course, with my trainers on.

'Put your hands down, I'm going to pass you this aid.' My out-of-date lifesaving training flooded back in this moment of crisis. 'Keep calm!'

The coach turned his head as I trod water. Suddenly I recognized the good-looking bloke from the previous day. What a ... 'Nick, stay calm! I'm going to rescue you.'

He glared at me as the catamaran slid underwater to its final resting place in the darkness below.

'I don't need bloody rescuing,' he bellowed. 'I can swim perfectly well. It's the outboard motor that needs bloody rescuing, not me.'

He turned over onto his back, holding the outboard out of the water like the Rugby World Cup. He kicked back to slipway and stood up, blonde hair still dry, outboard aloft. The rowers cheered. The sodden cox rushed forward to take the motor from him.

Meanwhile, Jason landed on the slip. He gave an almighty doggie shake, like the brushes in a car wash on max. The pressurised spray drenched everybody for a second time. Nick gave me and the *Iris* a dirty look.

Nonchalantly, I turned to swim through the cold muddiness back to the pontoon, still pushing the lifebuoy in front. By now I was too cold to smell the water.

The pontoon didn't have a way of boarding. I hung on a slimy vertical chain.

'Mum,' I called. It was quite bone-chilling in the water. No response.

'Mum,' I shouted. I'd be getting cramp any moment now.

'Help!' I screamed, like a full-screech soprano. My feet and hands were numbing fast. Manhandling the lifebuoy over my head, I clung to the chain with my fast-diminishing strength.

Several minutes later, two heads peered over the top at me. 'Are you alright?' A pair of hands relieved me of the lifebuoy.

In seconds, enough weight arrived to give the pontoon a dangerous list to leeward. The two lads, Delia, Mum, the owner of the lifebuoy and the Marina Manager hauled me out, between them. The dog, who'd found his own way back through the security gate, came up to inspect my landed-whale impression with a patronizing smirk on his face.

'Are you sure you're alright, dear?' asked Mum. I sipped hot tea aboard *Iris*, wrapped in a stringy beach towel and her duvet. My teeth ached from clamping their sporadic drum rolls.

'Yes, Mum, perfectly sure, it wasn't very cold.'

'Really? I've heard anyone who goes in the water here should have a stomach pump.'

'Mum, stop fussing. I'll be fine. Oh, how could I have been so stupid? Nick Smallwood is probably an Olympic swimmer.'

'It was very brave of you.' Delia rubbed Jason's fur dry with Mum's best white Egyptian bath towel. Gold and grey hairs spiked up from black. 'I'd never have had the courage to jump in.' She looked down at her long skirt and flowery blouse and smiled. Her dry hair, out of the turban, looked like straw stubble in a harvested field. Nevertheless, Delia exhibited a delicate feminine touch, which I sadly lacked.

'It was nothing,' I drew the safety curtain down over my embarrassment. 'Shame we couldn't save his boat. Does anyone have any spare clothes? I only have a nice, dry swimming costume in my ruckie.'

By the time I'd showered and changed, the rush hour had emptied out. Just as well, with a ballet-pink, fluffy housecoat over my Speedo.

***

At home I made a list of things to remember for the next day:

- Lunch
- Return Woodhouse and Rawlins
- Find ten articles
- Boots

Then I rooted round the drinks cupboard for an out-of-date can of Coke and settled down in the sitting room. My easy-read filled in years of missing academia. I took careful notes of the first three chapters. The central heating turned off at ten. With nine more chapters to go, I gave up at one-thirty.

I nestled into our warm bed, sneaking my icy toes under Paul's hot-water-bottle feet. A paintbrush of grey hair poked up from the duvet. Presumably he was comatose after another day's labour on the new garage. After two chaotic days, I felt well and truly knackered, too. Never mind. Only tomorrow at uni, then I'd have four free days at home, to steam ahead with my work.

1.5

The heating rumbled on at 6.00 am. I was on the road by 7.30 a.m., smarting eyes and limp hair notwithstanding.

'Bye, Paul, I'm definitely late home. It's the post-grad Reception, tonight. There's a pizza in the back of the freezer.' I leant over his cold tea to kiss him goodbye. 'Time to rise and shine.'

He groaned. 'I can hardly move this morning. I had to dig into the chalk with a spade.'

'Oh dear.' He never listened to my advice. 'Did you stretch last night when you finished?' He glared. A grin oozed out. 'Well, you know the best cure for stiffness is a little gentle exercise.'

***

I parked Smartie and started a focussed trot for the department, as the drizzle started. Damp darkened the lovely old limestone pavements, misting the droopy trees like water from a hairdresser's spray.

Season of mists and mellow fruitfulness .... 'Errm ...' I was never sure what came next, despite those learn-by-heart homeworks.

The triangle was strangely empty of muggers as I power-walked to the cash dispenser. I clinched my rucksack between my knees. I'd booked to be induced at the gym as painlessly as possible at lunchtime, and it bulged with trainers, towel and gym gear.

Nick Smallwood's mug shot smiled from the back of the Foyer. BSc Sydney, 1991; University team for rugby, rowing and water polo. Of course. A bit young for me, though. I congratulated myself on wearing my new *Cotton Traders* All-Blacks rugby shirt.

Thirty minutes early, I dumped my rucksack in the front row of the empty lecture theatre. At least I'd be able to see and hear. Then I settled down with Woodhouse and Rawlins, Chapter Four.

I'll swear the seating beamed out homing signals. Five minutes before the off, a noisy gang of young Greeks claimed the back row. The Asians drifted together then split into Chinese and Indian sub-continents. Clean-cut, American-speaking Scandinavians pigeon-holed themselves behind me. Middle-Eastern veils clung together, demure flashes of gold peeping out from toes and mobiles.

Xui sat down to my left. 'Hello, Nessie, how you today? Have you found false arm?' She grinned at me and shook her arm. The other Chinese girls joined in with early-teenage giggles.

'Morning, Nessie.' Cathy folded herself into the next chair, coffeeness wafting from the carton in her hand, thirty seconds early. 'Are you going to the Faculty Post-grad Reception?'

'I was planning to. Anyone else going?'

We looked at the five other mature students in the front row.

'Can't get a baby sitter,' apologised a stocky girl called Midge. My empty shell twanged. Her kids still needed daily doses of R and R to succour them against the great outside world.

'See you there at 6.30, Cathy?' Remembering Leah in South America, I fretted until Kirsty stood up, only a couple of metres away.

So far, I knew Kirsty loved chocolate and avoided varicose veins by not crossing her ex-runner's legs. As she bent over, her fabulous long mass of red curls and musky aura shouted sensual chic. She was decorated in beaten gold, except on her wedding finger. Was something going on between her and Nick?

'Good morning, everyone.'

Aah. My pencil tin was still in the rucksack. I probed, rustling surreptitiously through Kirsty's introduction. My hands felt round shininess. As it emerged, I dropped the pencil tin with a metallic rattle. Bollocks. Not again.

I looked up from my hot-faced scrabbling on the carpet at a hand, tapping lecture notes against a right leg. A tall man in jeans and brown leather bomber jacket stood easily next to Kirsty.

'Good morning. My name's Scott Woodhouse. I've been with this Department for nine years.' His thick hair, the colour of Jason's coat, looked windswept. So this was the star turn of Woodhouse and Rawlins. 'I started my career as a PE teacher.' The ex-PE teacher in me blanched at his single earring.

Really? Now that he mentioned it, his face still had the look of a man searching the far side of the football field for reluctant players gone AWOL.

'My PhD examined the cruciate ligaments of football players.' I tried to look riveted by the finer points of knee biomechanics. I was dying for a fag already. 'More recently, I've moved into qualitative research. Currently I'm interested in the identity of women rugby players. Anyone here?' On his Powerpoint slide, a woman grinned at an upheld ball.

A strapping lass with long, blonde straggling curls waved a powerful arm in the air.

'Excellent. I'd like to talk to you in the break very much. Are you thinking along those lines for your dissertation?'

'Probably. I participated in your research with the international youth team in 2000.'

'You must be Lucy Welsh, then. Any other international players here?'

'Just so we all feel better,' whispered Midge in my ear.

'Yeah, Ultimate Frisbee,' announced an efficient voice quietly, from half way back. We all turned to view an unobtrusive, clever face. Dr Woodhouse clicked again. A girl, perhaps this very girl, appeared on the screen with a Frisbee arching off into the distance.

I muttered at Cathy, 'Christ, how did he manage that?'

'Looked at our application forms and Googled, I expect.'

'And what about …?' A table tennis player zapped onto the screen. Xui's face flooded red. The other Chinese students fell about with tinkly giggles.

'Stand up, Xui Chang. Xui is far too modest to tell you, I'm sure, but she was the Chinese national Under-18 champion in 2001.' Xui fixed her eyes to the floor. I clapped into the silence, impressed to be sharing jokes with the famous.

A pair of sumo wrestlers appeared on screen. 'So we already know something about sport, then.' Did I catch a rolling Scots *r*, in that word *sport*? 'Most of us here are very healthy. Is it just coincidence that nobody in the room is obese?' He wasn't. Dr Woodhouse may have had academic scruffiness round the edges, but underneath was a purposeful P.E. core.

'Since the obesity epidemic took off, universities such as ours have won considerable funding for research on the health benefits of exercise. So, like everyone else in this fast-developing field, we've moved into studying general populations.' He clicked his fingers impatiently. He was a baby-boomer, like me. 'It's a very exciting time to be an exercise scientist.'

There was a discreet rustle as we all sat up straighter, hoping to be counted in.

I wondered what Scott Woodhouse did, when he wasn't being a researcher. Dinner table discussions with clever kids, probably.

'In this module, we will look at …' An All-cause Mortality pie chart swung into place. In less than a minute, Dr Woodhouse dispatched cardio-vascular disease, cancers, diabetes, infections, accidents and zoomed in a blank pie chart.

'Now, what's the biggest cause of mortality, acute and chronic disease, do you think?' He glanced at me for a moment. A smile crept its way up into his pale, prominent eyes. Then they sparkled icy-blue with something. Sarcasm? Sympathy? Anticipation, even? I couldn't tell, as yet.

'Poor diet?' hazarded Helen, a dietician.

'Actually, that comes in at number two.' A large slice of pie reddened. 'Any other ideas?' His eyelids drooped lazily over his eyes, like an alligator in waiting.

'Inactivity?' Was I really the rabbit venturing its head out of the hole, ready to get it bitten off?

'Surprisingly, sedentary behaviour is only number three.' Another slice turned blue.

'Poor living conditions?' Cathy tried.

'Ah, now that's interesting.' He glanced appreciatively at Cathy's immaculate physical self. 'You will be delving into that one this afternoon in *The Socio-Economic Basis of Health* lecture. A complex set of determinants built into a hugely important cultural gradient.'

There was a shuffling sort of silence. We'd all thought we were clever, up to this point.

'What is a major cause of respiratory and cardio-vascular diseases?' he primed encouragingly, lolling against the computer table. I dug deep. *Smoking*! I'd just confirm with one more clue.

'We've known about its damaging effects for more than fifty years.' I raised a clammy hand. 'Though it's an addiction, these days only the more unintelligent members of the population continue with this habit.' My hand faltered down.

'Smoking!' shouted Xiu triumphantly.

'Of course. It's still, after all these years, the biggest single threat to an individual's health, with the highest cost nationally to the NHS. Half of all smokers die of their habit before the age of seventy. In short, a no-win scenario, ladies and gentlemen.'

With a flourish, he zapped the biggest slice yellow. 'Actually, I'm surprised nobody thought of it. Does that mean there are no smokers here at all?'

A couple of young students smirked and fluttered hands.

'Incidentally, one of the smoke alarms in the Department triggered off the Fire Drill on Tuesday.' Dr Woodhouse gazed innocently at the far wall whilst the two smokers looked suitably guilty. As for me, I resolved to quit.

***

The gym upstairs reminded me of last year's giant uterus in the Engine Hall at Tate Modern. I slid over to the desk, face averted from the Duty Manager's office, in case Nick Smallwood recognized me. The thirty-year-younger trainer at the desk probably already had a PhD in gym inductions.

'Hav'ya come for cardiac rehab?' Darren pulled out a pile of papers.

'No.' I was mortified. 'I'm a Masters' student.'

'Oops, sorry. Would you fill this student fitness 'ssessment out first then, pl'se.' He ambled over to the fitness production line.

I hesitated over the form. Who should I list as my parent or guardian? Paul? Did they really want to know everything that was wrong with me? I settled on *Athlete's Foot* and left it at that.

'You can see on these charts what you have to do at each station, how many repetitions, that sort ov fing, s'quite easy, any questions? Right we'll move on to cardio-vasculah then.' I skipped, keeping up with Darren's pylon-sized legs.

'You set each machine up same way, press this t'activate your personal fitness programme, use th'other buttons t'adjust the setting to suit yer own requirements, don't forget to log ou' by pressing the blue button for five seconds, we can see at the desk how yer doing. What d'you wanna start on today?'

I gulped. I couldn't possibly work anything that required four buttons to get it going.

'I'll try the rowing machine.' I sank down, latched my feet in the straps and gripped the pulling bar. At least I could row. To my surprise, a display flickered into life. No blue buttons, then.

The display soared to 3.22 somethings. Next pull, it went even higher: 4.56. Rowing away with a Henley competitor's strength and grace, I topped out at 6.1. I glanced idly at my neighbour. 13.4, 15.8, 14.7! Wow, some strength. I looked up creased trainers, spindly legs, thin body, shiny head. Jonathan Griffiths gave a relaxed grin.

'Hello, Vanessa. You're pulling the watts there.'

How did everyone know my name? 'Dr Griffiths. I didn't recognise you without your clothes.'

He grinned again. 'They all say that.'

I ducked off the rower and retreated to the changing room. The gym didn't really appeal and, now that I'd witnessed a fire drill, avoiding nakedness precluded sweaty activities.

A small pair of steps blocked the exit downstairs. Keeping my head down, I sidled past, but it was too late. Nick Smallwood gave a double take. 'Oh … it's you.'

'Yes, err, sorry about yesterday.'

'Well … it wasn't your fault. It was that stupid woman on the narrow boat. She was far too close to the pontoons.' I ignored that, since he was probably right.

'Have you managed to recover your, err, boat?'

'It broke up. The bits floated ashore. No worries. It was due for the scrapheap, anyway.'

'Thank goodness for that.' Since he seemed friendly, I risked another question. 'Did you enjoy your unexpected swim?'

'Got the most terrible gut rot, today. That dock water is putrid.'

'Really? I always drink flat cocoa-cola if the water's dodgy. I'm fine today.'

'Straight up?'

I eyeballed the fuzz on his legs. 'Yeah.'

'I must see if Kirsty knows about that one.'

'Kirsty?' I asked, as innocently as I could manage.

'Kirsty Macdonald, you know, in Nuts 'n Ex. She's into dragon boat racing.'

'Oh, that Kirsty.'

He rested his screwdriving arm on top of the ladder and looked at me with a smidgeon of interest. 'Are you a new lecturer?'

'No, I'm a student on the MSc. Nessie Elliott.'

'Right. Gooday, err, pleased to meet you. Sorry I swore at you.'

'Not at all. What's this, then?' I gestured at his box of lights and screwdriver. 'I thought you were the manager?'

His lashes curled over his navy-blue eyes as he grinned. 'There's a surprise inspection by the Fire Service this afternoon. My bomb sweep today coincidentally includes checking out the emergency lighting.'

'Oh. Well, I'd better not keep you, then.'

I flowed downstairs. Nick wasn't angry at me and I'd discovered a little more about his interesting relationship with Kirsty. I sat on the wall outside the library like everyone else, to smoke my last cigarette.

The whole area vibrated with students after the long summer vacation. Groups crowded the café chairs and surrounding walls in the drizzle, laughing, chatting, texting. Scruffy gangs re-bonded with intimate shouts and screams. Neat freshers arrived uncertainly for library tours. I exhaled comfortable smoke, listening to accents and languages unknown in my little country village. Everywhere students, and I belonged.

I relaxed in a brief moment of triumph against the odds of this dream happening in real-time. Glanced at my watch. Five to two already. The heel of a best black shoe ground out my last cigarette on the pavement.

'The End,' I said aloud. 'I've quit.'

Reaching down, I felt for a missing rucksack. Fuck. Reviewing the evidence, I'd left it in the women's changing room. Double fuck. I'd be late for a lecture again.

I leapt off the wall and bolted for the Sports Centre. Waving my card at the receptionist, I took the stairs two at a time, thankful that Nick had disappeared from my through-route. I charged at the changing room door. Nothing happened.

I rammed with my shoulder, like an agent on a drugs raid. The *Closed* sign ripped away. The door gave in with a creaking scream. I fell in, my best black trousers tangling with a pair of steps, two Adidas trainers and a neatly-pressed Sports Centre polo shirt.

'Oh, sorry Nick, just looking for my rucksack.' I spotted it on the bench, grabbed it and was making off by the time Nick had untangled himself from the wreckage of steps and crushed lightbulbs.

'Bloody Sheila shit magnet,' I thought he shouted, as I bolted for the afternoon lecture.

1.6

The drizzle melded into a soft afternoon with watery lemon sun. The city smelled sharp, not summertime-dusty as I bobbed, ten feet tall, downhill to the centre. The shopping precinct was entrenched beyond the canal, twenty minutes' brisk walk away. Who needed cigarettes, anyway?

Boots. I found Vibram-soled, urban walking, in the outdoor shop.

'That'll be seventy-six pounds, ninety-nine, please.'

'Can I have a student discount, please?' She looked me up and down. Card ready, I savoured the moment. 'Yes, I really am a student.'

At 5.45 pm, I suddenly remembered why I'd written *Boots*. Dope! Maybe I still had time to find a pair of reading glasses.

My hand hovered between different identities. Should I buy half-moons, like Cathy and all the academics I'd seen, or something younger? Pounding uphill against the wind blasted all feeling from my face. I felt for my fag packet, then remembered I'd quit.

The converted house of a Post-graduate Centre bubbled with an unfamiliar casserole of languages. There was no sign of Cathy at the entrance. I slipped upstairs, smiling through the throng of foreign students.

I edged towards a young woman serving drinks from a large, white damask-covered table.

'Good evening. Would you like wine or orange juice?' A Welsh flavour tinged her voice.

'Juice, thank you. I'm driving.' She squashed up another Sainsbury carton and lobbed it ineffectually towards a black plastic bin liner.

Just then, a hiccup emitted from the carpet behind her, an unexpected sound for an academic party with so little alcohol. I dream it sometimes, even now, twenty years later. It's the whimper of a baby, gearing up for higher decibel action.

'It's a baby!' I exclaimed, like *Burglar Bill* himself.

'Yes.' She combed back her long blonde hair with cherry-shiny fingernails. 'Oh God, Bertie will wake up now, before it's even started. I thought he'd be fine until eight.' Dismay flitted across her eyes.

'How old is he?'

'Six weeks.'

'Ah. Will he go back to sleep before his next feed?'

'He might do. He's not really into a routine yet.'

'Would you like me to hold him? I'm always keen to practise my rusty mothering skills.'

'Oh would you? He goes to anyone.' She gestured at dozens of wine glasses. 'I'm supposed to be welcoming all the new post-grads into the Faculty family. Good thing most of the thousand haven't turned up.'

I untangled the baby from the straps on his carry chair and snuggled him into best fit against my shoulder. 'Is he always like this in the evening?'

'Yeah. My mother says all babies are restless in the evenings. Alan says he's got colic. This is Alan's third.'

A queue for wine materialized. I rocked Bertie through the exotic crowd over to the window, looking for Cathy. I didn't recognize a single student from my own Department. My cosy weight quieted, temporarily comforted. He unfocussed his velvety blue eyes on the middle distance, rooting gently in case a nipple might be lurking on my shoulder. Oh, how could I be too old for another baby?

On my next circuit round, I wandered back to Bertie's Mum. She looked about thirty, with a gym-honed figure and attractively foxy face. Apart from her panda eyes, I'd never have guessed she was only six weeks post-natal.

'How come Bertie's here tonight?'

'Well, I've come to support Alan, but the nanny won't work after six o'clock. Two of my new PhD students are here, too.'

'Oh.' I thought about it. 'What's your field?'

'Astrophysics.'

'I see.' The conversation stalled. I grounded in safety.

'My name's Nessie Elliott, by the way.'

'Elliott? Are you the new Hearing Impaired Reader?'

'Nobody's said anything about that,' I replied cautiously. Had the university discovered my weaknesses already? 'I'm an extra-mature student. MSc. Exercise and Health Science.'

'Oh sorry! Yes, Jenny Smith, in your department, joined my NCT class. I'm Sarah Rees.' The baby's head drooped on my shoulder. 'Oh look, he's asleep again.' She sounded surprised.

I remembered typing in Jenny's name to my e-mail group. 'I think Jenny's back after Christmas. Shall I put Bertie back in his recliner?'

She smiled at a gossamer women in a hijab, handed her a glass of orange juice and glanced at Bertie. 'Would you mind? Thank you so much.' The instant I put the baby down, he woke and whimpered again.

She sighed. 'I'd better heat up his bottle in the microwave.'

'Shall I do it?' I offered.

'Four dibs, I think it is.' She handed me the bottle. I wormed my way into the crowded kitchen. After five abortive attempts, I grabbed a Physics PhD. He heated the baby's bottle in thirty seconds flat and I shook it, until between us, it was roughly the right temperature.

Squeezing back through the crowd, I found Sarah standing next to the Dean. She smiled at me gratefully.

'Thanks, I really don't have much of a clue. Alan, this is Nessie, a Masters' student.'

'Pleased to meet you.' He was ceremonious, holding out a scholarly hand without recognizing me. His hair looked natural under artificial lighting.

'How do you do.' I turned slightly towards Sarah, Bertie in her arms. 'The bottle should be warm enough for him now.'

Grasping the bottle and cap, I twisted firmly. It was so stiff, that I had to exert full twist and pull on the cap. The bottle jerked, arching a thin jet of SMA milk sideways over Alan's hair and glasses.

'Mind out!' A small stream of white stuff trickled down his forehead and dripped from his chin.

'Oh, I'm so sorry.' I found a tissue in my best trousers, mainly unused from my admission interview. Alan looked at it doubtfully, but took it and dabbed at his damp suit. In the meantime, Sarah found a chair to sit down with Bertie. Alan and I stood together in embarrassed silence. I watched little Bertie guzzling his milk, while Alan cleaned his gold half-moons with irritable precision.

A bell tinkled from the front. More students crammed up the stairs and pressed through the overcrowded doorway.

'Must go. Four minutes, darling.' Sarah gave him the besotted look of a panda in love. He strode to the front, squaring his puny shoulders and smoothing down his jacket. He turned, tilted his gaunt chin and stared in a practised way over the top of the multi-national crowd to the stairwell outside.

'Good evening, and welcome to you all. My name is Alan Rathbone. I'm Dean of the Faculty of Science. May I welcome you to Post-graduate study at this highly prestigious institution, one of the most important research centres in Britain and one of the top fifty universities in the world. Here in the Faculty, we …' And he was off, cantering round the Faculty's more noteworthy achievements, like a champion jockey.

He wore the same tie as the other day. As well as the pattern of Oxbridge crests, it now had a large damp stain down the front.

I glanced at my neighbour. She looked adoringly up at the Dean, her mouth open slightly in wonder. I observed her large sparkly diamond and shiny wedding ring. Suddenly the penny dropped. Titania was quite a new Mrs Rathbone and Bertie was the Dean's baby.

'Now I'd like to introduce you to a couple of my colleagues here tonight. Professor Ron Rawlins is Chair of Exercise Science. His international stature … hmmph … is in the area of children's physical development through sport.' The Dean aimed a slightly-congratulatory nod at Ron. Professor Rawlins had positioned himself so as not to upstage the Dean, who was considerably shorter. His immaculate grey suit complemented his neat, silvery short back and sides. He looked distinguished and dignified, with the benevolent face of Father Christmas after a low-fat diet.

Already, I felt proud of Ron. My professor supported the Faculty after office hours.

'I invited Professor Rawlins here tonight, so that you overseas students would meet him once whilst you are in

Britain! Also somewhere around is my wife, Dr Sarah Rees, who studies the night stars in theory and in practice, since we have a new, small baby. Isn't that right, darling?' The Dean switched his gaze from the far corner of the stairwell and laughed indicatively at his own joke. A couple of seconds later, the rest of the audience finished translating and tittered politely.

Sarah thrust the baby and nearly empty bottle at me and wiggled through the crowd, to the front. Once she had flicked back her long blonde hair and arranged herself, she stood half a head taller than the Dean.

'Sarah has a very exciting peer-reviewed article published in the *International Journal of Astrophysics* next month, which you can all find in the Library.' He squeezed her hand affectionately and turned back to his audience.

'This is a wonderfully vibrant city in which to enjoy being a student. I'm sure you will make good use of its many facilities.' Ron, next to the Dean, gave the audience an encouraging smile, as if he had enjoyed student life here, in his time. The Dean gestured at Ron to go next.

'Do you have any advice for our newcomers, Professor Rawlins?'

'Welcome to you all. Yes, I do have one piece of advice for you. Quite simply, it's to buy an umbrella. Do you all know what that is?' Ron mimed opening up an umbrella, at which the English speakers from the Caribbean and India laughed. 'This city is in the southern half of England ...' The rest of the world caught up. '… and all the water in the clouds from their passage across the North Atlantic, is ready to drop on the British Isles before those clouds reach continental Europe. If you come from a dry country, you will be amazed to find that it rains here, nearly every day. I promise that you will never regret the modest financial outlay involved in an umbrella! Do enjoy the rest of your evening and your time here as a student.'

Ron smiled an impish smile until all the overseas students laughed too. Then he turned to Alan and Sarah. Since I was the only other person of the same generation in the room *and* I was left holding their baby, I decided to join them.

'Ron, this is Nessie Masters.' Alan introduced me.

'How are you, Nessie?' I transferred the baby to my left arm so I could shake the professor's hand.

'Vanessa Elliott, pleased to …'

'And this,' announced the proud father, 'is Bertie.' Sliding a firm arm round his middle, he swept the baby out of my grasp and wheeled him round expertly to face Ron. Bertie brought up his wind in true baby fashion with a vomit of projectile ferocity, which caught Ron totally unprepared.

'Bad luck, old man.' Alan brought out my second-hand tissue from his pocket. 'You just have to expect it with babies, you know.'

Ron produced a neatly folded white handkerchief from his pocket. 'So I'm told,' he murmured politely, mopping the curdy bits from his cheek. 'To be honest, I'm more used to students than babies.'

'Not much difference in Freshers' Week, Professor Rawlins.' Sarah stepped in with a muslin nappy and a couple of baby-wipes.

'I fear you're right, my dear.' Ron looked tired.

'I'm afraid your suit will need a dry clean. Milk goes off and smells awful if you leave it.'

Alan Rawlins glared at me.

'Thank you, Vanessa. I'll bear that in mind.' Ron finished mopping, though his jacket still looked saturated. 'I think I should be making a move. It's a good twenty minutes' walk home.'

'I should be going, too. My car's a fair distance away.' We squeezed ourselves out of the Tower of Babel and headed off in the same direction.

'Do you have far to travel?'

'Not too bad. I live about an hour away, if there's no traffic.'

'Of course.' He sighed. 'The city's biggest challenge. I'm fortunate to live within walking distance of the university. Unfortunately, I'm committed to London four days a week, this year.'

'Oh dear, Professor. Can't you get out of it? Video conferencing or e-mail or something?'

'Afraid not. The Chair has to be at every meeting.'

'What are you doing?'

'A Government review of children's physical activity levels. It's about ten months' work.'

'Does that mean you'll be out of the Department for most of the year? What a pity for all the students.'

'Yes, but the others are a good team. They'll look after you. What are you thinking of researching for your dissertation?'

'I've no idea yet.'

'A surprise, then,' said Ron, smiling. 'I'll look forward to reading it this time next year. Ah, here we are. Will you be alright on you own?'

'No problems, Professor, it's very well lit.' We looked up at the heritage-grade street lights, haloed with mist.

'Well then, goodnight, my dear.' He turned into the neat front garden of a three storey Georgian house in limestone. I imagined the terrace, high on the hill, overlooking a breathtaking view of the city. The first floor windows, traditionally the reception rooms, were lit up. Even from the pavement below, I could see that the rooms were renovated in period style. Someone in Ron's family had exquisite taste.

I walked back to the car feeling let-down. Without Ron, I suspected the Department would be missing its soul.

1.7

The next morning I woke late, to aliens clunking and whirring outside. Reluctantly, I hoisted myself out of bed. I wasn't at my best, before the first drag of the day.

Paul sat astride the orange giraffe, both hands on the controls, head stilled in concentration. Slowly he articulated the long arm forward until it was at full reach and then, delicately, angled the digger bowl to descend. The digger bit into the chalk, roaring and bucking, then scraped up a miniscule scoop of earth. Paul wheeled the arm round, until he emptied the spoil onto a tiny heap of streaky white mud.

I limped into the shower, aching from so much walking over the past three days. I felt exhausted, sore-throated and off-colour. However, there was work to be done and no time to laze in a hot bath. Within the hour, I sat, attempting to connect the university website proxy service to home.

***

'Quite straightforward,' Cathy Russell had said, but nothing happened, even with the miracle of reading glasses. I caved in at Page 4: I needed Bob the Builder to fix it. By the look of the steely cumulo-nimbus outside, he'd be available soon.

I phoned Mum, while I waited.

'How are you, Mum?'

'I'm very well, dear. How's everything with you?'

I took off my glasses so I could hear. 'Well, I haven't managed to start work yet.'

'Why ever not? It's nearly twelve.'

'There's such a lot to do, before you can get started these days.' My ashtray was by the computer. The smell of crushed ash made me queasy with longing. I must move it, now I'd quit.

'Oh, I see. Well now, when are you coming down again? I forgot to tell you my news on Wednesday. Were you going to call in today?'

I gritted my teeth. 'I'm working at home today. Is there anything wrong?' The first beads of rain hit the sitting room window.

'Oh, no, dear. I'm just being selfish, I know, but it would be so nice if we could go out to lunch together.'

I ground my teeth. 'OK, Mum. How about Wednesday, next week?'

'That would be lovely. There's another nice pub just along from the marina. We can walk there and sit outside if it's a nice day.' A scattergraph of water plopped on the glass.

'I'll come down about twelve, then.' The drops amalgamated into a dribble. 'I must dash. It's time for Paul's caffeine dose.'

He arrived at the kitchen table in his oiled wool socks, just as the kettle switched itself off.

'You must have smelled the coffee,' I said, for probably the three thousandth time in our marriage.

'Kettle needs de-scaling, Nessie.'

'Mmm. How are you getting on?' I put down his working mug, an embarrassingly twee Father's Day present, circa 1997. He picked up a banana, unzipped the skin systematically and took the first of four bites.

'It's rain stopped play,' he said, for perhaps the five hundredth time. I doubt Paul ever counted.

'What a pity! And you were getting on so well, love.' Elderflower and camomile scalded my tongue. 'Bloody hell,' I muttered sotto voce. 'Oh, for a cigarette.'

'I thought you'd given up?

My hands gripped the mug. 'I have. How many blocks to go?'

'About two hundred. Come and have a look, when the rain eases.' We both glanced at the kitchen window. The rain sleeted across, merging the distant hills in grey space. He chipped his limp banana skin into the bin.

'Paul, I wonder, could you help with the computer, while it's raining, please?'

He sighed. 'I hope you haven't messed up any software. What have you been trying to do?'

'Connect into the University's network.'

'Ah ha. How far have you got?'

'Well, I've got a sheet from Jonathan Griffiths, which tells you how to do it.'

'So what's the problem, then?' He paused, sighed again. 'OK, you make me another coffee. I'll look at it.'

Lightly-sprinkled mud trailed up the stairs to the nursery-small computer room we called a study. Mum's old bookcase squeezed down one wall, ready for all the books I'd need. Paul sat proprietorially on the only chair. I leant over his chalk-streaked fleece shoulder.

'Look. It's not coming up with the same message that's shown on Page 4.'

Paul compared the message on the screen with the printed instructions.

'Hmm. Let's see, now.' At Page 4, the computer aborted with a ring as unwelcome as an ice-cream van's chimes in December.

'What do we do now?'

'There's something wrong with the instructions! Can't you ask the IT Department ?'

'Well …'

'Explain the problem to them. See what they say.'

'But what is the problem?'

'I dunno. If I knew that …' Paul looked out of the window. 'You're the student.'

'But I need to be able to search databases and access journal articles,' I wailed.

'Your e-mail's working. Can't you get on with something else, until I can sort it out?'

'That's not the point.' I heard my voice escalate into panic mode. 'If I don't start soon, I'll never manage my first assignment.'

'Look, it's stopped raining. I must get on.'

Mr Reasonable left me to it. My blood pressure rose to dizzy heights. A headache kicked in, despite the camomile.

I made a start on Chapter One of Albert Bandura's six hundred page tome, printed on yellowing pages curiously untouched by human hand. Four hours and thirty-eight pages later, Leah's golden rule of student life rang in my ears. *Never read a book.* I decided to manage without Self-Efficacy and trawl for self-help.

'My name's Verruca Salt, and I want the poxy Server now!' I shouted to the empty house. Stamping my foot didn't help, either. Suddenly, I realised. In this new world, I had to slay the IT dragon myself. I jogged down to Anwar's. I lit a cigarette immediately, existed five seconds until the blissful rush, then settled down to business.

***

It was Wednesday morning before I managed a return visit to the library. By that time, I'd cobbled together a Proxy Server and two dozen printed references. Under pressure, the library catalogue was revealing its secrets.

The shelves upstairs provided a loan copy of Woodhouse and Rawlins. After that, I drew a blank. Browsing was bad. I was riveted in the most undiscriminating way: a starved man at the feast. Two-thirds down, I spotted a paperback, thin and colourful against the sombre academic texts. Its creased spine obscured the title. Intrigued, I wiggled it out.

'Prochaska and DiClemente,' I read out. '*Changing for Good*.' Only yesterday, we'd heard about the masters of behavioural Stages of Change from Kirsty. The little paperback was the shabbiest book on the block. Sinking onto a hop-up, I hoovered up its chatty style. Two hours later, my bum was numb and legs leaded. According to them, I was in Preparation for quitting smoking. In a moment of Self-liberation, I decided to nip into the doctor's for some patches before I tried again. Then, I'd be ready for Action.

Cheerfully, I clip-clopped downstairs and headed for the Library wall. Would anyone notice if I smoked two at once for a double fix?

***

A large, golden Indian pocketed his mobile phone. I sat down next to him in the Post-Grad Common Room and unpacked my first sandwich. His sparse goatee beard twitched as he shot out incomprehensible words.

'I'm sorry?' He looked surprised, pushing Hank Marvin glasses up his nose. 'Sorry,' I snailed. 'I .. did .. not .. understand .. what .. you said.'

'Ah, I see. Good afternoon, Nessie.' Elbows and knees knobbled out of his shiny blue track suit.

I bolted my first bite. 'Hi, how are you?'

'More slowly, please.' This could take a long time.

'Hi. What is your name?'

'Palapathy Srinivasula. Vasulu, I am called.' He lolled back, sliding a giant trainer over his knee. A blob of dried mud dropped onto the carpet.

'That's nice. Er … do you play football?'

His shiny conker-brown eyes glinted. 'Yes! Ars .. en … al.'

'Oh …' That floored me. Benjie played rugby. 'Are you enjoying the course, so far?'

'Yes, very much so.'

'Where do you come from?'

There was another incomprehensible stream.

'Oh yes.' I nodded sagely. 'And what do you do there?'

'Do?'

'Yes, did you have a job, or were you a student?' Taking a quick bite of sandwich, I tried to look encouraging and chew simultaneously.

'I have a BSc from University of Bangalore.'

'Why did you choose to come here to Britain?' I took another polite-bite.

'It is not so expensive in cost as Australia or the United States of America.'

'Oh ... You mean, it was the cheapest deal?'

'Yes. In the United States, it is maybe, three times the cost of Britain.' He smiled a wide, creamy-white smile at me. His shiny black hair nodded from side to side.

'And how did you find out about this university?' Such a long way from home, you poor little honey, I thought, feeling Mumsy again.

'The internet. And a man came to the University …' As he speeded up, I lost his drift. His wobbling head had a hypnotic quality. '… It was clearly a very good place of education, as is the University of Bangalore.'

'Oh yes.' We synchronised nods. 'This is one of the best universities in Britain.' I slowed down, and hewed another bite. Lumps of bread and ham jammed half-way down my oesophagus. My eyes watered. 'Where … are you living?'

'In the International Hostel in the town.' Johnny Depp's vulnerable dark eyes slid over his glasses. He pushed the black frames onto the bridge of his nose again. I groped in my rucksack.

'Do you like it there?'

'I'm sorry ...?'

'Sorry.' I swallowed a large mouthful from my water bottle. 'That's better. Are you enjoying the International Hostel?'

'Oh yes, I meet many different peoples there.'

'Are there other Indian students living there?'

'Oh yes, on my floor are seven computer scientists and two international economists.' He wobbled his head and volleyed more incomprehensible words. 'And there is an Indian take-away next door. Ah, three o'clock. It is open now.' He lolled back gracefully in the easy chair. 'Excuse me, please.'

Taking out his mobile phone, he thumbed a number, while I munched my apple. He broke into an Arkavathy of an Indian language with accompanying head noddings. Cosmopolitan life, here I come!

'I have ordered fish and chips for tonight. I like to try English food,' he wobbled at me happily. 'Excuse me, please.'

As he left the room, I remembered. Lunch with Mum. Shit. Bags full of it. I dredged my rucksack for my mobile.

'Hi, Mum.'

'Nessie!'

'Oh, Mum, I'm so sorry. I was, um, delayed.'

'I've been waiting three hours, young lady. The least you could have done was phone.'

'Oh dear, have you had some lunch? How about me coming down in an hour? Can we go out to the pub early this evening?'

'Phyllida's coming round now.'

'Well, can't we take her as well? I'll treat you both.'

I imagined Mum's pursed lips, considering the offer. 'All right, then. I'll see you in an hour.'

One hour to practise my search skills, before my new scholarly identity was guillotined for the day. My eyes watered. Yet again, a day of academic labour returning a nil result. I didn't know whether I was angry, frustrated, addicted, pathetic, or all of the above.

1.8

'Hi, Cathy.'

'How are you?' Cathy paused her gunfire touch typing, eyes still on the computer screen. I delved for my glasses in my rucksack and nipped into the only free computer station.

'Fine, thanks. Were you at the Post-grad Reception?'

'Sorry, Nessie, didn't you get my text?'

'Umm, I don't usually leave my mobile on.'

'Oh, I see. We had to entertain my partner's boss. What did I miss?'

I settled into my chair. 'Well, Professor Rawlins is out of the Department for the rest of the year.'

'No! I only came here because of him. Otherwise, I'd have stayed at Bir ...'

'Oh.' Ten pence dropped into the machine and a ticket came out the other end. 'Is he the Rawlins of Woodhouse and ...?'

'He most certainly is. Hadn't you heard of Ron Rawlins before you arrived?'

I shook my head. Cathy's eyebrows hitched up until they brushed the lines on her forehead. Clearly, I should feel embarrassed at my ignorance.

'Ron's probably the most famous exercise scientist in Britain, apart from Keen and Eiger. He was a Professor of Sport in the States by the age of thirty.'

Screens froze on travel bargains, Hotmail pages and cinema listings. Six students fell to serious listening. I slid down my glasses, so I could see her mobile face.

'He came back to Britain to continue working on his theory of children's emotional development through sport. Rawlins, 1988. After his article challenging Bandura in the

Annals of Behavioral Medicine, he got nicknamed Tiger of the Brits.'

'Really? Such a nice man, an academic tiger?'

She laughed wryly. 'Pussy cat now, Nessie. He's past his prime, these days.'

'Only his early sixties, surely? I thought professors went on to their eighties?'

'Maybe they still have a fan club, but brains are reckoned to peak around thirty.'

'Not much hope for us, then.'

'Not unless you're brilliant. So, how was the Reception?'

'Interesting. I met the Faculty Dean.'

'Oh ...'

'Alan Rawlins.'

'Yeah, I know. Redundant sociologist.' Cathy's typed sentence splatted onto the screen.

'What do you mean?'

'Obvious, isn't it? Twenty years ago, Sociology was fashionable. Nowadays kids don't want to do it. Half the lecturers have moved on.'

'Really?'

Cathy frowned, eyebrows dusted with loose powder from her forehead. 'What planet do you come from, Nessie? It's all about dumming down in a market economy. Look at the ever-increasing student numbers. Look at the number of Physics and Chemistry departments closing down.'

'But it doesn't feel like standards are falling from where I'm sitting. My kids had to work really hard for their places.'

Cathy wheeled her chair round. Her pointed toe twitched at the carpet. 'Maybe, for the best universities, but in general, it's survival of the fittest. Look at all the foreign students in town.' The students listening-in twitched as if she'd machine-gunned them.

'Foreign students?'

'Yeah. The non-European Union students pay three times as much for their year's MSc. The University would sink without their cash.' Cathy's voice vibrated in full battle cry.

The five non-EU students nodded vehemently. The other, a physiotherapist from Finland, nodded complicitly. I looked round my multi-ethnic fellow students, my fledgling friends.

'So all that pride in our vibrant ethnic community stuff is just ...'

The door clicked quietly open and Hugh Evans' head appeared. Eight students concentrated on eight computer screens. Hugh avoided looking anywhere in particular.

'Hello. Anyone seen Vasulu in the last half hour?'
We shook our heads, intent on our lonely studies.

'Everyone all right in here?'

'Yeah, fine thanks,' we murmured, far too busy to look up. The door clicked tentatively shut.

'I had no idea. That's shockingly ... Thatcheristic. What about the research ethic? You know, some off-the-wall theory that eventually saves the planet?'

Cathy's expression changed. She studied me with the curiosity of a paleontologist at the Natural History Museum. 'Research is ... what people are prepared to pay for.'

'What do you mean?'

'Research funding comes from politicians in the Government looking for their next election victory at one end, and charitable donations from old ladies in the street, at the other. Research projects merely reflect what's wanted and in fashion.'

'So where do we fit into that?'

'You look for a project that fits the Department's research profile, of course.' Cathy returned to typing. I hiked my glasses back into place. My sort of mollusc had disappeared half a century ago.

'Cathy, sorry to bother you again, but I'm really stuck on searching.'

'OK … can you find your way into Web of Knowledge?'

'Yeah, I think so.'

Ten minutes later, I arrived at my search engine. 'Now, type in your search terms and bingo, you'll get journal citations.'

'Search terms?'

'Yes. Well I suppose it's a bit more complicated than that. Type in a key word.'

How about *well-being*, my newest buzz-word? It would be good to know what, exactly, it meant. A recent landmark article or two would bring me bang up-to-date. I gasped: more than 200,000 articles.

'Um, Cathy?'

'Mmm?'

'There are far too many here to read.'

She glanced at my screen and laughed. 'Do you know about Boolean operators?'

'Something to do with knitting?'

'No.' She smiled at my feeble joke. 'You narrow your search down to, say, well-being in children. In most search engines you use AND to find articles which include both key words. Type in *well-being* AND *children* to isolate the stuff about both.'

WOK cooked with symbols I understood. Children turned up … oops, more than 300,000 articles since 1970! Then I stir-fried the two sets. Only 3,102 citations.

'Try the last five years. Nobody reads anything before 2000 these days.'

'371. That's amazing … but … I can't even read the titles in ten minutes.'

Never mind, I thought. For my first assignment, I need references to UK mortality. There's just time. I stirred in the key words and okayed. Nil.

'Cathy,' I wailed, hot, bothered, near to tears. 'Will I ever get the hang of these Noughties' student skills?'

Cathy hit return, full to the brim with satisfied smile. Her office chair whirled 180^0. 'Nessie?'

'How am I ever going to get together the resources to tackle this assignment?'

'Chill, babe. Vasulu was in here earlier, putting together a CD with all the papers you need for the first assignment. He's going to offer it round, in tomorrow's lecture.'

My voice came out puzzled as I packed my rucksack. 'Isn't that cheating?'

'No.' Cathy sounded amused. 'It's called co-operation.'

1.9

A female student, dressed like a young child, pushed past, weeping. My eyes suddenly watered, too. My initial high, correction, my positive affect, had been eroded by the frustrations of the past fortnight then breached by Cathy's bruising critique of the system. Everything was new and impossibly difficult. What chance did I stand of mastering it? I felt my antediluvian self-con… oops, sorry, my self-efficacy, trickling away.

I groped in my rucksack for the smooth oblong of the fag packet.

Untidy, black-clothed girls lounged outside the school. Youths disentangled themselves, small heads emerging unexpectedly above blazers and stick-insect grey flannel trousers. My shrinking uterus re-booted at the memory of my very own gangly ex-sixth former. I faltered to a walk.

Benjie hadn't phoned since we shuttled his gear to the Med School Hall, two weeks ago. I exhaled a furtive stream. As cognoscenti parents, we hadn't expected much else. After all, he'd gapped in Africa. If he could evade the crocs there, he should survive London. I'd start fussing at the weekend, if I hadn't heard anything.

***

A thin stream of smoke drifted from the little stainless steel chimney on the barge's coach roof. Mum's elderly geraniums matched *Iris'* bright graphics. An acrid, childhood whiff of burning coke permeated me as I stepped aboard. Through the open, varnished doors loud snorts blared up from the snug below. I stooped to look.

To my right, along the single bunk-cum-sofa, four elderly women perched, giggling at whatever was going on. On the other side, enthroned in the cane chair, a woman somewhere in her sixties, performed. She was a roly-poly sort of person, with a face like a red-cheeked Cox's apple emerging out of a bright-coloured kaftan. The mascara'd Biba look fossilised into a matching headscarf, from which long strands of henna-red hair straggled over gipsy earrings.

Mum stood in the galley area, filling the kettle. Several skeins of beads which I'd swear came from my circa-1958 dressing-up box dangled over her Marks and Spencer sweater and charity shop jeans.

'Vanessa!' Mum yelled, over the squawking. 'Come down, I'm sure we can squeeze you in somewhere.'

I clambered in. 'Hello, everyone!'

'This is Phyllida, and these are my U3A friends.' She gestured at the four women. I slid into the old nursing chair next to the galley. 'Phyllida's just been regaling us with her antics as a mature student at Sussex in the 1980's.'

'Oh, how interesting.' That seemed a bit of an understatement, judging by the startled silence when I'd arrived. 'Pleased to meet you, Phyllida. What did you read?'

'Psychology and sociology. Then I went on, by a very convoluted route,' she nodded knowingly at the parrots. They collapsed in paroxysms once more. '... to study the psychopathology of mystic role-models in transcendental religions.'

'Gosh, how er ... fascinating.'

'Yes, it *is* absolutely fascinating. Now I've retired from the university, I intend to spend more time out there.'

'Out there?' I didn't have a clue what she was talking about.

'And that's where my exciting news comes in.' Mum jumped up and down better than most octogenarians. 'Phyllida's invited me to go to India with her next month.' In her excitement, she slopped the tea out of the mugs she was filling.

'Right,' I echoed, to give me thinking time. 'How exciting.'

I passed round the plate of Mum's home-made rock buns, then munched through two myself. Nicotine deprivation had made me hungry.

Mum, although you would never know it from her hair, was eighty-two. She was thin and energetic. The climate might be a problem, but she wouldn't have any problems walking. She still had shed-loads of common sense, and never forgot to take her blood pressure pills. So far so good. Phyllida was the unknown quantity. I reserved judgement.

'Have you been to the travel agent, yet?'

'Of course, dear.' Mum beamed at me. 'It's only seven weeks away. I did it through the internet when I visited Benjie last Sunday. It's so easy to get the coach up from here,' she boasted to the others.

'Right. Did he help you, then?' I said weakly. Guilty as charged. Living on another planet.

'Of course, dear. He organised my medical insurance and looked up the injections I needed. There's no time to be wasted.'

'Good. So it's all sorted, then.' I felt totally out-gunned. 'Meal at The Baltic Trader, anyone?'

***

Much later that evening, bloated, I found Paul dozing in front of the News at Ten.

'Paul … wake up, it's bedtime.' He briefly came to. 'Would you like a cup of tea in bed?'

The tea revived Paul sufficiently for my purposes.

'Good day. I can play two notes now.'

I screwed on the toothpaste lid. 'Paul, do you know anything about Mum going to India?'

He sipped carefully.

'No. Are the teabags en flottant tonight?'

'Um, yes. I thought it wasn't worth making a whole pot. Do you want me to fish it out for you?'

'No, no. Just like to know what I'm up against. What's the gossip from Granny-land?'

I sat down on my side of the bed. 'Well, apparently, Mum's planning on going to Bangalore in November with Phyllida. She says Benjie helped her book the tickets and stuff.'

Paul leaned back against the headboard. 'Saves us the trouble.'

'That's all very well, but we hardly know anything about this Phyllida. How do we know if she's a suitable person … '

'… for Ella to go travelling with? Well, you met her today. What did you think?'

'Well, she's eccentric, to say the least. She used to be at the university. You know, the sort of person who's always had their head in the clouds …'

'… whilst the rest of us battled with the nitty-gritty of everyday life?' Paul finished my sentence for me. He often did that.

'Obviously still interested in Eastern philosophies. Now maybe, she's … just an ancient hippy who talks a lot? Maybe she's smoked so much cannabis …'

'… she's gone a bit loopy?'

'Mum's twenty years older, but she's a lot more down-to-earth.'

'Sounds like they'll look after one another. Will they get on each other's nerves?'

'Probably.' I grinned into my tea bag. Mum was getting more eccentric, year on year.

'I guess the bottom line is, do you think your Mum could get back safely …'

'… from Bangalore, on her own?' Yes, I admit it. I finished his sentences, too.

'Yeah.'

'I doubt it.'

'… I think she could. She travelled a lot in the nineties when your parents made all that money out of British Telecom. And look how well she organised the move onto *Iris*. We only helped with muscle power.'

'Mmm. And moral support? Paul, India isn't just fifty miles away.'

'Do you realize, we're talking about Ella here, not Leah or Benjie?'

He lay down and stretched his arm across the pillow, ready for my head. 'Sorry?'

'Well, did we go through this performance for Leah, travelling alone in South America, or Benjie, volunteering in Kenya?'

'No, but then, they're young enough to run away if they get in trouble.'

'I think this means we've moved into the next generation ...'

'… caring for the oldies,' I supplied. 'Not the kids, right?'

'Exactly.' He switched out his light. 'Quit worrying about her, Nessie. She's a tough old bird. Don't go there, just yet.'

I switched off my light. ‘Have you heard anything from Benjie?’

‘Yep, he phoned this afternoon.’

I snuggled down on Paul’s warm shoulder. ‘Is he alright?’

‘Of course. Didn’t say much. He was on his mobile. God, Nessie, you stink of garlic and smoke. I thought you said you’d quit?’

‘Well, I have … sort of. I’m going to get some patches so I can start properly.’

Paul pulled the duvet over his head. ‘Can you set the alarm for six-thirty, please,’ he mumbled from the depths. I rolled over, switched my light on again and spent a happy hour in bed with Woodhouse and Rawlins, instead.

1.10

Somewhere along University Road, my jacket gave up the unequal struggle against water ingress through the seams. After a personal best of 38.45, I puffed clouds of steam for the following hour. My soaked jeans chilled my thighs and sweat simmered under my arms.

'The first module finishes next week. The deadline to hand in written assignments is three weeks later.' Stress irradiated me. Today Versace scrawled across Kirsty's tee-shirt. She wore BTM-becoming tight pants and stiletto heels with winkle-picker grade pointed toes.

'What if we can't identify the landmark articles?'

'What if we get stuck?'

'What if we fail this assignment?'

Scott Woodhouse stood aside from the gathering clouds. Powerpoint popped up a cartoon knight in armour. 'Some of you have walls to scale before you even approach the question.' There was a wry laugh from the front row.

He was just explaining his template for opening paragraphs in forty-five slick seconds, 'Define key terms … own words … my thesis is that …,' while Powerpoint flew in points like carrier pigeons, when the door to the lecture room opened. Penny, the departmental secretary, dodged her face round the top half. A dog wandered through underneath.

Hugh was loading his file, ready to deliver the first lecture. If he noticed the dog, he was too polite to say anything. He was a sweet-looking young man, with something of the overgrown schoolboy mislaid somewhere about him.

Scott sat with Kirsty, over towards the far side. I guessed Hugh was a newish lecturer and they intended to help him out with some feedback on his presentation. Perhaps they didn't realize the fearsome array of skills with which the front row mature students already assessed any lecture.

The dog trotted down the gangway to Scott, a half-grown Labrador with a fluorescent yellow harness. He wiggled in, settling in the small space between them, leaning affectionately against Scott's leg. The dog-lovers in the room swivelled in their seats with a collective, 'Ahhh,' as the winsome one licked Scott's hand.

He half-rose.

'Sorry, Hugh. If I could just explain to anyone who doesn't know? It's *Take Your Dog to Work Day* today.' Scott looked at the Chinese students and slowed down. 'Research shows .. that domestic pets .. promote .. lower stress levels. In the UK .. many people have dogs .. as pets.'

There was a longer drawn, 'Aaahhh,' from the students, as the golden doggie stood up on cue, tongue lolling out of his grinning mouth, ready to go anywhere with Scott.

'My wife trains Guide Dogs for the Blind, so it seemed an ideal opportunity to give Jester here a taste of a different environment and a chance for everyone to lower their stress levels.' There was a corporate swell of humour as the translations kicked in. 'Sorry, Hugh, do carry on.'

Hugh pushed his Harry Potter glasses up his nose and clicked the first slide into touch. It was dark blue, with yellow words.

'Physical Activity patterns in the U.K.'

'Good morning everyone. I'm here today to talk about physical activity patterns in the UK.'

'Hugh Evans, University of Deepstraw, Wyoming. With acknowledgements to Ron Rawlins,' I read.

'With acknowledgements to Ron Rawlins, who originally wrote the lecture, but isn't er, here today to give it … and er,

Scott and Kirsty, of course.' There was an on-screen cloudburst and the Powerpoint slide morphed into a red background with blue words.

'The General Household Survey, 2002,' we chorused.

'Is there a handout, please Hugh?' asked Midge from the front row.

'Oh, yes, thanks Midge.' Hugh swerved into the table behind him. The sudden movement alerted the dog, who rose to his paws with a sharp woof. We laughed. Midge took the papers from Hugh, dispatching them to different destinations. Hugh waited as long as he dared for the handouts to reach the darker corners of the room and resumed. We focused on the screen again.

'Er, The General Household Survey, 2002.' Hugh blinked and clicked his remote control. The screen went blank. Hugh went pale. It was like the moment in the school play when your kid forgets his lines.

'Oh for goodness sake,' whispered Cathy. 'Hasn't he given a lecture before?'

'Give him a break,' said Midge. 'Every lecturer's got to start somewhere. He's probably a Powerpoint virgin.'

'Not In My Back Yard, thanks very much. I'm only seconded for a year.'

Scott and Kirsty leapt to the rescue. They pored over Hugh's laptop. Far-flung sections of Hugh's admirable and comprehensive filing system went on display. It seemed it might take a while to find the right menu.

'Do you think I've got time to …' I'd forgotten I'd quit smoking. 'Er .. what do you do, Cathy?'

'Part-time physiotherapy; part-time organizing training for the City NHS Trust.'

'Sounds interesting. What does …?'

The screen filled. Navy wording on pale blue marbling had suddenly down-sized two points. I had to switch to the handout. Some time later, an intermittent noise scored my concentration.

Losing focus was fatal. In the time I'd wondered about the sound, Hugh had moved on two slides and fourteen bullet points. I scrambled round the handout, as Hugh illuminated the leisure and sport section of the General Household Survey, 2002 with copious graphs. The permutations of assorted childhood groups seemed interminable. Someone else thought so, too. The wails escalated.

Hugh laboured through Ron's landmark research on children's sport in fifteen slides. I checked the back page of the handout. Nearly forty to go. How I needed a cigarette. Stimulus control, murmured Prochaska and DiClemente, over my shoulder. I sat on my hands.

'And this is an accelerometer.' Hugh held up an anonymous, plastic box. 'These are terrific because they measure all movement, not just walking steps. The data is fed ba ...'

An anguished yelp interrupted. I looked along the line. Kirsty sat, legs crossed, one long pointed toe idly swinging back and forward. I frowned.

'Dr Woodhouse,' I hissed. 'Is Jester alright?' Scott was scribbling in a notebook. He started, then bent forward to fondle Jester's beeswax-coloured head.

'Ouch,' yelled Scott, as Kirsty's winklepicker gored his hand. 'Look out!' Hugh's voice faded out of the reckoning as Scott nursed his hand.

Kirsty jumped up. 'Oh, Scott, I'm sorry. Sorry, Jester.' She leant down to the dog. Jester launched into a pathetic set of wails. 'Have I hurt you, boy?' She brought up a bloodied hand.

'Kirsty! You've drawn blood.'

'Oh no! I'm so sorry. What shall we do?'

Scott was already pressing the dog's ear with a handkerchief.

'Erm, would you like me to put on a bandage, until you can get him to the vet?' I heard myself offering.

'Would you?'

'Well, I can try, if you've got a first aid kit. I know how to bandage a human head.'

Scott half-stood, short-harnessing the dog with one hand, staunching the blood with the other.

As I joined Scott and Jester, I heard Kirsty. 'I think we should break for coffee now.'

'The nearest first aid box will be at Reception.' Scott held the door open for me and dropped the bloody hanky. I picked it up and held it to Jester's dripping ear, bent double. My back twanged. Not for the first time: bending over Leah's cot had started it.

Nick was leaning against the receptionist's desk. 'Scott! What's the go? Oh God, it's S.M. Sheila again.'

'Is there a first aid kit handy, Nick, please? Jester's got a bloody ear.'

'Sure, mate, bring him round here.' Nick led the way into the physiotherapist's treatment room. 'Shove him up on the couch, Scott.'

Together we hauled the dog up.

'I don't know what Yvonne will say.' Scott's cool persona evaporated in sweaty annoyance.

Nick stretched his hand to the wound. Jester backed off, head down and bottom up, growling. Scott grabbed his head to calm him.

He held Jester's mouth shut with one hand. 'Vanessa, can you catch him round the shoulders, please?'

Half-laying on Jester, I slid my arms round his neck. He smelled of ripe farmyard. It was far more intimate than I was usually prepared to go with a dog.

Nick approached with a gauze pad. Apart from the shorts, he could have been from Grey's Anatomy. I wished I'd thought of varnishing my nails.

'How did it happen?' Nick asked. The proximity of his designer stubble was quite disturbing. His hair was almost exactly the same blonde colour as Jester's.

'I didn't really see.'

Nick's cheek backed away.

Scott's jawbone was just the other side of the dog. I could see the sheen on his forehead, where his hair receded. The roots of his blond streaks were grey and scaly. Wiry hairs poked from the open collar of his blue shirt.

'Kirsty was kicking him.' His cheeks sucked in and out as he ground his teeth.

'What! Kirsty? Kicking a dog?' Nick paused, Steristrip waving from his finger. 'That's not like her.'

'Oh she didn't mean to,' I stuck in hastily. 'She'd just forgotten not to cross her legs.' Scott screwed-up his face. I suddenly remembered the garlic from last night.

Nick zoomed in with a Richard Branson look. 'Whatever are you talking about?' He'd made a bloodless coup with the Steri-strip, but didn't seem to have any idea what to do with a dog's ear and a roller bandage.

'Would you like me to have a go at the bandage, Nick?' I directed my voice hygienically downwards.

'Sorry? Err, sure, yes please.' Trouble was, I was locked, bottom sticking out like an old crone, trying to avoid breathing on either man. It wasn't enhancing my street cred.

'Where did you learn to bandage so neatly?' asked Scott, as I finished my reef knot. Even I had to admit that, for a dog, Jester looked fetching: a canine Pudsey Bear.

'Oh, PE teacher …plenty of practice.'

'So was I,' returned Scott. 'But I never got past the recovery position. Vanessa, I owe you one.' The smile reached up to the little circles of ice edging his pupils: contact lenses, without a doubt.

'And mine's a Castlemain. Now what's all this about Kirsty, then?' Nick packed the scissors away with large, deft fingers.

I inched upright. Oww. I clutched at the pain, but at least I was vertical. 'Well she told us in a lecture that she was trying not to cross her legs any more.'

The men exchanged glances. 'I didn't realize Kirsty had a libido issue,' Nick paused, deadpan. 'I'll have to ask her about it.'

'… because of varicose veins …' I added, too late.

Scott hurried off to the vet. Nick wandered off to report to Kirsty. As for me, I still had the second half of Hugh's lecture to survive.

***

I arrived home after a slow, painful journey. Paul was upstairs, judging by the tentative tuba sounds. As I closed the front door, he clattered down.

'How's your day been?' He was unusually cheerful. 'I can get three notes now!'

I clutched the back of the settle to ease the weight from my back. 'Terrific.'

Paul looked at me and sighed. 'You've had a hard day, haven't you? Shall I make you a cup of tea?'

'Oh, yes and yes, please.' I edged upstairs to the study.

'Here you are, Nessie. I'll spend another five minutes on the tuba and then I'll get some food.'

'Thanks, Paul.' I needed to be still.

Those soothing five minutes with a cup of tea were the ones I'd missed. My throat graunched from craving for the comforting fluffiness of cigarette smoke. My will-power reset to a record low.

With infinite care, I inched the ashtray onto the floor next to my rucksack. I crept myself down next to it. I slid one hand in the side pocket and found my cigarettes and lighter.

***

Half an hour later, Paul gently shook me. 'What's for supper?'

'Eergh … ' My back was as stiff as a witch's broomstick. I lay inert. 'What's in the freezer?'

He clumped downstairs. Hard objects thumped plastic. 'There's two loaves, a plastic box with something brown in it. There's a beef joint, a packet of scampi and er, a tub of ice cream. No it's not, it's rice. And some frozen veggies,' he called up.

'OK, scampi risotto. Or egg fried rice if there's any eggs left in the fridge.'

With extreme caution, I edged myself up and shuffled to the loo. Perhaps I did feel better for my power nap.

Paul opened a bottle of Cahors from our last trip to France as I slid the plates across the table. A glass of wine was an unusual concession for a Thursday. He gobbled his risotto.

'Are you sure you can cope with all this?' It was a fair question. Honest evaluation was called for. Taking my time, I picked at the scampi crumbs; scraped the last of the mango chutney out of its jar with my finger, rested my ache against the chair back.

'It's been a helluva fortnight. So much has happened: up, then down. Chaotic, scary and very frustrating. At the moment, it seems impossible.' I wormed out my shiny student card and studied my photo. 'I started as a frightened rabbit. Now I'm plain terrified.'

He leapt in, a lined face with a deep Y between his eyebrows. 'Is it wise to carry on? Why not give up now, before you get in any deeper? We'll still be able to get a refund, I imagine.'

I was tempted. No need to struggle with Vasulu's CD. A spot of gardening this weekend. We could spend the refund on a trip to somewhere very exciting indeed, like Greenland or the Gambia.

I braced my hands on either side of my chair to ease the penknife slicing across my back. I ached in every cell for more nicotine. 'Is that what you think I should …?'

'Well, you must admit, the past fortnight has been difficult for both of us. You've hardly been here and when you have, you've been very tetchy. Especially stopping smoking at the same time. That's been the final straw.'

'That's got nothing to do with it!'

Paul shrugged and stood to stack the dinner plates on the worn formica. Was it really only a couple of days since I felt euphoric? He turned on the hot water tap. 'What if this is just one of your fads, Nessie?'

'But what would I do, with the kids gone? I'm too old to be a PE teacher now, even if anyone wanted me. I couldn't bear to go back on the supply list until I retire.'

'What about getting a dog? We could do with a guard dog while there's all these building materials sculling around.'

'But that's not paid unless you mean training a Guide Dog,' I moaned.

The washing up liquid burped as he squeezed its emptiness. 'I could do with some labouring help for the new garage. You haven't even looked at what I've done, yet.'

My old identity had perished like an old rubber band. 'For goodness sake, there must be more to life for me than being Bob the Builder's mate!'

'OK then, your Mum needs looking after.' He rinsed the suds neatly off a plate.

'I've only just finished looking after ...'

'The kids? Get a job, then. The redundancy money will run out, eventually.' Mr Reasonable was nearly snarling as he picked up the blue and white tea-towel.

'When do I get the chance to fulfil myself? I could be an undiscovered Einstein, or a Bill Gates or … or Condoleezza Rice.' He lobbed me the cloth to wipe the table. I drew Manx with my finger in a trail of small suds. Paul didn't understand what I needed.

'Is that very likely? I thought it was a qualification in Exercise Science?'

'Well you never know where it will lead. I've never … ' The balance was tipping. Besides, I was stubborn. 'Yes, I am going to carry on. I think it will be fulfilling .... . It has infinite possibilities, like Lavinia at Project Trust always said.'

'I thought she said, *always have a raffle*? Perhaps you could …'

'Stop it, Paul, this is no joking matter. You can be so infuriating.' I wiped the wetness above my cheekbones with the back of my hand.

'Are you absolutely sure? I won't think any the less of you for not getting some poncy higher degree.' Paul tore a piece of kitchen towel from the roll and handed it to me.

His concerned eyes reminded me of Jester. 'Thanks, but no thanks. I just have more idea what I'm up against, now.' I blew my nose. 'I can do this.'

He smiled wryly. 'Don't say I didn't warn you.'

'You don't want me to do another degree, do you?'

'Well, let's put it this way. I've got along fine all these years without one.'

'Until now.'

'I can't do much about that, now. A degree at our age is obviously a lot more difficult than either of us imagined.'

'I'm only in my early fifties.'

'Fifty-six.'

The rubber band snapped. 'Oh, stop being so bloody negative! It's not at all helpful. I'm going to bed.' I stormed out of the chair. My back went into the worst spasm yet. Paul turned on the News at Ten.

PART TWO
Reviewing the Literature
2.1

'If I prescribed you nicotine replacement patches, would that help?' My GP wore a long skirt, ballet pumps and a posh voice. I hadn't met the newest incumbent before, but I already had the sinking feeling that further failure to quit smoking wouldn't be tolerated.

'Oh, yes, thanks very much.' I cosied up with a toothy beam. My back was on the mend and it hardly seemed worth mentioning my torturous week of challenged mobility until I could get an appointment. Besides, her own IT beast was roaring.

'Ah, no screen. Julie?' She listened, while I examined a photograph of two Gap-clad boys tumbling with a dog.

'Mrs Elliott, you haven't been into the surgery since 1998. You don't have a computer record.'

'Ooh, I'm sorry.' Had I somehow missed the call to log in my details on the NHS system? 'I haven't been ill ...'

'In that case, we'll just book you in for a Well-Woman check.'

'... but I've had a problem over the past week with my back.'

'Aha. While we're waiting for Julie, I'll take your blood pressure.'

The cuff squeezed on and off inside thirty seconds. 'Hmm. It's quite high today.'

I rolled my eyeballs round the corner of the screen. 180/105. 'Well, I'm quite stressed. I've just started a Masters' course.'

'Oh really?' She looked at me with a tinge of respect. 'What in?'

'Erm, sport science.' I spoke cagily, in case she thought I might tread on her professional toes. Her lip curled, even so. I forbore to mention it was a Russell Group university. One shouldn't pander to academic snobbery.

The computer nudged the printer into action. 'Here's your prescription, Mrs Elliott. I'll see you again in a month and check your back then.'

***

At home, an Urgent and Confidential letter waited on the doormat, in a thick wove envelope addressed to Mr L. Elliott. I e-mailed Leah as soon as I'd fixed the first patch on my arm.

> *If you can, please phone. Let me know if I should open mysterious letter and e-mail contents. Please confess if you have had sex change.*

That should do it. It took the best part of an hour to bring her up to date on the rest of my terrifying new lifestyle. Hopefully she'd reply quickly, before I died of curiosity.

Around 11.30, I settled down with Vasulu's CD. I had three weeks to produce a good enough paper. My first problem was to understand the piled research reports in front of me. Then, to amass any more information I needed from reputable sources. Finally I faced the mere detail of writing an assignment, the first in thirty years.

I reached the last sentence of the first paper eight hours later.

The language of the Literature invaded my brain: posited, somatic, chronic, meta-analysis, morbidities and cognitions. I noted each new glittering scrap of jargon, ready to sprinkle like fairy dust through my forthcoming essay.

The next time I surfaced was half way through Saturday afternoon. I found myself on the floor, surrounded by the spent forces of battle: a half-empty packet of chewing gum, balls of screwed-up paper, two cereal bowls, several empty coffee mugs, my big Oxford dictionary and an unintelligible harvest of hand-written notes.

Over the next week I discovered more about The Literature. References from one article lead into an academic hub, like clues in a detective story. I felt like a cab-driver, learning The Knowledge.

I developed a time-consuming soft spot for anything that nice James Prochaska published. In my dreams, he looked like Ron. When I read charismatic Voices, I imagined their personalities. After a while, I concentrated on granddaddies. They wrote pegs on which to hang the work of the rest.

My biggest problem with the Literature was its corrupting influence. Each morning I woke up, eager to engage. Each day I sidetracked. Intriguing hooks required instant perusal, before they disappeared forever, back into the mysterious Web. The *Journal of Happiness Studies* swallowed one whole afternoon.

An abstract might feed my habit, but often only the full article would satisfy. I feasted on the flexibility merits of T'ai chi or golf. I gorged on flow and watching the Winter Olympics on telly to increase well-being. I nibbled on support for anorexics from internet chat rooms. I wolfed weight loss strategies of successful dieters and Tom-peeped couples' intimate bed-talk. In a short time, I knew a little about a lot more.

Eventually I came up, gasping for air. With nine days left, a hundred pages of notes and no idea how to whip them in to shape, I e-mailed Kirsty for advice.

***

Kirsty was finishing up another meeting.

As I waited, the carpeted corridor around me reverberated. The gym floor above me oscillated. Down one wall were health-promoting cartoons. A row of kids sank gappy teeth into fruit and veg. A safety-conscious cyclist wobbled down the road to work. A swimmer ploughed through bubbly water. Further along, a girl and dog bounded joyfully into leisure-time physical activity. The other side boasted a plantation of articles published by the Department. I'd accessed two of Hugh's papers only last week and read them with the awe of a nobody.

Midge erupted from the office, clutching her handbag and a scuffle of papers. Her lipstick had all but disappeared.

'Midge, are you alright?'

'I think so.' Her urban warrior nurse's body usually topped a burst of cheeky freckles and a strong swirl of one-parent reality. To see Midge crumbling, of all the mature students, astonished me.

'Would you like a coffee when I've finished?'

'Yeah. I'll be in the IT workroom.' Midge stumbled towards the ladies' loo.

'Come in and sit down. I won't be a second: just sending an edit ...' Kirsty glanced up from her computer. '...

Midge'll be fine. She's very capable.' She swirled her chair. 'Now, how are you doing?'

I outlined how far, or rather, how little I'd moved with the paper.

'Which question are you answering?'

'The one on future directions of exercise research.'

'First off, that's only half the question. What's the other half?'

'Oh, the critique of recent studies. That's OK. I've got my six articles and I've started the table in Word. My only worry is how to set it out.'

'Have you looked in the cupboard yet?'

'The cupboard?'

'Yes, we told you about it on *Take your Dog to Work Day*.' Kirsty grinned. Today's fluffy, chocolate sweater made her warm and approachable.

'Really? It must have by-passed me.'

'Well, ask Penny to unlock the cupboard. Read last year's papers, to give you some idea what to do. All the A grades use tables, whatever the assignment. Always have a table.' That sounded familiar.

'OK, that's easy enough. What about the second part? I've got about a hundred pages of notes and only two thousand words left to write them up.'

'That's why you have a table or two. They aren't part of your word count. Now, what's your main message in one sentence?' Within five probing questions, a neat plan existed.

As I thanked her, she butted in. 'Oh, hang on, Vanessa, I've been meaning to ask you. Would you be the student representative on the Academic Committee?'

'What would I have to do?' I asked doubtfully.

'Oh, just attend a committee meeting every month to bring up any student issues. There aren't usually many. Our students are working too hard.'

'Well, I suppose I could, if it's only once a month. Thanks for thinking of me.'

'Frankly, it's quite hard to find someone. None of the younger students are interested. Thanks for volunteering. I'll let Ron know you've been co-opted.' And that's how I came to be at the Academic Staff Meeting the following week, when I should have been at home, writing my assignment.

***

Midge's tears seeped, despite the tissue. I sat her down on a café bar stool, and treated us both to tiffin squares and lattes. Sugar and caffeine are essential First aid sometimes, even at those prices and with cardboard cups.

'I just don't have enough time to write this assignment. I'm so tired from the late nights. Maybe I should give up now.' Midge's fingernails, cradling the carton, had taken a battering.

'What did Kirsty say?'

'She was very nice about it. She said, do what you can in the time, it's only your first attempt, there's still five more assignments to go.'

'How far have you got?'

'That's the trouble. I can only work three mornings a week, while Freya's at playgroup. She doesn't go to school until next September. I've hardly done anything yet.' Her eyes disappeared in teary, red rims below her sandy fringe.

'Do you get much time in the evenings?'

'Not really. Harry doesn't go to bed until eight, these days.'

'Mmm.' I flashbacked to my *golden days of childhood gallery*: a supper table, two parents, two lively, inquiring under-elevens in the spotlight, a blurry adolescent. I fast-forwarded from my empty nest back to Midge and her problems. 'What about weekends?'

'Well Mum and Dad usually have the children on Sunday, so I can get on.'

'That's not long, judging by the hours my assignment's swallowed up already. Are you full-time?'

'No, part-time, over two years.' She bit into the tiffin. 'Mmm, that's good. I want to go back to the NHS, when I can.'

'What did you do?'

'Well, I was a children's nurse. Now I'm interested in nutrition, this seemed like a good degree.'

'Yeah, I see. Is it going to qualify you as a dietician?'

'Well, no, unfortunately not, but it is local. I can't spend time travelling, like you do. It wouldn't be possible with two children to look after as well. So I'm thinking of moving into a nutrition-related area of nursing.'

'Oh Midge. What a good idea! Don't give up yet.'

'No, I'm not. I think I'll see how I do on this assignment, at any rate.'

There hadn't been any mention. 'Do you … have another half to help you?'

'No. He went off with a friend, a couple of years ago.' She smiled, suddenly fifty instead of thirty-four. 'Don't look like that, Nessie. We were washed up anyway. My Mum and Dad are around. They've even lent me the money to pay my fees.' She checked her mobile. 'I must go, it's nearly time for

Cinders to be at the school gate.' She drained the dregs of her cup. 'Thanks … my turn to buy the coffee next time.'

***

'Nessie.' It was Paul. 'What's for lunch?'

'I'll come down.' I sat up straight and reviewed my morning's output with a quiet glow.

> *'It is well-known that, in a general population, males and females age.*
> *However, today, due to advances in medical science, individuals do not necessarily die.*
> *This paper discusses the epidemiological relationship between exercise, the ageing process and disease.*
> *My thesis will explore the notion that reducing morbidities through exercise will eliminate All-Cause mortality. And we will have to find a new cause of death.'*

The last sentence wasn't quite right, but it would do for now. Triumphant, I found a tin of tuna lurking in the back of the store cupboard.

'I've all but finished the footings,' Paul slipped out of his boiler suit, arranging his mud-weighted shoes neatly on the back door mat. His walking socks had holes in both toes. He padded across the tiles to fill the kettle.

'There'll only be six concrete blocks left, so there's hardly any waste at all.' Paul surveyed the dings and grazes on his hands.

'Great.' My head was in the back of the fridge, casting for the bottle of lemon to add a dash of haute cuisine to the tuna paté. The bottle was five months out of date. I weighed up the odds ratio, scurvy versus food poisoning, and ground black pepper into the paté instead.

'I don't like lemon anyway.' Paul watched me jettison the bottle.

'Oh … sorry.' I returned from my theoretical meanderings. 'Yes, the footings.'

'The building inspector's coming tomorrow. Then they'll be backfilled, so it's your last chance to see them.' He laid his knife down. 'Any more bananas?'

'No, not at the moment, I'm afraid. I've bought some flapjack.'

'Oh … yes please. Then I must get on. It's dark by five, these days.'

At the end of the first page, I needed to insert a Word table. Table 1 itself was a two day hike and I was proud of it. Suddenly, I couldn't pick it up, let alone deposit it in its rightful home. This was much trickier than I'd expected. Oh, how I needed a new NRT patch. And an IT manager. But the weak winter sun shone all afternoon.

I found my gardening wellies and slipped out to the building site for advice. It was turning colder now, with a low mist over the fields and a clear view of the hills. The last unpicked apples lay strewn around, with late wasps excavating brown caves. I picked my way round the back, negotiating the remains of a pile of hard core on the way.

The hired cement mixer moodily churned out muck for the footings. I heard Edward's voice over its pervasive graunchiness.

'At least you hadn't finished.'

'Can you believe it, Nessie?' Paul crossed outraged arms, sparse grey hair spiked on end by the wind. 'The building inspector visited today. He's rejected the foundations.'

'What! Why's that?'

'No provision for a soakaway.'

'Whatever's that?'

'Wastewater drains into the soakaway.' Edward was used to placating clients enmeshed in the chains of house sales. He knew about buildings, in theory.

'I should have put it in on the plans.'

'Well, Building Regs should pick it up, even if the architect forgets it.'

I looked at the line of blocks. 'How do you put it right?'

The amateur architect looked ready to burst into tears. 'He's ordered me to break out the blocks and lay a drain over there.' Paul gestured through the concrete path and pile of hard core, to the middle of the back lawn. 'Before I carry on blinding.'

I gasped obligingly. 'Really? How do you do that?'

'I'll have to Kango through the concrete on the drive. Then the digger back again, I suppose. When I've had a cup of tea, I'm off down to the hire shop.'

'Would you like a cup of tea, Edward?' I offered.

'Erm, I think ... Oh, go on then, twist my arm.' He'd been our jocular neighbour in the new house next door for twelve years. 'How's the course going, Nessie?'

'Wonderfully, thanks.' Reluctantly I led him into the kitchen. I hadn't looked recently, but I pretty much knew what to expect.

The kitchen floor hadn't been washed for the past fortnight, due to an *it isn't worth it at the moment* stage. As well as man-sized muddy heelprints to the first aid box, pawprints led from the cat flap to the food bowl. Entrails from last night's hunting were displayed on the floor near the table. Breakfast bowls and plates from lunch piled by the sink, under the *pending* heading until supper time. Dead parsley crisped on the windowsill. Monday's rain-soaked labouring fingerprints still muddied the kettle.

'Do sit down.' Edward removed his shoes and tiptoed cautiously to the empty kitchen chair. I switched on the kettle and groped for a carton of long life milk, since we'd run out of fresh at lunchtime. I unloaded a chair to retrieve our remaining three best cups and saucers. Edward only drank out of bone china. There were no biscuits, so I cut the last of the syrup cake on offer from Anwar's shop into three spindly slices.

Half an hour later, the phone rang.

2.2

'Where are you?' Paul's face beamed: it could only be Leah. Edward tiptoed out, ostentatiously waving. I rushed upstairs for the letter.

'Yes, I didn't realise it needed a soakaway when I drew the plans ... yes … next time. Here's your mother now.' He handed the phone over. 'She's Skype-ing on a computer. There's a bit of an echo.'

'Hi Mum, how are you?'

'I'm fine, darling, where are you … you?'

'I'm in Arequipa. We arrived in town at six o'clock this morn-morning.'

'Arequipa? Is everything alright … right?'

'Sure Mum, I've been with some Australians this week, we've all come up together by overnight bus. We're thinking of making for Guatemala next-next.'

'Sounds fun … fun.' There's not much room for manoeuvre when your first born is three and a half thousand miles away.

'OK, so what's all this about a confidential letter?'

'Yes, it's here, addressed to Mr Leah Elliott.'

'How strange.'

At last, I slit open the envelope and pulled out the Croxley laid paper.

'It's headed, *Confidential: Dear Sir,*' I read out.

> *'I have responsibility for recruiting personnel for security services for Her Majesty's government. I am writing to ask whether you might have an interest in applying for a specialised international appointment that is not within the*

normal selection and training programme for a career in the Foreign and Commonwealth Office.'

'What on earth does that mean?'

'Hang on Leah, I haven't finished.'

'Please submit the enclosed form to me within two weeks should you wish to take this enquiry further. Applications are considered once a year and may take up to nine months to process.
Signed, Anya Ramonovich.'

'Is this some kind of wind-up?'

'I don't think so. It's from the Foreign Office. The envelope certainly looks *bona fide*.'

Paul moved round to my front and mouthed at me, 'M .. I .. 5.'

I nodded casually, as if letters like this thumped on our doormat every day.

'Sorry, what did you say, Leah?'

'I said, it sounds like the Secret Service.'

'Just what Dad's saying.'

'Ooh, how exciting. Shall I follow it up?'

'Well, darling, that might be a little difficult from Arequipa.'

'Yeah, but I don't want to ignore it. I could be the next Bond girl.'

I feared as much. 'I expect the Secret Service is very boring most of the time.'

'Can you give me Anya's e-mail address, please, Mum.'

'Umm, she doesn't have one.'

'The Foreign Office doesn't have an e-mail address? You must be joking.'

I searched the letter again. 'Nope, no e-mail address.'

'In that case, Mum, could you give them a ring for me, please. Explain the situation. Ask if I can apply when I get back to the UK?'

'I'm quite busy with my first assignment right now,' I fudged.

'Mum, a letter from me would never get there in time.' I understood exactly why they were head-hunting her, whoever *they* might be.

By the time the call finished, it was too late for Paul to get into Swindon or for me to ring the MI5 hotline. We made a deal. I cooked supper, while Paul magicked my Table into the position that I, rather than Microsoft, had appointed for it.

2.3

B.C. My last essay. Before Computers, that is. My blood pressure ascended Popacateptl as I struggled with the technology. And then my final draft didn't look good, even to me.

Now the study window reverberated to the punches of a pneumatic jackhammer exploding through concrete. In the background the phone rang apologetically.

'Hello?'

'Mum.' Benjie sounded cheerful as ever. 'Mum, I'm coming down to stay tonight. We're playing the uni at ...'

I stuck a finger in my other ear. 'Sorry? Say again more loudly, please.'

'I'm coming down this afternoon, to stay tonight,' he shouted.

'Great! Lovely To See You, Darling. What Time Are You Arriving?'

'About sixish?'

'OK, Six. Supper?'

'Yes please! Any crumble going?'

'I'll Look In The Freezer.'

That was the end of my academic endeavours for the day. Before domesticity prevailed, I sank into the lounge sofa and removed my glasses for the priority job.

'Good morning. The Foreign Office.'

'Ahh, good morning. Could I speak to Anya Ramonovich, please?'

'One moment please. Who's calling?'

'It's ... err ... Leah Elliott.' There was a long musical pause which muffled the thumping from the side of the house. I studied a faded little carton which Leah had brought home from Ireland. Why hadn't we ever burnt the blocks of turf inside the model croft? I sniffed. It didn't smell of peat or anything else after six years.

'I'm afraid Ms Ramonovich is not in the office today. Shall I put you through to someone else?'

'Urr … yes please.'

'Hallo, can I help you?' She sounded like an HRH.

'Errm, yes. I've received a letter addressed to Mr L. Elliott, with an application form for special appointment.'

'I'm afraid I don't deal with application forms.'

'No, I wanted to speak to Miss Ramon ...'

'She's left. Can I help?'

'Thank you. Well first of all, it's not Mr Elliott, but Miss Elliott, I'm afraid.'

'Yes?'

'Well, the thing is, Miss Elliott is away at the moment. I'm her mother. She asked me to ring, as she'd like her application to be considered on her return.'

'Oh yes. I see Mr Elliott's in … Leeds at present.'

'Well, no, actually Miss Elliott was in Arequipa, Peru, yesterday.'

'I see. Would you like a note on her file that the application form will be returned within one month?'

'Yes, thank you very much. I'll give you her e-mail address.'

'Oh no, I'm afraid we don't send out electronic versions of the application form.'

HRH sounded incredulous.

'Oh … oh … sorry. Would you like me to send the paper copy out to her?' I caught myself sitting up straight, knees jammed together.

'That is the only way she can be considered for specialised appointment. Shall we make it two months, Mrs Elliott?'

To complete the job, I e-mailed Leah for an address. I didn't even know where she lived.

Tidying the house took one and a half hours. I hoovered carpets for twenty minutes and scrubbed the kitchen floor of three weeks' worth of building work in twenty-eight minutes. Benjie's bedroom and the bathroom took forty-three minutes, which left one hour eighteen minutes to cook the fatted calf from the bottom of the freezer. As I congratulated myself on my domestic management skills, the phone rang.

'Sorry, Mum. Traffic's awful on the motorway tonight. See you about seven.'

***

Benjie sat with the last lickings of apple crumble. 'Do you know these bits are carcinogenic?' A half-spoonful of carbonised crumble dumped into his mouth.

'My timing was spot on, for six thirty, thank you, Benjie.'

'Please don't call me Benjie, Mum. You know I don't like it.' He smiled at me from Paul's narrow, serious face.

'It's a miracle there was any food for you at all.' Paul parked his spoon and fork. 'Your mum's been submerged for two weeks by her first assignment.

'Ah ...' My son sounded paternal. 'How's it going?'

'Well, nearly finished.' I paused, overcome by temptation. 'Not great. I'm not sure it's any good.'

'Would you like me to look?'

'Would you, please?'

'Well, I'm picking Stevie up in twenty minutes. I could read it tomorrow morning, before I visit Nan.'

'That would be fantastic. I'd be so grateful.'

'Mum …?'

'OK, just dump your washing by the machine.'

First thing next morning, Benjie sat on the top stair. With the ruthlessness of twenty years old, he operated on my draft with a pair of scissors. A hot flush swept up me.

'Is it that bad, Benjie?'

'Let's just say … unusual. At med school we're not allowed ideas; we only do robot learning.'

'Well, Scott and Kirsty both said that they wanted ideas not facts trotted-out.'

'In that case, don't panic. This box on the six studies is fine. Now … put this paragraph first, then this one. This following page is OK as it stands. How about global view next? This bit is repetition, chuck it out. Then your conclusion.' He bulldogged the cuttings in order.

'Wow.' I admired his certainty. '… and that's it?'

'Well, not quite. You haven't made your point in the first sentence of each paragraph. And the introduction and conclusion are crap. They don't say anything at all.'

'Ouch. How would you know?'

'Up to you, Mum. It's your assignment. I must be off, now.' I trailed downstairs after him to load part-dried washing in nine Tesco bags. We hugged each other and he swept outside. The Kango thunder ceased for a couple of minutes, as he chatted to Paul. I picked up the post from the doormat and trailed upstairs with a banana. Then, from the silent battlefield of my desk, I heard the car engine fade away. My only son evaporated from my life. The thumping started again.

***

By lunchtime, the blood swished round my ears, churning my brain into moribund spaghetti. While Paul washed his hands, I opened the card from Ella. 'Oh no! Do you realise, it's our thirty-first anniversary today?'

Paul groaned. 'Sorry, love, I clean forgot. It's been hard, getting through that concrete.' He dried his hands on the clean teacloth.

'Don't do that! It's not hygienic.' I stirred in milk to transform the mushroom soup into cream of. 'Yeah, I forgot too.' I placed the bowls, first. 'Look, Paul. I can't put up with that noise.'

'I should be finished in another couple of hours.'

'Thank God for that. Does that mean you're taking the monster back to Swindon this afternoon?'

'If I can get to the Hire Shop before five-thirty. I'll try to get a digger for Monday.'

'There's no food in the house ... Shall I come along for a supermarket shop?'

'How soon can you be ready?'

'I need to make a list.'

'Tell you what, how about going out for dinner tonight, after we've done the shopping?'

'Cool. Where shall we go?'

'I don't know. Not too far away …'

'Mmm. What about *Le Montagne*? Edward says it's good.'

'Good idea.'

I melted against him for a moment and swung back upstairs.

The afternoon bobbed along. I rewrote my conclusion three times, made out a three-page shopping list, phoned

Mum and wondered what to wear from my High Street collection.

I closed down the computer, dropped to the floor and stretched my back out like Manx. I used the last of the Jasmine shower gel, overdosed on hair conditioner and blow-dried my floppy hair into best bouncy.

Paul came in at four, as it started to rain. 'You look nice.'

'Thanks, hun. I'm looking forward to dinner.'

At four forty-five Paul hitched the trailer to the car. We battled round the Swindon ring road. Since the Hire Shop closed at lunchtime, we continued to the supermarket. The population of Swindon had pillaged it that afternoon. It took over an hour to forage enough food. Paul lost interest and wandered off to browse the wine. As I humped the bags into the trolley, he bounced back.

'Nessie, they've just reduced all the food in the café here.'

'Oh yes.'

'Well, I'm so hungry, I can't wait any longer.'

'Any longer?'

'And we can't really afford *Le Montagne* …'

'I see ...' I hesitated.

'Come and see what's on offer.'

I parked the trolley and trailed into the empty café after Paul. A couple of ladies polished stainless steel counters. I picked up a freshly-steamed tray.

'Look at this,' he beamed enthusiastically. 'What a bargain.' His plate was piled with gnarled chips and baked beans lurking in a generous crust of tomato sauce. The sausages curled strangely, the runts of the café's food production line. I read the menu. Pasta carbonara sounded good. I looked down empty silver bain maries. At the end, three dishes contained food. The Tesco lady paused her ladle in mid flight, tomato sauce gently gobbing from the handle, as she gave me a helpful smile.

'What would you like?'

'Chips, beans and sausages, I suppose.'

'They're all half price, love. How many sausages?'

'Just two, please. A small spoonful of beans. And a few chips.'

Paul was already buried in a weekend review lurking on the table, picking an elderly scab on the bony bridge of his nose as he read.

'How could you?'

'What do you mean?'

'This isn't what you promised for tonight.'

'Well, it was too good an offer to miss.'

'But it's not ... anything. Not nutritious, not freshly-cooked, not hot. I don't even like sausages and baked beans.'

'OK, you've made your point. But it only cost two pounds, sixty-five for both dinners.'

'Surely that's absolutely not the point when it's our wedding anniversary?'

'For goodness sake, Nessie, I'm unemployed, you're a student.' We've got to cut our cloth according to ... would you rather have a Chinese?'

The metal chair legs screeched across the marble chip floor. 'I'm sorry, I can't bear this unhealthy stuff, now I know more about it. I'll go and pack the car. See you in the car park.'

I stalked off, my only smart high heels resonating through the deserted cafeteria. Rain sprayed through the beams of street lights as I hit the entrance. The trolley needed constant tugging to avoid sailing off into the parent and child cars parked near the supermarket's front doors.

'Oops sorry,' I muttered to a near miss. The man sheltering inside the sports car glared at me. It was a long, damp trudge to the far end. I thumped the trolley up against the trailer and loaded the bags. Then I sat in the driver's seat, waiting for Paul to reappear and apologise. We drove home in silence. Paul stamped off to play his tuba. I sat in front of my assignment like Cinderella before the Fairy Godmother appears. By ten thirty, Paul and I occupied separate sides of the same bed.

2.4

A nauseous black hole swallowed Sunday and Monday. I hit the print button about nine o'clock. Finally I packed my rucksack for an early start the next morning. Downstairs, the tuba department was unusually silent.

'Would you like leaded or unleaded coffee?' We were at the glacier-melting stage.

'Already going, thanks.' Paul glanced up from his book, lifting his glass of Scotch with a 007 eyebrow. 'Would a little celebration be in order yet?' Manx took the opportunity to leap aboard *The Building Regulations, 2000.*

'Yes!' I punched the air, rubbed my hands and capitulated. 'First assignment done and dusted, ready to hand in tomorrow.'

'Well done. Would the intellectual streaker care for a wee dram?'

'Where did you hear that?'

'You said it, Nessie. Couple of weeks ago. I liked the idea.'

'Oh … oh yes, Scott told us that in Study Skills. How right he was. I feel drained. Only cotton wool left, instead of a brain and a body.'

'One down, five to go.'

'I will do it, Paul.' I collapsed on the rust-brown sofa to sip the smouldering warmth in my glass. Tight steel coiled round my rib-cage and spine. My shoulders ached from the neck down. 'Reading for my Mental Health assignment starts on Friday. At least it shouldn't be so noisy next time.'

'No, it was good to finish with the Kango today.'

I recognised that level tone. 'What have you hired, instead?'

'A digger, of course. To dig out the soakaway on the lawn. And I took a cement mixer again. Once the ground work is approved, I'll be on to the oversite.' Paul gentled the short fuzz from Manx's nose to his tabby forehead with a cracked forefinger.

'What does that involve?'

'Oh just mixing up concrete and pouring it onto the blinded hard core.'

'That sounds noisy.' I took a burning sip of Scotch and water.

'Yeah, but only on Wednesday or Thursday. You'll be well out of the way.'

'Thank God for that. The Kango pummelled all the ideas out of my head.'

'Well at least the cement mixer is a continuous graunch.' He pushed Manx off his lap and poured himself another large wee dram. 'Shame they only had a diesel one this time, they're a bit noisier.'

Manx tiptoed over to the rug and developed an elongated, bum-up stretch. Then he yawned outrageously wide, before settling down in front of the fire.

'Yeah.' I slipped down onto the rug next to Manx and stretched myself out. My back drifted into a soft, pain-free cloud. It only needed a cigarette in my hand, to perfect the ambience. I missed that contented feeling, these smokeless days.

'So what happens next?'

'Bricking the walls.'

'Good progress?' I glanced over at Paul. His worry lines had receded in the softer light. The dissatisfied pudginess on his face had disappeared and his arms and belly were tauter for five weeks of outdoor physical activity. I smoothed

Manx's neatly-gleaming back. The longer fur on his tummy vibrated as he purred. For a Grumpy Old Man, Paul was quite attractive ...

'Yep.'

'When will that be?'

'Friday, I hope.'

'Won't you have to wait until Monday?'

'Err, no.'

'What do you mean?'

'I'm decided to do it myself.'

'What!' Manx started and twitched his tail-stump. 'But you've hardly any experience of bricklaying. How on earth are you going to manage that?'

'It's a question of necessity.' Paul lifted his chin and glared. His worry lines frowned at me. 'Look, I got these out of the library today.' He pulled out *A Dummy's Guide to Bricklaying*; *Bricklaying for Beginners* and *Tricks of the Trade: Bricklaying*. 'I'm going to read up. I've always wanted to build a brick wall, and now's my chance.'

'OK, OK. Keep your hair on.'

'Yeah, my hair could do with a cut again.' He laughed ruefully. 'Could this herald a temporary return to normal services, now you've finished your assignment?'

'That depends, hun.' I considered how much better I felt about him, this minute. 'Maybe, you old grumpy!'

I cut his hair, retired to bed and intimated 'yes'. Just after eleven, the phone rang. Calls during the official hours of sleep never bode well, I've discovered. I rolled one way to switch on the bedside lamp and Paul rolled the other, to answer the phone. Was this Leah, or Benjie, or my Mum in trouble?

'Yes, she is. I'll hand you over. It's someone called Cathy.' His head flopped back onto his pillow.

'Hi, Cathy.' Cathy? Why on earth was Cathy phoning?

'Nessie, I'm sorry for calling you so late.'

'Not at all. We don't go to bed early.' Paul leant over and graunched a hand over my up-side buttock.

'Thank goodness you were still up. I have a problem with handing in my assignment. I wondered if you could possibly help.'

'Of course, Cathy, what can I do?' Surely Cathy, of all people, hadn't managed to mangle her assignment at the last minute? I picked Paul's hand off my bottom and replaced it in No Man's Land.

'Thanks, Nessie. I'm in Nottingham. Dad's been rushed into hospital with a heart attack. They're operating first thing tomorrow.'

'Oh no, how awful for you. Is he …?' I swiped at Paul's hand, which was marauding irritatingly towards my right boob. 'Stop it.' I glared at him.

'Sorry, what did you say?'

'Nothing, Cathy. Go on.'

'They think he'll be alright, but of course I need to be here with my mother for the next few days, while he's in intensive care. I've just remembered my assignment. It's all finished, here on my laptop, but I don't have any way of getting the paper copy to the Department by the deadline. I don't want to lose marks by submitting late.'

'No, of course not.' I rolled the tub of E45 towards Paul. 'Cathy, can you e-mail it to me? I could print it out and take it in tomorrow morning. I'm sure they'll accept it from me under the circumstances.' I pointed at his hands.

'Oh Nessie, I was hoping you'd say that. It'll only take a few minutes to print it off. I'll send it through now. Don't forget, it's two copies. Oh, and you'll need to make a disc copy for them to run through the plague programme. Is that alright? Do you know how to do that?'

'Plague programme?' The hairs on Paul's forearms were slathered with E45. His hands slobbered as he rubbed them together. He was not a man who understood the concept of little and often.

'Have you forgotten? They run each paper through a plagiarism programme, because students today are such an untrustworthy lot.'

'Oh, plagiarism … Right. Yeah, I can burn a CD or put it on a floppy disc for you. No problem.' Paul lay flat, airing both hands safely away from the sheets.

'In that case, I'll send it through now. Do you want me to wait up 'til you're done?'

'No, don't worry about it. Get some sleep, Cathy. I'll e-mail you when I'm through. Hope everything goes well for your dad, tomorrow.'

'Thanks, Nessie, from the bottom of my heart.'

As I sat up, Paul opened one eye. 'Paul, I am sorry. This is an emergency. I must help Cathy out, after all she's done for me over the past few weeks. It won't take long.' I put on my dressing gown and gently touched the tepee in the middle of his side of the duvet. Paul gave a disconsolate sigh and heaved over to face the window.

In less than ten minutes, the e-mail arrived. Apart from Paul's snoring, there was soft silence. Next door, Edward's house slept in darkness.

I saved the attachment to my file, opened it, and set the printer. My university inbox was full and while I waited for the print, I deleted all my dead e-mails. Through the quiet, the computer jangled discordantly. The printer stayed silent, until I remembered to turn it on. As the print run finally started, I slipped downstairs to make myself a mug of tea.

Now it was November, the window sucked warmth from the kitchen. The cat flap fidgeted. It sounded as if Manx was just outside, torturing a victim. I shifted from chilled foot to foot on the quarry tiles. In the boxroom, the printer congratulated itself on finishing as it spewed out the last page. Easy, I thought to myself. I'll just check through and I'm done. No disappointing Paul, after all. It's only taken twenty minutes.

But the fourth page was empty. My satisfaction dropped away like a lift lurching down three floors. I searched the text for clues. Page four was a stand-alone between a nicely expressed critique of Table One on pages three and five. Of course, the table was missing. Where was it? I scanned through to the References at the end of the paper. Nothing. I hid my face in the darkness of my hands to work it out.

I stumbled through View until I discovered Zoom. Table I had mysteriously vanished to page nineteen. I saved, before the missing page de-materialised. Now to cut Table I and paste it back in its rightful place. It was 00.45. The tea was cold. My patch had fallen off and there wasn't a cigarette in the house. I swigged cold tea and set to work.

Each time I picked up the table, it dropped into a whiteout. I'd already deleted the e-mail copy. The first time I panicked. Calm down, Nessie. Before the file disapparated for ever, I scrabbled wildly to Undo. I was losing, 5-nil, to Word's guerilla warfare. Cold air whispered up my legs.

Around two o'clock I made coffee, goose bumps on my arms inside my dressing gown. The quarry tiles iced my feet. Was there any alternative? Reluctantly, no.

I crept back to the stillness and placed the mug ready. In the darkness, I felt sore behind my eyelids. Very gently I put my hand on Paul's arm. He stirred.

'Paul.' I was a duplicitous heel. The cat flap rattled as Manx clattered through at full speed.

'Ergh. What's that?' He jerked upright.

'Cat's come in. Paul, sorry to have woken you.'

He rubbed his eyes and peered at the red digits on the alarm clock. 'Christ, haven't you come to bed yet? Whass going on?'

'I've hit a teeny problem with the Word document.' Oh what a deceitful Siren. 'Could you possibly wake up for a couple of minutes?'

He groaned, collapsed onto the pillow and screwed up his eyes. 'You're asking me to get up to help out some bird I've never met. Right.'

'Here's some coffee. You're my last hope.'

Paul groped for the handle, eyes closed, aim precise. He pushed himself up on his right elbow and took a tentative sip. The next gulp emptied an encouraging quarter of the mug. I turned on the bedside lamp. He opened both eyes by one third. They looked sore.

'Well, I suppose I've got to.' I couldn't blame him for sounding resentful. It was exactly how I'd have felt, too. There was a muted cacophony from downstairs, part scuffling, part wails.

'That bloody cat! If you go downstairs and sort Manx out, I'll look at your document. Is that a deal?' Cat casualties in the middle of the night were usually Paul's territory, but this was an emergency.

'Fantastic.' I kissed him and explained the problem. Paul groped for his pants from the floor where he'd abandoned them and found his dressing gown and slippers.

'Just show me before you go downstairs.'

The skirmishing sounds continued for another couple of minutes as I demonstrated the problem.

Manx's giant victim wasn't going to give him an easy victory. Downy featherettes skittered and floated across the floor. Manx was backed up in the corner next to the back door. As I opened the kitchen door, he bolted out of the cat flap, leaving me and a moorhen to fight it out.

The moorhen scuttered under the table. I looked around for the equivalent of a gladiatorial net. Tea towel in hand, I stooped down to look under the table. The moorhen cowered in the darkest corner. I dropped onto my knees and lunged. Breaking all previous webbed feet records, the moorhen skidded out from under the table and pelted for the gap between the washing machine and the freezer. I backed out from under the table, too late to head him off. There wasn't enough space behind the machines for him to hide any further away. He was trapped, for the time being. I ventured one arm down the gap. The moorhen fought for his life with a defensive flurry of wings and beak-pecking.

'Ouch, you bastard.' I yelled. He swore back, as I hauled him out backwards. My hand spat pain and I dropped him. Eyes watering, I staunched my bleeding forefinger with the tea towel. Before the moorhen could escape, I leapt for the kitchen door. How else I could corner him? Next moment, a head appeared through the squeaking cat flap, invoking terror in the moorhen. I leaped after him and launched the tea towel over his back. As neatly as Chris Packham, I caught him under my arm, safe from an aggrieved Manx, beak and webbed feet trapped against any further attempted ripostes.

I unlocked the kitchen door and hit the cold air. I fumble-footed into my wellies, last used and dropped by the back door a couple of weeks ago. The further ecology of their freezing, slimy interiors was unknown.

Manx's territory extended further than I'd thought, as I stamped off down the lane towards the stream. Under other circumstances, it would have been a exciting, ghostly night, full of frosty, swirling mist just a couple of hundred yards down the road. The chill whipped through the fleece material of my dressing gown and onto bare flesh. If only I'd thought of my windblocker.

Past Anwar's shop, I groped into blackness. Lightly-grassed mud sloped towards the stream. I slithered my way across on tiptoe. Near the edge of the stream, the moorhen blew up. One web tangled momentarily in the tea towel as he broke for freedom. I lost my balance. Then he was away, in a headlong slither down into the reeds. I picked one left cheek out of the mud and scrubbed at my dressing gown with a muddy, bloody tea towel.

Hugging my arms round my chest, I made tracks for home. The cold was bone-cracking in my dressing gown, with full-frontal shivers. Behind, a car engine chuffed down the lane. Headlights picked me out. The car slowed and I speeded up, glutes clenched, wondering whether to pelt into a neighbour's garden. I hoped my knickerless state wasn't obvious to the driver.

The car overtook and halted smoothly. I recognised the blue light box. Police car. The driver's window slid down.

I'd taught the driver, so long ago, he probably thought I was a geriatric wanderer from the local Rest Home.

'Hello, Mrs Elliott. How are you?'

'Fine thank you. Just on my way home, Oliver.'

'Are you alright?' He looked down at my muddied dressing gown.

'Yes, perfectly alright, thank you.' By now I was so agitated my teeth sounded like a percussion orchestra.

'Pleased to hear that. We haven't had any reports of missing persons or domestics tonight. So what brings you outside in your dressing gown, at twenty to three?'

'I've er ... just rescued a live moorhen from our cat, Manx. He er ... usually kills dormice and voles straight out.'

I could hear the grins. 'You do realise that the dormouse is a protected species, Mrs Elliott? Hop in, we'll give you a lift back to your house.' The back door swung open and I was inside a warm bubble. It was only a couple of hundred yards home, but then, I'd never been in a police car before, especially without knickers.

'It's just here. Thanks very much for the lift.'

Paul opened the front door and stood, arms folded.

'Are you sure you'll be alright, love?' asked the other officer.

'Yes, we haven't argued or anything. He's just been up sorting out my computer prog ...'

'OK, but take care. We're on duty until 8.00. Call us up if you need us.'

'Yeah, thanks.' I scrunched up the driveway and heeled off my boots by the front door.

'Whatever kept you, Nessie?'

'Catching the moorhen.' I closed and double-locked the front door. 'Did you manage to sort out Cathy's assignment?'

'Well … yes. I've been in bed for twenty minutes or more. Wondered what had happened to you. Yeah, it was just a glitsch. I've done a CD for Cathy and your one, too. Everything's ready to go.'

'Oh Paul, what would I do without you?' For the next fifteen minutes, until I reheated enough to fall asleep, I glowed with gratitude. Paul really does have the most amazingly warm feet and hands.

2.5

Three hours later it was my turn to make the tea.

The ironing mountain was unscaleable. I searched my wardrobe for inspiration. Brown polyester trousers offered themselves from the recycling end. They gripped my legs like an attached toddler.

'They'll do.' I kissed Paul. 'Thanks for all your help last night,' and sprinted for Smartie.

The city was foggy. I trotted through residential streets, bare horse chestnut branches spitting occasional cold blobs on my hair like shitting blackbirds. Conker cases spiked through crispy cinammon leaves and splatted green and white underfoot. Overnight, the army of student pedestrians and cyclists had donned scarves and hoodies, jackets and boots. Schoolkids disembarked from cars, still entrenched in white shirts. The sun tried to poke through as I entered the Sports Centre, bearing my precious cargo.

I joined a queue of people sagging along the corridor. Xui looked exhausted, but grinned widely when she saw me. Midge was missing. I re-checked: two paper copies and a CD in both sets. I smoothed my front page with its university crest, as if it were my child's hair.

'Hi Nessie, you have finished then?'

'Yes, and you too, Xiu! Congratulations!'

'Did you have difficulty with papers, Nessie?'

'Oh God, yes. I was …' I mimed. 'I was pulling out my hair.'

She laughed. 'Me too. Not until nearly the end, when I found some papers have Chinese translations, which makes it easier for me.'

'Of course: you had to do all this in English. I'm surprised you're not bald,' I said admiringly.

'It's a wig.' Xui's vocabulary had lifted-off, even in six weeks.

***

'Well done, you made it!' Kirsty wrote a receipt for my little pile of productivity. 'This first copy is anonymised, isn't it?' She scrawled a number and chucked a copy on an untidy pile in the corner.

My bra bulged with pride. 'Oh yes. I've got Cathy's here, too.'

'Oh, you're not supposed to hand in someone else's work. You might have copied it.'

'I wish I had. It looks fantastic.'

Kirsty looked suspicious. 'Why isn't she here herself?'

'She rang me late last night from Nottingham. Her dad's life and death. They're operating this morning. She asked me to print her assignment off and bring it in. That is all right, isn't it?'

'Oh, I see. I wish she'd told us. She could have just e-mailed it.'

'You're joking! Do you mean my husband and I were up til three o'clock printing out ...?'

'Yeah, we have ways round everything. Just ask,' she said casually. 'Here's Cathy's receipt. See you later.'

Kirsty came in with gorgeous Nick when we met up, that lunchtime. The Glass Belljar was a student pub, not salubrious, but handy to the Department. The wooden floor was sticky and the benches had rips in the maroon pvc upholstery. On the dark walls, mad Victorian scientists frolicked.

'Did Midge hand in her assignment?' My rucksack hid most of the cling-on trousers.

Kirsty dropped her voice. 'There's still a couple of people struggling. Why don't you ring Midge tonight?' She joined Nick at a separate table.

A celebratory glass of wine loosened my tongue, at last. 'What really puzzles me, is how did researchers managed to persuade a thousand people to walk on a treadmill four times a week for several months?'

'Why's that, then?' Jonathan sat next to me.

'Well I wouldn't have time to exercise four times a week, for a start. Life crises would intervene. Then I'd die of terminal boredom on a treadmill. The treadmill of life is quite enough for me.'

He grinned.

'And have you noticed it's always white, middle-class, young males in the studies?' Xiu spooned out pasta salad from a plastic lunchbox. I groped through the rucksack for my own surreptitious sandwich supplies.

'I have.' I munched into cheese-with-no-time-for-pickle. 'And they donate samples of blood for testing at the drop of a hat. Not to mention ECGs and those nasty fat- measuring callipers. I wouldn't volunteer for all that stuff.'

'I read study where eighteen youths swallowed body core temperature sensors the night before the experiment,' Xiu started, straight-faced. 'I wondered how many sensors dropped out the other end by the next morning.' She looked at me sideways and we sniggered hysterically. Sleep deprivation had put us high and the relief of finishing had pushed us over the edge, just for today.

‘Can they be recycled?’ I hauled my bottom upright on the slippery seat yet again. There were groans from the other students crammed round the copper-hammered tables.

‘In answer to Xiu’s question, it’s because they are student volunteers.’ Scott set down his pint and squeezed in. The beer mats were the cleanest feature of the hostelry. ‘In the States, it’s part of the credit for their undergraduate courses. And participants are often paid over there.’

‘Really? Is that ethical?’

‘Whether it’s ethical or not is debatable, but we can’t afford it in this country.’

Xiu nodded. ‘So that is how American studies recruit larger sample populations?’ ‘Yep. And the larger the sample size the more reliable the data is likely to be, of course.’

‘So samples outside the States are too small to be taken seriously?’ I ventured.

‘That’s a bit sweeping, Vanessa.’ Scott leant back, appropriating the discussion. ‘It depends what sort of research you’re doing. You can have perfectly robust qualitative research using one individual.’

‘Hmm.’ I noticed Kirsty and Nick, laughing together over plates of ‘home-made’ minestrone. I turned back to erudite, confident Scott, waiting to gobble up my puny arguments.

‘Another thing about The Literature, is that nobody has any pre-existing medical conditions.’

‘Well, you know, that levels the playing field in statistical terms.’

‘Yeah, I realise that. What I mean is, how many people do you know in their fifties and sixties with no health problems?

‘Not too many,’ agreed Jonathan. ‘Wasn’t it two medications for a man over 55 years and 2.3 for women, as an average, in the latest Health Survey?’

'So how biased a sample is that in the first place, just to use the one per cent who are completely healthy?'

'About 15%. But you may have a point there.' Scott looked at me with hooded eyes for a moment. Something I had said qualified as an academic gaffe.

Jonathan laughed. 'Nessie's learning, Scott. Watch out when she comes on the Statistics course. Anyone for a fill-up, before we get back to the marking pile?' Xiu, Vasulu and I shook our heads.

'I need to check my e-mails,' said Vasilu. 'May I call in to see you later, Scott?'

'Sure, Vasulu, about three? My round, Jono.' Scott swept the glasses up for refilling. I stood and reached for my rucksack. On the seat a v-shaped patch of polyester-engendered damp glistened. I gasped and collapsed to cover it. New jeans were urgent.

I hoisted my rucksack and walked out into the chilly sunshine with Xiu. I hadn't craved a cigarette the entire morning. The pub was smokeless and the others took it for granted that I was a non-smoker. For a moment, my mood soared and I was full of ... self-efficacy.

'My first visit to English pub.' Xiu bounced along beside me, face beaming enthusiasm and energy.

'My first student pub for thirty years.' I groped for my thoughts. I felt the same ... but it wasn't the same as ... . Being around young students was like ... well, sitting by an open fire, beside which I warmed and, yes, regenerated myself. Oh God, how mawkish.

***

During the graveyard shift after lunch, Alan Rathbone lectured. The sociology of mental health and illness was a fascinating subject. The Dean was held to be a good speaker. I'd looked forward to it all week. Me and my rucksack spread over two seats in the front row.

Kirsty introduced Alan, before diving off somewhere. Penny sent round the attendance sheet.

Alan moved the lectern to centre front, grasped the sides and cleared his throat. From my front row seat, wrinkly, clean pinkies came into close-up. The lectern obscured his mouth. His handlebar eyebrows took-off from his gold half moons, eyes soaring beyond the top of my head. Did he recognise me? He had baggy, dissatisfied lines to his cheeks and forehead. Broken nights with baby Bertie, I guessed.

Alan read his lecture. In six weeks, I'd habituated to Powerpoint with handouts. The notion of old-fashioned note-taking shocked me. By comparison with Jonathan's inspiring lecture that morning, Alan's cultural analysis was esoteric and difficult to bullet. Two points and I gave up.

My thoughts wandered. How could Sarah possibly have fallen for those podgy chipolata fingers, drumming the lectern? He had all the sex appeal of an ageing turtle. After twenty hard-going minutes, I came up with the aphrodisiac properties of power.

I hunkered in my seat, listening to his Oxbridge accent swishing along as level as a pair of sculling oars. The late night and wine at lunchtime snared me. Try as I might, my eyelids drooped for respite as he quartered his field. With a great effort, I jerked myself awake again. When that became too much, my head sunk down

***

I tried yawning with closed jaws when I woke. I stretched my stiff back from its kinked shape and braced alternate calf muscles to stop myself dozing again.

There were no questions at the end of the lecture. Alan avoided my eye as he tidied his papers. I slunk out, to rest my head on a library table for half an hour, before the final session of the day. If I had offended the Faculty Dean by breaking such an obvious taboo, did it matter? What was I, to a man of his importance?

Later that evening, I phoned Midge.

'No, I haven't finished yet. She's given me until Friday.'

'Is it going better now?' Poor Midge, still in the awful throes of that first paper. At least I knew that I was capable of completing an assignment.

'Oh yes, it's just grafting, now. I missed the lecture to spend all day writing. The first draft should be finished later tonight.'

'Was Kirsty all right with you?'

'Well, yes and no. She was sympathetic to a degree, but it's got to be on the table on Friday, or else.'

'Can I do anything to help? Babysitting?'

'That's very sweet of you, but I should be OK now, thanks.'

'So who was the other person in trouble with the assignment?'

'Oh, Rosa. You know, that very quiet Chinese student?'

'Is she the tiny, pretty one? Still struggling with her English? I tried to talk to her last week.'

'Yeah, the others have picked up, but she can hardly put a sentence together yet.'

'Maybe it's because Rosa only speaks to the other Chinese girls.'

'It must be so difficult to manage in a foreign language, especially with all the technical jargon on the course.'

'I feel ashamed to be whingeing.'

'Me too. You have to take your hat off to these kids. We've just about survived … they're doing it in a foreign language.'

2.6

I undressed as reluctantly as a teenager for cross-country on a wintry day. The couch crackled with paper towel as I lay back, breathing my shoulders and knees determinedly down.

'Just relax your knees.' I tensed, as my new friend, Dr Stainton-Jones, bent towards me in her beige crossover. I knew just how the corkscrew-shaped thingumyscope would feel.

'Excellent. You can put your knickers back on, now.' If she knew that already, why was she sending off a smear test of mucus on a glass plate?

'I'll examine your back, next. Stand up, please. Touch your toes. Good. Where exactly is the pain?' She poked. 'You said last time you weren't exercising very much?'

'I don't get much time,' I hedged.

'Well, there's nothing really wrong. But if you don't sort this out, it may become a chronic condition.' That sounded serious. 'Please try to exercise for half an hour every day. Brisk walking would be fine. Now let me see, what else did we have to do?'

Currently I was in the relaxed sector of my assignment cycle, reading about cardio-vascular events. I decided to be brave as she took off the cuff and let the blood flow round my arm again.

'What is my blood pressure today?'

'Oh, 145 over 95.'

That didn't sound too good to me. 'That's into hypertension, isn't it?'

'Well, it's borderline, we need to keep an eye on it over the next few weeks.'

'I see.' Surely the Americans worried about results like that?

'Are you concerned about it?'

'No, no … just taking an interest. I read an article yesterday about using breathing to control blood pressure.'

'Oh yes, you're doing a course, aren't you? How's that going?' Her cool eyes re-glued to my computer record.

'It's quite hard work.'

'Yes? How are you feeling about that?' She sounded as interested in me as I was in Paul's tuba playing.

'Well …' Whatever did she mean? 'I can't say I'm particularly optimistic about passing.'

'Hmm. Do you find yourself crying at all?'

'Sometimes.' She scrambled more words into the computer.

'How are you sleeping?'

'Oh, I feel tired at the moment. Well, I was up at three a.m. the other night, you see. The cat brought …'

'And your weight?'

'Well,' I said, cheering up. The forced marches against the clock were definitely working. 'Yes, I've lost some weight.'

'Hmm. Mrs Elliot, do you take any recreational drugs?'
I was flabbergasted. Surely she knew how old I was. Maybe she meant … other things.

'Umm, Omega-3 Fish Oils?'

'No, I didn't mean food supplements.' She spoke loudly and slowly. 'You seem a little confused. And you have seemed quite down, twice recently. Maybe we can lift your mood a bit. It might even help the blood pressure, if you're not so worried and stressed about everything. What do you think?'

Well, I thought, you don't go to a doctor to ignore their advice.

It wasn't until I was home, sitting among the articles on depression and exercise that I'd accessed, that I read the drug information. *What I should know* included a lot of side effects. The description packed a winding punch. She'd put me on to anti-depressants. I burst into tears immediately.

Benjie wasn't any help. When I finally managed to track him down, the background sounded like a pub. 'We haven't done depression yet. No, I can't tell you anything about anti-depressants.'

'What do you think I should do?'

'What do *you* think, Mum?'

'There's nothing wrong with me.'

'Well don't take them then, if you don't think you're depressed. You won't die without them. Half of all patients don't take their prescribed pills.'

'Oh.'

Later that week, Cathy gave me her well-researched take. 'The best outcomes were with the people who took anti-depressants and exercised as well, but it was only quite a small difference. Just doing the exercise was nearly as good, if you don't want to medicate.'

'Mmm … But the thing is, Cathy, will it work for me?'

'It helped the people in the research. Why should you be any different?'

'I don't know,' I wobbled.

***

The next morning I was up and running by eight o'clock. I just so wasn't depressed.

Two hundred metres and jogging, Edward's new BMW slowed beside me and the window slid down.

'Good morning, Nessie. Can I offer you a lift somewhere?'

'No thanks very much, Edward. I'm running for exercise.'

'You put me to shame!' He gave a cheery wave. The car swept away and disappeared round Anwar's corner. I heard my short puffs of breath, while my trainers slapped the tarmac. My legs hadn't much power left. I already felt like a box parcelled up with string. Five hundred metres in, I was power-walking. Don't be silly, I told myself. JFDI. I ran another five metres. Think positive. Running will make you fitter.

There were some new cards on the notice board and I stopped to read them. Was the missing budgie the remains Manx brought in yesterday?

'Morning, Nessie.' Anwar was washing his windows. We passed the time of day.

Twenty minutes later, I ran on. The tarmac petered out into a rough track after the racehorse stables. Old Man's Beard traced hawthorns, while spiders hung out under cobwebby blackberries and stiff, ginger beech leaves. The sun occulted brightly through the gaps, like the blinding strobe light of a disco. I turned uphill. The last dribbles of power in my legs disappeared and I limped to a halt.

Beyond the hedge, chalk downland rolled away into the misty distance. In the bottom of the valley, the stream swirled down to the Thames, partly hidden behind some decrepit farm buildings and a ploughed field. There was still a milking herd, grazing in the next field. Artificially inseminated, of course. Close by, young rabbits stalled in mid-leap, garden ornaments for a long gaze, before they swept into the bushes.

I took a deep breath of the warm stink of silage and listened to the rushing tide of the motorway. What an excellent idea to run every morning! *Far* better than drugs. This must be a good dose of, well maybe not pastoral, more agricultural … biophilia, that's what The Literature called it.

I walked on, struck by the picture of Nick and Kirsty in the pub. They made a perfect couple, attractive and sexy. But then, the Department thrummed; a far more exciting background to life than this habitual mundanity. Oh, I did so want more than … country retirement.

At the stables, I turned down the unmade lane to the farm. Halfway down, a sharp bend lead on to a six metre flooded stretch. I inched along the outside until my right foot slipped down a deep pothole, chilling one sock with muddy water. Paddling my way past booby-trap thorns and attacking nettles, I reached safe concrete again. I needed a level stretch to build up my running. I wouldn't come this way again, not in winter, anyway.

As I admired the bottle-grade water burbling alongside the lane, a milk tanker accelerated noisily out of the farmyard. Just in time, I ditched into nettles and dew-globated couch grass. The driver slowed and stuck his head out of the window.

'Nice morning for a walk.'

'Certainly is.' I was well past an age to worry about unsolicited advances. The Literature was right. Feel-good had factored in, without a doubt. He waved and pulled away from a standing start in a pothole, choking the air with diesel fumes. Gritty mud sprayed off the back tyres and splatted down my tee shirt, shorts and bare legs.

2.7

The pregnant elephant in labour inched closer, round the corner of the house and into undefended earshot. Ignoring the noise was impossible. In two hours, I was near screaming. By dusk, when Paul halted work, I was screaming.

'Great day. I've finished the trench. That gives me two days over the weekend for the oversite.' Paul switched on the kettle and popped two teabags in the teapot. Complacently.

'Look here,' I banged a tin of cat food on the empty patch of worktop, searching for the can opener. 'How am I expected to get on with my assignment? Are you trying to de-rail me off this course?'

'It's got to be done.' Paul opened the fridge, took the milk carton from the door and closed it with a disciplined thunk. He selected two clean mugs from the draining board and set them ready. I knew exactly what was coming next.

'There aren't any biscuits, Paul. They're just rubbish, I've stopped buying them.'

He ignored that. 'I'm sorry, but we're committed, now. I've bought the bricks and tiles.' The kettle bubbled for five seconds, then switched itself off. One second later, Paul picked it up to fill the teapot and changed the subject. 'The can opener's in the sink.'

I foraged the freezer for supper. Mince in the plastic box …that would do fine. I was overloaded with discontent. Paul's domestic expectations just didn't fit my new identity as a mature student.

I glared at him and bunged the mince into the microwave to defrost. 'You may be committed to it, but I'm equally committed to getting my MSc. Would you like some toast to go on with?'

'Yes, please.' He stirred the tea before tinging the spoon twice against the teapot. I flung bread slices into the toaster. 'The cement mixer's going to be just as bad over the weekend, isn't it? I can't concentrate, Paul. How am I supposed to finish this module in time?'

'You're winding yourself up again.' A mug of tea appeared next to the chopping board. He picked up his tuba and a music book from the worktop.

'Not now!' I screamed. Furious, I raked the larder in search of potatoes. 'You only ever think about yourself and your damn plans. Marriage is supposed to be a partnership. This one isn't. You over-ride everything I think or say.'

His tone stayed reasonable. 'You're always at the Uni or sitting at the computer half way through the night.'

'Well, yes, I'd say a fair bit of time's required, if you're going to do a post-graduate …' The microwave pinged far too quickly. '… course in one year.' There weren't enough potatoes for shepherd's pie, after all. Perhaps there was a packet of couscous?

'Fair enough, but that was your choice. Nobody pushed you into it. We still have responsibilities. When was the last time you went down to see Ella? It's been me sorting out her problems over the past few weeks, not you. I'm even supposed to take your mother to the airport tomorrow morning at six. Who took Manx to the vet? And how often have you rung Benjie, lately? '

'That's not fair! I phoned him on Tuesday evening.' The rest was true. Days slipped by without me thinking about Mum, let alone visiting her. As for the cat …

'You're putting up a smoke screen, Nessie.'

'What …?'

Blue smoke poured up towards the smoke alarm. The ripe smell of burning toast flooded the back of my nose. Paul leapt for the off switch.

'It's all right, I'll do it.' The alarm screamed, as he attacked the battery from a kitchen chair. He fished two large black crisps from the toaster. Finally, he altered the setting and replaced the crisps with two pristine slices of wholemeal.

I banged the half-defrosted box on the worktop, prised open the lid and poked at the hard, brown stuff, iced with crystals of frost.

'Where were we?'

'You were criticising my imperfect being.' As I spoke, I jettisoned the brown cube into a casserole dish. It shot out, slid over the worktop and skidded across the floor. When I'd rinsed the frost and cat hairs off, orangey lumps stuck out like broken bones. Were they carrots? I poked suspiciously. Buggar it, they were the stones from windfall plums.

'I'm not saying that at all, dear.' He fingered the tuba keys silently. 'For goodness sake, be reasonable.'

'I am being perfectly reasonable. You're telling me, I'm not up to standard. Well, I'll tell you what, Mr Reasonable. I'll collect Mum from the boat and …'

'… take her to the airport tomorrow morning? I'm all for that. Then I can get on with pushing the hard core into the soakaway.'

It wasn't the answer I wanted. 'If you think I'm that pathetic, why don't I just stay down there?'

'Good idea.' He picked evenly-tanned toast from the toaster. 'You're forever whingeing. Maybe you need some breathing space this weekend.'

I gasped. In a cascade, I was committed to independence.

'OK.' Always calm in an emergency. 'If you want me to, I'll go. There is some couscous in the cupboard, I think. Here are the plums ready to make into a crumble, which I'm sure you'll be able do with one arm tied behind your back. See you on Sunday night.'

Upstairs, one mature, reasonable daughter phoned Ella. 'Hi Mum. Are you all ready for India?'

'Oh, hello, dear. Yes, all ready for take-off!'

'Now, Mum, I'm going to drive you to the airport. What time do you have to check in?'

'Well Benjie said we should be there by six-thirty.'

'So it means leaving at four-thirty?'

'Oh, if not before.'

I gulped and thought of my two-seat Smartie. 'Right. Are we picking up Phyllida on the way?'

'Of course, dear. Paul said we should.'

'Four o'clock departure, then.' I was carefully breezy, wincing at the thought. 'Tell you what, shall I come down tonight and sleep on the boat? Then I won't have to make quite such an early start in the morning.'

'Ooh, that would be lovely. Paul said you were busy. I haven't seen you for so long, Vanessa.'

'OK, Mum, I'm sorry. I'll be down about nine o'clock. Don't worry about sheets or anything, I'll bring Benjie's old sleeping bag.'

'Nonsense, dear, it's no trouble at all.'

I went into our bedroom and picked out a tee-shirt from the pile of clean clothes. The downstairs ironing mountain yielded socks and knickers, but no clean bras. The best detritus from the underwear drawer featured my boobs busting out like Diana Dors. I hesitated. By the look of it, my current bra had been on at least two days. I couldn't remember any further back than that.

I rushed through the shower and pulled on the old pink bra. Flaccid lumps of breast drooped out beneath, half-captured by the soggy elastic. Maybe I'd put on weight since I stopped smoking. As a side silhouette in the mirror, it didn't look too bad. I wriggled the bra a bit further down and stuck a jumper on top. I wouldn't be tucking my teeshirt in, tonight.

I packed clothes into a zip bag and unplugged the laptop from various appendages it had accumulated over the past few weeks. It was nearly seven when I bumped the bag downstairs.

'May I take your car?'

Paul silently proffered his car keys.

***

We sat with glasses of white wine. Water clap-lapped loudly against the hull and pontoon, inches from my ears. *Iris* leant and grabbed at her mooring lines as the current scoured through the basin, swirling down the plughole and into the river outside.

Below, the saloon nudged gently to port or starboard, as if I was slightly drunk already. Through the portholes, urban streetlights dipped and bobbed. The Saturday night city sounded close. Traffic ebbed and flowed noisily along the street opposite; police cars wailed and ambulances whined; youths shouted and girls shrieked.

'Cheers Mum, here's to a wonderful trip. So, where are you heading first?'

'Oh, we're going straight to Bangalore. Phyllida has friends there. She says it's a very large city in a very beautiful part of India. We'll see what happens from there.'

'How strange! One of the students on my course comes from Bangalore.'

'Well, it does have several million inhabitants.'

'Have you booked all your hotels ahead?'

'Oh no, dear, that's part of the excitement of travelling, Ben says. Not knowing where you're going to stay next.'

'But you have organised your first night?'

'Of course. It will be very early Monday morning when we arrive, what with the time difference.'

'Oh yes.'

Mum looked at me almost crossly. 'Don't worry about me, Nessie. I've been ready these last three weeks. Everything will be alright.'

'I can't help worrying. You're my Mum.'

'I'm not in my dotage yet, young lady.' She leaned forward, glass of wine in hand, narrowing her eyes. 'We've been doing some self-defence with U3A. I can give 'em what for. No little rat is going to get my handbag!'

'Mum, you're not really taking a handbag?'

'Well where else could I put everything I need to hand?'

'Not that old crocodile thing though?'

Mum shook her head, sighed, and gave me an indulgent smile. 'No, of course not, dear. It's a sort of handbag with straps. Paul took me over to that camping shop where you always go.'

'Cotswold?'

'Yes, that's the place.' She jumped up to go to her cabin in the bow. The pause gave my bad feeling just long enough to swell into guilt. She returned with a tough-looking daysack for me to admire.

'I'm sorry I've been so busy lately, Mum.'

'Don't be silly, it's been good for me to get off my backside and sort it all out for myself. I don't need to be a burden to you yet. D'you know, I can't believe I'm so old and still going on this big adventure.'

I handed the daysack back to her, and picked up my glass of wine. 'How old do you feel inside, Mum?'

'Ooh, about forty, I'd say.'

'Really? I wish I felt as young as that.'

She eyed me sharply. 'You surprise me. I thought everything was going your way with the course?'

'Well … oh yes, everything's fine.'

'So what's wrong?'

'Nothing's wrong, Mum. Everything's just fine.'

'How's Paul?'

'Yep, still going strong on the building works.' I could feel smarting behind my eyes.

'So now, I'm going to be the one who's worrying.'

'No, you don't need to. I'm a big girl, now. You just go and have a good holiday. What do you want me to look after, while you're away?'

'Well, Delia said she'd keep an eye on the boat. But I've discovered this week that the bilge needs pumping out every fortnight. Could you do that for me?'

'Of course I can. Would you like me to water your plants?'

'I think I'll give you my key tomorrow. Then you can come and go as you like.' She appraised me with her hypothesising-mother look. 'You could always sleep on board. You'd have some peace and quiet and the boat would be looked after.'

'Good idea. That'd be fun. Maybe I'll think about it.'

'Well I don't want to hear about any noisy late night parties if you do stay. You and your student friends, I don't know what you might get up to!'

'Mum!' We both giggled. 'Would you like a cup of tea before bed?'

'No thanks, dear, I don't drink anything after eight o'clock at night, these days. I'll go and see about some sheets.'

'Mum ... I've brought Benjie's sleeping bag.'

'Are you sure? Then I could leave you without any dirty washing.'

As I undressed, my mood lightened. I saw myself, swanning off to City restaurants and concert halls. I imagined unobtrusive appearances at fun student events. It sounded a lot more exciting than building sites and late night shopping at the supermarket.

The mattress on the saloon berth felt strangely narrow after the king-sized double bed at home. I'd forgotten my travelling alarm clock and hadn't a clue how to set up the alarm on my mobile. The early night before the three-thirty am start dribbled away, worrying if Mum would be alright. It didn't seem such a good idea to stay on board, as unfamiliar bells tolled twelve and one.

In the first few moments after I fell asleep, Mum woke me with a cup of tea. The cabin wasn't dark. There was a back-lit orange glow from streetlamps. Outside the sleeping bag felt icily-wet, as I clutched my mug. The little solid fuel stove had petered out, where I'd forgotten to bank it up.

'OK, Mum, I am getting up.' My eyes ached from the effort of waking. Fortunately, I'd slept in my teeshirt and underwear. Now, I only had to add last night's layers, to be ready. Twenty minutes later, the pontoon boards glittered with the first frost of the winter as we clumped up to the car park. Mum's suitcase wheels drew long dark lines in our wake.

Up in town, Phyllida looked pale and tense in purple.

I switched off to concentrate on a fast, efficient drive to the airport, before I fell asleep again. In the back, Mum and Phyllida giggled and chatted like excited Girl Guides in a bell tent after lights out.

I tuned into my name, further along the motorway. 'Vanessa's going to pump me out every fortnight.'

'One never knows if these things will become a problem or not.'

'Well, why not ask her? I'm sure she'd pop up to your boat.'

'What's up, Phyllida?' I caught her rosy face and dangly ear-rings in the rearview mirror.

'Oh, nothing really, just that up in town I worry about vandals getting on board.'

'None of the boats around you have liveaboards, do they?' put in Mum.

'No, that young couple have moved into a flat, now she's expecting.'

'Would you like me to check your boat as well?'

'Would you, Nessie? I'd be very grateful.'

'What's the name of your boat?'

'*Aqua Nymph*. Shall I give you my keys? Then if anything seems wrong down below, perhaps you could unlock and have a quick look.'

I swallowed a snort at the boat's name. 'And what should I do if there is anything wrong?'

'Oh well, sort it out, I suppose.' Phyllida was no help at all.

Mum wormed Phyllida's keys onto her own keyring and handed them over. I zipped them carefully into my pocket for safety. Negotiating the spaghetti round Heathrow would demand courage and fast reactions, even at six a.m. on a Sunday morning.

***

It was just coming up light, when I arrived back at eight o'clock. It felt like lunchtime. The marina was deserted, our crisp wheel and footprints still delineating the sparkly pontoon.

As I approached *Iris*, I unzipped my pocket to fish the keys out. A cup of coffee and more sleep were only five minutes away. I relaxed. In a framed instant, the keys arched cleanly from my hand. Impotent, I observed their slow slip and sparkling spin through the murky-dark yellow water, until they disappeared into darkness. Only two hours in possession and I'd lost them already. I returned to the warm car to contemplate the dichotomous nature of reality and wonder what to do next.

2.8

I didn't really know about the possibilities for retrieving sunken keys. I thought Mum had a spare set on board, if I could somehow break in. On the other hand, that didn't help with the keyless *Aqua Nymph*. My first instinct was to phone Paul. No, I had to sort this out for myself.

I was totally stumped, so I walked up to town in search of some breakfast. An hour or so wasn't going to make any difference, except there might be a few more people around to uncover a solution.

The marina development lay to the south side of the basin. I broke into a jog: marginally faster and definitely warmer than walking. Past the marina, I padded across the bottom end of a car park and into the concourse of a newly-finished building development. Faded flags fluttered and tired hoardings advertised prestigious apartments.

Near the dockside, an old railway line ran alongside. I turned down to follow the tracks alongside the old warehouses. A couple of hundred yards ahead, a dark shape streaked across the path of a cyclist in shorts. One hand on the handlebars, the cyclist wobbled as he approached. Just as I recognised the honeyed tautness of Nick Smallwood's Achilles' tendons, his front wheel lurched into the railway track and he sprawled onto the concrete on his left side. His obese Sunday newspaper fractured into supplements as he went.

'Nick!' I ran the last fifty yards. 'Are you alright?'

He sat up slowly.

'Yeah, think so, mate. Oh, hello, Sheila.' Did he know my real name?

'Hey! Whose fault is it this time?'

He shook his head slowly, like a bemused koala. 'Didn't pick up on the bloody rat until the last moment. D'you know, that's the first time I've ever come off a bike. Been cycling ever since I was a kid.'

Mumsy intuition stepped in. 'But not your first Sunday morning hangover?'

'Well no ... We did have a few beers yesterday evening after the game.'

'So, any injuries from this little incident?' I asked brightly, ever the first aider.

'No, I don't think so. The bruises are from yesterday.' He looked down at a Burgundy-coloured selection on his right thigh with a veteran's pride. 'The bike took a bit of punishment, though.' He pushed himself up slowly and righted the bike. 'Front wheel's well buckled.' He looked at me speculatively. 'What are you doing down here this morning?'

I suppose he thought I'd come from the apartments. I pictured myself on a balcony overlooking the water, sipping from one of those 1930's cocktail glasses, in a slinky long evening dress, attentive man behind me.

'Well, I … I've just taken my Mum and her friend up to Heathrow. She's off to India. I came back to work on her canal boat in the Marina today but …' I wondered how silly I looked. 'But I've just managed to drop her keys into the dock.'

'Talk about Shit Magnet Sheila. What are you going to do now?'

'I've no idea.'

'Tell you what, come and have a cup of coffee while we both have a think about it. I'm not due at the rowing club until eleven.'

'Oh Nick, thanks. That would be great.' I picked up the newspaper sections for him and smoothed them back into a complete wodge again. Nick wheeled the buckled bike slowly back to the concourse. He had a small apartment, up two flights of stairs. He took the stairs running.

My shoes tapped across the varnished wooden floor of the living room. 'This is very nice, Nick.' I admired the view of a windswept empty car park and adjoining derelict warehouse, which rather let down the contemporary chic of the room.

'Yes, it was the last one left, so they knocked the price right down for me. I wanted somewhere handy for the town and the Sports Centre.'

I sat down on the edge of the cream material sofa, both feet parked on the russet rug in front of me. The room smelled clean. There was no sign of another occupant; in fact there was very little sign that Nick lived there. A whiff of coffee drifted through as I remembered the pink bra and wiggled my over-egged boobs back into place.

'Would you like milk?' There was a jug of milk with the cafetière and two bowls of perfectly-cooked organic porridge.

'Oh, er, yes please.'

'Here we are, then, Sheila.' He sat down on the sofa next to me, placing his own mug neatly in the middle of a coaster on the glass coffee table. Something incongruous hit me about the scene, although I hadn't a clue why. Perhaps I still hadn't come to terms with his designer stubble.

'Now then, how can we get your keys back?'

In the end, Nick was as clueless as me, though we finished warm and fed. Around nine-thirty, we walked back to the Marina. A couple of joggers overtook; Delia appeared from the Ladies in her dressing gown and slippers. She paused at the entry gate as we told the tale. I don't think she recognised Nick.

'Mike should be around by now. Let's ask him.'

The three of us walked down the gangway and round to the trawler. Delia tapped on the wheelhouse window.

'Mike. Mike.'

After a few seconds a large hand appeared, followed by a sunburnt forehead and then a grubby white teeshirt covering a voluptuous paunch. He threw open the wheelhouse door. The scrub on his chin rivalled Desperate Dan's.

'Good morning, Mike. We need your help, please,' said Delia, all pink, fluffy and female.

Mike gave a loud yawn, showing gaps between the yellow posts of his teeth.

'What on earth time do you call this, Delia?'

'It's, erm, five to ten, Mike.' She smiled prettily at him.

Mike groped for his wrist and stared at his Rolex diver's watch in silence. Eventually, he said, 'Whadya want?'

Delia winked. It was my turn. 'Sorry to bother you so early, Mike. I've dropped a set of keys for the *Iris* into the water. I've got no idea at all how to find them. Can you help, please?' As I spoke, I felt the panic rising through me. It was now two hours since I'd dropped the keys. Was there any chance of finding them?

'Oh,' he grunted and disappeared.

'I didn't realise the *Iris* was your boat,' said Nick, after we'd waited a while.

'Erm, no, it belongs to my Mum. The one who's gone off to India.'

'Was she the one …?'

'Yeah, 'fraid so.' Delia looked more closely at Nick.

'Shit magnet sort of runs in the family, then, does it?' Delia gasped discreetly.

'Try this.' Mike erupted into his wheelhouse again. He had a tatty, oil-spattered cardboard box in his hands, which he thrust through the door at me.

'Oh, er, thank you, Mike. What is it?'

'Magnet. Works well.' He grinned. 'You'll be surprised what you find.'

***

There was something big on the bottom under *Iris.* We felt the magnet lifting and dropping the thing, whatever it was. It was about a metre and a half wide and two metres long, with lots of holes. Trouble was, it was right where I'd dropped the keys. Until we fished it out, we stood little chance of locating an insignificant keyring.

Nick and I took turns. We probed through three metres of water. As we drew up the rope attached to the magnet, three metres of mud, weed and general gunk found its way over the pontoon. Very soon, my trousers and trainers were sodden from the knees down.

Nick was determined. 'Houston, we have lift off … get ready to grab it, Sheila.' Hand over hand, he inched the magnet towards the surface. Whatever it was, weighed a lot more than a bunch of keys.

I lay flat out on the pontoon deck and reached down. 'Look at this. Just what I need, Nick.' Despite the layer of mud, a woman's bicycle appeared, with a wattle and daub basket on the front handlebar.

'I wonder how long this has been on the bottom?'

'D'you know, I think that might be Ella's.' Delia stepped back to avoid mud rivulets dripping on to her still-pristine pink fluffiness. 'I'm sure she had a bike when she came here.'

'Yeah, it was stolen, wasn't it?'

'Maybe not,' said Delia. 'Perhaps someone pushed it in for fun.'

I sighed. 'Messy cleaning job.' I leant it up against the electricity stand to dry off. 'Well, look at this!' Nick wound up a rusty saw.

'My turn!' I plumbed the line until the magnet made contact. An old paint tin, full of eggy-smelling mud, emerged. Nick and I arranged the trophies on the pontoon, like a couple of kids fishing for crabs on a summer's day.

'Could I have a go next, please, Nessie?'

'Sure. I dropped the keys just as I was stepping aboard, round about here.'

'OK. Here goes then.' Delia dangled the line, dipping the front hems of her dressing gown into the muddy water.

'Nick!' There was a shout from the shore. I glanced at Nick. His immaculate white shorts had muddy water marks soaking up the backside; he had smears of black round his designer stubble and across his teeshirt. His hands were coated in mud. I smirked. 'So who's the shit magnet now then, Nick?'

Nick looked down at himself and grinned. 'You got me there, Sheila.'

'Nick!'

'Oh Christ, it's twenty past eleven. I must go. Hope you find the keys soon, ladies.'

Next thing, he was waving from the wheel of a pristine RIB inflatable, wearing a brand-new lifejacket.

'Good looking guy.' Delia watched him buzz off towards the waiting fours.

'And nice with it,' I hauled, very gently, very carefully … 'But not nearly as good-looking as these little beauties.'

'Nessie, you got them! Oh no.'

'What's wrong?'

'Sorry, I just wasn't thinking straight. I remember now. Your Mum left a spare set of keys in the Marina office.'

'No matter.' A glow-worm of confidence nudged through me. I'd retrieved the keys, in the end.

Around two o'clock I sat down, plugged in my lead and started work. Nobody knew I was there. I ignored the enticing noises off. Two depression papers tucked themselves under my belt that afternoon. My productivity rate was improving! I reached home about seven, my joie de vivre restored.

There was, of course, no dinner. The plums, now fully defrosted, took pride of place in the fridge. The couscous remained dehydrated. Paul was reading at the kitchen table, arms and legs sprawled out as if *nonchalant* was his middle name.

I discovered a tin of chicken in the larder and turned it into a saucepan. The couscous only needed boiling water. And I wasn't about to waste the plums after their value-added period in the freezer.

'What did you do last night for dinner?'

'Oh, I went out for fish and chips. What did you do?'

'I … went out for fish and chips, of course.' The tight silence could go either way. 'The people at the Marina were really helpful. Delia invited me on board her boat for a sandwich at lunchtime. The guy who lent me the magnet was as rough as old boots, but Delia says his boat is stacked with all sorts of gear, if you ever need to borrow anything.'

'Do you mean the *Argosy*?'

'Yeah, that big fishing boat over by the far wall.'

'I've chatted to him. He goes in the pub over the way, every lunchtime.'

'Doesn't he work?'

'Dunno. Doesn't seem to. So did you get your peace and quiet down there?'

'Yep, I really steamed on with my articles.' Suddenly I realised what a brilliant opportunity Mum had offered. My heart thumped with enthusiasm. 'Look, would you mind if I went back to *Iris?* While Mum's away, I could really get down to this assignment and get it nailed, if I could concentrate without any distractions.'

'Why should I mind?' Paul turned back to *Bricklaying for Beginners*.

'Well ... I thought you might.' My fine mood snuffed out. Didn't I even have to fight for my independence?

After dinner, I trudged upstairs and hauled out our largest bag. I stuffed in a pathetically inadequate pile of clean clothes with which to leave home for four weeks. Then I slung the slightly-mouldering laundry into bags as well, hoping there was a drying-room at the marina. By the time I had loaded the remaining detritus of my student identity into the rucksack and my clothes into the passenger seat, Smartie was stuffed to bursting and I was knackered.

I drove slowly down to the marina and unloaded. Once everything was trundled on board, my conscience erupted.

'Paul? I've arrived safely. Are you OK?'

'I'm sitting down with my book and a glass of Scotch. Quite OK, thanks.'

My insides tweaked. ‘Are you sure you can manage on your own?’

‘Of course.’ There was a rustle as a page turned.

‘And is Manx all right?’

‘Fine. Are you frightened on your own down there or something?’

‘Certainly not! Well, if everything’s all right, I’ll get to bed early.’

‘Bye.’ He put the phone down.

I cried into the chilly sheets. A faint scent of washing powder overlaid Mum’s distinctive essence. It exhausted me, but I defined the feeling exactly. I was crying from being alone in a double bunk and the premonition that Paul would get along very well without me.

2.9

It took forty nine minutes to walk up to the university. Only a couple of miles for a herring gull, but for the rest of us, a trail round the Victorian basin. Gentrified warehouses and contemporary waterside terraces straddled the marina. After the pub, renovated workshops overtook the original dockside. Round every corner a surprise waited: a rigging specialist or a reclamation yard; a commune of artists or an antique yacht being rebuilt. Once, walking down after dark, I spotted stadium lights and heard the shouts of the home football crowd.

A couple of floating restaurants lined the North bank, dusty in the early morning grey. Of a lunchtime, they transformed with white damask tablecloths to an affluence I ignored, on principle. If you were lucky of a Wednesday afternoon, canoeists larked, sailing dinghies becalmed and rowers splashed up and down. Usually it was derelict of life, except for swans and an occasional plastic bag, running down on the breeze.

Early on in my independence, I discovered a shortcut of stone passages leading up the steep hillside, avoiding the dirt and traffic of the main road. There were far too many steps to count. Gulls whining overhead evoked family holidays, which made me tearful the first time. Later on, I'd arrive at the top with a smile on my overheated face, enjoying my heart thumping. The old Regency rows and crescents started here, far above the hoi polloi. I looked for Ron, every time I passed.

Next, I slipped through a high, black-painted gate, mindful of the worn paving stones under my feet. Other students scurried through the boneyard from their Hall of Residence.

The stones' inscriptions had worn away after two hundred years, the graves dismal, un-named beds. The anonymity of the dead still bothered me.

When I was early enough, I walked by the grim Sixties Students' Union. More often, I was late and edgy, and I'd scuttle, half-running, half-walking, to make the Department by nine-thirty.

The first assignments weren't returned before we handed in the Mental Health papers, three weeks later. Several students flagged up the problem. I queried it at the next Academic Staff Meeting, in early December.

'They have all been first marked, but some of them haven't been second-marked yet.' Kirsty gave Scott a cool smile.

'I've been working on a proposal for a Type 2 children's physical activity trial. It goes in on Friday,' returned Scott, stony-faced. 'I'm afraid that comes first.'

'Of course.' I felt embarrassed to have made a fuss. 'When will they be cooked?'

'They'll be ready next Tuesday. That's always been the situation.'

'I could give you a hand, if you're pressed for time,' Jonathan offered.

'No, I don't think we should change anything. I just think it would have been courteous to let the students know what's going on.'

It seemed a good idea to change a tetchy subject. 'I didn't know there were different types of children,' I muttered to Hugh, sitting next to me.

'I don't think there are.' He sounded puzzled.

Scott looked over. 'It's Type 1 and Type 2 diabetes,' he said, in the patient tones of a maligned man.

'Oh, sorry, of course.' I'd compounded my idiocy.

By Friday tea-time, the horizontal trend of my learning curve was undeniable. I raided the supermarket for some extras. The store was more crowded than I expected. Tired parents wheeled family trolleys of crying children, negotiating erratic elderly ladies with vacant looks and empty trolleys.

I succumbed to two packs of chocolate caramel shortcakes: double the calories and fat, for the price of one. A man with an untidy carpet fringing his baldness moved in behind to pick up his own supplies. He must spend weeks at a time sitting on the creased bottom half of his battered, beige raincoat.

Hmm, I thought to myself, what a slob! You can see why he's obese. Now let's have a look at the ready meals.

A deliciously evil, French flaky pastry tart crammed with goat's cheese and roasted vegetables tempted me. Not too expensive, just for one. I added a bottle of wine and some crisps, ready for guests. Navigating the hazards at full speed ahead, reduced sausage rolls caught my eye and I fell for them, too. Why I thought nearly out-of-date saturated fat was a bargain escapes me now.

Next door to my checkout, Mr Raincoat unloaded his wire basket. His collar trapped rolls of fat below his bald head.

The next customers moved behind me. Half-turning, I recognised Professor Rawlins. He smiled at me, but I guessed he wasn't sure of my identity. A tall, fiftyish man stood with him, in an old pair of fawn trousers and a worn army jumper. Affluent gentry, in spite of his grimy artisan's nails.

'Hello, my dear, how are you?'

'Good, thank you. And yourself?' The reduced label shouted its identity from the top of my trolley load. Reluctantly, I heaped my purchases into a mountain at the far end of the belt, hiding my sinful shopping behind my backed-up body. As the belt trundled forward, the sausage rolls slid off in slow motion and thwacked onto the floor.

Ron's friend stooped down and retrieved the sausage rolls from his brown polished shoes. Ron observed them with scientific interest.

'Oh, oh thank you.' Pink crept up my face.

'Yes, we're very well, thank you, Vanessa.' The Professor of Exercise and Health placed his organic, low fat and finest quality purchases neatly onto the belt, behind mine.

'Hi, Nessie.'

'Oh hi, er … ' The checkout operator was a Taiwanese PhD nutritionist. 'Are you taking a break from the Department?'

'Yes, I need to earn money, too.' She smiled at Ron, unashamedly AWOL, as she finished swiping through my pile of unhealthy eating. 'Enjoying the course?'

'Very much. Thanks … er, goodbye.' I fled with a besieged smile. Healthy Eating joined my in-tray.

I arrived back on board *Iris* to find the phone ringing.

'Vanessa? It's me. I've been trying to get hold of you for days. Paul said you were on the boat.'

'Yes, Mum, give me your number and I'll ring you back.'

'No that's all right dear. I'm speaking from a house in Bangalore … well, it's virtually a palace.' Her voice dropped to a whisper. 'I've gone to bed; the phone's in my room. They won't mind. It would almost be an insult if I let you phone me.'

'OK, so how are you, Mum?'

'Wonderful, thank you. Everything's just fine.' She sounded extremely proud of herself. I smiled back down the phone.

'What have you been doing with yourself, then?'

'Well we came up here on the train. I can't tell you what an experience that was.'

There was a pause. OK, fair enough. 'How long have you been in Bangalore?'

'Oh, the whole time. Phyllida's friends are very hospitable. It's like a large family living together. They're making a big fuss of me; they've even given me the largest bedroom. It's got marble floors!'

'That sounds fun.'

'Oh yes … treating me like the Queen. There's a society based here … they've been teaching me about meditation.' Oh God, Mum was into transcendental meditation. Next thing, she'd be in bed for a week with India's answer to John Lennon. 'And about computers.'

'Ooh, does that mean you'll be e-mailing me soon?'

'I've sent some e-mails already, but you haven't answered,' she said in a dignified voice.

'Oh, no, sorry Mum, I didn't realise. I'll start checking. I've only been looking at my university in-box. Have you taken lots of photographs?'

'Yes and I've put all my photos up on my website.'

'Right.' I gulped. It was one thing to have my Mum travelling to exotic places, and quite another to have her outstripping me on the IT front. 'Erm, would you like to send me an e-mail with the address on it? I can't wait to see the photos.'

'Yes, we put the first blog up today.'

'Blog …?'

'Yes, you know, dear, it's a chance to have my say about India. Bangalore is …' she dropped her voice, '…squalidly poor in many parts. It is *encapsulated in poverty, despite its high-tech persona*.'

'Oh, I see. Well, good for you Mum.' The Literature stressed the importance of elderly people taking an interest in current affairs. 'When are you moving on?'

'Well, that's the other reason I'm ringing. We've delayed our flight back.'

'Oh yes? What's the new date, then?' I picked up a pen to jot down the flight details.

'We haven't re-booked, as yet.'

'Well, you'll need to get a move on, or all the seats will be filled for Christmas.'

'Oh, we're not intending to come back then. We thought about the end of February. Phyllida is researching for her next book. Really, they have made us so welcome, we may decide to stay longer than that.'

'But … but … you'll be away for Christmas! Won't you miss us?'

'Well, I suppose so, dear.' It didn't sound as if that thought had occurred to Mum. 'But really, this is a once-in-a-lifetime opportunity. Once I get to eighty five, I'll be too old to travel.'

'Right.' Nothing more to say, really.

'Well, I must get some sleep now. It's nearly one o'clock.'

'OK, take care, Mum. Send me your address.' As if she took any notice whatsoever of what I said.

On Monday morning I ran the basin perimeter for the first time. Four kilometres still took more than thirty minutes, so that according to Jonathan, I wasn't technically running. Generally, I couldn't manage more than two minutes of continuous jogging. I'd get hot in my face, my lungs heaved uncontrollably and my legs stripped of everything except pain. Then I walked again, until I could persuade my body to accept some more abuse.

A cold mist of rain permeated my tee-shirt and my current state of mind. I was about to challenge my emerging self-efficacy by starting my third assignment without a whisper of feedback. Was I aiming too high?

A man of about my age shuffled along, partnering a waddling Westie.

'Morning!' I ran, showing off my long strides.

He gawped as I passed. 'Rather you than me, love.'

Within a couple of hundred metres, I smiled. I bounded along, until pain tweaked the front of my shins. Forced to slow up, I wondered about warm up. And warm down.

My way took me around my favourite, west side of the dock, first. Car-clogged roads ribboned high above the spindly bridges, as I crossed the lock down to the sea. Beyond the old engine room, new terraces with different-flavoured pocket-gardens clustered round a conserved quay. A dressing-gowned old man breakfasted with a broadsheet behind a french window. Next door, contemporary furniture and unwashed plates revealed hurried departures to professional offices in town. Further on, children had disappeared into the Monday whirlpool, leaving wheeled toys abandoned.

Here I was, a fortunate student with space in my life to observe. I jogged on, cooled by the mist, my mind freewheeling on rhythmic movement. Then it hit home.

Mum would be away. Fifty-five traditional Christmases imploded. Come to think of it, what was Benjie doing? Leah, of course, would be in darkest Peru or somewhere. I haven't heard from her for a month. Reflexive fear jiggled its way up my body. I elbowed Leah out again.

Just Paul and me, then. I was too busy to make social arrangements and Paul never would. I slowed to a walk as the inevitable conclusion occurred. We were on course for the worst Christmas ever. The idea crashed a wave of dreariness over me. I came to, considering an abandoned ceramic pot of mushy black stalks. The only solution was to run.

A launch chuntered officiously up to town, too fast to pace me. Every day dribs and drabs of workmen and office workers, shop assistants and school children straggled down worn stone steps for the ferry pick-up. My mood plummeted. I concentrated on breathing.

It was never a good idea to turn into the town during the morning rush hour. For some reason, today, the traffic was still log-jammed at a quarter to ten. Ron was right. I risked passive asphyxiation. I could feel the eyes of queuing drivers, silently weighing up my legs and boobs.

I jogged through the tourist precinct in the centre of town and over a footbridge. Cobbles slapped my running soles down to a walk. Near the end of the quay, an ancient mariner eyeballed his way out, through the concrete reefs to the sea. I patted his chilly bronze thigh in passing, admiring his wanderlust.

By the time I'd run over the final bridge and out of the heritage area, I was feeling good again. An hour's running and my positive affect was strong enough to withstand any further vagaries the day presented. Who needed anti-depressants anyway?

***

In the first few seconds after waking on Tuesday, the lump of reckoning weighed in. I arrived at the Department far too early. Scott was still reading papers. Kirsty told us all to come back in half an hour.

'How are you feeling?' Cathy and I paced to the IT workroom.

'Nervous. Ridiculous at my age. How's your Dad?'

'Oh, the operation went fine, thanks. He's still in hospital.'

'How long will he be in for?'

'We … don't know. He's in barrier nursing. He's picked up *Clostridium difficile*, so he's quite poorly.' Flat voice; she concentrated on the screen.

'Whatever's that?'

'Oh you know, one of these antibiotic resistant nasties. You go into hospital fit and well and come out feet first having wretched your guts up in between.'

'Oh, Cathy, I'm sorry.' I swallowed. 'How's your Mum coping?'

'Giving the staff hell. She's a retired sister herself.'

'I see.' My fingers hovered over the mouse. I clicked on my home e-mails.

'Are you going to the Christmas party?'

'First I've heard about it.' By now I was adept at multi-tasking. I scanned through Mum's e-mails and replied to her latest. There were one hundred and fifty four photographs up in her gallery.

'It's at the Grapevine Hotel, on Wednesday week.'

'How much does it cost?' Twenty un-named, teeming railway stations later, I quitted out of Mum's adventurous life-style.

'No idea.'

'I haven't heard anything about it. Yes, of course I'll go.' Probably the only bit of Christmas cheer in my carol book this year. Must make the most of it. *Not that I'm complaining*, said Eeyore. I closed my e-mails. No hope of concentrating on them at the mo.

'I'll definitely be going,' Cathy was reapplying scarlet lippie, scanning a neat little mirror and pressing her lips together. 'By the way, I've decided on my dissertation.'

'Really?'

'Yeah. I've talked to Kirsty. It seems that the right person to advise me is Jenny. She's not back until after Christmas. A bit disappointing, but I'm getting on with the literature review.'

'Oh … are you? Where do you get the time and energy, with your father ill and a job as well?'

'Erm …' For once, Cathy didn't have a ready answer. 'I suppose … I make up my mind and focus. Don't let distractions get in the way? Oh, it's probably the HRT.'

'HRT?' The door clicked open and Vasulu walked in.

'Well?'

He flashed his assignment at us with a modest grin. The topsheet was typed, with a couple of handwritten lines and a large A in a circle.

'Wow, well done, you. You must be proud of yourself.' I looked round to share his triumph, but Cathy had already disappeared to Kirsty's office.

2.10

I couldn't tell how Cathy had done. She walked back, core body language firm as ever, paper tucked away in her bag.

'Everything OK, Cathy?'

'Great, thanks. No problems.'

Rosa came out, looking flattened. Now it was my turn.

'Hi, Kirsty, do you have mine, please?'

'Yes, it's here, somewhere.' I could feel my triceps quaking. 'Relax, it's alright.'

She started leafing through the pile of assignments. Were they sorted worst or best first? I couldn't look any more. I stared out of the window at the continuing grey world outside.

'To have two As for the first module is quite exciting, don't you think?' Kirsty said casually. Scott was lounging with an elbow on the filing cabinet. The wire in-trays on the file teetered excitingly close to the edge. Could it be me? My guts leapt upward to pummel my heart. Cathy was pulling out my paper with a complimentary smile. Yes, I was heading for gold. After the weeks of uncertainty, the relief was wonderful.

'Elliott … Here we are. Nice try. Read the feedback and come and talk to us if there's anything you don't understand.'

I glanced down at the circle. I gave a small gasp and my guts slithered over the cliff-edge. There was no mistaking the ringed C.

'What's the matter?'

'Well, I …' I gulped, my vision fuzzing faster than I could clear it. 'I'd hoped for more than a C.'

'You passed, didn't you? That's really all that matters at this stage.'

'Come on, Vanessa.' Surprised, I blinked a couple more times. 'We'll look at it together.' Scott propelled me out, leaving the trap clear for the next victim.

'This was a truly innovative idea, but there are two issues you need to address. First, you haven't supported it with the right evidence. I had the feeling you just banged in everything you could find. Second, the idea isn't developed. At the moment, it's just the statement that mortality statistics don't tell the whole story.'

I wiped my nose on a pensionable tissue. The last few minutes had steam-rollered me below the tarmac. Scott looked at me and changed gear.

'You know, sometimes less is more. You could transform this into a strong argument for a new take on mortality statistics, if you reviewed and distilled the evidence from …' He leafed through my overblown reference list, '… this, this and these two meta-analyses. Take the ideas, push them on. Score the goals. Get the references accurate, next time.' He shuffled the papers back together. The C glared at me again.

'Well, yes.' I wasn't sure which way was up in the wind tunnel of my existence. Scott leaned back and crinkled his eyes. For an academic of such honed precision only a few seconds earlier, he looked almost relaxed.

'How are you feeling?'

'Well, erm … flattened?' It was the best I could do. Could I conceivably scour my brain for more power?

'Persevere, and you'll build up to a good result in the end.' The ejector seat activated, and next thing I knew, I was sitting in front of my laptop on the boat, working on the next assignment.

***

I drove back to the village to see Dr Stainton-Jones early on a dreary Friday morning, punching through the city rush hour. This time, I meant business.

'How are you today, Mrs Elliott?' Above a duty smile, her eyes strayed to her computer screen like a teleprompt.

'Well, the patches have worked … I stopped them two weeks ago and I hardly noticed.'

'Well done! Now, how about your back?'

'That's fine.' I remembered the pain in my shin. 'I've been running,' … must put that in, I thought, 'and that's helped it, I think.' Sod it, I couldn't cope with too many things wrong at once.

She nodded, fiddling with a teensy flower-shaped button on her cardigan. 'Excellent! I'll check your blood pressure again.' My heart sank, but The Literature was shouting at me that more exercise would help. Did I trust The Literature, or not? I sat up straight, and breathed my blood pressure down.

'Oh yes, much improved.'

'Really?' I squeaked. It worked!

'Oh yes, well within normal limits. We'll check it again next year.'

'Next year? All that worrying I've done about it and it's normal?'

'Oh yes, it will fluctuate up and down.'

'Huh,' I said. 'I feel cheated! I'm not going to worry about that any more!'

'And how is the depression?'

'I don't have depression,' I snapped. 'At least, I don't think so.'

Dr Stainton-Jones sat up straight, as if she'd suddenly spotted a fellow human in a jungle clearing. 'Are you saying you are well again, now?'

'No, I'm not saying that.' I launched into my collected thoughts. 'Just that … err, lots of things are wrong in my life right now, so that when something else goes wrong, I don't have any spare resources. But I'm not down all the time. When I'm running, I feel good. I don't think anti-depressants are right for me, that's all.'

'When you say, lots of things are wrong in your life, what do you mean?'

'Oh, everyone's flown the nest; there doesn't seem much point to life; I don't have as much energy as I'd like. Usual stuff about the menopause, dry fanny, hot flushes and all that.'

'And your libido, how …?'

I laughed. 'Over the last twenty-five days or the last twenty-five years?'

'Have you ever taken Hormone Replacement Therapy?'

'HRT? No, I wouldn't take drugs I don't need.'

'Well, it's not so much a drug as a replacement for naturally-occurring female hormones. You might find it a more palatable choice than an SSRI, for short-term use.'

What was she talking about? Wasn't that something to do with wild flowers? Something clicked. In an instant, I decided that if HRT was all right for Cathy, it would be all right for me. I hardly listened to the rest. I'd look it up on the internet later.

Armed with a month's supply, I drove round to see Paul. The brickwork was a metre and a half high. There was no sign of action on the muddy, rain-lashed building site. I opened the back door to the squawk of the tuba, and my spirits drooped.

'Hello, Paul.' I filled the kettle at the sink. Paul and the tuba stopped embracing.

'Oh, hello. What are you doing here?'

'I've popped in to see how you're doing,' popped out brightly, as if he was an elderly uncle.

'I'm very well, thank you.'

There was a pause. I leaned against the sink and looked round. The worktops were clean, clear of old letters, manky oranges and superfluous breadcrumbs. Three washed plates and a mug drained by the shiny sink. On the clean floor, Manx's bowls were freshly filled with food. It hardly looked the same kitchen I'd left, four weeks ago.

Paul studied his music book. He'd upgraded to the trousers he wore the day he was made redundant.

'How's the garage coming on?'

'Very well, thank you.'

'How much longer for the brickwork?' I gave him his mug of tea and sat down opposite. He had ageing elastoplasts on two fingers.

He stretched out his hand to study them. 'Oh, another week or ten days.'

'Good.' I tried to rustle up another sentence. I stood up. Taking the dishcloth, I scrubbed at the limescale on the taps. 'How are you managing?'

'Fine, thank you.'

The kettle boiled and switched off. I jumped in to make the tea.

'Mum's planning on staying out in Bangalore for a bit longer.'

'Right.'

'It means she won't be home for Christmas.'

He gave a transient smile. 'Yes, she told me.'

'Er, I was wondering what we should do about it. Have you heard when Benjie's home?'

'Benjie's been invited to South Africa with the rugby club.'

'Really? When? He hasn't he told me.' Paul shrugged his shoulders. 'That's fantastic news. He must be so excited.' Normality suddenly intervened. 'I thought he was overdrawn? How's he going to pay for it?'

'I think it's our Christmas present.' He looked at me sideways. He seemed to have temporarily lost the will to look straight at me. 'Is that alright with you?'

'Yes, of course … Can we afford it?'

Paul sighed. 'It more or less cleans us out of our reserves. I reckon if I can finish the garage in two months and then get a job, we'll just about manage.'

'Maybe it's just as well that we're not planning much of a spending spree over Christmas.'

'Ah, Christmas.'

'Mmm.' I looked at his hunched shoulders as he sat at the table with his hands cupping the tea. 'So what are we planning for Christmas?'

'So far as I'm concerned, I'd be quite happy to forget all about Christmas.' He said that every year.

'Really?'

'I mean it. I can't see what all the fuss is about, especially if your Mum's not here. Can't we just forget about it and have a normal day?'

'We can't do that.'

'Why not?'

'Because it's a family celebration. Let's invite the Chinese students up here and give them a nice, traditional, family Christmas.'

'If you want to do that, go ahead. Count me out. I am going to have a nice, quiet, unsociable Christmas.'

'Are you sure?'

'Quite sure.'

'In that case, I'll stay at the marina. It will be more convenient for them.'

Paul stood up. 'Have you finished your tea?' I shook my head. He rinsed his mug at the sink. 'Excuse me. Now it's stopped raining, I need to get on.' With that, he opened the back door and pulled on a chalk-streaked boiler suit and wellies.

One flattened hour later, I arrived back at the Marina. One minute later, I remembered the boat keys left on the kitchen work top. In view of my resulting mood, I drove back home very carefully, to avoid accidents. Two and a quarter hours after my departure, Paul met me at the door.

'Are these what you're looking for?' Tears were off-limits. I took the keys from him, turned round and drove the hour back. On board *Iris* at last, I opened the bottle of wine. It wasn't a minute before time to take my first HRT pill.

2.11

I added my Christmas post to the seasonal logjam and nipped into ASDA before it closed. I hadn't a vast choice of party clothing. A low-cut sparkly tee-shirt in purple, reduced by 20%, looked very nice on the teenage model in the photograph and would go with the inevitable black trousers. Near the entrance, a hollow-cheeked Eastern European sold large boxes of liqueur chocolates for a pound. What a bargain. I fell for two boxes, before he moved on.

The neckline was a good inch lower than the left-over smear of last summer's suntan. I had a black balcony bra, which I'd not worn much. The mirror reflected a spectacular uplift, worthy of Barbara Windsor in a Carry On film, but at least I only bulged spare tyre over the top of my trousers. Somehow I'd put on half a stone or so in the last couple of months, but there wasn't time to worry. It wasn't as if anyone was going to grab my boobs.

Of course I was late, but the Grapevine was quiet. A few students sat in booths at the far end. I slipped off my coat and re-arranged my shoulders to cover the uplifted cleavage. After being as well covered as a polar bear over the past couple of months, my bare arms invited hypothermia.

On the far side of the bar, the lecturers had dressed for the occasion. Kirsty, in velvet pants, posed close to Nick. Even in December, Nick glowed with a surfer's tan. Jonathan and Hugh were dressed down, or perhaps it was up, in jeans. Scott, in his usual jeans and leather jacket, didn't look as if he'd made any effort at all.

'Nice top.'

I turned back. 'Oh, thanks, Cathy. I thought I was going to be alone all night.'

'Don't you know any of the students here?'

'Well, no,' I admitted. 'Although I've seen most of them before on odd occasions, I wouldn't say I know anyone here well enough to plonk myself down next to them and start a conversation. I've really only made friends with the other mature students and the Chinese girls.'

'I see what you mean. We're only in a couple of days a week and apart from that … This degree's quite a solitary business, isn't it?' Cathy smoothed down the front of her little black Christmas number, a league above me in youth and looks.

'And expensive,' I added, factoring in yet another visit to the cash dispenser on my way up.

The Greek student gang erupted into the bar. Someone shouted, 'Hi, Nessie.'

'Hi!' I smiled vaguely into a middle distance that encompassed them all. I turned back to Cathy. 'Basically, I can't put names to faces, even if I remembered the names in the first place. I'm not even sure who the e-mail names are, in the flesh. It's quite embarrassing really, being the Student Rep and all.'

'Oh dear, I'm not looking forward to getting old. Good evening, you two.'

Midge had made a heroic effort with the slap. She looked as bland-faced as a Geisha girl. Her lycra top didn't pull over the spare tyre left over from two kids, she was wobbling on her stilettos and her stolid bare shins below the pants looked candle-pale cold. This wasn't Midge's cockle-warming everyday self. 'Have you just arrived?'

'No, I've been sitting over there ever since you turned up.'

'I didn't see you. My night vision must be worse than I thought.'

'Are you coming over?'

'Yeah, we'll just get a couple …'

'Good evening. Can I buy you ladies a drink?'

'Hello Scott. Hey, it should be us buying you one,' said Cathy. 'What would you like?'

'No, no, it's Christmas. Midge?'

'Just a lemonade, please. I'm driving.'

'Nessie?'

'Erm, ... fizzy water. Thank you, Dr Woodhouse.'

'Scott, please.'

'Oh, oh sorry, Sco ...'

'Cathy?'

'White wine would be great, thanks.' Scott turned to order, leaving me to wonder. Did Scott fancy the sophisticated Cathy, to distinguish us so obviously?

He smiled as he handed over Cathy's wine-glass. 'You're drinking tonight, then?'

'Only the one, I've got to drive back at the end.'

'Are you clubbing first?'

'Oh Scott!'

He smiled again. I'd never seen him so relaxed. 'What do you mean, *Oh Scott*?'

'Student night clubs aren't really my scene.'

He laughed. 'Personally, I can't stand dancing.'

I joined in. 'Really? My husband's just the same, never dances. I've given up on him, now.' Scott handed me a bottle with a straw.

'Mmm, I know what you mean,' Cathy said, 'but it's easy, Scott, you just stand there and keep time to the music. No-one's expecting a *Strictly Come Dancing* performance.'

'Maybe not. But I just can't see any point to it, unless you're a teenage girl.'

'So, what's your game?' Cathy asked him.

'Gym, mostly, up at the Centre.'

'I haven't seen you up in the gym, for a while.' Nick came across carrying empties. 'In fact, I think I've seen more of Nessie up there, this term.'

I checked the state of my bust and slouched a bit more to hide the outline. 'An exercise scientist without enough time to exercise,' I offered. There was the slightest pause. Nick turned to the bar to buy his wine and beer. Cathy talked about her plans for Christmas. And then the first dance track erupted, smelling hot and Latino. The Greeks flowed on to the dance floor.

'Are you dancing tonight, Scott?' Cathy asked.

'No thanks Cathy. I'd … better get back to Yvonne.'

We looked over: Hugh held hands with the lovely Louise; Kirsty stood close to Nick. Yvonne closed the circle. I could see a plump back, hear her assured laugh. Her straight swing of lightened hair could have been mine. I sighed. They were out of my reach.

'Have a good Christmas, Scott,' said Midge.

'Yeah, you, too.' He smiled all round and wandered back. Nick moved aside to let him in, next to Kirsty.

We skirted the dance floor, avoiding droopy gold stalactites tumbling from the ceiling. We beat the incoming Scandinavian students by an arm's length to a plummy velvet booth. I passed round my box of chocolate liqueurs. Greeks rolled off the floor to stack at the bar. The DJ's voice whined off the walls and lost itself on the empty dance floor. Students dribbled in. The background noise level rose against the competition from newcomers.

I caught, 'What do you …..?' from Midge, next door. I smiled appreciatively back, trying to guess what the hell she had said. She waited for my reply. It was no good, I didn't have a clue. She offered me the box.

'Just one more,' I shouted. She smiled and turned away. When I bit into the barrel, the syrup spurted out down my chin. No-one else seemed to have such an obvious hearing problem. Disconnected, I panned round my fellow students like a cameraman. I was the oldest. Maybe I'm too old to cope. What on earth am I doing here?

I watched Nick buy more drinks. Jonathan arrived with a partner. Or wife, or girl friend or something. Yvonne put on her coat, kissed everyone in the group and disappeared. Maybe she had to walk Jester, I posited. That entertaining word again: posited. Was Yvonne Miss Muffet, I wondered?

The DJ's voice cajoled. One couple stood up to salsa: Jonathan and his partner. Their practised panache put everyone else off. The DJ changed tracks.

Noisily, Nick and Kirsty moved onto the floor, then Hugh and Louise. Scott, bottom leaning against the bar, watched them alone, beerglass in hand. Half a dozen uninhibited students followed. They weren't yet at the tottery stage. Vasulu looked like a gangly scarecrow in his dark suit, looming over the smaller girls.

'Come on Nessie, are you dancing?' Cathy had loosened up but I shook my head. Stony-sober and blatantly miserable, I just wasn't up for dancing. In a while, the patch of dance floor boxed in a squeeze of bodies. Uplighters on the walls dimmed light and creamy as the music slowed. In the soft surrounding twilight, the carpet's square patterns bounced through the spaces between empty chairs and glass-littered tables. I missed the feel of a cigarette in my hand. I switched off. Perhaps I dozed off.

Next thing, I came to, as Scott and Cathy danced. They circled slowly, talking. Cathy's top reflected back the spotlights in myriad sparkling bursts. Scott bent his head an inch or so. Cathy, who was much taller than me, had her arms round his neck, so their mouths were on a level. She leant forward and kissed him langorously.

Oh no, Cathy. Don't do that.

'Sorry, Sheila?' said a voice.

I turned. 'Oh, hi, Nick. Why aren't you dancing?'

'Well, I might ask you the same.'

'I'm far too old a lady.'

'Rubbish, Sheila. C'mon.'

I looked up at him and he smiled the invitation. I couldn't help smiling back. In for a penny, in for a pound, I thought. I stood up, worming my boobs surreptitiously into action stations. 'OK, let's go.'

Nick's dance style didn't extend to bodily contact. It felt awkward, dancing opposite such a virile youngster. I admired his jawline yet again, feeling twinges of admiration stirring deep within the bowels of my earth. He leaned his deep blue eyes towards me.

'Did you bring your car up?'

'Yeah.'

'Do you think I could scrounge a lift, when you leave?'

'Sure, Nick, course I can give you a lift.'

'You going down town now, Nessie?' Xiu was dancing close by.

'In a little while, Xiu. Why, do you want a lift too?'

'A lift?' She looked at me uncertainly. 'Why … an elevator, Nessie?'

'Oh, sorry Xiu. I meant, would you like me to take you in the car?' She looked from me to Nick.

'In … car? We're going to *Copacabana* in the precinct. Are you coming with Nick? Why you take car?' Xiu craned admiringly up at Nick.

I swallowed. This was getting a little out of hand. Was I really ready for a city nightclub with such an attractive piece of male crumpet?

'What do you think, Nick?'

'I'm on the early shift tomorrow. I'm happy to get home any time.'

'Erm, yeah, Xiu. I think we'll be making tracks. I mean, I think we'll go now.' I turned to Nick.

'… offered me a lift home, thanks.'

Kirsty stood next to him. She wasn't looking too chipper. 'Oh well, goodnight, then,' she spat out and marched off to join Hugh and Louise. Xiu reached up to kiss me goodbye.

'Take care. See you on Christmas Day.'

'I can't wait!' She sounded like a big kid.

'What was all that about?' I asked Nick, as we left the hotel. It was chilly, now we were outside. The moon, lit up above the stone spire on the skyline, was fuzzy-ringed in the damp night.

'Oh, er, Kirsty brought me up this evening, but I think she was intending to make a late night of it.' He sounded cagey.

I smelled rat. 'Did you enjoy the party?'

'Uh, yeah. Good do,' he said, with all the enthusiasm of a surfer looking at a mirror-calm sea.

'I enjoyed watching the young students letting their hair down.' My God, I sounded Mumsy. Not my intention, at all. 'It's been hard work for all of us, this term.'

'Yeah, I think you've got to celebrate and let go on a regular basis, otherwise the stress builds up.'

'Is that what Cathy was doing with Scott?'

'Scott can look after himself.'

I unlocked the car and quickly shunted six library books from the passenger seat to the Smartie's minute boot. 'How long have you been at the Sports Centre?'

'Oh I started last March. Before that, I was in London for three years.'

'So you've been in Britain for some time?'

'Yeah, came over … oh, five years ago.'

'And where were you from, originally?'

'Perth, in Western Australia.'

'So what on earth did you come here for?' I peered through the mottled windscreen, levitating the car onto sun-baked beaches.

'Mainly for the rugby. I came over to be a professional player. I was in Harlequins' first team for two seasons.' I gulped. Maybe I should have heard of him before. What a privilege it was, to be taken for granted by the famous Nick.

'Oh.' The road was very dark, in the rain. 'What happened?' I concentrated on the difficult conditions.

'Sheila.'

'Yeah?'

'Do you have some windscreen wipers on this car?'

I clicked them on. 'Yes of course. How stupid of me. Sorry Nick.'

'I expect you're tired.'

'You're right, it has been a long day.' I indicated to turn right and concentrated on driving down the hill to the dock, without anything else going wrong. Although he chatted easily, I was conscious of Nick braced beside me, and I slowed until he took his hand off the dashboard. I didn't want him to think I was a crazy driver.

'So have you ever been in a … what on earth?' Bright blue light swept through the side window. In front of me, a red sign flashed. I jolted to attention and braked hard. Had I somehow bumped off the road and onto a pavement?

2.12

'Good evening, madam.' A dark lump blocked the view. A fist knocked at the window.

'Oh my God!' I jumped and banged my hand on the central locking. The locks clunked. I took a deep breath before panicking.

'Nick, someone's trying to break in.'

'Sheila,' Nick's voice was level. 'You'll need to open up and find out what's wrong. It's the police.'

'Erm, yes, you're right.' I couldn't find the window button. In its own time, the window descended. A hairy beard peered in at me.

'Good evening, madam.'

'Good evening, Officer.'

'Have you any idea of why your car is not complying with the Law?' He glared at me.

'No, I … I didn't know anything was wrong.'

'Well, madam, the Road Traffic Act states that during the hours of darkness, vehicles must display front and rear lights, as well as brake lights.'

'Has a brake light gone?' I never looked. Paul's job, until now.

'No, madam.'

'Oh …'

Nick looked startled. 'Sheila, we don't have any lights on.'

'Oh no!'

'Were you aware that you were on the public highway without any lights?'

Fire ringed my heart. 'No, of course I wasn't.'

'Are your front and rear lights in working order?'

'Yes, of course.' In my panic, I found the rear washer, the indicators and the front washers.

'Can I inspect your insurance documents and driving licence, please?' They were supposed to be on board *Iris*. Fortunately, I found them in the car. The policeman looked at my documents for so long that I felt sure my insurance was out of date. Blue light swept the car as regularly as the loom of a lighthouse.

'Thank you, madam. Now have you consumed any alcohol in the last few hours?'

'Erm, no, of course not.'

'Well, madam, everything seems to be in order. Provided that you are willing to comply with a breathyliser, which shows you within legal limits, I will let you off on this occasion. Please get out of your car.' Exhaling for the first time, I felt my lips stretch in a huge smile of relief.

Suddenly I remembered the liqueur chocolates. I'd eaten three … or was it four? The chill hand of inevitability showed disqualification or imprisonment. I climbed out of the car and followed the police officer. He wrote busily. Then he dug out the breathyliser.

'Have you ever been breathylised before?'

I shook my head, screwing up my eyes. 'No. Never in nearly thirty-nine years of driving.' He looked at me sternly. 'Excuse me, officer. I've just remembered that I have had something alcoholic.'

It was too late: he was already demonstrating the breathyliser. I had perjured myself, as well as committing an offence. Taking a large breath, I puffed into the machine for as long as I could.

'It's registering nil,' he said.

Freedom!

'I was really worried there for a minute,' I babbled. 'You see, I had some liqueur chocolates, earlier on.'

'Well, monitor your alcoholic intake more carefully, and make sure your lights are on in future, please, madam. Then we won't have any cause to pull you over.'

The bargainous chocolates were alcohol-free. So much for goodwill to all men, I thought, walking back to the car.

I plumped myself into my car seat, clicked my seat belt, looked in my rear view mirror, signalled, checked my wing mirror, looked behind, pulled out into the road and snivelled into tears.

'Do you think you should pull over again?' said Nick.

'No, I just want to get home, now.' I wiped my hand across the back of my nose in the absence of a spare hand to ferret for a hankie.

'Here, have this,' supplied Nick.

'That was so humiliating.'

'You got away with it. How many had you drunk tonight?'

'Three liqueur chocolates.'

Nick giggled.

'Well, they were supposed to be alcoholic.'

'You should have seen your face, when he asked you to get out of the car.'

'Oh Nick, I've never been stopped before. It was awful.'

Nick patted my arm. 'Stop stressing, you're bound to get pulled over occasionally.'

'I suppose so. Has it ever happened to you?'

'No, but then I haven't driven over here. I do have a driving licence, but .... Next turning on the left, please Sheila.'

'Oh, right.' I turned into the parking area.

'My slot's over there.' He pointed towards an empty expanse.

'Oh yes.' I pulled in at an angle. 'Let me have another go. Oh, still not right. Sorry.'

'What do you keep saying sorry for?'

'I don't know. Silly habit really.'

'It is. I'm really grateful for the lift down. It would have been a long cold walk, tonight. Hey, you still look shocked. Why don't you come up for some hot sweet tea, or something?'

How thoughtful. I looked at Nick. He looked … gentle. He smiled toothsomely at me: I could feel my eyes widening. Surely not? Me? I flushed hot and clammy. Perhaps he was the man in the background of my dream.

'Er …' I sat up straight. You don't have to be young to be cool, as they used to say at *Saga*. 'Yes, that would be nice.'

It was dark round the back of the building. I couldn't see past the first concrete step.

'Sorry, Nessie, I haven't organised an outside light yet.' I felt his hand on my elbow, guiding me gently round to the second flight.

At the top, his front door had a porthole inset, through which the flat was dimly lit. I stood aside for him to unlock the door. He opened the door and motioned for me to enter. I stopped to take a sideways peek through an open door, into the bedroom, where a suitcase lay on the deep red duvet. Nick went ahead.

'… expecting you until tomorrow morning.'

Nick and his twin were standing in a close embrace.

'Come in!'

I stared, gulping for air.

'This is my friend, Andy. He's down from London, to stay over Christmas.'

'Right. Hello, Andy, pleased to meet you.' I shook his hand and we sat on the sofa.

'Hello there. Would you be Kirsty?'

'No, this is Nessie, one of the students, aka Shit Magnet Sheila. What would you like? Tea? Coffee? Wine?'

'So where's this Kirsty you've been telling me about?' asked Andy, when Nick came back with a tray of tea.

'Tell you in a minute. First up, we need to de-stress Nessie, she's still looking very white.'

'I'm alright now, thanks Nick. It was only a storm in a teacup.'

I took a swig from my mug and grimaced. Sweet tea. I set it down carefully on the coffee table.

'What happened?' asked Andy, making sympathetic eyes at me. He was another handsome man.

'I was stopped by the police. They breathylised me, then let me off with a caution.' My face flushed at my lack of aplomb.

'I see. Is that why Nick calls you, er … Shit Magnet Sheila?'

'Could be. She's been a cautionary kick up the backside, all term.'

'I've never heard you talk like that before, Nick.' Andy sounded proprietorial.

'Sorry. It's my public face speaking. The rugby-playing dude.'

'Huh.' I'd get my own back, anyway. 'So what happened tonight with Kirsty then, Nick?'

Andy smiled and raised his eyebrows. 'Sounds interesting.'

'Yeah, well. Kirsty was coming on a bit strong at the party. So I used Nessie here as a decoy to bring me safely home.'

'Decoy?' The rosy smoke drifted away from my eyes.

'To get Kirsty off the scent?'

'Something like that. I don't think she's realised.'

'I don't understand.'

Andy looked at Nick. 'Need to know basis?'

Nick paused for a couple of ticks. 'It's not generally known, but I'm gay.' And then, quickly, 'It's really difficult to come out in a sport like rugby, even today.'

'Oh. I see.' I kept the casual, sophisticated grin fixed to my face. How could I have been so dumb?

'So I've just kept quiet about it, at work. Developed another identity.'

'Not the real you.'

'No, it's not. You don't … mind me telling you straight out, eh? I thought that with your experience, you, of all people in the Department would understand why I stayed undercover.'

'Of course I don't mind Nick. Do I seem like the homophobic type?'

'Well, no. You seemed so open-minded, being on the course at your age.'

'At my age …?'

'Well, you're old enough to be my Mum, and you're still up for it.' I crossed my arms over my low neck and balcony bra. Embarrassment ignited the embers of my hot flush. What exactly did he think I was up for?

'I'd have to have been a very young virgin.' It came out more dryly than I'd intended. They both laughed.

It was nearly one o'clock before I sat on Mum's bunk to take the pill. I looked at the white speck of hormone in my hand. I hadn't forgotten it once, yet. It reminded me of college: I suppose that's why I fallen for the pleasure of calling HRT 'the pill'. Already I felt years younger.

I didn't know much about rugby, off the field. I had a vague vision of steamy baths full of eleven, or was it fifteen muddy men in a bath, singing about fannies and fucking. He must have had a bad time, to stay quiet. And I thought ... I flushed again retrospectively, which heated up my chilly bed quite nicely.

That lead me on to flashbacks about blue lights and my inept driving. On nights like this I missed having Paul in bed to talk me back to my senses. From there it was a small step on to the wider agenda of life, the universe, and rowing the Atlantic with Nick Smallwood. As his Mum, of course.

I hadn't yet bought Paul a Christmas present. After a dithery while, I decided on a jumper. *Plus ça change*, and all that. It was nearly three o'clock before my confused brain settled itself to sleep.

PART THREE
Method
3.1

'The next item on the agenda is the Research Assessment Exercise.' I must have looked puzzled. 'The national exercise to evaluate the quality of research in every university department ,' Scott threw in my direction.

I nodded. I was an OFSTED survivor. 'Oh. How did that go, last time?'

'Well … we got a 3a.'

'What does that mean?'

Scott hesitated. Kirsty chipped in. 'A five grade means the research is of international quality; a four indicates national importance, and so on.'

'I see.' A three didn't sound too good.

'This time we intend to get a five.' That didn't sound too likely.

'I wasn't here last time round,' said Hugh. 'What issues were thrown up?'

'Last time, the assessment covered all staff, even those not currently engaged in research. We suffered because departments elsewhere didn't do that. We've already sorted out our research-active staff, for next time.' Hugh nodded. 'Second, we need to ensure that all our research is written up and submitted to journals, so we are credited with everything we do.'

'I've only just got my two projects off the ground. They're a long way off publication.'

'Will you be able to publish interim results, Hugh?'

'Not yet.'

The staff looked gloomy. 'How about you, Kirsty?'

'Yeah, well my article for *Journal of Sport Sciences* was finally accepted last week, after two rewrites.'

'Congratulations! Any more in the pipeline?'

'Maybe Jonathan and I could squeeze another one out of children's weekend activity.'

'Sure. And what about you, Jenny?'

Jenny looked up from her notepad. It was the first time I'd seen her. She should have been beautiful, but that day she looked exhausted. Her long brown hair straggled down, nearly to the table. 'My two papers were accepted before I went on maternity leave, Scott. They're in press now. Faria's PhD thesis will support another paper when she finishes in a couple of months. Apart from that, I'm waiting to hear which projects you want to re-allocate my way. Then I'll shape up a new research programme.'

Everyone fastened their eyes on their Agenda sheets. The air-con took up the silence.

'There's plenty of time, yet,' I said, in my best encouraging-Mum mode. No-one replied.

'That's only three papers accepted,' Kirsty said.

'Could we make something out of the obesity camp that didn't come off last year?'

'That would really be scraping the barrel. I don't know if Ron would approve of that.'

I cast around the pessimism for a positive re-frame. 'How … do you get paid lots for these articles?' Round the conference table, stolid faces jerked. Kirsty sniggered into the silence.

'No. We don't get paid anything for these articles.'

'You don't get paid? You don't generate any income from them? Then, why on earth do you write them?'

'Peer review and publication is the only way for academic research to be accepted as evidence.'

'It's the means of establishing an academic reputation.' added Scott.

'So it's about … academic … kudos?'

'You could put it that way.' Scott returned to the coal-face. 'Any of last year's MSc dissertations worth writing up?'

Jonathan spoke. 'Andy Harris and I are planning a poster for the European conference in Belgrade.'

'Great. How about some more posters?' Scott turned to me. 'They count, too.'

Another depressed pause spanned out. The fluorescent lights invaded, overly bright in the windowless space. I squinted, adjusting my perspective.

'I know! Your epidemiology assignment, Nessie. I told you it would be easy for you to convert it into an exciting paper slanted towards mortality statistics. How about making it into a poster?' Across the table, Scott's eyes glittered, frost blue.

'Poster …?' I squeaked. This was out of my league.

'Yeah, knock up a poster for the … how about Birmingham? The call for papers and posters is out now.'

'Birmingham?'

'Yeah, the annual sport, health and exercise research and professionals' conference. You have joined *SHERPA* as a student member? '

'D..Do you mean, an a.. academic conference?' My voice squeaked, even higher.

'Yeah,' he replied casually. 'If your submission is accepted, you get to attend the conference. We usually have two or three posters displayed.'

'A poster? Could I do that?' More to the point, would my voice ever regain its mature pulse?

'Jonathan will help you out.'

'But I've never used Powerpoint. Could I manage it, Jonathan?'

'Sure, it's easy. Come and talk to me about it.'

'Well, if you think I'm up to it.'

'Of course.' Scott crinkled his eyes winningly at me. 'It will look good on your cv.' As if I didn't know I was being stitched up. 'Now what we need, ladies and gentlemen, is another large project to write up.'

'We don't even have any other grant applications in.'

'There's nothing in the wind for the next twelve months.'

'So it needs to be internally generated,' remarked Scott. 'As Nessie has noticed, it's the only research we can afford.'

'Planning and ethics will take six months. The earliest we could run it, would be, er, the summer term.' Kirsty looked round for agreement.

'Could students be involved?' I asked. 'What a great opportunity that would be.'

'There'd almost certainly be sections students could dip into, for their dissertations. Trouble is, there aren't enough Masters' students to make much of a sample for a double-blinded randomised controlled trial.'

There were a few grim smiles.

I didn't like the negative attitude I was hearing. 'OK, so what about the rest of the student body, then?'

'Timing wouldn't be ideal for them. Our undergrads have exams in May.'

'No-one would want to participate.'

'Unless it was something they were motivated to do.'

'Any ideas?' Scott looked round.

'Summer term? Easy. Exercise and exam stress,' I said.

'Very difficult to show anything. There'd be too many variables.' Kirsty sounded definite. She wasn't going to support anything I proposed, since the Christmas party.

'I don't agree,' Jenny chipped in. 'The research question would be: can exercise improve exam marks? There are hundreds of potential participants for a robust sample size; we could match pairs to make a randomised controlled trial.'

'What's the minimum for a significant difference?' asked Hugh.

'A couple of months? We could check that out in the literature search.'

'But how do you get them to go to the gym often enough before exams to make a difference?' asked Kirsty.

'The ones who didn't go often enough would form the control.'

'A big event.' Everyone looked at me. 'Err … you know, the sort of thing kids get enthusiastic about. Something like a …a …'

'A sponsored something. Gymathon, training, football tournament?' suggested Hugh.

Kirsty groaned. 'Please no. The world is awash with sponsored events.'

'I'm hearing something attractive, that we can put a physical spin on,' Scott sounded like Gus in *Drop the De* …

'I've got it! Campus run. Five or ten k race.' There was a round-table silence, like the Emperor's new clothes. 'How about: Run for Results?'

Then Kirsty laughed. 'It might just work. Would it pass Ethics?'

'Why ever not?' Scott frowned.

'Well, you might be disadvantaging those who didn't run.'

'Oh come on, Kirsty, it's unlikely to make a significant difference to their exam results.'

'I'm not so sure,' said Jenny. 'Look at strength training in old people. Improving strength improves their memories.'

'Is it worth spending some time on a literature search?' asked Scott, looking round for a volunteer.

Jenny caved into the ringing silence first. 'OK, I will.'

'Thank you. Would you be prepared to write up the proposal, too?'

'Provided I don't have to organise the whole event as well.'

'Of course not. I think we should put a committee of staff and students together. You're right, to be good, this will need to have good publicity and at least Faculty, if not university-wide support. I'll co-ordinate that. Would you like me to chair as well?'

Jenny nodded. 'Yes, please.'

'Then I'll speak to Nick and Alan today. We'll need to talk to the university Athletics Club. Anyone a member?' Scott looked round.

'I used to run,' said Kirsty.

'Louise's into running,' said Hugh. 'She belongs.'

OK, we'll bring you two on board as the experts then.' Scott grinned. 'Then Nessie can be the student input, as she came up with the idea.'

'I've started to run,' I boasted.

'Even better. Jonathan, will you have time to lead on the statistics?' Jonathan nodded. 'Now, Jenny, how long do you need to put the proposal together? You'll need to motor.'

'Two weeks?'

'Right, two weeks today. I'll invite the Faculty and Sports Centre to send reps too. Well done, everyone. Let's get the show on the road. Now, what else is on the agenda?'

When I bumped into her outside the Library, I realised that I hadn't seen Cathy since the Christmas party. We fought downhill to the *Mad Hatter* for cappuccinos, my hood battened up against the rain and gusty wind. It was opportunistic physical activity with a vengeance. Inside, the bitter, grainy smell of ground coffee enveloped the gale. Upstairs was dead: the new term hadn't started yet.

A balding, middle-aged man sat on the battered leather sofa in the bay, reading a newspaper with his coffee. I couldn't place the man, though I'd seen him before. The thin, sweet smell of his cigarette smoke drifted across. Thirteen, nearly fourteen weeks since my last cigarette: almost, but not quite, long enough to past-tense the habit.

'Did you have a good Christmas?' I realised my gaffe, as soon as I'd said it.

'Very quiet without Dad. We brought Mum down here to make a bit of a break for her. How was yours with the Chinese girls?'

'Surprisingly good. It was all such a novelty for them. Really refreshing. When it's the same old traditional stuff year after year, you wonder if anyone really enjoys it,' I burbled, spooning up the chocolate powder and froth from the top of my coffee.

'You're not usually so cynical, Nessie. Didn't you miss your two?'

'Well … funnily enough, I did miss them trailing in at all hours after clubbing.' I bent to take a lukewarm sip, though I didn't really like cappuccino. 'You're right. We used to enjoy Christmas evening, playing games.' I sighed. 'Life had to change.

I loved having them as teenagers. Not very fashionable, but it's true.'

'I wouldn't know. I don't have any children.' She gave me the sort of enigmatic smile that means, don't ask. Her oversized white cup held a perfect imprint of plummy lipstick.

'My kids and their friends filled the house with their energy. Without them … oh, it's just a living space we rattle round.' Cathy let hang a pause.

'And the Chinese girls?'

'Yeah, that Xiu was a little firecracker. You can see why she shot to the top in table tennis.'

'Did you cook a traditional Christmas dinner for them?'

'Of course! It's small in Mum's galley, but I managed. They loved all the trimmings with the turkey. Not the Christmas pudding, though.'

'How was Rosa?' Cathy smoothed her unwrinkled trousers. She did that quite a bit, when she was thinking.

'Quiet, as usual. The others ribbed her for missing her boyfriend in Shanghai.'

'So, she's got a boyfriend? Well that's a start.'

'I feel sorry for her, Cathy. She's so immature.'

'She never seems very happy, does she?'

'She hasn't made herself at home here. Do you know how she's getting on with her assignments?'

'Not really.' Cathy always knew everything. 'Only that she re-submitted the first one. The others haven't said a dickey bird.'

'I expect the lecturers will jolly her along, if she's struggling.'

'Is that an evidence-based observation, Nessie?' Cathy was probably right. The Department wasn't a nursery school.

She repositioned her saucer. 'So, did Paul turn up on Christmas Day?'

'No.' My cup rattled the teaspoon, as I set it down. 'I invited him when I took his present up, but he said he was quite happy to stay put.'

'You look sad.'

'Yeah. Well, it was his choice, wasn't it?'

Cathy looked at me steadily over her cup. 'Have you two split up?'

'No!' It came out emphatically. The man looked over. He collected his sodden raincoat from the curly coat stand before clumping down the wooden staircase. I sat up. 'Cathy, do you know what happened this morning? Scott wants me to do a poster for the SHERPA Conference!'

'Really? Do you have time?'

'Well, the statistics exam isn't til February. Probably I could squeeze it into the end of this month.'

'Won't you be reading for your dissertation?'

'Christ, Cathy, I don't even know what I'm doing for my dissertation, yet.'

We sat silent, while I scrabbled an answer to the real question. Rain drops, suspended on the misty window, quivered in the wind. The man stepped outside and turned his collar up, before disappearing into greyness.

'We haven't split up, Cathy. It's good for me to cope on my own. Oh … do you think it's just a polite fiction, the time out from each other? Is that …?'

'What do you think?'

I looked at her. ' … It's the f..freedom. You know, I haven't been my own woman for … oh, twenty-five years, since the children were born … and Paul is such a grumpy old man ...' I tailed off, twisting a tail of hair round and round my finger.

'But?'

'But I don't …' I stopped short. 'Is that what he wants now, freedom?'

'What are *you* looking for?'

'No idea.'

'Something new?'

'Yes … no … I … don't really know. It's all been … so much more exciting than I expected.'

'Mmm.'

'My future's full of optimism again. I don't want to be old just yet. I guess … it's this place, throbbing with life ... It's opened up my brain, given me a new lease of life.'

'This place? The Department or the city?'

'Everything! City, students, university. I love it all. I want in.'

She nodded. 'It's on your face. You're alive here, aren't you?'

Our drinks were cold by then.

***

We headed down into town. On an impulse, I decided to raid M and S après-Christmas reduced rails for a bra. I'd ditch the embarrassingly over-crowded balcony.

The biggest of the small sizes was a 32DD, and the smallest of the bigger sizes was a 40AA. Judging by the cleavage I'd been showing, my cup was full to overflowing. I dithered for so long, a sales assistant came over to offer help.

'Would you like me to measure you?'

'Maybe that would be a good idea.' I'd lost Cathy to Next.

The clear light of the fitting room revealed the greyfulness of my current bra.

'I don't think either of those would be quite right for you.' The sales lady led me tactfully over to the more expensive stands. Some of the bras looked like Madonna's conical erotica on the *Blonde Ambition* tour. I goggled and scuttled back to white, firm support, next door to nursing and sport. But somehow, the practical ambience no longer appealed, now I'd tasted the apple of excitement. I sidled back to lacy, nipple-revealing netting.

It was the first time I'd tried on exotic bras, after the motherhood years. I posed into the mirror, as if I was a photograph from *Good Housekeeping* or something. I felt suddenly and startingly sexy, in leopard skin lycra. I humped my back like Manx, so I couldn't see the fatty bumps below the bra, left over from Christmas. It was all right, so long as I didn't catch sight of the lumpy creases elsewhere. I smiled at myself like a model.

The white bra adopted a more business-like approach, with underwiring on a translucent netting that clamped my boobs upwards and stood the nipples on end. Also a first in twenty five years, I bought both bras and matching pants, without considering the price, then headed back out into the gale.

Now I was in town, I remembered that Phyllida's boat needed checking every fortnight. Mum and Phyllida had been gone five and a half weeks. To my surprise, I was still carrying Phyllida's keys in my jacket when I checked. Good. I could tick the job off this afternoon, before it got dark.

3.2

Within ten minutes, I'd re-entered the real world.

Aqua Nymph squatted, grey and dismal, amongst a pontoon of boats laid up for the winter. From the swing bridge, I could just make out choppy water, drooping tarpaulins and a grimy fibreglass coach roof. Above the noise of the wind, loose lines and covers frapped and frayed. Pontoons graunched and groaned together. Boats tugged and stretched at creaking mooring lines.

Phyllida's berth was a couple of hundred metres away. I'd better go and have a proper look, I thought. One of her keys let me through the gate. I paced carefully down the jerking pontoons, aware there was no-one around to rescue me.

Aqua Nymph was a motor cruiser, about twenty five feet long, with a large open cockpit in the stern. In this weather, its ancient fitted cover bloomed green and black lichen. Star-cracks spotted the fibreglass decks. Bare, teak hand rails were leached fossil-grey from the dirt and sun. I tested a mooring line: stiff and grey, like old manilla, but secure enough. The boat looked a little down on her marks at the stern. Maybe she needs a pump-out, I thought suspiciously.

The tarpaulin was cold and rigid. I gripped my M & S carrier between my knees, in case I lost my new bras to the gale. With a tussle, I wrenched nine stiff turnbuckles and climbed into the gloomy cockpit. To my right, at the after end of the boat, was a large dim shape. To my left, varnish peeled off wooden doors. I fumbled around with the rusty padlock and eventually managed to fiddle the lock open.

Down in the chilly saloon, the sharp stench of damp boat hit me. The galley window was slightly open on its runners, allowing a crack of air. A couple of dirty dishes grew penicillin in the sink. Elbows, jaws and buttocks clenched, I tiptoed through to check forward. Grey mould flowered in the loo compartment and round the roof linings above the forward bunk. Damp, unmade bedding and a scarlet kimono partly covered the bunk. Presumably Phyllida slept here. It would need more than an open window to dry out this mould factory.

Satisfied that the boat wasn't sinking, I decided to leave Phyllida to face her own cleaning. With difficulty, I re-locked the cabin door. Turning to the stern, I took three paces towards the mysterious dark lump, a large, varnished, mahogany something. I searched my brain for some item of boat's gear that I could identify.

Maybe Phyllida collected antiques from passenger liners? Was it some kind of wheel housing or skylight? I stooped down to inspect the brass marquetry inlaid in the wood before I realised. Long ago, it must have been valuable. But that was yesterday. The piano was now irretrievably past its use-by date.

An unmistakeable scuttling sound rustled inside and I wondered for a millisecond if it could be the sound of water against the GRP hull. It was no use kidding myself. It was a rat. Probably more than one. In the middle of a city like this, there must be rats everywhere.

Within ten seconds I retreated to the pontoon. My heart pounded even while my brain was sneering at me, 'It's only a rat.' I was shivering from the close encounter. Shit. I buttoned up the canvas, pulled up my hood and made a plan.

***

Back on board *Iris*, I checked, double-checked and triple-checked for vermin. After a shower and an aural maze of a phone call to Environmental Health, I cooked supper. Ratty rustles filled the quiet boat. Dishcloth in hand, I found myself cleaning round the sink, perpetually alert. I faltered up the pontoon, but Delia's boat was closed up. I didn't know anyone else well enough to visit. After half an hour of uncomprehending reading, I locked *Iris* and set off home. I hadn't seen Paul for two weeks and that suddenly seemed important.

Paul lay slumped in the bath with a glass of red wine. It was a pine bathroom, with a circa 1980, large avocado corner bath and a pile of DIY magazines handy to both bath and loo. In contrast, Iris' miniscule shower cubicle was suitable mainly for three-quarter size midgets. Generally I braved the chilly shower block next to the car park, which felt like a P.E. lesson in the rain.

It was only eight o'clock. I awarded myself a glass of red wine and sat on the loo to talk to Paul, as steam condensed up the draughty window.

'Have you seen what I've done?'

'Er, no it was dark.' I hadn't even thought about it.

'The walls are finished and the roof trusses are up.'

'Fantastic.'

'I've finished the felting.' He didn't sound as doggedly pragmatic as usual.

'You have done well, Paul. What's left to do?'

'The next job is the roof tiles. They're being delivered on Wednesday.' The downturn in his mouth scored creases down his chin.

'Is that all? You've nearly finished!' I was back in my old role as *Tigger*.

'Yes. But, after that, there's the garage doors to fit.'

'It'll be exciting, to see it done.'

'And the fascias and gutters.'

'Yes?'

'And the glazing.'

'Oh.'

'And the wiring.'

'Ah.'

'And the entrance ramp. And the drive to make good.'

'So how long before you stop making a noise?'

'I can't help the banging. I've got to use a hammer, a drill and a saw. They all make a noise.'

What Paul needed, I decided, was positive self-talk. 'Hey, what's the problem? I can stay down on the *Iris* for now. It's just as well, what with rats around the dock area. I'll come back up when you've finished. Surely it can only be a couple of weeks, now?'

'I don't know about that. Couple of months, more like.' Pessimism saturated him like a cold sponge.

'Does that matter?'

'We had our bank statement in this morning. Christmas was much more expensive than I expected.' *Eeyore* looked away, the weight of depression drooping his shoulders. 'I've had to transfer three thousand in this month. That only leaves three left from my redundancy money.'

'Oh dear.' And I'd just made it even worse with the new bras. My stomach held a hollow cave of massed fear. 'I'll go on an economy drive. I'll hide my Barclaycard. It must be cheaper to live on board the *Iris* than on dry land. After all, I'm only paying for the electricity.'

'But all the expenses here are the same. Council Tax, heating and lighting. It's only food that's cheaper. I don't spend out on anything else.' His knees disappeared under the soapy surface as he sat up. He kneaded his hands with the soap.

'Hmm … Council Tax! I know. Full-time students can get a reduction. Cathy told me that, but I haven't chased it up yet. Leave it with me.'

'It won't be worth having,' predicted *Eeyore* mournfully, smoothing white lather up to his armpits.

'Well, you'll get another job soon, won't you?'

'I'm not so sure about that. How many production manager jobs have I seen in the last three months? Zilch.' He rinsed his arms. Splashing swallowed his voice.

'Have you been round the agencies recently?'

'This week. At my age, I'm wasting my time.' He soaped his ears as if they were the main obstacle to his employability.

'Oh Paul, I'm sorry.' What else could I say? I'd hardly ever heard him so down. He needed a concession. 'Look, would you like me to come in the bath with you?'

'Only if you want to.'

'I do. You can't believe how much I miss having a bath.'

'I'll put some more water in, then.' He turned on the hot tap and started mumbling.

'I can't hear you,' I shouted from inside my tee-shirt, above the sound of the water splashing.

'I said, I'm glad we've paid your fees up front.'

'Oh, for goodness' sake! Stop being so gloomy.' I prodded his tummy with my big toe. 'Something will turn up.' I stepped in gingerly and sat down at the other end of the bath.

'Well at the moment, that something is down to me, isn't it?' He stood up, stepped out and reached for his towel. 'Here, have the bath to yourself for a bit.'

I swirled the sudsy grey water into a whirlpool with my hand, bitten by the bitterness in his voice. Annual General Meetings in the bath had always worked efficiently in the past. Why not this time?

Paul is losing his confidence, I told Me. Especially without anyone to jolly him along. Furthermore, he resents you being at uni. But what else can I do? I'm far too busy to consider getting a part-time job. I need to concentrate, just to survive. If we can just soldier on through this year, maybe I'll land something lucrative next autumn, with the MSc under my belt. Paul appeared in the doorway with the half-empty bottle of wine.

'How's the course going?' he murmured apologetically.

'I was just thinking about it. Good, thanks. I'm going to do a Powerpoint poster for an academic conference.'

'Wow, I'm impressed.' So was I, with such a cool aside. 'Do you know how to use Powerpoint, Nessie?'

'No, not a clue. I expect I'll find out soon.' I grinned. Suddenly, I could manage the most impressive parts of my academic cv without him.

'Well, let me know if you come unstuck.' He ran a line of toothpaste along his brush from the neatly-rolled fag end of a tube.

'Yeah, thanks Paul. But I'm going to do it for myself.' I slurped from a dew-drenched wine glass. 'Here's to a happy New Year.'

When the bath water was too cold to enjoy, I searched out the best, fluffy, white guest towel from the airing cupboard. I sat for a while, finishing my wine and enjoying the rat-free luxury of home, despite the tuba, playing in the background. *Iris* always seemed more like camping out, than real life.

Then I wandered into our familiar bedroom. The wind whined over the roof tiles and slammed against the windows. Manx was washing his face on my side of the bed.

My toes squelched into my shabby, 1980's deep pile carpet. 'I'd better get back.'

Paul abandoned the tuba and slid into bed. 'How much wine have you had?'

'Well, two glasses.'

'You'd better stay here then.' It wasn't a very romantic proposition, but I felt surprisingly ready to join him. I shooed Manx off.

'Paul, I'm afraid I bought some underwear in Marks and Spencer today. It's more expensive there, but it does last well.'

He rolled over and dug his arm under my back.

'Ouch!'

'Sorry, it was the mention of underwear. It's OK, Nessie, if you need it.' He snuggled his body a bit nearer. 'Would you feel like …?'

'I don't know …'

After the years of practice, we still fitted together. Later on, in the middle of the night, I half woke, in a tingling panic because I hadn't taken my pill. It took a minute to realise that, whatever my slippery vagina was telling me, biological necessity had transformed into a hobby. And it cheered Paul up.

The next morning, I couldn't run, because my trainers were on the boat. I hadn't brought my pills or any clean knickers, so I was keen to get back.

'By the way …' I chewed through muesli at high-speed.

'Yes ..?.'

'Smartie's making a strange noise.'

'Where?'

'I dunno.'

'What sort of noise?'

'Well, a kind of whirry noise.'

'All the time, or intermittently?'

'Yep, it's been all the time, recently.'

'OK.' He gave his habitual sigh. 'Sounds like the alternator. I'll have a look at it. Tell you what, you have to be back for the rat man. Take the Audi back with you.'

'Do you need it this week?'

'No. I don't need anything bulky. Shouldn't need the trailer. No, keep it for as long as you want.'

'Thanks Paul. It's not as if I drive many miles. I'll look after it.'

He kissed me before I went. 'It just needs some fuel.'

'No problem.'

'See you next week?'

I filled the car with petrol and picked up a pint of milk. It was foul: the sort of morning where Attention All Shipping gale warnings for Rockall, Malin, Hebrides, Minches, Bailey *and* the Irish Sea follow the news on Radio Four. It was raining so hard, I could see the exhaust smoke hanging in the half light of the other cars' headlights on the motorway. The back windscreen clogged up with oily muck thrown up off the road. Even screenwash couldn't clear it.

Yesterday evening had been something of a surprise, and I needed to think about it. I chugged along, trying to deal with my feelings like the new, scientific me. On the one hand, when it was good, I could only describe life with Paul as *Flow*. There hadn't been much of that lately, but it could still be invoked, given the right atmosphere. On the other, I knew that I needed to assert my own identity, no longer justa-wife and justa-mother.

A warning sign flashed on the gantry overhead. I glanced at the speedometer, making sure I wasn't too far over fifty miles an hour. Only forty one. That's odd. I accelerated. In the rear-view mirror, exhaust smoke splayed out. The car chugged up to forty-five. Below the speedometer, the fuel consumption showed thirty. That didn't seem right. Whatever's normal? The truth was, that I had no idea if the display showed miles or kilometres per litre or per gallon.

I was glad when my junction appeared out of the mist. Apprehensively, I followed the dual carriageway into town until I hit the first set of traffic lights. As I drew up, they changed to red. The car in front skittered across, but mindful of my recent brush with the law, I stopped. The engine stalled. OK, ignition off. I wiggled the steering wheel to loosen the steering lock and flicked the ignition over. Everything lit up, except the engine. I'd been driving for too many years to be fazed, even when the lights changed to green.

'Ignition off, wiggle the wheel, turn ignition on,' I said aloud. Nothing.

OK. One more time. No luck. OK. What next, Nessie? I turned on the hazard lights and a chorus of hoots answered like ship's sirens on New Years' Eve.

Oh God, what now? I tried one final time, and the engine reluctantly fired.

There's something wrong. Mustn't stop again between here and the marina. Double de-clutching like a veteran racing driver, I stormed across town. The engine stalled again as I approached the marina car park barrier. Luckily, there was a spare parking spot in front. I coasted in and sprinted up to *Aqua Nymph*.

I needn't have run. The environmental guy arrived half an hour late. By this time, my fleece from last night was heavy, wet and chilly. Down the inside, of course.

'Morning,' he said cheerily. 'Rats is it then, love?' I shivered. He was reminiscent of a rodent himself. He had grey, curly hair and a pointed, wary face above a torn waxed jacket.

'Well probably.' We clattered down the gangway. 'I haven't actually seen one. Can you exterminate rats on a boat?'

'Oh, we take them on anywhere in the city.' He had a smooth, sure-footed step across the boards.

'Are there a lot of them around?'

'Hundreds! They get everywhere. All the places humans go and lots of smaller ones besides.'

I shuddered as a cold trickle ran down my shoulder. 'Urggh. Sounds like they're taking the city over.'

'Well they are, in these warmer winters.' He looked at me with beady, rodent eyes. 'Where there's nothing to stop them, they're growing bigger and bigger all the time.' As we reached the boat, I'd have sworn he sniffed the air.

'So why do you think they're in here?' He cracked back the cover on *Aqua Nymph*.

'I've heard them. Good Lord, I know the sound a rat makes, after all these years.'

The rat man climbed into an enormous pair of gloves and clambered inside the cockpit. 'Right. Show me where you heard them.' I pointed at the piano and started unlocking the cabin doors.

'What on earth …?'

'It's a piano.' What a bizarre conversation to have at the best of times, particularly with a giant rat.

'Do you get much chance to play? Arr, I used to play when I was a lad.'

'No. No, this isn't my boat,' I said hastily, in case he thought I was the sort of person who inhabited a vermin-infested sewer. 'The owner's on holiday in India.'

'And you've been left in charge? Well now, there's no droppings round here. I'll just check in the cabin.' He disappeared into the gloom below and crept around for a couple of minutes, muttering to himself.

'No, nothing there.' He returned to the piano and poked an inquiring hand round the back. Taking a firm grasp, he heaved the piano out of the way. For a rat, he had powerful shoulders. There was a rumble of disintegration from the piano's innards. He shone his torch around.

'Well, I'll be jiggered. Now, you're supposed to be asleep, right now.' He beckoned me forward to have a look. The carpet was a still mess of slimy brown sticks and sticky green mud. Then a stick jerked and I saw it was a frog.

'What on earth is that doing here?'

'It's the environment today, my love.' The rat catcher sounded disappointed. 'They've moved out of their natural habitats looking for something that suits them better. Though this is beginning to look quite natural.' He spun his torch round the mud. I saw a glitter of water through the splintered hull.

'I'm so sorry.' It didn't really help to say it, as we walked back up the pontoon. 'What do I owe you?

'Nothing at all. Them rats are public enemy number one down here.' If he had a tail, he would have groomed it as he spoke. We arrived at his dirt-spattered white van. 'Call us any time you have a problem.' He extricated himself from his gloves, opened the grimy door and groped in the dim interior.

'Sorry it's a bit of a mess.' He wiped a damp hand over his grubby contact card. 'This is me bolt 'ole. Everything in here but the kitchen sink! Here you are, my love, keep this by you.'

'Thank you,' I said. 'That's a lovely idea.'

3.3

The car wouldn't start. I was ten, clanky, gearless minutes late on the bike.

'Nick Smallwood and Ron send their apologies,' said Scott.

'Does that mean we're on our own?' Jenny was in battleship grey. Domestic battle stations, perhaps. I massaged my jellied quads beneath the table.

'No, not at all. Nick says to count him in. He's at Fit Men today in Sheffield. Ron sends his blessing.'

'What about the Faculty?'

'Good response. Alan Rathbone's asked me to write a piece for the next Faculty news. He's coming today. Now, who else?'

Jonathan re-settled his new, trendy glasses. 'Where's Hugh?'

'Should be here. He's around.'

'Shall I pop down the corridor to his office?' My legs creaked upright.

'Please.' Jenny stood up to pass round some papers as I left.

It only took a minute to knock Hugh up, since he was chatting to Vasulu.

On the way back, the door to the Department rumbled. Hugh and I looked at each other and stepped over. Alan Rathbone gesticulated at us through the glass window.

'Doesn't he have a swipe card?' I asked Hugh.

'Probably not. He doesn't normally bother us much.' He switched the door open. 'Good morning.'

Alan was towing a three-wheel buggy, the sort athletic parents use for running and cross-country. Little Bertie was fast asleep. Alan was red and perspiring. 'Sorry I'm late. Important business.'

He had a 90° turn to execute with the buggy. I held one door open and stepped aside. It's a well-known fact of life that Mums, even those towing several small children, always operate baby equipment far more efficiently single-handed, than with help. Not so Dads. Alan chewed the inside wheel into the nicely-veneered ash door, bringing that side to a sudden halt, whilst the other side careered on round. Hugh and I winced. The jerk woke Bertie. His cries revealed that he wasn't so little any more.

'How's Bertie?' Alan looked surprised at my insider knowledge.

'Oh, fine, thank you. Well, not strictly speaking today, as it happens. Bertie has a temperature and I've had to dose him up with Calpol until I could get to the doctor ...'

'Oh dear.' I looked at Bertie. 'Poor chap.' He had a dirty orange trail with pink edges from his nose to his chin. It looked like recently-administered Calpol in carrot purée.

'So the university nursery won't take him today.' Alan sounded as if people rarely said 'no' to him.

'I thought you had a nanny?'

'She walked out last week.'

'Oh no, bad luck. In here, please.' Hugh and I opened a door each so he had a two metre target area. He swept the buggy through, with Bertie providing the sound effects.

The others looked up from Jenny's proposal. Scott raised his eyebrows until he looked like Tintin.

'Alan's baby isn't very well, today.'

'Where's Sarah?' asked Jenny pointedly.

'She's at the Canaries observatory this week. It's my turn to manage Bertie's arrangements. The doctor says he has a virus.' Alan whipped out a bottle of milk from a large, fluffy, teddy-decorated holdall. An open jar of organic sweet potato tumbled out. Orange remains spewed out onto the carpet. He slipped the bottle in Bertie's mouth. I poked around the holdall until I found a baby wipe to scrub up the mess from the floor.

'But he goes to the university crèche every day.' Jenny sounded almost sympathetic.

'The crèche have refused to take him today, because of his illness.' He sounded aggrieved. 'That's why I am obliged to bring my son here, until I can make other arrangements.'

'Like firing the crèche staff?' muttered Hugh.

'Now, I don't have much time. How far have you got?' barked Alan.

'We have a proposal from Jenny.' Scott nodded at Jenny, who handed a copy to Alan. Scott tapped the top of his biro on the table a couple of times. 'The purpose of the study is to examine the cognitive benefits of a two month exercise schedule on examination performance in a less-active population. In order to fit within the constraints of the academic year, we are proposing to hold a 5k student run on Whit Monday. This year, it's the last Monday in May. Examinations start on Tuesday, 31st May.'

'The study design is a matched pairs randomised blind control trial. Participants will be recruited from the student body,' Jenny chipped in.

'My good man! You'll never get it through Ethics and recruit sufficient volunteers in …' He scrabbled over Bertie's bottle to consult his watch, '… in only four months.'

'Jonathan and I intend to submit the proposal to the Ethics committee meeting next Wednesday,' Jenny put in quietly.

The Dean ignored her and concentrated on Bertie's slurping noises. 'So you're proposing a running race round the campus for what, several hundred students? Who will be organising that, Dr Woodman?' Hugh stifled a giggle.

'The department have already made outline plans.' Scott put down his biro to concentrate on the Department's case. 'I've spoken to the Bursar's Office and the local Police about the proposed 5km route. We need permits to close the roads and the immediate campus area, which isn't an issue on a Bank Holiday. Once we've agreed the risk assessment with the Safety Committee, we'll be in a position to apply for the permits. The main cost is the police presence, but it's not as if there's likely to be any trouble.'

'Louise's Dad has volunteered to negotiate that for us.' Hugh grinned. 'He was Chief Constable until a few years ago.'

Alan ignored Hugh. Scott went on. 'We're proposing to harness the Student Union capability to provide the organisational structure on the day. They're very keen to support the event and have already agreed to the marshalling in principle. Nessie here is going to head up the support arrangements.' He nodded at me.

'Ah yes,' Alan paused to look me over. 'Dr err, Masters, the Hearing Impaired Reader?'

Scott looked puzzled. 'No, this is Nessie Elliott, one of our Masters' students.' There was silence, except for the slurping noises. I watched Alan's face as he digested the unwelcome news and recollected our last encounter. My heart sank in readiness.

'Hmmph. Try to use staff members, if you can, Dr Woodhouse.'

'Nick Smallwood at the Sports Centre will provide initial fitness assessments. We are liaising with Psychology over the cognitive testing arrangements at the end of March. Professor Burbage has allocated a member of her research group to the team.' Scott leaned back in the chair, hands behind his head.

'All gone, darling.' The Dean looked sadly at the empty milk bottle and shook his head regretfully at Bertie. 'How will you ensure the safety of participants while they're training?' he barked.

'Kirsty will be getting together with the Running Club to produce some training guidelines.'

Bertie grizzled. Alan licked a fluorescent green dummy and popped it in Bertie's zigzaggy mouth. 'I hope Dr Macdonald will take the lead. The Running Club aren't scientists.'

'Of course …' murmured Kirsty.

'What's the budget for this venture and where's it coming from, Dr Woodgreen?' cut in Alan, looking over his half moons. 'You're not expecting any more from the Faculty pot this financial year are you?'

'No, no,' soothed Scott, eying Bertie with disgust. 'The Student Union are interested in the proposed research: they're talking of £5K funding. Participants will pay to enter, too. I think that will cover the expenses of the race. Of course, we would hardly charge outside research rates to the Student Union, would we, Dean?'

'Hmmph. Have you put anything in for insurance yet?'

'Not as yet, I'll look into that this afternoon. Would a thousand cover it?'

'No idea, ask Rob Power in the Faculty Office. He always sorts out my car insurance. Hmmph.' Bertie's miserable grizzle punctuated Alan's grumpy quiet.

I can't ignore crying babies for long. 'Come on, Bertie.' I fumbled at the harness, wiggled Bertie out and joggled him up and down the corridor outside. We inspected the cartoons, until he stopped crying. I skipped back into the conference room with the temporarily-acquiescent time bomb, just in time for the verdict.

'I suggest you to put your proposal to the Faculty meeting in February. If it is approved, you may enlist the help of other departments to enrol student participants. You may use the Faculty photocopying services for a limited number of posters. Furthermore, I will speak to the VC during our weekly meeting about your venture. Now if you'll excuse me, I must be off to my next meeting.'

'Oops, Bertie,' I said. 'Let's get you back in your pushchair.'

'Thank you, Dean. We're very grateful for your support. We'll keep you informed.'

'Yes, please do, er, Scott.' Bertie cried again. Alan gave the meeting a ghoulish smile. 'Keep it up, everyone.'

Hugh leapt up to open the door. Wails reverberated down the corridor. Then the outside door banged and muted Bertie's decibels.

'I think that was a yes,' whispered Jenny into the Departmental peace.

'He's lost the plot,' said Kirsty. 'Something happened to him when he hit fifty-five and Sarah dug her claws in. He used to be a nice old geezer.'

I happened to catch Scott's scandalised expression. 'What a lot of work people have put in over the last fortnight,' I said hastily. 'I had no idea that I should have been liaising with the Student Union.' Kirsty and Hugh laughed and even Scott smiled at my naïvety.

'Actually,' said Kirsty, 'I think it's more, now we've been briefed about what Scott expects, we can all get on with it.'

'Ah.'

'I've asked Penny in the office to help out with the organisation. No need for you to get more involved than you want, at this stage,' said Scott.

'Thank goodness for that! There's the poster, the statistics exam, the physiology module …'

'Of course … we don't want you to feel at a loose end.'

'Hmmph!' It came out like Alan.

Laughter rippled round as I gathered up my things and loaded them in the rucksack.

'Bye Nessie.'

'Thanks for helping out.'

'See you tomorrow.' I left the room feeling as if I had a fingerhold in the magic circle.

***

Back on board *Iris*, I phoned Paul.

'There seemed to be something wrong with the car when I tried to start it this morning.'

'Tried to start it?'

'Well, yes, in the rain. Not very successfully.' There was a scuffling sound from the galley. I wondered for the ninety-fifth time if a rat was rustling.

'How was it, last time you drove it?'

'Err … fine. I think. I can't really remember.'

'Well I couldn't find the whirring noise on Smartie. The disc brakes were jamming a bit. I've had the wheels off, but I've just greased them up. I couldn't find anything wrong in the engine. Nothing to worry about, anyway.'

'Good, because I've just remembered your car was making a sort of zooming noise as I came down the motorway, last week. And it wouldn't go very fast. It was the day I had to be back for the rat man.'

'Well, I'd better come down and have a look, if it won't start. Are you around tomorrow morning?'

'No, I'm meeting Scott and Jonathan about the poster. Can't you come this afternoon?'

'No, I've got an appointment booked with the agency later today.'

'About a job?'

'Yeah.'

'Good luck, Paul. I'll be back down around lunch-time. See you then?'

Intimations of mortality statistics swallowed up the rest of the day, and half the night.

***

Scott and Jonathan had a book open, the next morning. They moved the easy chairs around Scott's little, square coffee table.

'How are you getting on?'

'Not very well, I'm afraid. I can open Powerpoint and I've précised my ideas into seven hundred words …'

'Ah,' said Jonathan.

Scott picked up the book. 'Have you heard of Jessica Boyd?' He and Jonathan made eyes like slavering spaniels at the sound of her name. I inferred she was good-looking.

'N .. no, I don't think so.'

'Jess was terrific. For her PhD, she interviewed older people, mostly women, on their exercise experiences.'

'Yes?'

'She gathered nearly a hundred lines of transcript on emotional response to partner's death, which so far we haven't used. I'm sure some of the responses could illustrate the point about activity, mental health and survival rates.'

'Are we allowed to do that?'

'I think so. We keep the transcripts for seven years in a security store. The participants will have agreed to continued academic analysis, when we recruited them. I'll e-mail her later today. She's at Liverpool, now. I'm sure she'll be pleased to contribute her ideas. Especially if she's a co-author.'

'I see. So it's not just me?' I sat back in the chair. My shoulders relaxed as an uncool 'phew' escaped.

'Oh no, that wouldn't be fair at your stage of development. We'll help you along and make sure it's up to standard. Now, let's see what you've done.'

I dug the CD out of my rucksack and handed it to Scott to load. Their joint expertise left me feeling almost totally inept and I didn't want to embarrass myself with fumbling fingers.

Scott and Jonathan read my effort silently. 'Four paragraphs, do you think, Jonathan?'

'That's about it.'

'It would be timely to involve an epidemiologist from the Faculty of Health. I'll see if Roger's interested.'

'Have you forgotten, he moved out to …?'

'No, he's back here, if he ever went. The RAE is biting already. The university couldn't afford to lose him.'

I could feel my head ratcheting from side to side like a Wimbledon spectator, though I didn't have a clue what they were talking about. I basked in the moment. This was the stuff, after all, from which recycled dreams are made.

'Four quotations from Jess would be ample, supported by her analysis. Say another three hundred words.'

'I was wondering if we could use some of the photographs I took for her presentation at SHERPA last year.'

'Oh yes! What about using one in soft focus as the background?' Scott had a steely look in his eyes.

'Yeah, there's two or three possible ones. Shall we let Nessie choose?'

'Ooh, me?' I suddenly twigged that Jonathan was encouraging me.

'Fine. Do we have a title?' Scott's prominent eyes targeted me.

'Err, not as yet.'

'Well. I'll leave that to you as well. It needs to be something punchy that encompasses the key ideas.'

'Something like: 'Teaching your grandmother to suck eggs?' I offered.

'Possibly … it … well, no. What about the lived experience of …?'

' …decreasing mortality …?'

'No, they do die, eventually.' Scott gave me an amused look.

'OK, delayed mortality …'

'That's better.'

' … of an ageing population?' I was getting the hang of this.

‘ … in a sample of women from the U.K.’s ageing population,’ finished Jonathan, with a slight smile.

‘Err, right. Can you say that punchy title again slowly, while I write it down, please.’

‘Sure,’ said Scott. ‘And I’ll edit your text this afternoon and e-mail it back to you. Then you can have another look. Are you happy to put all this stuff onto the slide?’

‘I don’t know how to import the photo in as a background.’

‘Come and choose which one you want. I’ll send it down to you as a slide. Then you can just drop your text boxes onto my existing slide,’ said Jonathan. ‘That’ll be a bit easier for you.’

‘Send it back to both of us after that,’ said Scott. ‘Then we’ll all have a second draft to work on. Thanks for your time, Nessie.’

The entire process took thirteen minutes.

3.4

Paul was locking up the Audi as I clanked into the marina. I thought of the repair bill and altered my high-optimism profile into a more suitable expression of concern.

Paul looked at me grimly as I clanked to a halt. 'Is that bike roadworthy?'

'Oh er, just needs oiling. How's the …?'

'I don't know exactly what's wrong. The electronics and battery are fine, but they're not turning the engine over.'

'That's strange,' I posited.

'Yes. You did fill up with fuel last Sunday? It's not just an empty tank?'

'Of course I did. I put … hang on, the bill's in the front somewhere.' I unlocked the door and searched. 'Here we are. Forty litres of unleaded, debit card transaction for …'

'Unleaded!'

'Yep, forty litres.'

'Nessie. This is a diesel car.' A rusty drawing pin pricked my balloon. He glowered at me.

'I'm sorry.'

'So am I.' He sighed, obviously staying calm. 'Well … that explains the problem.'

'Oh good. Does it make much of a difference?' I looked at his face. 'Ah. Can you sort it out?'

'Probably not. It's highly likely the engine and the injectors are damaged, since you drove a fair way on it.' He paused for maximum deflation. I thought of money we couldn't afford and lusted for a prop-up cigarette.

'The only thing I can do, is empty the fuel tank, flush out the fuel lines, replace the filter and try to get the engine turning over. Which it probably won't.'

'Come down to the boat and we'll have some lunch, first.'
Paul whistled quietly to himself as we walked down the pontoon. 'I wonder if Mike has any spare jerry cans for fuel?'

'I'll put the kettle on, while you ask him.'

***

Within a couple of hours, Scott's draft and the photograph dropped into my inbox. I saved it immediately, just in case. I was as cunning as a cat so far as IT was concerned, these days.

When I looked at the file, I recognised my idea. But, in two hundred and twenty three precise words, Scott had built a strong, logical argument from my waffle. Its force derived from its simple, direct style of writing. I suddenly understood what he had meant in Study Skills by 'Voice'. Scott's voice came over as loud and clear as if he were behind my shoulder, talking into my ear.

'Wow,' I said to the imaginary rat who lived on board with me. 'I want some of that.'

About four o'clock, there was a thump into the cockpit as the barge moved slightly.
Paul climbed down into the saloon. 'Do you have some rag I can use on my hands?'

'Err, here take this.' Mum would never notice her Grand Union Canal tea towel had gone.

'There's a strange smell in here.' Paul paused, rubbing his hands.

'Oh? What sort of a smell?'

'Don't know. I can't quite place it. It's only faint. Perhaps it's outside in the dock.'

'Maybe. Have you …?' I was too scared to go on.

'Yes, I've done it. The fuel's drained and in Mike's tank. We now have a car than runs. I don't know what permanent damage has been done yet.'

'Oh. Did Mike help you?'

'Yeah, he cleaned out the fuel lines for me. There's something strange about the fuel tank. It's as pressurised as a bottle of bubbly, but at least the engine's running.' He gave me a wispy smile.

'What do you want to do now?'

'I'd better make tracks before the evening rush hour starts. I don't want to be stuck in traffic, if the car's giving trouble.'

'No …' He didn't want to stay with me. 'Paul, you haven't told me about the agency interview, yesterday.'

His face closed down. 'No good. There's just nothing out there for an engineer of nearly sixty.'

'Have you thought of anything else, yet?'

'I'm working on it.'

I spent the evening fiddling round to make a layout worthy of the wonderful people with whom I was working. The poster went back to Scott and Jonathan just before one a.m.

3.5

Thursday dawned bright. Now the days were lengthening, it was theoretically possible to run first thing, before heading for the Department. I hadn't yet managed a single morning. After a late night, my bunk was far too cosy at seven a.m. Quitting the warm boat for the draughty delights of the shower block was just as unappealing. Several times recently, I'd showered on the boat, despite the clammy touch of formica walls on my bare hips and shoulders.

My glumness was grounded in a tough day of statistical methods and the return date for the Children's Activity and Nutrition assignment. In any case, I told myself, as I trudged up several hundred stone steps, forty minutes walking, there and back, was more than enough exercise for one day.

'Yes, but.' It was my Superego again. 'You are capable of running and walking each day. Why don't you do that?'

True. I'd ample energy again, now I was on an exercise roll. The man I was passing on the steps was unfit. He was breathing heavily, struggling to keep up with me. It's always the same with men, they just have to win. I pounded upwards, unzipping my jacket.

Best news of all, only days without any physical activity left me limp and morose. In short, I was living proof of what I read in The Literature. I had convinced myself of the health benefits of exercise.

'Oh no,' I muttered, stopping short on a narrow footpath by one of the Halls. 'Maybe I'm addicted.' The man behind cannoned into me.

'Mind out,' he gasped. It was the obese man from the Mad Hatter. I recognised the raincoat. How strange. But then again, if he worked for the University, seeing him was hardly surprising.

'Oops, sorry, I was far away.'

***

I psyched myself up for my assignment result. The module, writing and deadline had sped by in a cognitive pea-souper. What could *the worst* be? My first C had been followed by a promising B for my paper on activity and depression. I had spent far less time on the third module, although my citations these days were guaranteed diamond-cut Harvard. I was the only person I knew who proof-read End Note, our citation software.

Maybe I should expect something between the two. I trotted between limestone Wrenesque buildings, thankful for the Vibram shoes. After all, I knew heaps about children's activity levels after twenty years on the playing fields of school PE. On the other hand, I was low on the academic learning curve. Although I knew what *they* wanted, I couldn't produce it. The best I could hope for was a B-. Logically, the result should be better than the epidemiological juvenilia I'd written first time round.

This positive thought landed me outside Jonathan's office at the appointed time. Returns had become quite the social occasion in my otherwise Chaucerian student life. Midge and Rosa waited in front of me.

'Hello, you two.'

Rosa smiled at me without speaking. Midge shook. She eyed Vasulu's satisfied smile.

'I don't know why I can't wait until last thing in the afternoon, when everyone else has gone in.'

'Another *A*?' we chorused. Vasulu, the specially gifted, darted us another modest grin.

Bracing myself long and thin, I went in. Jonathan was complimentary.

'This was a superb piece of work. Well done, Nessie.' Had he made a mistake? No, there was the A in a ring on the front, endorsed by Jenny, the second marker.

'Wow. Thank you very much.' Ingenuous and inarticulate as the chorus in *Grease*, I bolted outside.

'How did you do?'

'An A!' I fanned my hot flush with the paper. 'I can't believe it.'

'Well done!'

'Good for you!'

I couldn't wipe the clockwork smirk from my face for the rest of the day. The world grinned back. I found a bargainous après-Christmas Chardonnay. I charmed the student at the checkout with my encyclopaedic knowledge of exotic fruit. Even the rat on *Iris* finally stopped rustling.

The statistics exam approached alarmingly fast, but I had the poster nearly nailed and a complete week to climb from my 'O' Level baseline. For one night only, I felt sufficiently in hand to relax and celebrate. I wandered up the pontoon to see Delia, bottle of wine in hand. She'd invited me, often enough.

'Have you heard from Ella recently?'

'Well, I had an e-mail last week ... oh dear, I haven't replied to it yet. She's still in India.' The Chardonnay had chilled outside in my cockpit for an hour. 'Salud!'

'Happy New Year, Nessie. Santé. How is your Mum? I miss her, she's a dear.'

I didn't have anything up-to-date to pass on to Delia. Mum had eschewed stuffy old e-mail in favour of texting Benjie and Paul on a daily basis. I didn't understand her abbreviations. 'So far as I know, she's very well. She's learning meditation and IT at some temple in Bangalore.'

'Do you know when she's back?'

'Not exactly. She mentioned the middle of February. Your guess is as good as mine.'

'It's a good thing you're there to look after the barge for her, what with all the rats around.' Jason, safely caged under the worktop, pricked up his ears. 'Does your Paul mind you being away so long?'

'No, he's very good-natured.' I didn't know her well enough to sabotage niceties with the truth.

'And what about your other travellers?'

'Oh, my son? Benjie's fine. He's safely back at med school again now after his rugby tour. I never have to worry about him. Leah's been at the monkey sanctuary since December. She's planning to move on, with a group of friends, at the end of the month.'

'And when is she due back?'

'Well her round the world ticket runs out at the end of August.'

'What is she planning next?'

'I've no idea. Her first degree is in ecology. It remains to be seen if there are any jobs in that field.'

'Do you think she might do something else?'

'The er … civil service have approached her. Hopefully the year away has inspired her in some way. The university wanted her to carry straight on to a PhD.'

'But she didn't, eh?'

'She wasn't at all interested. Said academic research was far too boring and esoteric for her.'

Delia laughed. 'Is it?'

'I don't think so. It seems exciting and relevant to me. But then, I'm just a boring old fart who doesn't have any relevancy herself these days.' With an A and a couple of glasses of wine under my belt, I could afford to chuckle.

'I don't think so.' Delia looked me over in her kindly way. 'You don't come over like that.'

'Well, no, I don't really feel like that tonight.' Modesty compelled me to shield my academic brilliance from my new friend. 'Look, Delia.' We were sitting next to her large windows. Snow flurries landed inches from my nose.

'I hope it's not going to settle.'

'Oh, but it's lovely, like sparkling icing sugar.'

'The pontoons are lethal in the ice.' Delia shivered. 'So what's next for you, Nessie?'

'I'd love to do a PhD, myself, but I'm not clever enough.'

'How will you know, if you don't try?'

'Well, trying involves my first exam in thirty-four years, in less than a fortnight.'

Delia poured out the rest of the bottle in my glass, as best she could. 'Lesh drink to you passing,' she said.

'Blesh you.'

She was right. The icy crust sparkled prettily over the pontoon until I left. Half way home, I sliced across the pontoon. I levered my icy BTM up from within a smidgeon of the pontoon edge. So nearly the cold, black water: I must be more careful, under the influence. Tomorrow morning, I definitely wouldn't be running.

3.6

My back was as stiff as a frozen shirt. I inched painfully into the loo. Clean socks were beyond reach. For the rest of the day, I lay on the cabin floor with numb bare feet, viewing the snow-encrusted boom of the yacht next door. I held the lightest and thinnest book I could find, upside down, above my headache.

Jonathan had recommended his maths-teaching friend's 'A' Level guide. It was perfect, a belt and braces job for the statistically illiterate. The questions at the end of each chapter rested my arms for a very long time, while I thought out the answers. Fortunately, the correct answers were at the back. Over three days, I married them up and remembered I always came top in Numbers at Junior School.

After that, Cathy arrived and pummelled me back onto my feet, muttering, 'Active rest,' like a witches' curse, until life painfully returned to normal.

The day before the exam, I sat with a cup of green tea, my head back against the cushions, resting my tired eyes for a minute. I was refrigerated from the long cycle back from uni at half speed. I needed a final evening on psychological statistical methods from the course text, although I didn't feel like it. The cabin was dark. Rush hour traffic whirred past the basin in a soporific stream of red lights reflecting along the cabin side opposite. Someone knocked on the hull.

'Mum.' Who …?

There was a double thump as feet landed in the cockpit. A dark head appeared as the doors creaked open. It could have been Paul, as a gawky young electrical engineer .

'Benjie!' Now he stood below, drooping in his dark jacket, I saw something was wrong.

'Ben,' he snarled back in a teenagerly kind of way. I snapped back into real time.

'Sorry, darling, I forgot.'

I bundled over to hug him, mothering urge temporarily out of control. 'Lovely to see you. Would you like some tea? How long can you stay?'

He took off his coat, tossed it to the back of the berth, avoiding any reason to look at me. 'I'm fine.'

'So … so … what's all this about, then?' I turned away to fill the kettle, trying not to envision anything too awful, before the evidence emerged. Dropped out of med school? Girl friend pregnant? Murder. No, not Benjie. It would be manslaughter.

'Nan's having a good time in India,' he remarked, picking up her postcard of Bangalore from the back of the settee berth.

'Have you heard …?'

'Yeah, she was fine, yesterday. She sent a text.'

'As in fine fine, or politely fine?' I asked.

'Really fine, I think.' There was a silence. I slipped a mug in front of Benjie. I knelt down to the Wendy house stove, opened its door, added a small shovel of coke and adjusted the draught so it would burn up again. Then I sat down. Benjie was staring at the stove.

'Have you eaten, yet?'

Benjie shook his head.

'Shall we go out, later on? What's up, Benjie … Ben?' Benjie gave me an assessing look. I put an arm round his shoulder as my earth mother identity swept back. He pulled away stiffly. I'd forgotten he'd returned to Kevin-land.

'God, I can never fucking hide anything, can I?'

We had a session on counselling in sport psychology last week. I decided to give it a try.

There was a pause while I figured out what to say. 'Well, no.' Another longish pause dragged, expectant on both sides. I cracked. 'What have you done that's so dreadful, then?'

I was being watched. I smoothed the denim on my leg, like Cathy would have done. 'I promise not to moan,' I added, just in case and waited again.

He put his face in his hands. There was a quiet snort that put me in mind of little Bertie in low gear. Then I heard a sigh. I noticed my body, leant forward, mirroring his distress. Yes! It was going to work. I was 'with' my client.

' ----take,' he whispered.

'Sorry, I didn't quite hear …'

'I said, ----take.'

'Mistake?'

'Re-take, Mum,' he said irritably. 'For God's sake, you need to get your ears checked out. I ballsed my Life Systems 1 last week. Re-take in two weeks.'

'Two weeks,' I reflected back. 'Oh.'

'Is that all?'

I plunged back in. 'Well, what do you want me to say?'

'Well, you usually tell me off next, when I fail at something.'

'But I've promised not to, so I can't. Besides, it looks to me as if you're doing a pretty good job on that front yourself.' I reminded myself, that as Egan's *Skilled Helper*, I should be of few but empathic words.

'Yeah, well … I s'pose I shouldn't have gone on the rugby tour.'

'So, how are you feeling about that right now?'

Benjie gave me a surprised look. 'Feeling?'

'Yeah, how does it make you feel?'

'Well, how do you think you'd feel, doing a fucking exam with a hangover and then failing?'

It was no good. I got down to the business. 'What happens if you fail again?'

'Three hits and you're out.' I noticed that somehow he had snuggled into my waiting arm. He leant his head on my shoulder. It probably wasn't much help, but it made me feel better.

'Mm. So what you gonna do about it?' Ghostbusters had always worked just fine when he was young.

***

The next morning I left Benjie … sorry, Ben to his work and tramped up to the department for study skills. There was an expectant air to the lecture theatre. This morning kicked-off the dissertations. The statistics exam followed.

Scott surprised me with his enthusiasm for Race for Results. 'There'll be several hundred students. We'll match our volunteers in pairs. Before the race, we'll collect demographic, educational and psychological data, measure their fitness status, and provide training input for the runners. After the race, we'll feed in times and exam results. This could provide you with quantitative data from a much larger sample than is usually available at Masters' level. Jenny has developed the major research question, but if you have smaller parameters to investigate, or want to plan some qualitative research, come and talk to us. Your research could be published quite soon, boosting your cv and future prospects.'

The packed house buzzed.

Jonathan jumped up. 'Can I just put in a quick plug for some volunteers to help with preparations? We're developing a web-site for publicity, on-line entries, a training programme, nutritional information and so on. If you have expertise that you'd like to see represented on your cv, we need your help now. And we need lots of volunteers to marshal on the day. See Nessie for that.' He nodded at me and caught some questions.

***

'Why this sudden enthusiasm for a student race, Nessie? Do you know anything about it?' I twitched back to the present. Five of us sat in the Sports Centre café, waiting for the exam.

'Well, yes, I'm organising the marshalls. I was press-ganged because of being on the Academic committee.'

'Sounds like a lot of work.'

'Not too bad. I've only been to the Student Union a couple of times, so far. It's all going on around me.' I was surprised how calm my voice sounded, considering my entrails were submerged in gooey ectoplasm.

'Jenny wrote the research proposal and got it through Ethics in three weeks. Scott seems to know everyone who matters. In the last month, he's nailed the race route, charmed the health and safety lot and squeezed most of the funding we need from the Student Union. Oh yes, and co-opted Jonathan onto the committee, when he discovered how much work was involved in the risk assessment.'

'Why? We know Jenny's conscientious, but Scott's hardly famous for his overtime.' Scott lifted a hand as he wandered past. His bum swung, moulded in denim below the bomber jacket.

'It's the RAE.' Had I pulled one over on Cathy at long last?

'Oh, I see.' She only needed three seconds. 'The Department needs to upgrade its publication record. So, Scott's getting the students to write lots of articles. Typical Scott. I guess we'll all get plenty of help with our dissertations, then.'

'That's a bit unfair. I think it's a great idea for us all to work together on a major research project. When I came, I thought we'd help with research as part of the course. I've been disappointed up to now.'

Cathy laughed. 'Oh Nessie, you are funny! They're not going to let the plebs loose on their precious research participants. You have to be a PhD student before they let you do anything for real.'

'We'll see. We should all get a look-in this year, if Scott has his way about the race. Are you going to join in, Midge?'

'Maybe. Thank God I don't start my dissertation until next year. I'd like to do something about nutritional status. Maybe I'll measure exam performance.'

'Do you mean all that stuff about oily fish to make your brain work better?'

'Possibly. Either that or caffeine intake. I don't really know yet. Yours is buttoned up, isn't it Cathy?'

'Yeah, my line manager and I have been planning motivational interviewing with cardiac rehab patients since the autumn. We're off to the workshop next week.' Cathy's eye was twitching and she was massaging both legs, today.

'How about you, Xui?'

'I wanted to do something about promoting water intake in schoolchildren. I will have to find a school or two, I think. Have you thought of something yet, Nessie?'

My background and interests crystallised into an idea. 'Well, I'm not sure. I've been thinking about the Stages of Change for smoking in the Transtheoretical Model and …' I peaked for an instant. '… and exercise. Well, I suppose it depends on the supervisor to some extent.'

'Who's your supervisor, then? Does anyone know, yet?'

'I don't. I'm hoping it will be Jenny. She's very grounded.'

Last year's lot said she was terrific at sorting them out.'

Xiu's face was extra-perky; today her eyes glittered. She looked ready for a challenge. 'I have asked Hugh.'

'What did he say?'

'He said,' Xiu grinned. 'Yes he will.'

'I've heard he only takes on young students in short skirts,' said Cathy.

'Perhaps I'll try my luck with him tomorrow, then,' said Midge. 'I've still got one mini-skirt left. After that first assignment, I'm not sure I could put up with Kirsty again. She was terrifying, one-to-one.'

'What about Jonathan? He's calm and ever-so-helpful.' My own fingers were chattering with nerves.

'But he's a devoted quantitative man. His places will already be full of stats buffs.'

'What are your plans, Rosa?' Rosa was the only one who hadn't spoken.

'I think training of runners, is the area of me.'

'Good, good,' we chorused, grinning like a row of encouraging Cheshire cats. Exam nerves had made her talkative.

***

It wasn't long before we were in the café again.

'Who needs more caffeine?' Midge went to the counter for us all.

'Well that was easy, after all,' Cathy murmured. 'I was expecting something far worse.'

'Me too,' I said. 'Did anyone else think the questions had a familiar feel to them?'

My friends looked puzzled.

'I never got round to much time with that thick Stats book. But I'm sure I've already worked through most of the questions and knew the answers.'

'Who set the exam?'

'Scott?'

'I remember now! They came from the 'A' Level primer.'

'Cheeky sod. That must have saved him a load of work.'

'Can that be right?'

Helen appeared at the table, carrying a coffee carton. 'I've been meaning to collar you about the exam.' I felt hot wetness, seeping down the back of my neck, as Helen dodged behind to steal Midge's unoccupied seat.

'Err, what's that? Hi, Helen, haven't seen you for ages. What's up?'

'Well …' She dripped black coffee onto the table. 'I want to complain about the statistics exam. I don't think we should be assessed by exams on any part of the course. It's nothing like real life, to be sat down for two hours to solve a raft of problems.'

'Sometimes I'm not even given two hours, in my job,' said Cathy. 'You're right.'

'You know what I mean. With an assignment, you show your best work, over a period of time. It's a fair assessment of your capability. If you're the sort of person who gets exam nerves, you'll never do as well, when you're put on the spot.' She dabbed at the spilt coffee with her serviette.

'OK,' I said. 'Fair comment. Two other people have said the same. I'll bring it up at the next Academic meeting.'

'Don't you agree with me, then? They just sprung it on us and you have to pass, to get through the Statistical Methods module.' She dismembered the serviette into thin, sodden strips, multiplying the mess on the table. I felt like shouting, *For goodness sake, stop it.* But of course, Helen was a middle-aged woman, not one of my kids.

'Yeah, I don't like the idea of an exam. No-one does. But I think the Faculty insisted on it. Why are you so worked up, Helen? Do you think you've failed?'

'I've never been any good at exams.' Her face drooped like Moaning Myrtle in the Hogwarts' loo. 'If I don't pass, I'm complaining to Faculty. I didn't pay all this money to be treated like a school kid.' She stomped up from the chair.

'Well, see how you do first, before you go shouting your head off. And I'll put your point of view to the lecturers.'

'She's really stressed.' Midge look at her grumpy backside receding. She put down a limp cardboard tray of coffees. 'I've never seen her like that before.'

'I've not seen that much of her to judge, we've only done one module together,' I said. 'I hope I didn't sound sanctimonious, did I?'

This time, I was focussing on success. Hopefully, diligence would have its reward.

***

‘I can’t afford to miss any more time.’ Benjie lay on the saloon bunk.

‘Are you sure you’re OK to go back, now?’ I’d made mugs of tea and foraged in the locker for Christmas cake remnants.

‘Yep.’ On the floor was a poster-sized blank sheet, half-filled with a flow chart. I smiled at him. My little boy had stopped wobbling. Benjie was coping with a failure that could wreck his career at the first hurdle.

‘Well, not the first.’ I dried a knife to cut the cake.

‘Sorry?’

‘You’ve jumped so many hurdles to get this far, haven’t you?’

He grinned. ‘Fair few. Wiping old people’s bottoms for work experience wasn’t much fun.’

‘I never thought you’d pass your Chemistry exam, when you only got 30% in the mocks and Mr Smith was away.’

‘That was easy, once I got my head round it.’ He cut two slices of cake.

‘Do you remember your Cycling Proficiency Test with those dreadful women examiners who failed nearly everyone?’

‘Hiker Badge in Scouts was even worse.’

‘I complained about that man to the District Commissioner. Do you know …’

‘It’s all right, Mum. I’ve got the message. I’m resigning from the first team, and I’ll make sure I pass the re-take.’

‘You’re clever enough, Benjie. You’ll pass once you set your mind to it.’

‘One thing about med school I’ve learned already, is that there’s always someone cleverer than you are. At school I came out top most of the time, but up there, I’m only average. I've just got to work harder.' He swigged the last of his tea. 'Is there any more cake going? I missed all the Christmas goodies, being in South Africa.'

'All that fat, you mean. It won't do you any good, my boy. Let me look at the box … uh huh, eight grams in every slice. Oh go on, take the rest of it back with you. Enough slices there to last until exam day.'

'Mmm, sounds good to me. By the way, Mum. Have you noticed the horrible stench?'

3.7

Benjie was right. There was a pervasive, foetid pong about the boat, whenever I went back, now my non-smoking nose was in full working order again. I was glad to get out and air my clothes, after sitting in the saloon all night. Did I smell like that to other people? A chance dip into a text-book on mental illness suggested that imaginary smells were a sign of neuroticism. I made an executive decision to ignore it.

The Obesity module trundled through, like an overstuffed London bus. By now, my literature searches were honing to a fine art. I enjoyed tracking evidence down, every bit as much as Sherlock Holmes at a crime scene in his overcoat and deerstalker hat. I'd already put in a fair amount of work towards my assignment, in the three weeks of the module.

Writing was still a hazardous pursuit, but at least I wasn't totally nude. I'd pulled a few skills about me. Just a light thermal layer at present, maybe, but my clothes were thickening up all the time.

That afternoon, a preppy Professor from up North lectured us on the metabolic syndrome. He showed clips from his recent television series: close-ups of a cowlick, warm brown eyes, worried frown and sympathetic answers to difficult questions. Even Cathy succumbed.

He looked the same age as Benjie. Perhaps they have trouble finding professors, these days, I thought. Perhaps there's an academic future for me, after all. Midge, Cathy and I stayed on for the evening debate with the local Obesity Forum.

In between times, we holed up in the IT workroom. Mum had written a long e-mail to me. She'd enjoyed travelling to Sri Lanka to renew her visa, and was staying in Bangalore for another three months. At least I didn't have to worry about her. I wrote back to Mum.

Good to hear you're enjoying yourself.

'Which sort … ' Cathy asked Midge in the background.

I am surviving. I have finished three modules, now.

'Well personally I've tried several kinds, but I do like ...' I didn't catch the next bit.

'Do you mean the basic …'

'Yeah, I've had it for over … '

I have started thinking about my dissertation. I've been reading up on The Literature to fill in my missing background.

'Not so messy as a relationship, in any respect.'

Cathy laughed. 'What about you, Nessie?'

'Hmm?'

Benjie came down for …

'Do you have a Rampant Rabbit?'

'No, just a pussy,' I said absently. 'He's called Manx.'

… the evening a couple of weeks back, he seems fine. He sends his love. He was telling me how much he enjoys your texts.

Cathy and Midge were both smirking now. I paused in my typing.

'What's the matter?'

'You weren't listening at all, were you?'

'Yes … rabbit. Well, no. I'm trying to wing this e-mail off to Mum as well.'

We had a good evening together, except that when we got to the Tapas bar, he had to pay,

'Would you like to come to my girlie …'

because I couldn't find my Barclaycard, which was a little embarrassing.

'… next Saturday?'

I have hidden it somewhere on the boat so I won't be tempted to use it, but I can't remember where!

'Oh, I'd love to come, but I'm seriously busy at present. Sorry. My New Year's Resolution was a better social life.'

Good way to avoid spending money!

'Well don't give up yet,' said Midge. 'I could always get you one. I'm keen to make some profit from you.'

'Yeah, that would be good.' I re-read the last couple of sentences. 'Err, what would?'

'You enjoying …'

Iris is just fine. You don't have to worry '…

some money. I'm pretty sure it's £19.99. Would you like one?'

'Sure.'

... about her at all. I am on board very often, checking her out. There are no signs of rats at all, either on Iris or Aqua Nymph, tell Phyllida.

'What colour would you like?'

'What are the choices?'

Paul is getting on really well with the tuba. I almost recognise the odd notes he plays, now.

'... possibly blue.'

He has very nearly finished the new garage. He's seriously looking for a job, but still nothing in any of the specialist agencies.

'Oh, anything would be fine,' I finished off the e-mail, pressing send.

'Thanks, Nessie, you're a pal. It will be here on Tuesday week.'

'Return date for the Physiology module,' commented Cathy.

'Err, girls, I think we need to run if we're to get back to Gorgeous Gary on time.'

Everyone was there. Afterwards, the lecturers mobbed him like bees on a buttercup. I hung around, hoping for a dinner invitation from the gang. But he'd studied for his PhD in the Department and no-one was inviting newcomers. I arrived back at the marina about half past eight, head replete with ideas, but an empty stomach.

'You're a nobody.' I crept down the pontoon, bunny ears drooping. 'Fancy thinking they would ask you. The lecturers never socialise with students. Even when the student is everyone's Mum.'

I opened the lock on the cabin door and stepped through the evil stench into a cold, dark boat. My left foot squodged into dank carpet.

'Eergh,' I screeched, as the cold, wet shock connected. I groped for the light switch. At least the electricity still worked. I looked down. An inch or so of dirty, greyish liquid swirled over the carpet and round my shoes.

'The boat's sinking.' I would have leapt for the bilge pump switch, but I had to think where it was, first. The electric pump whirred immediately and I breathed out. The next thing, assuming the pump could keep up with the ingress, was to find the leak. There was a lot of hull to inspect. Even as I started worrying about how I could find a leak in the dark, the pump made a choking sound, and stalled.

'Oh no!' The carpet was still awash, but at least the water wasn't any deeper. In fact, it didn't seem as if *Iris* was sinking imminently, now I wasn't in a complete panic.

'What do I do next?' I had no idea how to fix the pump or the leak. There was one single, shameful solution.

Ten minutes later I caved in. 'Never again,' I vowed to my steely-eyed Superego as I lifted the phone.

'Paul? Are you busy at the moment?'

'No, just practising my scales. What's up?'

'Well, I don't think *Iris* is sinking, but there's quite a lot of water inside.'

'Sinking! Nessie, switch the bilge pump on!'

'I have.' I felt momentarily proud of myself for doing the right thing. 'But it stopped before it pumped out very much.'

'So has more water come in, since the pump stopped?'

'Err, I don't think so. The level seems about the same.'

'OK. There's a hand pump in the cockpit. The handle's in the box seat. Try pumping it out with that, until I get down to you.'

'How long will you be?'

'I'm leaving now. If you have to, get off the boat and go and sit in the car. I'll be right there.'

It took a little while to find the Smartie's keys. I added my memory stick, pills and best new underwear in a survival bag, just in case.

Then I searched for the torch. The pump handle wasn't under the seat. I found it in the engine compartment, with the rest of the tools left on board by the previous owner. By the time I'd found the bilge pump, sited inconspicuously under the bulwark and worked out where to put the pump handle, it was nearly half past nine.

I bent over and started to pump as strongly as I could. Up to now, I'd been on automatic pilot. It was the first chance for my brain to think again. As I pumped, I connected the foul stench and the leak.

Pumping knackered my right arm. I switched to my left. In an even shorter time, that one faded, too. Had I pumped the bilge dry yet?

Leaving the pump, I peered down into the cabin. The water was a smidgeon lower. Still over the carpet, but only half an inch deep now. I leapt back to the pump for another go, but my triceps and biceps weren't really used to the activity and soon shouted even louder.

Planks clanked down the pontoon. Paul thumped two tool boxes down outside the barge, clambered in and put his arms round me.

'Are you alright, Nessie?'

'Yes, of course.' My relief at seeing him was humiliating; I hid it against his jumper. 'You arrived very quickly.'

'Yeah, there's no traffic at this time of night so I could really step on it. Now let's have a look.'

Paul ducked down into the cabin. 'Phew, what a stink.' He slip-slopped forward. I pulled feebly a couple more times on the pump handle. There were thumps and creaks as lockers opened. In a couple of minutes, Paul appeared. He rummaged heavily through his tool boxes for a couple of spanners and said, 'You don't need to pump any more.'

I looked hopefully into the cabin. The carpet was saturated, of course, but I'd cleared the water half an inch, back to floor level. Beyond that, Paul's trousers blocked the entrance to the loo compartment. He had stacked floor sections against the bulkhead, and *Iris* immediately entered workshop mode. Paul backed slowly out.

'Do you have some dry cloth I can use?'

I grabbed Mum's Canalmania tea towel, and he wiped his filthy hands to drag out the suspense. You can't be married to a man for over thirty years and not be aware of his attempts at dramatic timing.

'Panic over. *Iris* isn't sinking. There was a leak on the pipe joining the loo to the holding tank. I've tightened both the Jubilee clips. Cor, how long have you had this smell?'

'Err, not sure. Two or three weeks, maybe?'

'And you didn't think there might be something wrong? Oh, Nessie, that's probably how long it's been leaking. Have you ever emptied … no, of course you haven't. Right.' He handed back the mucky rag. 'I'll clear the electric bilge pump next.'

'Do you think we should be pumping raw sewage out into the Dock?' I dumped Mum's tea towel in the bin.

'No, definitely not. But what else can we do?'

'Can you refill the holding tank?'

'Yes, but it only takes a hundred gallons, I reckon there's more than that swilling round the bilge.'

'Can you do anything else?'

'I'll sort out a way of draining the pipe into the loo, once I've cleared the bilge pump. At least the lock's on open flow at the moment. You make me a cup of coffee. I'll think of something. Do you have any rubber gloves?'

'Er, no, sorry. Would you like me to clear the blockage?' I volunteered in my smallest voice.

'No, it's alright. I'll do it. You'll have to phone the Environment Agency in the morning and confess. What is it, that your friend Nick calls you?'

'Shit magnet Sheila.'

'Not far wrong, is he? Here goes." He gave a manly smile and dived down below again.

With the floorboards up, the stench from the bilge was overpowering. How Paul was breathing, I had no idea. For myself, I held my breath while I put on the kettle, then rushed outside for a fresh lungful. By the time the kettle had boiled, the electric pump was whirring again.

'You can't stay here tonight, Nessie.'

'It does smell pretty bad.' We were hunched up on the little seat in the cockpit together, in the cold darkness, contaminated hands round hot mugs.

'The carpets are far too wet to walk on.'

'They'll need replacing before Mum gets back.' We looked at each other. More money. He sighed. I shrank into the incompetent wife of his nightmares.

'Let's come back tomorrow morning. We can take *Iris* up into town to pump her out.'

'You're taking over again, Paul. No, leave it to me, I'll do it.'

'You can't manage *Iris* on your own. And you wouldn't know what to do when you got to the Pump Out, anyway.'

'Don't worry about me. I'll get some help. I'll ask Mike. Or Nick. Or the boys from the yard will help, if I ask them nicely.' I sat up straight, demonstrating my confidence.

Paul bridled, ever so slightly. I'd noticed a feral atmosphere, a couple of times recently.

'If you're sure.' He sounded super-calm as he left. 'The pipe into the bilge is connected up to the tank, all ready. Just don't use the shower or loo, until everything's clear and reconnected.'

'I can't do anything, first thing tomorrow. It's the Academic meeting. I can't miss it. It will have to be tomorrow afternoon.'

Paul was right. After he left, it was a long, anxious, miserable, hungry night.

3.8

The Conference Room was empty, when I arrived. Strange: it wasn't like me to be early. Jenny's was the only open office door.

'Morning, Jenny. Is this the right day for the Academic meeting?'

'Yeah.' Jenny looked up from her computer. 'We've delayed the start for an hour, until everyone's in.'

'Oh?'

She grinned. 'Don't ask about last night.'

'You didn't go, then?'

'No, sleep's hard enough to accumulate at present, without voluntarily relinquishing it in late night socialising.'

An hour later, a shambolic assortment slumped round the table in the conference room. Jenny looked grim. Jonathan had the pinched, sallow face of a man with a bad head. Hugh was white-faced and silent, huddled in his overcoat. Kirsty was blowing into a man-size hankie, as if she had a cold. I doubt I looked my best.

Scott won the worse-for-wear competition. He held his hands round his head, propped up by his elbows on the table. The other men had shaved, while Kirsty had managed near-normal warpaint. Under the hands, I could see Scott's closed eyes and the dark stubble scribbled round his white face. The others wore subdued clothes. Scott was wearing the same jeans and jacket, but more crumpled and what looked like last night's shirt. The others acknowledged my good-morning with assorted grunts. Scott looked as if he tried, but no juice squeezed out.

I sat down in the empty chair next to Jenny, wondering if poor Scott's dehydration was serious.

'Penny's just getting some coffee.'

'Did Scott sleep in his clothes?' I whispered.

'Very likely,' she muttered back.

I used my most strident, cheerful, mumsy voice. They deserved it, for not inviting me. 'You had a good evening, then?' There were a couple of groans. Scott screwed up his face, presumably at the intrusive noise.

'Are you OK, Scott?' He looked up at me with dull, red eyes, like an adorably scruffy hamster, disturbed in his nest. My heart lurched.

'Yeah, give me a minute,' he managed eventually.

Penny brought in a cardboard tray, filled with paper cups. It was another ten minutes before Jenny prodded the revellers into action. Time enough for me to have taken *Iris* up to town and back again. Time enough for me to imagine caring for Scott, so he wouldn't want to get into this state again.

We went through the agenda until it was my turn.

'I've received a few comments about the Statistics exam. Several students have pointed out that an exam seems rather unfair, when everything else is written assessment.'

Scott's eyes slowly opened. They were scarlet-rimmed, as if he'd left his contact lenses in all night.

'We've pushed hard to get the course modules assessed by assignments. The Faculty would much rather it was total examinations. They insist on us leaving the Stats exam in. Maybe it is an anachronism, but we won't change the current Faculty climate, other than slowly.'

'People who get anxious with exams feel they are being disadvantaged.' I persevered, wishing I could tuck him up in bed for the morning. Crossing Scott was the last thing I felt like today.

Scott scowled. 'Exams are just part of student life, Nessie. You have to understand, that's the deal when you come here. Just because you're a mature student, doesn't mean you get preferential treatment.'

'Oh.' I collapsed, quite flattened.

'That's a bit unfair, Scott,' said Jenny. 'Nessie said *several* people had given negative feedback. It's not just her. Don't shoot the messenger.'

Kirsty re-entered the planet. 'I agree. The students have brought it up, so we should minute and action it. You're the Faculty representative. I think you must feed it back to the Dean, even if you don't think it will work.'

I took my eyes off Scott's private hell and nodded gratefully at them. I could never dream up strong counter-arguments on the spot. Somehow, he always turned my brain into frog spawn. Even now, when he was rat-arsed.

***

For the rest of that week, I dreamed up my Obesity intervention and moved the heater round from damp patch to damp patch.

Being in the middle of an assignment, I didn't think. Other than about writing, that is. All my hours of the day, creativity, energy, memory, critical reasoning and logic were consumed. The task was insatiable, for my perfectionist self had taken over by this stage in the course. I ate carbs. I drank caffeine. At night, I dropped into my bunk exhausted by the complexities of the day, and mentally re-ran Scott's lecture on Powerpoint presentations for guidance, until I dropped into a murky pit of sleep. In a word, I was happy.

I came up for air the following Wednesday: the deadline for the conference poster was four o'clock.

During my draughty shower in the communal block, I decided to launch my new underwear. I peeled the labels off and covered them with an inconspicuous tee-shirt and my new jeans. I set off on the long walk up to the Department, feeling like a clandestine leopard dressed as a domestic cat.

First, my physiology paper boomeranged in. A highly satisfactory B. I was as upbeat as Pollyanna.

Midge met me, as I left the IT workroom. I'd just spent ten minutes gossiping with Cathy, to recuperate from my latest scholarly success.

'Nessie, I've got it.'

'Got what?'

She hauled a red plastic carrier out of her bag and handed it over. 'Roger Rabbit, of course.'

'Oh … oh, thanks, Midge.' I'd forgotten.

'You can return it within twenty eight days if it's unused. Otherwise it's £19.99 as soon as possible, please.' I reached into my rucksack and proferred most of the morning's booty from the cash dispenser.

'I'm sure it will be fine.' I kept my voice casually sophisticated. Red bag in hand, I strolled down the corridor to Jonathan's orderly office, for our meeting at noon. It was empty. I looked at my watch. Bang on time, for a change. I retrieved my reading glasses and unrolled my A3 print of the poster, ready to show.

Still no sign of the others.

As a diversion, I peered at my twenty quid's worth of red bag. Inside was a square box, which gave off a muffled rattle as I pulled it out. I turned it right way up, opened the flap and extracted the layer of card on the top. Inside the Fisher

Price look-alike carton was something like a Darth Vader puppet. I still couldn't see exactly what it was. I tried to worm it out, to keep the packaging pristine. Then I gave a sharp tug and the contents ejected in my hand. It bounced out, neatly pinned to a packaged stand: a turgidly red, erect penis.

My heart gave a great bound as I recognised it. I was in a precarious position, sitting in Jonathan's office, waiting for two deadpan academics to arrive. I tried to push it back inside, but like Mr Punch, the Rampant Rabbit wasn't going to be battered to death. The more I panicked, the less likely the stand to allow itself to be seduced back inside.

Even with no-one around, I fried red-hot. Voices sounded down the corridor. I crammed RR violently back down into its box, raping the virginal card and cellophane housing irrevocably.

'Jess, then Roger?' Scott entered first.

'I don't think he'd put up with that.'

I squashed down the top of the red bag. The package wouldn't stuff into my rucksack. Clearly, this wasn't the moment for a major re-pack. I kicked the carrier under my seat with my foot and hoped the box was hidden.

Jonathan looked at me. 'Hot flush.' I flapped my hand in front of my face, before he had a chance to ask.

Jonathan looked embarrassed. 'Ah … erm … would you like the window open?'

'No, no, I'll be fine in a moment. Just carry on.'

Scott sat down in the chair next to me. I needed to exorcise Roger Rabbit, but my nipples had found a rampant, leopard-skin identity of their own. Scott picked up the poster. It was only one-eighth size, but you could see how it would look.

'The layout's good. Really eye-catching.' He looked at me admiringly. 'You've put in a lot of work.'

'Well, yes. I got to twenty-four hours and stopped counting.'

The guys smiled at me. 'It takes a long time at first, doesn't it?' said Jonathan. Blimey, I thought. The new underwear must be working.

'I think it was mostly the terror of doing something for real,' I admitted. 'What do you think of the font size for the title? I wasn't sure if that was too small, or too big. I tried it both ways, but still wasn't sure.'

'Well, you've still need space for the authors' names. So you can't go too big with the title.'

'Oh no, I've put the three names down there, Scott.' I pointed to a small box in the bottom right hand corner.

'If this is displayed at *SHERPA*, it needs to highlight the authors and the institution. So, the names go directly under the title, as large as possible.'

'OK, I can do that. Do I just put surnames and initials, or full handles?'

'What do you think, Jono?'

'Initials won't take up so much space.' That was strange. How many authors were there?

'You'd better dictate them to me, so I don't get any wrong spellings or anything.'

'Sure. Let me write them out for you.' Scott pulled over a piece of copy paper and wrote *Woodhouse, S.M., Griffiths, J.D., Lawson, R.E.P., Boyd, J.A., Elliott, V.* He handed the sheet to me.

I read the names. 'I've got a middle name, too.'

'Well, I'm sure you're allowed to add it in,' soothed Scott, crinkling up his eyes like Jeremy Paxman in a conciliatory mood.

I couldn't help smiling back. 'Is the title OK?'

'Fab … except, it's usually the *lived* experience, not living. Can you change that?'

'Of course, Scott. So it's now: *The lived experience of decreasing mortality rates in a sample of women from the U.K.'s ageing population*?'

'Yeah, then the authors and then, name of institution. You'll be able to get the University logo in as well, on the left there.'

I added a note to Scott's paper. 'Got it.'

'We'll leave that in your capable hands. Now, I've edited the abstract you e-mailed me last week.' He handed me a single sheet of paper summarising the poster, which I read.

'Oh, that's perfect. You make it sound so clear. Thank you.'

'I'll shoot the abstract in this afternoon. I suggest you make those changes and we'll be ready to send the file to reprographics.' He twinkled at me. 'I'm sure we can squeeze your poster out of the Departmental budget.'

'Oh is it very expensive? I'm sure I could fund it, if need be.'

'No, no.' Jonathan frowned at Scott. 'That really isn't necessary, it's a Departmental effort.'

'When will I hear if it's accepted?'

'Oh, it will be three or four months, yet. They'll contact me. I'll let you know straight away, of course.'

'Err, would you like a drink?' I gushed. They looked startled. 'It's the least I can do, for all the help you two have given me with this poster.'

Jonathan smiled nicely at me. 'Thanks but no thanks. You won't know this until next week, but you've scored 100% for your Stats exam. I wouldn't like anyone to accuse me of favouritism.'

'100%! You're joking!'

'No, straight up. Superb result.' I didn't disagree. I was incapable of speech.

'Congratulations, Nessie.' Scott seemed to have forgotten about our argument at the Academic meeting. 'I'm sorry, too. I'm having lunch over at Senate House at one, but why don't we fix up a time for us to have a chat about your dissertation plans? I've an interesting proposition for you.'

Scott and I exited the room together and walked to the Sports Centre entrance.

'So, what have you been reading lately?'

'Well, statistics and obesity.'

Scott grimaced and glanced at his watch. 'Yeah, Nessie. I meant, what ideas have you come up with for your dissertation?'

'Oh, sorry. Erm, I was thinking about smoking and exercise. Maybe take people in one of the Stages of Change like Preparation and see…'

'Old hat, Nessie. Have you read the paper Julie Prudent's just published?'

'Do you mean, where they tested the effect of carbohydrate drinks on elite rowers' affect and rate of perceived exertion? Yeah, I've had a look at it.' I was, after all, a woman of the research world.

'I was interested in whether we might find the same sort of effects with recreational runners.'

'You think there might be?'

'Sure. Why not? Vasulu wants to do blood tests. What about you picking up another angle?'

'Me?' I squeaked. 'I was planning a qualitative study.'

'Oh come on, Nessie. Don't waste your time on that woosy stuff.'

'Really? I thought qualitative research was just as important as quantitative?'

'This will be more publishable. And that's what you need at this stage in your career. Go and read the article. Think about it. Come and see me next Tuesday.'

'Bollocks,' I remembered. 'Oh, nothing, Scott … I've forgotten … err, something. See you next Tuesday, then?'

'Sure, about four-thirty. I'll look forward to it.'

When I arrived back at Jonathan's office, the room was empty. No red carrier. What was I to do? I teetered for half a minute, a pair of eyes caught in headlights. I bolted for the safety of the outside world, before anyone ran me over.

'Put it aside. Glory in transitory triumph. You, young lady, are an ace performer. Who else do you know who has *ever* got one hundred per cent for an exam?' Chest thrust forth, I shimmied through the gridlocked traffic massed by the shops.

'Well, Paul's friend got 105% for a maths exam in 1969,' snitched my Superego.

'Stop it! Ian was a maths genius, and, and … that's years ago when we were young and bright-eyed! This is me, Nessie. No more science than a Biology 'O' Level to my name. A supernumerary player in the game of life.' I swept down the hill on a roller-coaster of air, Superego kicked into touch.

'Scott wants to be my dissertation supervisor.' My voice trailed off into imagination. I re-ran yesterday, several times.

My new bra scratched my nipples. Scott's vulnerability grabbed my guts, and smashed them back, upside down.

I watched the ferry launch chug up the dock, and thought, 'if he's proposed that topic, it must be viable. Stop doubting, Thomas. Go fr'it.'

***

I didn't manage to get through to Paul until Sunday evening.

'Are you alright?' I could feel my frown as I tried to read his voice.

'Sure, just tired.'

'What have you been doing, Paul?'

'Oh, nothing really. Bit of running about.'

'Well, I've tried to phone you five or six times. All I've got is the answerphone.'

'I'm sorry, I got your messages, but I just haven't had time. I was out several nights last week. Been out on the bike this afternoon. Thought I ought to be getting a bit more exercise.'

'Oh …' Immediately, I had a prescient feeling that he was seeing someone. After thirty-three years, I could tell …

'You have emptied the holding tank, haven't you?'

'Yeah, a week ago, now. All done and dusted. I steered *Iris* all the way and into the pump out berth with a cross wind and all the way back.'

'Did you find someone to help?'

'Yep, in the end Mike and Nick both came along.'

'Oh.' I thought the syllable carried a smidgeon of disappointment.

'Mike was a rather abrupt pilot. Single word commands. You know, *port*, *slow*, *stop* and *bloody 'ell*.'

'Not much help, then.'

'Oh yes! He knew what he was talking about. I just followed what he said. And he looked the engine over, first.'

'There wasn't anything wrong with it.'

'And topped up the antifreeze for me when we got back.'

'I did the anti-freeze in November, before your Mum went away.' He sounded cross.

'Mike couldn't have been more charming. He invited Nick and me on board *Argosy* for a cup of tea when we got back to the marina.'

'What was the *Argosy* like, down below?'

'A bit shy on female comforts! Stacked out with gear. Do you know, he had a carpet cleaner and an industrial heater tucked away, which he lent me. Mind you, I didn't think I'd take him up on his offer of a dry bunk for the night.' I laughed. Paul didn't.

'So are you working hard?'

'I am. Just spent another afternoon on final tidying up of the poster. It took ages to sort out the title and authors. I had to re-type the same box eight times, because it kept disappearing. But it's gone to Scott now, ready for photocopying.'

'Glad you're enjoying yourself.' That sounded flat. 'Is the carpet drying out?'

'Yeah. It's nearly dry. It smelled putrid before I shampooed it. I think it will be alright, but we'll see what Mum says when she gets back. It wouldn't cost that much to re-carpet the whole of the boat. It's not that many square metres.'

'Well, the money should get a little easier soon. You didn't really need Nick as well, did you?'

'Well, Nick rode shotgun up in the bow. With the two of them to handle the ropes, it went very smoothly. Mike only had to say *bloody 'ell* twice.'

'Did you remember to switch back to the holding tank when you'd …?'

'Of course. Mike did all that for me.'

'And how is Nick?'

'Oh, he's fine,' I said airily. I do feel it's important not to betray confidences, even to close family members. 'So, have you seen anyone lately?'

'I went into supper with Edward and Margaret last night. Anwar was asking after you. Ben phoned to say he'd passed …'

'Yeah, he phoned me too,' I cut in. That wasn't what I'd meant at all.

***

'Look at that,' Xiu pointed out of the Sports Centre window. The others craned round.

'It's almost obscene in a man of his age.'

'Steady on, Midge.' I put down the inevitable rucksack. 'He must be at least fifteen years younger than me.'

'I think it's romantic,' Cathy said. 'Steve would never neck with me so passionately in the street, these days. And we're not even married.'

'Is that his wife?' asked Midge.

'Well it might be his mistress, but I rather think she was his wife at the Christmas party. She's French.'

'We would not do that in China.'

'Really, Xiu?'

'No. My parents would not allow it.'

'What do you think, Nessie?'

'I'm with Cathy. I think it's rather nice to see a married couple who still show affection in public.'

'It's so OTT, it's almost like he's trying to make a point,' said Cathy.

We watched Jonathan walk away, hand in hand with his missus.

'Midge, have you got a moment?' I hissed, as the others got up to leave.

'What's up, Nessie?'

'I've got your money here … and …' I took a breath. There was no alternative. I needed help. 'Midge, Roger Rabbit's disappeared.'

'Who's nicked him, then? Has the barge been burgled?'

'No, I left it in Jonathan's office and it's gone.'

'Blimey!' Midge burst out laughing. 'No wonder he was so enthusiastic. Have you asked him about it?' I shook my head. She looked at me steadily.

I could feel my cheeks burning again. Would I ever be grown up enough to talk about sex aids without betraying my embarrassment within one millisecond?

'Midge, if he knows about it, I'll be far too embarrassed ever to face him again.'

'Would you like me to go and ask Penny if it's been handed in?'

I nodded. 'Would you mind?'

'No, not at all.'

Five minutes later she was back, with a large Marks and Spencer bag. She handed me a postcard. 'Look what's been pinned up in the common room for a fortnight.'

I read the message. *Found. One framed Roger Rabbit.*

'Well, at least someone in the Department has a sense of humour, Nessie.'

'Did Penny say anything?'

'No. Very businesslike.' She laughed at me again. 'Come on, it's a fact of life for the unattached. You'll need to grow a thicker skin to manage on your own, Nessie.'

'Yeah, thanks Midge.'

3.9

Our discussion was booked for four thirty, but I didn't get inside Scott's office until five to five. He'd been meeting students since lunchtime. He sighed as I came through the door. His hair was messy, as if it had been a troublesome afternoon.

'Would you rather postpone until tomorrow?' I hoped he wouldn't take me up on the offer. I'd been looking forward to the session all week.

'No, no, not at all. Come on in.' I dumped my rucksack and sat down, glowing gently in all respects. Scott slumped back in his office chair and wheeled to face me. He scaffolded hand, elbow, belly and knuckle to cup his chin, emphasising his ennui.

'How are you getting on? Any more thoughts?'

'I have. I think the design from that paper could be adapted to our runners in the race.'

'Good girl. You're going to pick it up?'

'Yes, I think so.'

He sat up. 'Cool! Now, how will your study be different from the rowing one? We don't want it labelled *Me Too* research.'

'Well I guess the student runners might react differently, both mentally and physically, because they'll be less fit.'

'Anything else?'

'Rowing and running are different in several respects.'

'OK. That'll be the starting point for your literature review, then. I'll leave you with them, for now. Let's move on to the method. What are your initial thoughts?'

'Erm, I thought, before and after the race ...'

'What testing protocol will you use?'

'I guess, give them the glucose drink or a placebo, take blood, psychological testing.'

'Are you a nurse?' He frowned, his eyes seriously icy.

'No …' It was pretty scary, fielding a brain the speed of Scott's.

'I told you, Vasulu's going to take blood.'

'Maybe I could just compare their times?'

'Yeah. Keep it simple, for now. What statistical design have you chosen?'

I stared at him aghast. My recent reliance on an 'A' Level text was my sole source of statistical expertise.

'You need to decide on your design early on, to inform your method,' he prompted.

'Erm … well you could do several tests and give them the drink or the placebo at different times, without their knowledge.' I fumbled to clarify a wisp of an idea. 'Or you could set up an er … blind, randomised, …' I groped for a word that had gone spinning away. 'Er … er, trial and compare similar participants.'

'What variables are you controlling for, in your statistical calculations?'

I looked at him helplessly. I had the sensation that he was squeezing me through a tightly-fitting dark tunnel. 'Erm … '

'What other reasons might one person run better than another, apart from the carbohydrate drink or placebo?' he translated for me.

'Erm … gender … err, physical activity history, health?'

'Good. What else?'

Bloody hell. 'Erm … fitness level, smoking?'

'Do you think a student from this course might run faster than someone from Drama?'

'Well, it depends on lots of other things. I doubt I could run as fast as a twenty year old, whatever subject they were studying.'

'But there might be a significant difference, taking the students as two groups?'

'Possibly,' I conceded. A cautious answer, but I didn't have a clue what he was getting at. I wriggled on my seat and made a stab.

'The exercise students might try harder in the race itself.'

'Certainly. In your stats, you have to control for all of those, for example by using regression analysis. In other words, think your design through at this early stage. Now, how many individuals do you envisage using as a sample?'

'I don't know.' My stomach contracted in panic.

'Never mind. We can work that out later. You mentioned an RCT. Do you know how you would go about setting that up?'

'No idea. I'm sorry, I haven't a clue.' In the silence, the gap between what I wanted to achieve and my current knowledge state seemed unbridgeable. I'd been through the wringer. Now I wished I could disappear into the floor through the gap between the legs of my jeans.

Scott gave me the concerned look that Sir Bob might bestow on an African child.

'We can work it out together, Nessie. Don't look so worried. You don't need all the answers today. Carry on with your literature search and come up with a research question for next time.'

'I'm sorry. It's just that I haven't done a proper dissertation before.'

'What's wrong?' He looked as if he cared. 'You can do this. You've already proved you can cope with a steep learning curve.'

'I … er, nothing, really.' How could I say that his brain scared me?

'Am I moving too fast for you?'

'Well, I don't even know what a dissertation looks like, at the moment.'

'That problem's easily solved. I'll lend you one.' He stood up and made for the bookcase. 'I'm sorry, I'm far too impatient. Now, Sara Haines, last year. She wrote an excellent one on students' exercise patterns. … I've got it somewhere here, she was my …'

Unsurprisingly, he couldn't locate the copy in his untidy office.

'Hmm, must have lent it out to someone. C'mon, there'll be a copy in the Dissertation cupboard, let's go and find that one.'

Scott whistled quietly through his teeth as we prowled along the corridor. The Dissertation cupboard was as attractive as most windowless stock cupboards, though too new for spiders, or a dusty smell. At one end locked steel cabinets housed confidential research data. Apart from that, several hundred dissertations awaited perusal by future generations.

Scott ran a finger along last year's shelf.

'Here we are, Sara Haines. I'm sure this will help.' As he turned to give it to me, I heard a click. We stared at the closed door for a nano-second, then at one another. How had that happened?

Scott walked three paces to the doorway and probed the closed woodwork in disbelief.

'Nessie, we're locked in.' He pushed the door. 'How can they damn well build a cupboard that you can get locked in?'

The first aider in me noticed sweat glowing on his upper lip, his pallor. I dabbed a smile on my face.

'Calm down, Scott. We'll get out in a moment. Is there a release button on the architrave?'

'No … there's … not.' He swallowed. He banged on the door, but the corridor outside remained silent. 'This Centre is a disgrace, the builders cut so many corners …'

'Ah … how about trying plastic …?' I fished out my student swipe card. Scott jilled from foot to foot, like Manx stalking a prospective supper. His edginess was catching. There was a grille, air breezed in, but I had to concentrate on staying calm myself.

'No, looks like it's a deadlock.'

'They must have beefed up security for the confidential stuff.'

'OK. Let's just think it through. There's always a solution.' I sat down facing the door, and rested my head back against the bookshelves. A white-faced Scott sat down next to me, biting his lower lip, pulling at his earring.

Eventually desperation triumphed. 'Mobile!'

'Of course, thank the Lord.'

I giggled. 'You sound like Lionel Blume! Erm, I'm afraid I've forgotten mine.'

He propped his feet against the steel shelving opposite. 'I'll phone Jonathan to let us out.' He hauled his mobile out of his jeans pocket and thumbed buttons. Ten seconds later, he glanced down at the display.

'Only one bar, we're right in the middle of the building here.' He shook the mobile, as if to make it work better. 'What now?'

'Well, it's only … ' I looked at my watch, ' … ten to six. People must still be around.'

'Yeah … Alison and her staff will have gone by now, but Kirsty and Jono were in their offices, and there's nearly always someone in the IT workroom or the open plan. Trouble is, hearing them pass by on the carpet.'

'How about putting an SOS on a piece of paper and slipping it under the door, so anyone going by spots it and rescues us?'

'Cool.'

I glanced at Scott as I sat down again. He didn't look as pale, now. Somewhere deep inside my jeans, redundant ovaries flipped.

'Do you want to carry on with the tutorial?'

'Well, not right now, if you don't mind. Err, I think I might find it difficult to concentrate.'

'At the very worst, we might have to wait all night.'

'Good thing there's a light, then. Oh God,' I smiled at his strained face. 'I do hope not, I think I'll need a pee before then.'

'You're good at this sort of stuff, aren't you?'

'Yeah … s'pose I've had lots of practice. I've been in lots of tight corners.'

'Such as …?'

'You're forever dealing with emergencies as a Mum. I remember once, when Benjie was about two, he locked himself in the bathroom, and I had to talk him out. It took about three hours.' I decided to pass on more recent exploits. 'And I guess you get self-reliant when you travel out of tourist areas. Paul got arrested in Nepal, once.'

Scott looked respectful. 'My education has clearly been sadly lacking: I never go beyond a pavement and I don't have any children.'

I looked down, creasing denim into folds. A brain like that, lost for ever? Meanwhile, he sidled a comb out to smooth his hair.

'Scott, we're gonna have to keep quiet, or we won't hear them coming through.'

'I was just thinking that, myself.' He slid an arm round my shoulder. The silence hyperventilated. 'Would this be more comfortable for you?'

I sat up, rigid, astonished as the heroine of any novel. It was just as well we didn't speak. Elizabeth's confusion, meeting Darcy at Pemberton, had nothing on me. I needed a geriatric moment, to sort it out.

Scott was playing with the buttons on his mobile, and the movements transmitted up his arm to his collar bone, like the rhythm of a song, to my head. Eventually I closed my eyes. I suppose I relaxed. The next thing I noticed was a light touch on my jeans leg, gently rubbing, like tickling a cat's head.

'*Dar* … Scott … ?'

'Don't you like it?'

'I … ' His hand paused solicitously. I really didn't know how to answer. This was moving a lot faster than my readiness levels. In terms of the Transtheoretical Model, I wasn't ready for Action in a different reality plane.

Eventually I settled on the cautious truth, ' … It's … ' I snuggled down into his arm, regretting that both sets of new underwear were in the dirty washing pile. He stroked even more tentatively.

'You know, I like you a lot, Nessie.' My blood drained out, to be replaced by fuzzy felt.

Whilst I considered a suitably maidenly reply, Scott graunched stubble against my skin, as he turned his mouth towards my forehead.

'What the hell's going on?' I heard Kirsty's voice and opened my eyes. She was staring at Scott, hand to mouth. 'I was just off home when I saw the message on the carpet.'

'Hi Kirsty' said Scott pleasantly, 'we got locked in. Thanks for rescuing us.'

Kirsty flung back her fizzy hair and grinned at Scott.

'Oh yeah!'

'It's not what you think, Kirsty,' Oh God, he's turned into a cliché. He rose to his feet and distanced himself down at *Participants' Consent Forms 1999-2004.*

'Well it's a good thing I found you. I'm the last one left on the corridor tonight.'

I picked up Sara Haines' bound copy. 'Do you mind if I keep this until tomorrow?' I eventually managed.

'No not at all,' Scott replied, as urbane as Ron Rawlins in the supermarket queue.

'Because I must go, now. I'm absolutely dying for the loo,' I said, making a swift dive for the exit.

PART FOUR
Results
4.1

For the next month, I lived in a crazy bubble. I wandered round, inoculated against the stress of mundane research proposals and risk assessments. I re-discovered Scott in every morsel of nonsense I sang. *I'm hypnotised, petrified, every time you walk by … maybe we get together, maybe forever, maybe just for a while…..* Oh God.

Could it be manic depression? I kept my head down, as a natural alternative to lithium. It turned out to be flu. I found myself drinking in tea, toast and *Persuasion.* At such moments, it's either that or cream of tomato soup, *Pride and Prejudice.*

'She learned romance as she grew older'. I'd never noticed that line before. That's me, I thought, studying Mum's pink and green flowery duvet cover. A working lifetime of looking after others, and now I'm emerging like the butterfly from *The Very Hungry Caterpillar.*

Perhaps more like a leopard from within a domesticated pussy-cat, popped up in my brain. My sweaty body contracted at the reference to my bra. Then I realised the little hole round the back of the pants was for someone like Scott to rip off, which made me feel even more feverish. I even briefly considered Roger Rabbit, hiding in the back of the clothes locker, before I fell asleep.

The white and chrome room always recurred in my dream. The pink hillock obstructed my field of vision. I felt again that tight, passing sensation of the slippery baby corkscrewing through. I caught my first sight of a face, like a squashed-up lemon without ears. This time, the crumpled body's limbs unfolded and jerked. The gummy mouth opened and distorted for a first breath and living pink swept across the waxy grey body. The baby cried into the silence: me, the midwife … Scott. Not the frantic rest of them crowding round, like that first time.

I plunged down a tunnel of air. My eyes latched onto Mum's stern line, secured to a cleat on deck with a couple of half hitches, just outside the window. I shut my eyes, hoping to encourage more, but the image had ghosted back to my subconscious. Only an essence lingered: ' … *joy, senseless joy'.*

From the window, an eye level view of wooden boards stretched grey and deserted into the cold, rainy afternoon. This is all about Scott, I thought in a flash of cold sweaty sanity, until the loop of film recurred.

'You know, I like you a lot.' I had to imagine the look in Scott's eyes, since we were both staring at different shelves at the time. His glacier-cool eyes melted into something warmer and deeper. An Adriatic-blue sky, perhaps.

I focussed on the half hitches. What attributes, precisely, did he like? My brains … or my body? I didn't know much about Scott Woodhouse's likes and dislikes. Frederick Wentworth applauded spirit. *'My first wish, for all whom I am interested in, is that they should be firm'.* Did that mean standing firm to my principles? What principles anyway, in my inverted, hypomanic world? Did my principles, for example, exclude sex with another man? I read on. *'A strong sense of duty is no bad part of a woman's portion'.* Shit.

What about Paul? Had I stopped loving him? I didn't know. Paul. The place-in-my-heart seemed the same, when I felt it. But you can't love two men at once, Nessie. 'Why not?' tempted my Id. 'There's at least two children in your heart, not to mention Ella, several relatives and assorted friends.'

Years of monogamy hadn't equipped me to deal with the situation. I couldn't even think of anyone to talk to, since my primary advisor on all matters personal hitherto had been Paul. *Persuasion* wasn't much help with modern morals. I wished I'd enough energy to fetch *The Times.*

***

After two further days I finished *Pride and Prejudice*, the tomato soup ran out and I'd had my fill of bed. I resumed a tottery service on the research proposal. Saturday night was earmarked. I'd invited Cathy, Midge and Xiu out to dinner with … well, Paul. *'A commonplace business, too numerous for intimacy, too small for variety'.* Oh, stop it, Nessie. It's your birthday bash. My centrally-heated overpowering happiness swelled into a cosy nest again.

***

We turned right, and right again, along a gloomy, half-lit street. Chill gusts of wind swilled up my skimpy trousers and launched icy draughts down my open front. I pulled my best jacket closer and wished I'd dressed in my urban hill-walking gear. Tucked half way down the square, a short parade of shops skulked in darkness.

'Here we are,' I said brightly. 'No 84, *Casa Nuestra.*' I pushed open the pale blue doorway and motioned the others into the dingy restaurant. Midge stopped short as a ghostly-pale waiter appeared. We piled in behind her. I was eager to shut the door.

'I've booked a table for five for eight o'clock. The name's, Elliott.'

'James Elliott,' Midge muttered in the background.

The waiter looked us, unsmiling. 'Ah yes, come this way.' No-one seemed anxious to follow his long black trousers and waxy-white neck. He led us though the semi-darkness to a pine table in the front window bay.

'At least the passers-by will have a last sighting of us,' said Cathy wryly, as she sat down with her back to the glass.

'There aren't many other diners here, are there?' commented Midge. One couple sat on the other side of the door.

'Oh, stop winding me up, you two. It's early, yet.'

'How did you find out about it, Nessie?'

'I thought it would be fun to try something different. OK, there was an advert up in the Union. They give a 10% student discount. Has anyone tried Portugese, before?'

'I've been to the Algarve,' said Midge. 'There were lots of little open air bars barbecuing yummy sardines. I'm really looking forward to it.'

'That might be a bit difficult, in this weather. Is Paul still coming?' asked Cathy.

'Yeah, I don't know where he is. I expect he'll be here soon.'

Mr Horror Movie arrived at the table. 'You order now?'

'What is this?' I asked, pointing at the Starter menu. 'Is it soup?'

'*Sopa.* Vegetables and … fish. And meat.'

'Oh, that sounds just right. I'm cold.' I mimed shivering. 'I'll have that first.'

He whipped out a notebook and pen and raised funereal eyebrows at everyone in turn.

'And one more,' I said, pointing at the empty chair. 'One person to come.'

'What is this?'

'*Cataplana.* Is a stew, with fish, with vegetable … and *chourico.*'

'And this?'

'This is … ' He groped for a precise definition. 'This a stew. Is meat, fish, and … vegetable.'

'I see. What sort of meat?' I smiled at him encouragingly.

'Err … pig. And sheep. And cow … big stew.' He petered out into silence.

'Do you have sardines?' Midge tried, but it was no good. He'd given 100%, already.

'So, what will it be, girls? Meat stew, fish stew or vegetable stew? Pot luck, or …?'

'Let's just have one of each, and five plates. If we're having soup first … '

'I'll try,' I said, 'but I'm not promising I can make him understand that we only want three.' I turned back to Mr Horror Movie.

'OK.' He wrote spidery words on his pad. 'And to drink?'

'Shall we have some *casa vinho verde*, girls?' I asked. 'And, a jug of water, please.' He shuffled off to the kitchen. The door gusted open and Paul arrived. He looked better, more like his old self.

'Where on earth have you been?'

'Sorry, love, I've only just finished work.' He took off a navy coat that I hadn't seen before. 'Good evening everyone, I'm Paul. Nessie: happy birthday.' He didn't kiss me, but sat down opposite, next to Midge.

'This is Xiu … Midge … Cathy.' He smiled round the group and half-rose to shake his rough builder's hand round the table.

'Hello.' He started his glass of wine, leaning back in the basic wooden chair. I could see the girls' warmth had already disarmed him.

'I tried to phone your mobile, but I couldn't get through.'

'No, it wasn't on …'

'Anyway, I found the place. So, how's everyone? Research Proposals in yet?'

'Tuesday,' we chorused.

A large figure opened the door. Mr Horror scuttled over and led him to a table near ours. From the corner of my eye, I noticed the man shrug off his coat and settle down with *The Sun* and a bottle of wine. His balding head looked familiar. It was the man on the path, near the university. How strange, I thought, for a lecturer to be reading *The Sun.*

I floated in again. Cathy was just finishing Paul off. She'd described her research proposal in some detail, and he looked like a man who needed a breath of air.

I rescued him. 'So what's the work you've found, Paul?'

He stiffened. 'Err, I'm sub-contracting at the university.'

'Are you! You didn't tell me. That's wonderful news.'

'Yes.' He sounded unconvinced. 'I only started last week. The agency found it for me.'

Midge leant forward with an interested smile. 'So what project are you working on?'

'Umm, well, several. That is … inter-departmental communications.'

'Really.' Midge fluttered her eyelids at him. 'I didn't realise you were working so close by.'

Paul eyed her. 'Oh, er, no.'

The waiter came up with a basket and offered stiff, grey rolls round. The *sopa* arrived, thick, greasy and colourless. It tasted of rancid marina water. Earthenware bowls carried enough liquid to fill the hungriest Portugese fisherman.

I breathed through my mouth, to avoid the cabbage-mashed-with-fish smell. 'This is interestingly spicy.' Cathy and I concentrated on our rolls.

'It's not that bad, if you imagine … oh hell. Sorry, Nessie, it's horrible.' Paul pushed half the bowl away.

Xiu tucked it away without comment. 'It is … quite good, although too thick, I think. At home, our soup is always thin.' She looked at our leavings. 'You didn't like that, Cathy?'

'No, a bit salty for me.'

We tried smiling at Mr Horror. 'Very good. Mmmm,' we murmured.

A tempting smell of seared meat wafted from the kitchen after him. I imagined a wholesome meat stew overflowing with veg. 'I expect the next course will be better.'

Paul turned my way. 'How are the preparations for the race going? I've seen several flyers advertising it, round the uni.'

'Not too bad. Only ten weeks away, now.'

'Have many people entered?'

'A few. Not nearly as many as we'd like.'

'What about some telly coverage? I've got a friend in the studio here.' That was Cathy, of course.

'Maybe it's best to start small,' said Midge.

'We're hoping for several hundred in the end.'

'Even so, I can't see how they will ever recruit several hundred participants into the experiments. Usually they only recruit a small percentage of all the eligible people.'

'Don't say that, Cathy. Somehow I've got to recruit enough pairs of people willing to drink my carbohydrate drink or a placebo. What on earth will I do, if no-one volunteers?'

'How many do you need?'

'We reckon, at least twenty.'

'There you are, Paul, you could go in for the race, now you're part of the university,' smiled Midge. 'Help Nessie out.'

Paul smiled back. 'I expect I'll be working. How are you going to manage marshalling on the day and your own experiment as well, Nessie?'

'Oh, I'll find someone to else to deal with my participants on the day. To ensure it's blind, only I should know who is given what drink. The person who actually delivers the drink doesn't know.'

'Oh, I see. So then the participants don't get any clues from the way it's given out?'

'That's right. I'm hoping one of these guys will help me out.' I looked round. 'It's what's called a research team in The Literature.'

'Yeah I'll do that,' said Cathy. 'It sounds more interesting than being a marshal.'

Eventually, our *cataplana* arrived in six huge bowls. A pallid selection of lumps squatted, camouflaged by huge humps of half-submerged potato. Firm, grey lumps were squid; fatty lumps, mutton. We shared the identical bowls round, leaving the sixth one to congeal in the middle.

'What's your carbohydrate drink made from, Nessie?' Midge dredged her *cataplana*.

'It's 6.2% maltodextrine. You buy it as powder from the specialist mail order shops, then mix it with water.'

'Urr, that sounds disgusting.' A piece of light grey fish appeared. 'What does it taste of?'

'Lemon, I think.'

She chewed speculatively for some time before swallowing. 'So you think they'll run faster as a result?'

'So The Literature and Scott seem to think.'

'Does that make it a performance-enhancing drug?' asked Paul.

'No, of course not, it's only an ordinary foodstuff.'

'You'll have to get a move on, with the race only a month away.' Paul speared a lump of potato. As he raised it towards his mouth, it disintegrated off his fork.

'Yeah, I must ring up, this week. Trouble is, I don't know how much to order, yet.'

'Well, don't leave it too late. And put in on the Barclaycard. Then if it gets lost in the post, we won't lose the money.'

'Ah …,' I wondered how to break the news to Paul. 'Good point. I … I haven't been able to use my Barclaycard for a week or two.'

Paul looked at me. 'The new one hasn't come through yet?'

'Err, I haven't ord …'

'Haven't you stopped the stolen one?' Paul looked stern.

'Well, no, because it's not stolen. I just can't find it, right now.'

Paul looked daggers at me, but he was too well-contained to make a fuss in public. 'Well, if you haven't found it by the end of the wee …'

I looked away. The lecturer's steak and chips arrived, leaching a wonderfully robust, meaty smell. On the debit side, he wasn't getting any vegetables either. A slight grin rolled up his chubby face. I wondered if he'd been listening in. Or was it just olfactory anticipation? I regrouped the congealing lumps on my plate and discovered a third prawn. My appetite for international food sated, I left the rest.

We finished around ten. The couple had long gone and the lecturer disappeared a few minutes before. Mr Horror Movie looked like he was keen to close.

'I'm sorry everyone,' I started to say, once we were safely round the corner. 'Not quite what I was expecting. Come back for …'

'What on earth …?' said Midge.

A swarm of vans and minibuses laboured up hill, filling the narrow street with diesel exhaust smoke.

'Were they police vans?' asked Paul, looking back. There was the sound of shouting and doors slamming.

'Perhaps they were desperate to catch final orders at the restaurant?' said Cathy. We sniggered and turned downhill towards *Iris*.

4.2

Midge and Cathy left around midnight, just as my birthday started.

'Happy birthday, Nessie.' Paul produced a small, brightly-wrapped box from his pocket. Perfume!

'Oh, thank you. Shall I open it now?' I smiled, exaggerating the nose-wrinkling to show him how pleased I was.

'Go ahead.'

'A memory stick! Oh, Paul, thank you.' On an impulse, I got out of the cane chair and slipped onto the seat beside him. I put my arms round his neck to give him a quick kiss. 'It's … err, just what I need.'

'Do you really mean that?' His voice sounded cautious.

'I do! I'll use it tomorrow.'

Paul relaxed back with the bottle of Islay whisky.

'Are you sure that's a good idea, sweetie?' I asked quickly, before he could start pouring.

'Why not? I've only had two.'

'And three glasses of wine at the Casa.'

'I was hoping you might invite me to stay.' He looked over at me, one eyebrow up, a look he had adopted around the time Sean Connery was James Bond.

'Maybe.' I tried not to sound keen. 'The amount you've had, you shouldn't be driving home.' Beneath the thin patch, his scalp shone familiarly in the lamplight.

'It's good to be sitting here with you, again.'

I was conscious of my interested body. What's going on? 'Well, I think I'm going to bed now,' I found myself saying.

He looked pleased. 'Won't be a minute, just finishing this off.'

I undressed, leaving the leopard-skin underwear for Paul to discover. Once in bed, the duvet cosied my readiness in warmth. In a few minutes, I'd dozed off.

I came to when a foreign object, probably a nude Innuit, slapped into bed beside me.

'What time is it?' I groped to focus my eyes on the clock. 'Urr, one o'clock. You've been a long time.' I rolled over on to my front and put a reluctant hand on Paul's icy chest.

'Ergh, don't do that.'

'What's up?'

'The cabin's going round.'

'Oh, no.'

'Is the boat rocking, or is it just me?'

'No, 'fraid not. It's dead calm tonight.' I waited for a response. Paul lay like a lump of meat on a butcher's slab. In the end, I said, 'Are you alright?'

There was a long pause. 'Err … Sorry, Nessie, I think I'm feeling sick. Do you mind …?' He sat up, shivering, to grope his way to the loo.

'No … that's OK.'

Around four am, that is, after Paul had been sick three times, a strange blue light reflected across the cabin roof. I slipped out of bed and peered through the curtains. There was furtive activity at the top of the pontoon. Several black figures scurried along the far side of the marina.

'Hey Paul, do you think Mike's taking delivery of some stolen goods?' Paul wasn't even slightly interested. He groaned. 'Well, something's happening. I'm sure it's Mike with a whole gang of men, up at the entry gate.'

Paul sighed, sat up, gulped for air a couple of times and disappeared into the loo compartment once more. Everything went quiet, but for Paul retching, as he emptied out the final morsels of his meal. I returned to bed. The oscillating light made it difficult to shut my eyes, let alone sleep. Suddenly, the blue light danced round the roof and slid down the far wall.

I leapt out of bed again. 'It's moving off.' There was no sign of Mike. 'Paul, Mike's been arrested!' Paul slid back into the small bed. He lay like a stranded slug. 'How are you feeling?'

'Terrible.' Own goal. I almost felt sorry for him.

***

Late Sunday afternoon, Paul recovered enough to go home. By then I'd put in five more hours on my research proposal. I'd lined up a select row of birthday cards and baptised the memory stick. As I sedated Word to infiltrate the last diagram, Ella phoned from somewhere in India.

'Mum, you are coming back?'

'Yes dear, the flight's booked for the 15th of April. We get in at midday.'

'That's wonderful Mum, I'm really looking forward to hearing your traveller's tales.'

'Ah … ' My heart sank at her tone. What was wrong? 'I'll only be around for two nights. I just want to sort out some suitable clothes for the colder weather.'

'Do you mean up at the house? Of course the boat will be ready for you to move back on board as soon as ...'

'No, I didn't mean that, dear. Have you looked at the photographs on the web-site recently?'

'Err, no Mum.' Last time I looked, there were eight hundred unnamed, long-distance shots.

'Well, I'm going up to Doncaster, with Wolfgang, one of my new friends, on the 17th.'

'Wolfgang? Have you got a toy-boy?' I heard Mum's quick breath.

'Don't be childish, Nessie. Wolfgang is very special. I am going to visit his family.'

Mum had outgunned me. 'I see.'

Within seconds I had clawed my way onto the website. Several minutes later I had his snapshot in front of me.

He was an older man, but stood so straight, it was difficult to guess his age. He had the body of a plump pear, with the waist:hip ratio of a man who enjoyed life. I saw a row of grinning pearlies. I didn't much like the way he looked into my Mum's eyes and held her hand. That's not an objective, scientific reaction, I told myself sternly. Emotional, and therefore psychological, nodded The Literature.

I ate through Midge's birthday chocolates, chewing over Mum's news. The caffeine and sugar were just what I needed. Did I really have any right to resent a man who might make my Mum happy at her age? *Just because it's not your old Dad*, my Superego chimed in knowingly. Obviously one should judge Wolfgang on his merits, when one met him.

Oh my God, should I talk to my Mum about sexually transmitted diseases?

Paul and I walked slowly up to the car park, while I spilled the news. The sparse clumps of daffodils at the dockhead were over, and the brown, papery heads drooped with their own little hangovers. In the car park, Paul walked up to a new white Transit van, grimy round the back. My chat dried.

'Oh, have you … where's the Audi?' He didn't say anything, just unlocked the door.

My excitement evaporated. 'What's …? Have you sold it, or something?'

'Yes.'

'Oh.' He jiggled his keys instead of replying. 'But we always said … we'd keep … was it a part exchange?'

'No.'

'What do you mean? Doesn't it run properly any more, since …?'

'No, fortunately, it's running fine.' He looked at me, a grey-white man against the silvery March sun.

'How much did it cost? Why didn't you ask me first, Paul?'

He climbed into the front seat. 'I'm using this for work, so we don't need the Audi any more.' He shut the door with infuriating calm and zizzed the window down. 'We've still got Smartie, when we need to go out together.'

That presumed so many things about our relationship, that I felt quite tight-chested. I breathed in carefully, in case it was a cardiac infarction. A taxicab blocked the roadway. Mike stepped out and paid the driver. Paul started the van and pulled forward, waiting. I walked alongside. The taxi shunted neatly round.

'Mike!' I feigned a social smile. 'How are you?'

He hesitated, then turned towards us as the taxi pulled away in a cloud of steam and CO_2. 'Yeah. Hello there.' Paul grunted back.

'What happened? I saw you disappear in the middle of the night.'

Even his stubble had frown marks. 'Been helping the police with their inquiries, as they say.'

'Oh?' Paul perked up, interested in something other than his digestive system once more.

‘They’re ransacked the boat and found nothing. They’ve questioned me on drugs charges and released me.’ Mike was usually a man of few words. He wasn’t trying to hide anything, then.

‘No! I’m sorry to hear that.’

Mike creaked with suppressed anger. ‘Yeah, so will they be, when I get my lawyer on to it, tomorrow.’

‘But they’re not charging you?’

‘No. You should see the state of the boat, when they’d finished.’ He clanked down the gangway and stomped off along the pontoon to his violated pride and joy.

‘He’ll have to tidy his boat up, now.’ Paul leant his arm on the open van window.

‘Do you think that happened at the restaurant as well?’

‘What?’

‘Drugs raid?’

‘Could be.’

‘I’m glad we left when we did. Just think, if we’d still been sitting there, we might have been arrested.’

‘When Customs rummage a boat, it’s very thorough. If I’m not mistaken, they don’t even make good the damage.’

‘No! I’d have something to say about that!’

‘Anyway,’ he said, ‘it’s nearly six. I’d better be off. I’m on the early shift tomorrow.’

‘Early shift?’

‘Yep. Six a.m. Week of earlies, then a week of lates.’

You’ve left me more confused than ever, I thought as I walked back down to the boat. What on earth are you up to? Why do you need a white van for an IT job? And if you’ve found a job, why do you need to sell the Audi?

A shadowy vibe about our relationship temporarily eclipsed my generic *joie de vivre*. Mum was home in April.

Decisions would have to be made by then. On top of that, Leah hadn't phoned on my birthday. That worried me.

Then the need to lose five hundred and fifty four words from my research proposal before Tuesday lunchtime, became a wave of fear that engulfed everything. Except, of course, the bladder of romantic air I walked on, these days.

***

Every time I went into the department, I saw Scott. Every week, he nudged my research along, like a dolphin wet-nurse. He didn't tell me what to do. Occasionally he'd e-mail, or put a paper in my pigeon hole. Neither he nor Kirsty alluded to the cupboard. No gossip surfaced, that I heard. I began to wonder if I'd dreamed it all, like an ageing Titania.

When he spoke, I turned as red as a Valentine's heart and shook. On the whole, it was easier coping when I told myself I'd imagined everything. When the evidence fingered that way, I felt disappointed.

Unfortunately, I'd tested the water, and now I was wet and drippy. The Literature told me that love was one of five basic emotions. As for me, I diagnosed an obsessive disorder, and *reined in* my smiles, as best I could.

***

Heathrow, April 15. Paul and I waited. A mêlée of people thronged Terminal 3, leaving nowhere to sit. Paul supplied a running commentary on the state of the arrivals board. I pencilled marshalling notes on the eighteen pages of Jonathan's risk assessment. Job done, we still waited. I checked and re-checked that Mum's plane had safely landed. Was she really going to appear, after all this time? My trepidation stirred at the thought of this Wolfgang she'd picked up. We were in for a bad time.

Hours, or perhaps only ten minutes later, Phyllida wandered through from the baggage hall. She looked vague and lost, until we claimed her. Five minutes later, Ella and Wolfgang scurried through, holding hands and giggling like a couple of teenagers. Behind, a uniform pushed a trolley piled with plastic bags, unfamiliar suitcases and travel bags.

'Mum!' My eyes bubbled like a chalk-fed spring. I ducked under the barrier and grabbed. She dropped his hand and flung her arms round me.

When I could see again, Paul was shaking his hand. Wolfgang's face shone with health. The photo hadn't captured his effervescent well-being, sweating out of every pore along with the mingled smells of curry and perspiration.

'Hello,' he said in a strong German accent, 'you must be Vanessa. It is …' he took my right hand in two warm, cuddly paws. '… a very great pleasure to meet you.' He stooped over with a little difficulty, to kiss my hand. After that, I was putty. Paul capitulated half way along the motorway on the National Express coach.

The Literature on older age is explicit. Optimists with partners live longer. Sociable people with good quality of life measures and high levels of well-being are the darlings of epidemiology. There was no doubt about it. Mum had done herself proud.

4.3

Among the empty Exercise shelves, I spotted a figure hunched on a hop-up stool.

'Rosa.' Tears streamed silently down her face. I made my way along the narrow gangway and hefted off my rucksack. Crouching down, I stroked her arm. 'What's the matter?'

'Nessie … ' I waited. Tears streamed faster. Rosa was not a friend, like Xiu. All I really knew about her was that she was from Shanghai. I reached into my rucksack pocket. Rosa studied the tissue I handed her for a few seconds, then collapsed her face in it. She looked about fourteen, although she was at least twenty-two.

Here I was, Mum again. 'What happened?' She looked at me blankly. 'No hurry, take your time.'

Eventually, Rosa straightened a bit. 'Jenny says I have to … ' She still stumbled over every long word, even after eight months in England. 'Re ... re-submit my last assign ... ment in two weeks.' She kneaded the tissue into a chewed-up sausage.

'Re-submit in two weeks?'

'It did not pass. It got D.' The tears started all over again.

'Oh, that's awful.'

'No, Nessie, that is not all.'

'There is more?'

'Oh yes.' I waited, while she cried some more. The difficulty of explaining her misery in a second language made me ashamed I still didn't know a single word of Chinese.

'I am already late with my re ... search prop ... osal. It should be in … '

'I know. It should have been in six weeks ago. What does Jenny say?'

'She is very good to me. She sits with me today to help with assign ... ment. She shows me what sec ... tions to write again.'

'And is she helping with your proposal?

'She is not my diss ... diss ... er ... tation super ... visor. Scott is super ... vising me.'

'And what does he say?'

'He say,' she said so quietly, I barely understood. 'I no work hard enough. I don't read enough papers for my proposal to ready. He give me one week more. If I don't have proposal ready in one week, he say I cannot research in this year.'

'Oh Rosa!' I took a breath, scared by the real thing. 'How do you feel about that?'

'It make me feel I can't go on,' she said urgently, in tears again.

'You feel you can't go on with the course?'

She looked at me for a moment. 'No,' she whispered. 'I can't go home if I fail course. My mother and father will not take me back home.'

I closed my eyes. I imagined pressure from all the grown-ups, squeezing her. I listened to her breathing, waiting for it to slow again. In a while I said carefully, 'So you're behind on two assignments. Now Scott is saying he won't let you get on to the research and finish the course. I understand that bit. Tell me about your parents not taking you back home.'

'In China is impor ... tant. My mother and father are doctors. My mother is heart surgeon in Shanghai and my father is ... emer ... gency room doctor. Very impor ... tant people in Shanghai. They expect me to be doctor too, but I want to be, you know, sport scientist.' She leant her head against the grey metal bookrack, her face pale and exhausted.

'Uh-huh.' So China had pushy parents, too.

'We have many argu ... ments. In the end they say, you come here get Masters then take PhD back home. But since I come here, I get low marks all way through. I work hard all time, Nessie, but still I don't get good marks to pass for PhD.' I don't think she'd ever looked straight at me, before today.

I nodded. High marks were elusive on the course. When she didn't say any more, I probed. 'Not good enough for a PhD?'

'Not in England but maybe in Chinese, if I can finish Masters here.'

'Mmm … Rosa, you must be really clever to have passed at all, writing in English.' She looked me, but said nothing. I pressed on. 'Does anyone help you with your work?'

'We all help each other with the assign ... ments.'

'The Chinese students …?'

'Yes, but now the others have fin ... ished all their assign .. ments and have started research. I am late by six weeks … so they do not have time to help me now.'

'Have you asked Scott to help you?'

She shook her head. 'Scott is always busy.'

'Would you like me to talk to Scott? I am your student rep, after all.'

'You will talk to Scott?'

'When do you think you can finish the proposal?'

Rosa wrinkled her forehead. 'I think two weeks after my assignment for Jenny.'

'That would take you to the end of April. That will be too late for the race.'

'Yes, I know.'

'But you can still finish your dissertation by the middle of September?'

'I think so.'

'I'll e-mail you as soon as I've seen Scott.' I collected up my rucksack and confidently doubled back to the Department. Years of teaching suggested that Rosa wasn't as desperate as she'd first appeared. She'd cheered up reasonably quickly. On the other hand, I thought she deserved better customer service than that.

Ron Rawlins was with Scott. 'Come in, Nessie. What can I do for you?' Scott's smile lit me up. I basked. He should be a pushover.

Ron Rawlins looked up. It was strange to see a tie in the department. 'Good morning, my dear. How are you?'

'I'm very well. What a nice surprise to see you.' I wondered if he remembered our last meeting. 'Hi Scott. Ahm, I've just been talking to Rosa in the Library.'

'Mmm?'

'She was really upset. I said I'd come and talk to you.'

Ron raised an eyebrow. Scott glanced over at him. 'Why would that be, Nessie?'

'Rosa was in a panic about the two assignments she has to complete before she can start on her research. She can't see how she is going to finish both assignments, within two weeks.'

'Why is that your problem, Nessie?' Scott's voice stayed level.

'Err.' Scott's face set in a lined mask. 'Well two reasons really.' I ploughed on, ignoring the signs. 'One, I'm the student rep and she asked me to. Rosa's English isn't that good that she can stick up for herself in an argument, so it seemed like a reasonable thing to offer to do for her. Second

…' I paused. 'She … she's being pressurized by her parents back in Shanghai, so I was concerned. Maybe she's desperate enough to … you know, do something silly.'

There was a pause.

'What does she want?'

'Four more weeks, to complete both pieces of work.'

Ron stood up. 'If you'll excuse me, I'll get on with this.' He lifted a sheet of paper with another university logo, full of handwritten boxes. 'Come back to me, once you've sorted out Vanessa's concerns, Scott.'

'Thanks very much, Ron. I appreciate it.'

'Goodbye, my dear.'

Scott turned back to me, looking grim. The lines on either side of his mouth creased in deep verticals. 'She'll take four weeks, if we give it and then ask for more.'

'She knows she's missed the research window for the race.'

'She had no hope of getting her act together for that. That's only for the fast-track few.'

'Oh?'

'She shouldn't be on this course in the first place, Nessie. We have people like this every year with inadequate intellectual or English language skills. That is despite our best efforts to monitor their qualifications before we accept them.'

'But the Department did take her on and accepted her fees. Surely you have some sort of obligation to see her through?'

Scott folded his arms, switched off. 'No, none at all. If she chose to come here, she must accept the consequences of her decision, whether that means success or failure. She'll go back to her parents with a certificate or diploma for what she has achieved.'

'That's hard, Scott. She's not speaking or writing in her own language. The marks she's getting can't be a valid reflection of her intellectual ability, surely?

'Those are the rules of the game. You're over-reacting, Nessie.'

'But Scott, Jenny is helping Rosa with her referred assignment.'

'That's Jenny's choice. I don't have that sort of time to waste on non-starters.'

'But …'

'No buts.' And that was the best I could do for Rosa. He turned back to his computer. 'Oh yes, one other thing. Can you send me your poster again, please. I'm afraid Reprographics have lost it.'

It occurred to me, when I was outside in the corridor. I'd been too angry on Rosa's behalf, to feel embarrassed. And, that I'd left my rucksack in his office.

***

Plans for the race were going well. Once Nick and Kirsty had potted a regional news spot, punters poured in. Jonathan and Hugh managed the burgeoning website and Kirsty persuaded all sorts of experts to contribute to the on-line training Pit Stop. Each week, more and more students turned up at the gym for their free sessions in return for participating in the exam research. Even I started training again.

'Hi, Nick,' I shouted, flitting by one lunchtime. I couldn't hear his answer over the hum of people, machines and an underlying bass thump.

There was an empty saddle on the cycle next to Sarah Rees. She recognised me and looped her headset down, still peddling. 'Busy, isn't it?'

'Yeah, it's all the extra people training for *Run for Results*.'

'*Run* …?'

'*Run for Results*. Haven't you heard about it?'

'No, 'fraid not. Is it a marathon or something?'

'No, only 5k. We wanted to encourage inactive students to run, and it's part of a bigger research project for the department. You're welcome to join in.'

She sounded vague. 'When is it?'

'Whit Monday.'

'Yeah, … I might do. I'm still here then.'

'Oh, are you off to the Canaries again?'

'No. As a matter of fact, I've got a new job.'

'Really? Whereabouts?'

'Cambridge.'

'Oh.' I cranked up the resistance on the bike, so I was cycling up a steep hill. 'Not … at the University?'

'Yes indeed.'

'Sarah! Congratulations! What fantastic news. When do you start?'

'1st July.'

'Oh … What will you do about Bertie?'

'I think he'll stay here during the week. He's settled, now. We've found, or rather, Alan found, an au pair last week. I'm not too worried about him.' Did she normally worry about either of her menfolk?

'Bertie must have grown. He'll be … seven months? What's he doing now?'

'Oh usual things: lots of giggling … sitting up, reaching out. He loves Rosa.'

'Rosa?'

'Yes, the new au pair. She's a Chinese student from the university who's dropped out.'

'Dropped out? Rosa? Do you mean Rosa from our Department?'

'I've no idea where she came from. Alan would know. He's after the scalp of the person who was so unhelpful to her. Something about the pastoral care of post-grad students. If she gets as far as complaining formally, it will show up on the next assessment.'

'But … but, I know Rosa. I, er, approached someone in the Department on her behalf, last week. She didn't say anything to me about quitting.'

'Well, I wouldn't get involved in too much complaining if I were you. It's not good for your career prospects. Let Alan sort it out. Ah, that's me done. Time for lunch.' She dismounted and towelled the bike saddle dry. 'I'll ask Alan if he's interested in the run. He started fitness training after Christmas, too.'

'How are you doing, Sarah?' Nick looked more like Wills every time I saw him.

'Nick, hi there.' Sarah stuck out her now-deflated boobs as she dried the handlebars.

'Nessie!' Nick stepped past her and gave me a fulsome kiss on the cheek. 'Howya doing?' I cosied up and returned the kiss.

'Good, thank you, Nick. How are the entries?' Sarah looked startled and melted away.

'Inundated! Passed five hundred, yesterday.' Nick flashed me a toothy white smile. I didn't know him well enough to ask if he'd just had an NHS Scale and Polish or was it one of the new private bleach jobbies.

'Fantastic!'

'I'm not sure if the gym can cope with many more. But it's great to see it buzzing.'

'I'm seeing more runners outside, too.'

'Running training's completely full. As a matter of fact, I came over to ask if you could take on someone as their mentor. Just once a week, until the race. I know you run regularly.'

'Right, er sure.' I last ran in December, but I wasn't going to broadcast that.

'She could do with some encouragement. Here's her e-mail address. Honestly, Nessie, it will be easy, Sophie's a bit of a pathetic girlie-wobbler.'

'Nick!' I took the scrap of paper. 'Poor girl, of course I'll help her.'

'You'll see what I mean. Have you persuaded the Prof to join today?'

'Prof? Do you mean Alan Rathbone? He might do, Sarah said.'

'No I was talking about Mrs Rathbone, our ex-English track star.'

'Really?'

'The new Professor Rees.'

'What!'

'Sarah's pulled a chair at Cambridge.'

'And I asked her if her new job was at the University! No wonder she laughed.'

'Rumour has it …' Nick started and half-turned to wave. 'Bye Sarah. See you later, Scott.' He turned back to me. 'Now have you got time to sit down and go through …'

'I'm sorry, Nick, there's an SPSS workshop at two, down in the nuclear bunker. Can we make it tomorrow?'

4.4

A couple of weeks later, Scott's e-mail arrived.

Good news. The poster has been accepted. See you later?

I sped up to the department, bright-eyed with the implied forgiveness. Scott's door stood open. 'Hi, I got your e-mail.'

He looked up from his screen. 'Pleased?'

'Thrilled, more like!'

He looked amused. 'Are you going to book for the conference now?'

I put my rucksack down for a moment. 'Well, er, yes, I think so. Will I enjoy it?'

'Of course you will. I'll send the details through. You'll get a student rate.' He turned back to his computer, then paused. 'Have you finished that first chapter of yours yet?

'No, Scott.' I was aghast. 'I've been much too busy with my Ageing module.'

'When will that be finished?' He gave me a full-on Lovejoy look.

'Friday, I think. I'm going as fast as I can,' I panicked.

'The clock ticks ever faster.'

'Yeah ... That pretty much sums it up.' He still had that amused glint in his eyes. The contact lenses, I told myself.

'Someone needs to pick up the poster from Reprographics.'

'Oh, I can do that on Friday.'

'Great. Now, is your introduction ready to go?'

'I guess ...' He clicked the mouse and stood up. He walked over to his easy chairs and flopped down, motioning me down, too.

'Sure of your research problem?' His sudden interest spun a warm cocoon round me. My aura, could he have seen it, was deep rose-pink.

'Well,' I took a breath. I wasn't ready for a consultation. 'I think the problem is, whether a carbohydrate drink can make a real difference to an average exerciser.'

'And what's your gut feeling?' I looked into his eyes. Was Scott making a joke or not? I frowned, forcing myself back on track.

'It seems likely to me, from what I've read, that water is just as good, for an hour of recreational exercise.'

'Why's that a problem?'

'Because there's a vast industry out there selling carbohydrate drinks in the sports marketplace.'

'And why's that a problem?'

Where's this going? I could hardly throw a question back, so I stayed schtum.

He said, after a pause, 'So how do you attribute the better results that you've read about with elite athletes?'

'I don't really think we're comparing apples with pears here,' I launched off, confidently enough. 'Athletes are different. Their psychological motivation, standards of fitness and skill levels are all honed by comparison with recreational exercisers, so their performance is much more …' Up to that point, I had been fine. I had stunned myself by my articulate delivery, a first in front of Scott.

I groped for a word, hidden away in the geriatric regions of my memory, which immediately refused to reveal itself. 'Well … err …. on a level … you know.' I teetered off the tightrope and felt myself falling. I screwed up my eyes, to avoid Scott's confused expression.

Scott frowned. '… inherently stable; less dependent on unstable mediators?'

'Y ... yeah,' I said, my notebook and pencil sliding to the floor in embarrassment.

'So the promising results after a carb drink, might either come from ingestion in the gut or still, maybe, from something else?'

'Mmm,' I tried, groping on the floor with my foot. It was no good, the pen had disappeared.

'And the something else?'

I girded my loins to enter the fray again. It was the only way to impress him. 'Psy ... psychological, or maybe other, phsi … shit … physio ... log ... ic ... al … er … things.'

'Ah,' he said, 'that's pretty much where the literature brings us. You've been reading the mouthwash study.'

'I can't put in a mouthwash as well, Scott,' I panicked. 'It's complicated enough organising a glucose solution and a placebo drink that taste exactly the same.'

'No, no.' I was mortified to realise that he was trying not to laugh at me. 'I thought you were going to measure well-being? I'm sure that's what you put in your research proposal. What about your ordinary populations?' Scott used a clean, academic nail to rub some speck from his forefinger.

'I think,' I grabbed a definite lifeline. 'Positive results are much more likely, simply from believing the drink will do you good.'

Scott looked at his watch and smiled sweetly. 'Nearly lunchtime. I think that's enough for one day. Remember what I said in lectures. Just keep refining your research question, so in the end you reach the tiny part that's solvable out of the bigger problem.'

'Yeah, thanks Scott.' I smiled back at him. Now I was looking, he really did have the nicest hands.

***

'Good afternoon, I've come to collect the poster for Dr Woodhouse in Exercise and Nutrition.' I rested my elbows inquiringly on several reams of paper mounded on the Print Services counter. The background swishing and clunking of the photocopier sounded like a speeding train.

'I'll just go and check, love.' The Print lady disappeared. There was a pause. I studied the price list and samples on the wall. I tried leaning a shoulder against the metal racks or a bottom against the counter. I recalled Hugh's research on increased physical activity in the university workplace, and wondered if he was to blame for the lack of chairs.

'It's just being done now. Won't be a jiffy.' She wriggled her maroon overall. 'Chilly wind this afternoon, isn't it?' She set to work on the invoice.

'Yeah, it's not very summery yet.' Outside, a brown paper bag was chasing a McDonald's carton round and round the cobbled alleyway. It must be freezing up here in the middle of winter.

'Can you sign this, please.' She disappeared again. 'Here we are.'

My poster, in all its glory.

'Wow!' I said. 'That looks wonderful. *The lived experience of decreased … morality … rates in a sample of the U.K.'s ageing population.* Ohh.'

'What's the matter?' She turned back to me.

'There's a typo,' I said apologetically.

'Oh no. Where?' She settled her glasses half-way down her nose.

'You see this? It's only one letter. It should be *the lived experience of decreased mortality*, but it's come out as *morality* instead.'

She peered at the title. 'Does it make any difference, then, dearie?'

'It's vital.' I said, wondering if I could afford the replacement.

'Wait a minute. I'll go and have a word.'

A thirty-ish woman with a beach-blond crewcut and a pincushion full of pierced appendages appeared. I sized her up.

'Err, well you see, I'm afraid I made a typing mistake and …'

'That's a good one,' she said, transferring her chewing gum to the side of her cheek. 'Down to you, is it?'

'Yeah, it was me, I'm afraid. It's been accepted for a conference.'

'No problem. We'll sort it out for you right away.'

'What shall I do with this one?' I asked as they rolled the corrected version up for me. 'Oh, you'd better lose it quietly. Give it here, I'll tuck them both in together.'

***

I woke up sweating, in the middle of the night. In a few seconds I was bolt-upright awake. Arrangements crowded my head.

I'd briefed the marshals yesterday lunchtime. In any case, with Kirsty on the public address system, I was no longer solely responsible for incident control, thank goodness. The area round the university and roads up to the common were closing at 12.00, ready for the runners. There would be diversions and traffic chaos, but that was a police issue. Five finely-tuned brains and one recycled other had spent several hours anticipating problems. The event we'd planned so meticulously had finally arrived. Perhaps it was just excitement. I humped over in bed.

My own experiment was ready, apart from mixing the carbohydrate drink and the placebo, first thing in the morning. No reason to be nervous. I'd pilot-tested everything in sight, booked experimental psychology booths for testing my participants, before and after the race. Cathy was geared up, ready to go. The affect instrument was photocopied ready to capture the data. I even had twenty fully-signed up, consenting participants.

Dawn was breaking. I pushed the duvet down. Considering it was a Bank Holiday, the weather forecast was unbelievably good. After all that worrying about rain, snow or gales, it was going to be hot. Water! Yes, I must phone Kirsty first thing. We needed to organise more water for the competitors.

I woke again at 6.30 am, alert and ready. I pottered round, making tea and muesli, going up for a shower.

Mum's large green jug held a litre of liquid. I filled two plastic containers with water, ready to dilute the solution. Then, I realised. The carbohydrate wasn't on board. The large plastic tub of white powder was sitting in the women's changing room of the gym, where I'd left it last night. I looked at my watch. Eight-thirty. The Sports Centre would be open already. Just time to get up there and back if I got a move on.

I whipped Smartie into full-on acceleration, only to find the university precinct already closed to traffic. A big-enough gap appeared for my tiny car. I drove full into the kerb, leaving the stern abeam with the Mercedes to my left, jumped out and sprinted up to the precinct. There were several white police vehicles cruising around already. White-suited figures were cordoning off the area. How efficient. It reminded me of the fire drill at the beginning of the year. I smiled to myself. It would be me insisting on getting into the Sports Centre this time.

4.5

'Can I come through?' I used my jolly hockey sticks voice on the police woman at the entrance.

'I'm afraid not, madam. The building is closed for the time being.' My smile slipped.

'Closed? Oh no, I need to get in. I'm the race committee, you see.' I sounded like Alan, at the beginning of the year.

'I'm afraid we have closed the whole area. We are waiting for the Bomb Disposal Incident Team to arrive. I must ask you to move back, please.'

I ran to Smartie. What was I to do?

This was an emergency. Paul wasn't in. I sent a text message.

left carb powder in womens at sports centre they wont let me collect it phone me please nessie xxx

Not wanting to be flummoxed for long, I decided that my best bet was to buy some sport drink. I drove as fast as I dared to the university swimming pool. Three bottles wasn't ten, but it was a start.

Nine-twenty. I picked up my mobile again.

'Midge, what do you think I should do? When I went up to the Sports Centre for my carbohydrate solution, it was closed by a bomb scare. I don't know when I'll be able to get in. The solution's got to be up there by 11.45, just before the race starts.'

'Hang on, I'm nearly ready to leave. I'll come down, but I'll have to bring the kids.'

'Oh Midge, thanks.'

'Now, have you got any lemon squash?'

'Err, yes, I think so.'

'Sugar, or low calorie?'

'Low calorie. That's for the placebo.'

'Well, you need the sugary stuff, as well.'

'Do I? For the kids?'

'No Nessie, not for the kids. Enough to make up ten litres of solution. Get up to ASDA now!'

She arrived at the boat at 10.11 a.m.

'Sit down there, Freya. No you can't go outside, Harry.' She glared at them until they subsided onto the saloon berth. Freya was dressed in a pink fairy costume and plastic see-through raincoat. She took off her pink fairy rucksack and started unpacking the contents. Pink ballet shoes, pink alice band … 'We've just got back from ballet lesson.' Midge looked embarrassed to the depths of her urban combat hot weather gear.

'You're wonderful to help! Now, here's the lemon squash …'

'We're going to make up a dioralyte solution. You've got some salt, haven't you?'

'Yes. Why is Freya wearing a raincoat in this heat?'

Midge solemnly added ten pinches of salt to each plastic can of squash. 'Got it for her birthday last week and she's insisted on wearing it ever since. Thinks she's a fairy, packaged up for her imaginary friend. Ta-da. What do you think?' We compared our samples carefully.

'The sports drink looks more orangey than lemon. Oh, why didn't I buy orange squash?'

'Too late now. Harry, where are you? Nessie, is it alright if they explore the boat?'

'Fine. Just be careful, kids.' Harry reappeared. He dropped his jeans in a heap on the floor and stepped out. He emptied the contents of a Tesco carrier into another heap.

'It should be a more golden colour. Not as obviously lemon squashy as this is.'

'What do you have that's golden and liquid? Any food colouring?'

'No …'

'Drat, I've got some at home, from Freya's birthday cake last week. No time now.'

'Worcester sauce?'

'Try a teaspoon.' A diminutive Captain Jack Sparrow started to emerge from the clothes pile. When he'd done, he disappeared up forward into my cabin.

We looked at a sample. 'No, too dirty-looking.'

'Syrup?'

'It'll make the placebo too full of calories.'

'Tomato ketchup?'

'Let's try.'

I transferred a little squash into another glass and stirred red gloop round with a teaspoon. 'Oh no, there's all bits in the solution now. That won't do. Midge, we've only got ten minutes.' I looked round the cabin, determined to succeed. 'Got it!' I dove for the food locker, grabbing the bottle of Islay. 'This is dark and golden.'

'Alcohol?' She gauged my desperation for a moment. 'OK. Let's do it.'

'What do you think the Ethics Committee would say?' I asked, nervously adding a tablespoonsful to each ten litres.

'They won't know. For goodness sake, get on with it. Look, hold the funnel still.' Midge grabbed the bottle from me and slopped a cupful into each canister. 'It's no good if it looks like gnat's pee.'

'Midge! We can't have them getting drunk.'

'Oh for goodness sake. This is medicinal.' She shook one of the canisters. 'How do they look now?'

'Perfect. Quick, let's get them into the litre bottles.'

'I'll do that, while you get the rest of your stuff together. Are your tests ready to go?'

'Yeah, they're here.'

'Kids! Come and put these lids on for Nessie,' she yelled, flicking the funnel into the next bottle.

Harry re-appeared. He was still minus any trousers, but he had picked up my only high heels en route. His hands and forearms were grubby from the mascara he'd brushed into his long curly lashes.

'Be careful you don't spill any, Harry.' Sticking his tongue out through his teeth, Harry started on the plastic lids with infinite care.

Freya's round, pink face looked even hotter and sweatier.

I said, 'I've marked up the names. Can you stick the labels on for me, please, Freya?'

'I want some orange, Mummy.'

'What do you say, Freya?'

'What about some smoothie? I've got a very special one here.' When I came back from delving in the fridge, the labels were finished. Each one had its own artistic slant and dark, sweaty signature.

'No time to change it. I just hope she didn't get them mixed up.'

'Well you certainly can't tell the difference now,' said Midge. 'Have you got a cloth?'

'Yes, next to the stove.' Midge whizzed round my tiny kitchen area. Within five minutes, the evidence disappeared. *Iris* looked shipshape and Bristol fashion, on the surface at least.

'Right, GO!' shouted Midge. 'I'll lock up. See you up there.'

'Thanks, you guys,' I said. Johnny Depp shook his cutlass at me. 'I would have been keel-hauled, without you three.'

***

The runners gathered in the remaining part of the precinct.

'Everything OK?' I looked round the empty room. It was 11.15. 'Where are they all?'

'They're students. It will be fine. You get on with all your other jobs. See you back here with the papers, at the end.' I left Cathy with two crates of jungle juice.

My next task was to locate the ambulance men and check the marshals into position round the course. After that, if everything ran smoothly, I'd be superfluous. At 11.45, I sneaked back to the experimental lab. Students sat in booths, ticking little boxes. Cathy and Steve stood at the door, checking in participants and checking out bottles of carbohydrate and placebo drink.

Cathy smirked. 'Told you it would be alright.' I breathed a sigh. We were back on track. My little senior moment could be forgotten.

Jonathan and the IT team had set up makeshift tables in the concourse to process the throng. Vasulu sat, absorbed in his laptop. His regression analyses, probably. I grabbed Hugh.

'Morning Nessie. Loop this round your ear. Here's the mike.' He clipped it on for me. I began to feel like Madonna and perked up. 'OK you don't have to change into a black suit.'

'What?'

'Security for Mr President?' I looked down my front. I still wore my grubby jeans, which I'd thrown on first thing this morning. Yesterday's teeshirt was crumpled, hot and humid. Hugh was cool in baggy shorts and a pristine Blooper teeshirt.

'Joke?' he faltered. Goodness, he was scared of me.

I was too hot already. 'Sorry, yeah ... So long as I hear any shouts.'

The Azores high had steamed up Britain. Shocking-green leaves on the lime trees shimmied in a feeble, northerly breeze against an electric-blue background. In the roads round the university, cars bumped up on pavements, playing sticky witch with police no waiting signs. Bunches of onlookers gathered in the interstices, buffering dehydration with cans and bottles.

A television car parked close by the starting tape. Adjacent to Senate House, Scott and Kirsty lounged against the staging. Ron joined them, with the friend I'd seen in the supermarket. Scott shook hands; Kirsty kissed him. Then the metallic shell of Kirsty's voice boomed out over the loudspeakers.

Five hundred runners massed. Most of them wore casual summer shorts and tees, but every now and then a serious runner in lycra stretched and crouched and made little jogging starts.

About five minutes to twelve, the Vice Chancellor and his wife appeared from Senate House to start the race. The VC had grizzled grey hair, a spotless, open-neck silk shirt and trim waist. He was instantly recognisable. His sandy-coloured suit and panama hat were probably indispensable in the diplomatic tropics. They shook hands all round, chatting to Ron, until Kirsty was ready. He mouthed a short speech which I couldn't hear and let fly the start ribbon.

Practically the first runners through were Sarah in lycra and Alan, in singlet and shorts, self-consciously smiling for the television camera. As they passed me, Sarah spurted off with the other front runners, leaving Alan in her wake.

Judging by his face, Alan wanted to wail, 'Wait for me!' but didn't have enough breath.

I cheered them on. By the time Lucy Welsh and Jenny trotted by, nostalgia welled in my eyes. It reminded me of all the other sports days I'd organised.

A bottleneck of bodies waited to turn right as I set off for the Common. The last hundred walkers caught them up, briskly chatting. Fifty metres down the road, Rosa pushed Bertie. She looked even tinier than usual, behind the man-sized buggy, deep-loaded with designer-baby impedimenta.

I slowed. 'Hello Rosa. How are you?'

She looked happier. 'I'm good, Nessie. How you?'

'I'm excited. Are you following the race round?'

'I don't know. I have camera to take pictures of Alan and Sarah.'

'I know a short cut to the common. Do you want to follow me?'

We trotted off down the deserted return route, hearing disjointed claps and cheers a street away. We jogged the deserted tarmac road, since bikes and cars cluttered the stone pavement. Even pushing the buggy, it wasn't far, only a kilometre. Scott had cunningly worked out a route to take the runners all round the houses, before they reached the common.

'You've only missed the leaders by about a minute,' Midge said, as we panted up to the turning onto the common. 'Lucy Welsh was first through.'

'Hello, Freya. Aren't you hot, still in that plastic mac? What about Sarah?'

'Oh, comfortably in the first twenty.'

'Where's Harry?'

'Over there.' Captain Sparrow was engaged in hand to hand fighting, still minus his trousers.

A gaggle of runners pounded by. 'Go fr'it!' I yelled into the morning. Rosa jumped.

'Help!'

What was that? I looked round wildly, before I realised that my headset was bleating.

I nearly gave my phone number. 'Hello, Nessie here.'

'Nessie, it's Xiu. There's a pile up.'

'Where are you?'

'At the 3K marker. Most of the runners have already come through. Get the First Aiders! Oh …' and she lurched into Mandarin.

'OK,' Kirsty broke in. 'Did you read that, Pete? Can you get the ambulance down there, please?'

'Roger, 3K marker. The traffic's jammed right round the common. I'll try overland. Four minutes.'

'Quick,' I said to Rosa, 'there's some trouble at the … oh, look, over there.' I pelted for the mangle of bodies, leaving Rosa and Midge to follow.

Already, the heap was sorting out. Between laughter and good-natured raillery, most of the participants were up and running again. At the bottom of the pile, a singlet and pair of shorts lay in the road. Xiu diverted the runners round him. I dodged through the crowd.

The casualty was on his back. 'Alan, Alan! Can you hear me?'

No response. Oh my God. I bent down to open his airway. His skin was dry, but much warmer than Resusci-Annie's. I bent my head to feel and listen for signs of breathing. Nothing. Quickly, I put the heel of my left hand on his breastbone between the light blue bumps of his nipples. I linked my right hand over my left and compressed firmly. It was shockingly real after practising with cool plastic and mechanical tubing only a month earlier.

'Urrrgh,' said the body. He was hot, dry, pale, and alive. I breathed again.

'Kirsty, Kirsty, there is one breathing casualty.' I turned back to the casualty. 'Are you OK?'

Alan opened his eyelids and immediately screwed them up against the sun overhead.

'Errrgh …'

'Can we have the ambulance and first aid team here, now! Hurry!' I yelled into my mike.

'OK, Nessie, they'll be along in a couple of minutes, now.' Kirsty sounded calm from the other end.

'Are you in pain?' I asked Alan.

'I don't …,'

'Alan!' Rosa cleared the crowd with Bertie's buggy. 'What happened, Alan?'

'Just lay there,' I said authoritatively, as he tried to sit up. Wait for the paramedic before you start moving please, er, sir.'

Alan was at eye level with Bertie, strapped in his pushchair like a geriatric Biggles. 'Darling, Daddy will be alright in a moment. No, don't cry. Daddy be with you in a minute.'

'Please, Alan,' I put my hand firmly on his chest, as he tried to pull himself up. 'We don't know what's wrong. Please just lay there quietly.'

I thought to myself. He's not grey and clammy. No chest pain. And where's his sense of impending doom? You can't have a heart attack in a first aid book without a sense of impending doom.

'How are you feeling?'

Alan put a tentative hand up to feel his neck. 'My neck ...'

'Where's the casualty,' Steve steamed up like a heart surgeon from a tv documentary. Within seconds, he had ploughed into deep assessment. I stood by, like a spare part.

'There's an ECG in the van,' he said. 'We need to get this gentleman inside. In view of his age and recent strenuous physical activity, I'd like to be driving down to the hospital as we wire him up.'

'Sure,' I said. Paramedics know best, don't they?

'Alan is in danger, I go with him,' said a voice from under my arm.

The paramedic looked round at the gridlock of traffic. 'We'll have trouble, getting through this lot. I'd best call in the Air Ambulance.' He spoke into his mike.

'Rosa, we need to get hold of Sarah. Can you find her?'

'Sarah will finish race soon. You look after Bertie. Take him to Sarah. Here, car keys.'

'NO! I protest,' bellowed Alan, behind me. Rosa thrust the set of keys at me.

'Sir, you must be strapped in for the helicopter.'

'I am not going in any helicopter!'

A minute and a half later, Alan was strapped onto the stretcher, neck encased in a support like a Bedlam patient in a strait-jacket. Rosa caught up and held one hand, still protesting from the straps. He was loaded into an ambulance, ten fat sausages waving furiously. The doors closed. The ambulance set off, inching along. I turned to leave, fumbling for the buggy brake with my foot. Much better than finding out what the Faculty Dean thought of the situation.

An overwhelmingly raucous clatter overhead set Bertie off again. As the helicopter came in to land, the ambulance stopped two hundred metres down the road and opened up, ready to transfer Alan.

Oh my God, I realised. I'm going to have to run like the wind to catch Sarah.

I set off at a fast trot, pushing the buggy in front of me like a chariot. Now the runners were through, their outward route would be clear. I dodged through jammed cars, trying to return to their usual parking spaces, while two policemen harvested traffic cones. Bertie stopped crying as his buggy joggled violently over cobblestones.

I could hear shouting, as the runners entered the final strait, uphill to the Senate House. I sprinted along, glad of my fitness and the short cut. The cheers grew louder. My back started to tweak in the old place. The roads converged at the top of the hill, near the finish line. My breath was short and my jeans chafed my jelly legs. I was no match for Sarah. She was in the lead, with the next runner nearly two hundred metres behind. Beyond the finishing line, the whole of the university precinct was cordoned off by new, fluttery incident tapes. Goodness knows where the finished runners would go. The confusion of people about to descend on that narrow strip of road, didn't bear thinking about.

'Sarah!' I shouted, as I hit the finishing line. She was a hundred metres away, leaning forward on her thighs, lost in the exhaustion of the moment. 'Sarah!' I shouted again, just as a camera nosed over the shoulder of an immaculate woman in full war-paint, carrying a microphone.

'Splendid! What a fantastic level of fitness to run the race in under 20 minutes, pushing a buggy. Well done, Paula Radcliffe. Your many fans will be delighted to hear you're back, after your pregnancy.'

'Paula?' I gasped, confused, but smiling at the cameraman, in case he was filming me. 'Paula who? My name's Nessie Elliott.'

'Oh, I'm err…' The reporter's smile tailed off, as she took in my bedraggled and sweaty, anonymous physical self.

The helicopter roared overhead, drowning out her words. It flew so low, the windows of the Senate House rattled. A down draught of air blasted the returning runners and waiting spectators, so that everyone stopped short. A Mum next to me hastily pulled her children into her skirt to protect them. On the podium, Ron, his partner, Scott, Kirsty, the VC and his wife crouched and held their ears like a Battle of Britain ground crew. Just behind the finishing line, runners stalled in painful slow motion.

The cameraman was already twenty metres away, filming the developing chaos around us. He jumped onto a low wall, but was overwhelmed by a scrum of runners, crossing the line. Finishers piled up, second by second, until it began to look like the final battleground from *The Lord of the Rings*.

'Oh er, thank you.' The reporter turned to battle towards his camera crew. I pulled my hands away from Bertie's ears.

He looked at me and giggled. I could imagine how Alan was taking it. There'd be hell to pay. Sarah was pulling away, heading for Ron and the VC. I lunged and pushed through the milling crowd. Bertie's battering-ram buggy barked the shins of several unwary runners.

Sarah already stood on the podium, talking to the VC and Scott.

'Sarah,' I hissed. 'Here's Bertie.'

'Excuse me, madam,' said a low voice by my side. 'I wonder if you could come this way, please?'

I looked round. A familiarly-bearded policeman stood alongside.

'Err … sure. What's the problem? Hang on a minute, I need to pass the baby.'

'Sarah? I've brought Bertie …'

Sarah bent down over the railing. 'If Rosa has gone with him, Alan will be fine. Can you look after Bertie, Nessie, while I change?'

'Sorry, I'm needed by the police.' Sarah looked startled. 'No, not like that,' I added quickly, in case she thought I was a criminal.

'Oh, alright.'

I walked a few steps. 'Buggar, I've still got Sarah's car keys.' I dodged back. 'Now, how can I help?' We cleared through the crowd.

4.6

'Come this way.' He showed me into one of the white vans: an incident control version of a mobile Breast Screening Unit. Motioned me to sit down.

'Are you Ms Nessie Elliott?'

'Erm, yes.'

'Now Ms Elliott, we have a few questions to ask.'

'Fire away.' I was cheerful. The race had been a success. I basked in the buzz.

'I wonder if I can ask you about your visits to the Sports Centre over the last few days?'

'Why yes, I've been up and down to the Sports Centre no end of times this last week, getting ready for the race.'

'And have you ever had in your possession a parcel addressed to you, which you took to the women's changing room of the gym?'

'Oh yes. You've found it?'

'What are the contents of the parcel, please madam?'

'Oh, a glucose powder, to mix up for the race today. Have you brought it down for me?'

'No, Mrs Elliott, the Bomb Disposal Team is just examining it. They've had several incidents to investigate, today. Animal rights activists working overtime, so it seems. Would you be an animal lover yourself?'

Yes, of course, I am. I've got a cat.'

'And would you describe yourself as anti-vivisectionist?'

There was a knock on the door. 'Excuse me, please.' The uniform left. I had a sudden prescient feeling that all was not well.

The small room was swelteringly hot. I couldn't remember whether I'd put on any anti-perspirant this morning, either. I stood up. There was a small pane of glass, looking out over the Sports Centre, and another into the reception area of the van. The interior window was partly blocked by a light blue shirt, but I could see across, through a remaining strip. A tubby man stood by the open door, mobile phone clapped to his ear.

Out of the other, exterior window, I saw a white van stop. A figure climbed down from the driver's seat. It looked like Paul. I stared. It was Paul.

A security man went over and they chatted for a couple of minutes. Then Paul went round to the back of his van and pulled on a white suit and rubber gloves, still talking. Poor man, having to wear painter's overalls on such a hot afternoon. Whatever was he doing, decorating the IT department?

I watched Paul disappear inside the Sports Centre. A couple of minutes later, he returned carrying a large plastic tub of paint, waved at the security guard, got into his van, and drove away at walking pace through the departing crowd.

I sat smoothing my new jeans. On the left leg, a dried patch of stickiness caught my hand, left over from the lemon squash this morning. I'd have to wash them, now. Whatever was going on? What on earth was Paul doing in the white van? He looked as if he knew the security guard quite well. Just as I listed some alternative theories in my head, the plain-clothes man opened the door.

He looked vaguely familiar, although I couldn't place him. His pneumatic waist rolled over the top of a worn black belt. Round his balding forehead and across his plump, flat nose, sweat beads glinted in the heat. I took an instant dislike to him. He looked as if he'd duff you over as soon as look at you.

'Good afternoon, my name is Fenton Squires, City Surveillance Unit. I'd like to ask you some questions.' His accent was pure East Enders.

I could feel the heat of battle-fury. 'Well, I'd like to ask you a question or two, first.' I countered. 'What's going on here? I'm supposed to be collecting in my research data, and I'm stuck here, waiting for you people to chat amongst yourselves.'

He drew back a little. Maybe he wasn't used to Viking warriorettes.

'Ms Elliott, this is no way to carry on if you want to get a job in government service when you leave university.'

'I beg your pardon? What are you talking about?'

'Ms Elliott. You live on a canal boat in the City Marina?'

'Yes that's correct.'

'Well, Ms Elliott, I don't know how much of a surprise this will be to you. The suspicious package found in this morning's bomb sweep didn't contain explosives.'

I put two and two together. I hadn't got 100% in my statistics exam for nothing. 'If it's the package I lost, it certainly doesn't.' I stood up ready to leave, angry as hell. 'Well, it's no use to me, now. Do what you like with it. You've wasted enough of my time.'

'Sit down, please. I'm just waiting for the Drugs Enforcement Agency to arrive, to examine the package. In the meantime, I have several more questions for you.'

'For me? What else do you need to ask me?'

'We'd like to know about your relationship with Mr Michael Hall, owner of the motor yacht, *Argosy*.'

'Mike? Yes, I know him. Not very well.'

'Have you ever been on board his vessel?'

'Once or twice.'

'Have you ever seen any illegal substances on board his yacht?'

'Errm. I don't think so, but it's always pretty full of gear.'

'And do you want to tell me about any illegal substances that you may have aboard your own vessel at present?'

'No, there aren't any.'

The bearded policeman knocked on the door. Fenton glanced at the photocopy he gave him. 'There seems to be some confusion about your name. Is your full name Vanessa Leah Elliott?

'Not quite. I'm Vanessa Geraldine Elliott.'

'But you're also known as Leah Elliott?'

'No. Leah Vanessa Elliott is my daughter.'

'So you occasionally use your daughter's name, instead of your own?'

'No!' I could feel adrenalin pumping round my heart, the beat thumping loud enough for Fenton to hear.

'Ms Elliott, we'd like to search your vessel for illegal substances, this afternoon.'

'Now? I hope you're not going to make a mess inside. I'm expecting my mother, the owner, back any day now.'

'And you're positive that you don't have any illegal substances such as cocaine, crack, heroin or marijuana that you would like to tell me about at this point?'

'Err, no. Not unless Mum has some ganja that she hasn't told me about.' I let slip a nervous giggle.

'How old is your mother, Ms Elliott?'

'Eighty-two.'

'So that's quite unlikely, isn't it?' He put down the sheet of paper. 'Are you prepared to accompany me down to the Marina?'

'Err, yes, I suppose so.'

He didn't use handcuffs, but he stayed so close, it felt like it. A crowd of people lolled around a day too nice to rush. Fortunately I didn't see anyone I knew, though the rest of the world stared. Fenton adroitly handled me into a police car and sat in beside me. I remembered my last police ride.

When we reached the marina, Paul waited in the car park. He followed us down to *Iris*. Three bruisers tailed him.

'Can you tell me what's going on here?' He spoke pleasantly enough, but Fenton pulled up short. Paul wielded the old aura of power, despite his casual shirt and shorts. He put an arm round my shoulder.

'Ms Elliott has given her permission to search this vessel.'

'What for?'

'We're searching for illegal substances.' I looked at the other men. They had bulges on their chests. Were they obese, too, or wearing guns?

Paul turned to me. 'You've agreed?'

'Why yes, I've got nothing to hide.'

'No damage,' said Paul firmly. 'If you need access, I'll open anywhere up for you.' He disappeared to fetch his tool box. Five of us crammed below. I sat stiff and silent on the saloon berth, as the three men searched. Once my imagination took hold, I shook. Paul read his newspaper, tool box at his feet. Fenton overloaded the cane chair and observed us steadily.

Over the next hour, suspicious objects filtered out from the searchers. Fenton examined each one, lining them up neatly along the table. A nearly empty tin of athlete's foot powder arrived which Fenton sniffed carefully. He discarded the perspex sea salt mill immediately. The dried milk powder, he tasted. My HRT tablets appeared next.

'Please don't pop them out,' I pleaded, too late. 'I haven't got any more at the moment.'

After a pause, a Marks and Spencer bag appeared. Fenton pulled out the box, and emptied Roger Rabbit, handling him delicately, like an unexploded bomb. He took the package to bits, examining the inside of the penis meticulously. 'Yours, sir, madam?'

'No, it must be my Mum's.' I squirmed bright red. I didn't dare look at Paul.

'It's ours,' lied Paul firmly, at the same time. Fenton looked at us speculatively, and added a Rampant Rabbit to the line of exhibits.

Then one of the guys appeared with a Barclaycard. Paul and I looked at one another. Fenton caught the look and pounced. 'Why was the Barclaycard secreted in the bilge?'

'No comment.'

His mobile rang. 'Yes.' He listened to a long spiel with raised eyebrows. 'How did that happen?' Suddenly, I sensed victory. I picked up my plastic card. It looked OK. I wondered if the magnetic stripe was affected by sewage.

'Really? I'll be up straight away.' He looked at me appraisingly. 'It seems the powder has disappeared. Someone's just left the packaging.' He paused. 'I haven't collected any evidence of wrongdoing. In fact, my guess is that you're clean.'

'Why do you think that?'

'We've taken an occasional interest in you, since you applied for government service.'

'But, I haven't applied for government service. The only person in the family who's that way inclined is … my daughter, Leah.' Fenton and I eyed each other up. 'And she is in South America.'

'Not according to my information.' He pulled out his BlackBerry. 'Let's see:

> *30 hour surveillance report requested for Leah Elliott, last known address Leeds, now living narrow boat, City Marina.*
> *See SIS application received 15th December. Please return result to this office.*
> *Regards, Anya Ramonovich.*

She obviously thinks you are Leah Elliott.'

'Well Anya Ramonovich doesn't exist, anymore. She's been a figment of the Foreign Office's imagination for some months now. Some incompetent other thought I was Leah.'

'Maybe you should check your facts more carefully in future, Officer,' said Paul in his Mr Reasonable voice.

Fenton shook his head regretfully. 'These days, you can only rely on the stuff you do yourself.'

Fenton stood up to shake Paul's hand and slipped him a card. 'Good day, sir. Very sorry to have bothered you both. If you do happen to notice any drugs changing hands down here, I'd be much obliged if you'd contact me immediately.'

He looked at me with his clever piggy eyes as he shook my hand. 'Nice work, Mrs Elliott. If you really managed to pull that one off, I'm sure they'd be very interested in employing you.'

***

We sat on the warm cabin roof that evening. There wasn't time to chill the wine: I was desperate. Small groups strolled round the side of the basin. Glass in hand, I watched a young couple with two tiny children and a large Labrador meander pub-wards.

'Aaah.' The couple stopped for a full-on kiss. 'Do you think Leah's alright? I've only heard from her a couple of times since Easter.'

Paul studied a blossoming vapour trail headed by a silver, westward-bound jet, thousands of feet up. 'She wouldn't have travelled this long in South America without a degree in survivability. She'd let us know if she wasn't.'

'I suppose so. Sometimes I go for the whole week without thinking about her. Do you think that's uncaring?' I pinched the buds of geraniums from the new crop in the painted bucket, now pole-vaulting over the weeds. I hoped Alan Titchmarsh would approve, as I crushed the green, growing smell on my fingers.

'I don't know. It's probably the ultimate accolade, if your children don't have to rely on you. You can get on with your own life with a clear conscience.'

'She was such good fun to have around.'

'I miss her like hell, you know.' The first hot-air balloons of the evening drifted northwards. 'We lost something when they left, didn't we? It was like the heart had gone from the family.'

'Paul, you've never said anything like that before in your life!'

He squirmed, looking back at me. 'Well, perhaps I've never had long enough to put such a profound thought together, before.'

We watched the owner of the tiny yacht tidy his tools back into the cockpit. He straightened up in his rust-streaked boiler suit. Slowly, he picked up a decrepit sea toilet and wandered along the pontoon towards us.

'You've had a good day, then?' I nodded at the rust-streaked loo.

'Yeah, but you're never finished on a boat, are you?'

Paul nodded. 'You're right there. I must check the bilges before Ella comes back again.'

'I didn't leave the Barclaycard in the bilge, you know,' I said, staring at Mum's still-unoiled bike chain.

'Oh? So where did you leave it?'

'I put it in the back of the loo locker, next to the fly screens. It must have slipped down behind the lining. Maybe the card blocked up the bilge pump, that night.'

'I don't think so. I fished out a load of disgusting gunk from the tube. You really must be more careful in future, Nessie.'

'Paul!' I warned him.

He studied his hands. 'Sorry.'

'Well …' I decided to leave it. 'You've probably serviced the loo for the next twenty years, you know.'

'Talking of services, where would you like your unused tub of powder?'

I could feel my laugh turning hysterical. 'Should I hide it in the loo?' I relaxed back on an elbow. 'Thanks for rescuing it for me, Paul.'

'Forget it. 'Twas easy.' He took another mouthful of warmish white. 'So … where did the willy come from?'

'Roger Rabbit? I bought him from Midge … by mistake.'

'Oh yes and how do you find it?'

'Oh, impossible to lose!' I wasn't going into detail with anyone. Not even my husband.

'Can I … persuade you to use me instead? I come equipped with all mod cons.'

'I don't know.' I didn't move, watching his profile. Had our power relations changed enough? 'I still need time to be myself, you know.'

'Sorry … not a done deal then?'

'I really … don't know.' Paul and Scott were muddled up in my mind. I didn't want to choose. Not yet. 'What were you doing up at the uni in your white van this afternoon?'

'Oh you'd be surprised where I get to.' His face shuttered as Delia came by with Jason on a choke collar.

'Are you two OK? I didn't like the look of those men you had with you this afternoon.'

'The local drugs squad.'

'Really? They looked more like baddies than goodies. What did they want?'

There was an infinitesimal difference about Delia. 'Oh, just a few questions and a quick rummage. You haven't arrived until your boat's been searched these days.'

She laughed. 'Oh, I hope not.' I glanced at Paul. I guessed he was thinking the same as me. Somebody down here was attracting suspicion, to have searched two boats for drugs. I'd put my money on the least likely person in the whole marina.

Delia stood her ground. 'Did you see the news on telly? Traffic's been gridlocked all day. Animal rights people have been planting bombs all round the area. It was chaos up there at the university.'

4.7

I swiped in the Department through the other door. No-one mentioned my criminal activities. Whether they'd heard anything, I don't know.

We gathered for our wash-up meeting, later that morning. Scott bowled into the conference room a few minutes late, carrying a carton.

'Buildings Maintenance send their Apologies. The air conditioning's broken down. Anyone feeling too hot?' He didn't need the lethargic silence: we all had sweaty faces. 'Here, try these.'

Hugh delved in and passed the carton, with a surprised smile. When it was my turn, I sank my hand into abrupt coldness and brought out an ice cream cone. The rest of the committee crowed with childish pleasure when it was their turn.

I edged a finger nail under the top wrapper cautiously, in case the ice cream was already melting. Rocky nuts sprinkled the top. My tongue dug through, delving into cool creaminess. As Scott talked, I sat back in my chair. I explored the ice with the tip of my tongue, making it last.

'The VC was delighted with the race. He liked the concept of a fun run and is talking of repeating it next year. He wanted me to pass on congratulations and thanks for all your efforts.' The feel-good ran the table at high water mark.

'What did he make of the television coverage? I didn't think it showed the university in a good light.' Jenny teased her wrapper round and round like a helter skelter, exposing the bare cone. She looked at it for a moment with academic scrutiny and executed a neat bite. The wrapper hung in a long coil from the bottom, like an apple peeling at Hallowe'en.

'This morning, he said the publicity was a balanced plus for the university.'

'I expect most people blamed the chaos on the animal rights activist.' Hugh's cone disappeared in four mouthfuls. 'They don't generate much sympathy from the general public. Maybe the university reaped the benefit.'

'Mmm.' Jonathan licked his ice cream energetically. 'It wasn't our fault the helicopter buzzed in so low.'

'Until the police stepped in, the crowd control was pretty much out of hand, though.'

'There wouldn't have been a problem at all, if the precinct hadn't been closed by the police during the race.' Kirsty pleated her wrapper into a fan, as if she regretted finishing her ice cream so soon. 'I think we did well, under the circumstances.'

'What exactly happened, Scott?' Jonathan wiped his mouth.

'It seems that Nick found a package upstairs somewhere in the gym, when he did his early morning bomb sweep. He called the police. They cordoned off the area.

Unfortunately, there was a long delay while the Bomb Disposal Squad investigated several suspicious packages around the City, apparently planted by animal rights protestors. Even when Bomb Disposal freed the area, the police had to wait for the Drugs Team, to identify the package contents. I understand the police finally closed the incident about six.'

'And what was it?'

'I don't know. Does anyone else have any more information?' Scott picked up the last cone. He swept the top off and hoovered up the melting ice cream in energetic bursts, eyes pivoting round.

I assumed as non-committal a face as everyone else.

'Have you heard how Alan is?' I asked, as soon as I dared.

'Yep, he's fine,' said Kirsty. 'He was discharged later in the afternoon. Sarah says he'll be back at work tomorrow, still steaming gently after all the tests.'

'What was wrong with him, then?'

'Heatstroke, apparently.'

'Yes!' I shouted triumphantly, punching the remains of my Cornetto in the air. 'I knew it! He wasn't cold and clammy, he was dry and hot.'

'Mrs Incredible, again,' Scott teased.

'She's still licking her ice cream, when all the rest of us have finished,' Jonathan pointed out. I felt myself blushing. A romantic heroine can hardly have a hot flush. I bolted my remaining half a thimble full.

'That reminds me, one limitation to our findings will be the moderating effects of dehydration in the unexpectedly hot weather. We'll put that in all our reportage. Any comments on the data collection, Jonathan?'

'We finished the experimental work as planned. We're just waiting for the exam results, now. About three weeks, and we can start number crunching.'

'What's the likely sample size?'

'Over six hundred individuals enrolled. Around a hundred didn't do any training, but ran on the day. Another hundred didn't turn up at all. They'll form a sizeable control group. We'll lose a few more over the exam period. Probably around four hundred participants in all, excluding outliers. We've doubled our sample minimum of a hundred in each of the experimental and control groups.'

‘I lost some of my participants between the pre- and post-tests,’ I said. ‘Two of them didn’t complete the race, and four disappeared. That puts me down to only six complete pairs.’

‘Went to the pub, probably,’ Jenny said.

Scott shrugged his shoulders. ‘Luck of the draw. Now, is there anything else we could have done better, before we close the file?’

Afterwards, Scott came over. He perched on the edge of the table. ‘Are you worried about your small sample?’

I leaned back on my chair legs. ‘Should I be?’

‘Probably, but we’ll scrape something together. When are you going to enter your data?’

‘Soon as I can. This afternoon, probably.’

‘Do you need any help, setting the programme up?’

‘Well, I might. I was going to use the IT workroom, so I can find someone if I get stuck.’

‘I’ll be around.’

‘Thanks, Scott. And for the ice cream. It was a lovely idea.’

He looked at me and crinkled up his eyes in a way I loved to watch. It creased deep fishtails of laughter lines above his cheekbones. Sudden, deep dimples cragged lower down on his cheeks. Just who was he deriding? ‘A small price for such a good meeting.’

***

I was sitting in the deserted IT workroom when he wandered in and pulled up a chair, so close his breath warmed my neck.

‘I’m at a loose end. Come on, I’ll give you a hand.’

Fiddling around to set up took a lot longer than the data entry. For once, Scott wasn't totally concentrated.

'What's up Scott?'

'Oh, nothing.'

'Yes there is,' I said idly, tapping in my first set of results. 'It's not like you to lose concentration.' I peered at the screen, as if I were Dr Stainton-Jones herself. 'That's why I asked, what's up.' I kept the quiet click of keys steady.

'I've got an interview tomorrow.'

'Really. What for?

'Professor.' He was grinning slyly. I boinged upright on the seat and lost my place in the column of data entries. My fuzzy bubble of happiness exploded in a lead-lined shot of adrenaline.

'Professor! Scott, that's great. You'd make a wonderful professor.'

'Shh. Thanks for the vote of confidence,' he said wrily.

'No, seriously. You'll get it. Well, I suppose it depends who else is in the field.'

'The field's not too hot. It's a new chair and the department doesn't currently have the academic credibility to attract many good applicants.'

'Surely tons of people apply for a professorship, wherever it is?' He didn't reply immediately, so I returned to the screen.

'The current head of department is applying. He'll be the strong competition. The rest are mostly youngsters, without much research behind them. Most of the department don't even have doctorates.'

'Uh huh. So, why leave here?'

'Several reasons. But if I don't get something soon, I'll be too old.'

'You can't say that at an interview.' I still peered at the screen.

'Oh, I was just telling you. No, Ron and I sorted out my pitch some time ago.'

'Has he given you a good reference?'

'And the Dean. Alan really encouraged me to go for it, when I saw him, last week.'

'Where is it?' I glanced round.

'You're very nosy, aren't you?' He leaned over and touched my nose gently.

'No … yes. I'm interested in …' I tailed off. I couldn't say any more. The thought of him going swelled up into a miserable ball of certainty.

'Aren't you going to wish me luck, then?' He looked at me with glinting eyes. I wondered if the expression, that I'd seen so often before, was really self-mockery, or even self-doubt.

I grasped my adrenaline in both hands, stood up and hugged him. 'Of course I am. Hope you get it.' Without thinking, I leaned forward. I'd coveted that high, thin cheekbone for ages. It was warm and taut, when I kissed it. 'Good luck.' I grabbed my rucksack and disappeared to the Ladies, for a while. *Anne Elliott* would have disinherited me.

The next day, I sat in the IT workroom, cleaning my data, and pestered Jonathan at frequent intervals, instead.

E-mails pinged in and out.

I've been offered the job.
Great news! Are you going to accept?
Probably.
Congratulations Professor! When are you back?

It was strange that no-one else seemed to know what was going on. But I was learning how the Department ticked. I kept mum. When Scott returned, he wasn't around much. He said nothing publicly. I lobbed e-mails to Scott over the next fortnight, which he volleyed or not, as he saw fit.

Kirsty and Jonathan went on holiday, before dissertation fever started in earnest. Scott told me he was going to his new place for a couple of days, then external examining in Wales. It was as if Ron didn't exist.

Relentless optimism gave way to something else in the Department. A huge ball of tangled knitting wool that everyone was trying to unravel. When they reached inside, the ends were hidden in woolly softness. When they pulled, the knots tightened. I sensed bewilderment and frustration.

***

It was difficult to meet up, now the modules had finished. We beavered away at lonely research programmes and dissertation writing. I wanted to thank the girls for their help and decided on my old favourite, the *Mad Hatter*. At least I knew its idiosyncracies. Since I was late, Midge and Cathy's lunches had already arrived.

'I've got some news.' Midge announced, once I'd sat down with my umbrella upended, to drip onto the floor. 'I've got a date on Friday.'

'Midge, why haven't you told us?'

'A date! That's terrific. Who with?'

'Guy called James.' She looked as shiny and attractive as a polished red apple, now something was going right. Beside her, I felt like a slug-damaged cabbage.

'Come on then, spill the beans. How did you meet him?'

She looked shamefaced. 'Internet dating agency.'

'Wow, how cool is that,' I said, to be supportive.

Cathy looked interested. 'Where does he live?'

'Oh, only just the other side of the motorway. It couldn't be handier.'

'I didn't know you were up for romance. I thought you'd had enough of all men forever.'

'Well ... it's not much fun being on your own.'

'Really,' I said. 'I'm enjoying the solitude.' No, Midge didn't want to hear that. 'Correction. I'm enjoying standing on my own two feet.'

'But when you've proved you can do that, a real partnership ... would be ... well ... lovely.'

'So is this love?' I teased.

'Oh goodness. I've only e-mailed him so far, we haven't met.'

'Fingers crossed then.' Cathy's smile was indulgent.

'That's a coincidence. Scott was talking about some research on internet dating, when we had a meeting last week.' It was funny, I found myself talking about him incessantly. He was like a drug.

'You're getting on well with him, aren't you?' Midge leant forward, her freckled face suddenly up close.

'Yeah, he's being very helpful at the moment. SPSS is a nightmare.' I wondered how much *sensibility* I was betraying.

'SPSS was bound to be a nightmare. You've never used a stats program before.'

'When are you off to SHERPA?'

'Oh, three weeks.'

'Well just watch out.'

'What do you mean?'

'Midge,' said Cathy warningly. 'It's up to Nessie.'

'Where is Scott? His door's been closed all week.' Midge was hanging in. 'Has he gone on holiday, Nessie?'

'No, I don't think so. I think he's … er, visiting another university.'

'Oh yes? Which one?' Cathy smoothed a long magenta sleeve precisely down to her watch strap.

'I don't know exactly, Cathy. Somewhere near Cambridge, I think. But not *the* Cambridge.'

'Really? How interesting. Sarah's off to the real Cambridge, soon.'

'Yeah. So what?' Midge and Cathy looked at one another.

'Just be careful,' said Midge, defying Cathy's warning glance.

'Why's that, then?'

'I think.' She looked at her pasta, hovering in mid air, 'Scott's slimy.'

'Do you?'

'Maybe I'm wrong. It's just how he comes across to me.' I looked at her plate. What with the smell of Italian food and my dash through the June monsoons to get to the café, I was starving. 'He's very manipulative. Look how he got rid of Rosa.'

'Well, aren't all psychologists like that? They're so knowing, they can't just behave normally like other people ...'

'Jenny does. Jonathan does.' Cathy pointed out.

'Scott does, too. He's very thoughtful. D'you know, he bought everyone an ice-cream on Tuesday, to cheer them up, because the air-conditioning was broken.' My damp face frazzled dry.

'Exactly,' said Midge. 'That's what I mean.'

'Well, if you think he's manipulative if he does that sort of thing, he's damned when he does and damned when he doesn't! Why do you say that, Midge?'

'Well, I must come clean. I really like your Paul. Look how he saved your bacon with the carbohydrate powder. And all the other things he's done for you, over the year. He's a decent guy. I think it would be a shame if your marriage broke up because of Scott.'

'You don't understand, Midge. Paul acts more like my dad, most of the time. He can be very controlling. It's like … well, that's the down side of a long partnership. You know, in the end, you fall into fixed roles that turn out to be a bear pit. You can't get out of it.'

Midge looked unconvinced. 'Sorry.' She attacked her salad. 'I've probably said too much. What do you think Nessie should do, Cathy?'

'How can we advise her? We don't know how it will turn out, Midge.'

'But you're so clear-sighted, Cathy. You must have an opinion.'

'Only that she should think about her motives, before she acts.'

'You sound like a fortune-teller at the fair,' I said lightly.

'It feels like that sometimes. But there again, I don't believe in predestination. What was it Becker said? You know, *chance is the way things happen*. We have to take advantage of chance. Deciding whether it's to my advantage or not, has always been my problem.' She put her knife and fork tidily on the plate, just as my quiche materialised.

Since she wasn't going to say any more, we got down to the serious business of bemoaning the number of days until our dissertations were due in.

***

I sat quietly in the IT workroom, tapping away. Chapter 3 was a mechanical report of the method, easy to write, already tedious. For once, I was aware of the environment beyond my screen. It was stickily hot. The door was open and a fan wheeled quietly, helping out the air circulation. I wondered for a moment how Benjie was getting along with his exams. Important exams.

As I moved back into the SPSS data to check my last result, I heard Kirsty's clear voice. She was talking to someone directly outside. I didn't recognise the other voice, but assorted PhD students shared desks in the open-plan. Then Hugh chimed in too.

'… the last three.'

'Would that mean any jobs?'

'Almost certainly. It's a half-million contract.'

Kirsty's voice. 'We'd expand more into nutrition.'

'When will you hear?

'About two weeks.'

'Was Jonathan the lead applicant?

'No, Scott.'

'Oh. So what happens if he goes?'

'We lose it, unless Ron can negotiate a partnership agreement.' Hugh sounded pessimistic.

'Sounds dire. I'll have to see what else is around.'

Kirsty spoke. 'I wouldn't say that. Ron is back full time soon, and he's already negotiating for two other contracts. There's cholesterol and activity in childhood coming up from a Department of Health/BHF consortium. And we're just about to put in one from Ron and Jenny, on childhood obesity and thermogenesis.'

'Is there any chance Scott will stay on here? I really wanted a slice of that diabetic study.'

There was a silence.

'It's a difficult decision.' Kirsty sounded cautious.

'Why is he hesitating? It's a professorship. Who knows how long he'll have to wait for Ron to retire. Maybe I should move over there with him.'

'Well I wouldn't even consider that,' said Hugh.

The student sounded surprised. 'Why ever not?'

'Once you leave the Russell Group, you'll never get back in.'

'So? The new universities do lots of useful research.'

'Frankly, the research in a place like that just doesn't bear comparison. It's like the different leagues in football.'

My fingers stiffened. Kirsty sounded piqued. 'Scott's ready to do something bigger. I think he should go.'

So the knitting wool was Scott's decision. Not wool at all, but a stone balanced on top of a rock.

The computer bleeped at me. Still nettled, I turned back to my screen. My rows and columns of data had been replaced by a forest of gobbledegook. Positive affect, multiplied by eight thousand. My fingers rested innocently back on the home keys. It took half an hour to sort out. One step forward and two back, I thought. My own positive affect plummeted for the rest of the day.

***

Around chapter four, I hit a technical hitch. I printed out all my results and returned to *Iris*, where I laid them out over the saloon floor. Over three cups of coffee, I pondered. That got me nowhere, so I phoned Scott. He'd given me his home phone number, ready for the inevitable, I suppose.

'Hello … er, could I speak to Scott, please.'

'Who is it please?' It was the first time I'd spoken to Yvonne. She sounded chilly.

'It's Nessie, one of his Masters' students.'

'I'll ask him to call back, when he's out of the shower.'

It was hot again. Although it was good to be near any water in this weather, an odour of festering dock permeated the boat.

I rang back half an hour later.

'Hello, Nessie.' My heart thumped.

'Oh Scott, sorry to bother you at home. Are you busy?'

'What do you want?'

'Well, it's … I've come to a bit of a stopper. I've tried it all the ways I can think of, but my data's just not making any sense.'

'And you want to get on over the weekend?'

'I'm afraid so.'

'Well I'm off to Liverpool first thing, so I can't help you tomorrow. Can you get up here now?'

I looked round at the pages of data and comments, laid out in order, my laptop, the open statistics books and draft dissertation pages. 'I suppose you couldn't come down here? I haven't quite arrived at a paper-free office scenario yet.'

He laughed. 'OK, I can give you half an hour.'

'Right, I'll meet you at the marina pass gate. How long will you be?'

'Oh, about … fifteen minutes?'

I put down the phone and felt the thrill start somewhere at my knees and course through until it reached my neck.

'Calm,' I told Me, feeling like a clockwork toy.

First I rushed to the sink, to tackle the dirty washing up left over from a half-day of thinking. Then I raced up to the loo compartment and cleaned the toilet bowl and seat. There was just time to straighten out the duvet on Mum's bed. Certainly not time to change the sheets. As I powered back down to the saloon, I peered out. No sign of Scott at the dockhead yet.

My eyes took in the saloon with the appraising glance of a desperate housewife. I swept up two empty mugs and washed them, then used the wet dishcloth to lick the dust from the table and stove. I squirted Mum's air freshener, until the air smelled sickly-sweet. Sixteen minutes gone. No time to change. Smoothing my tee shirt down over my shorts, I realised I hadn't looked at my hair. I gave it a desperately quick brush and climbed out of the boat.

Scott was lounging at the dockhead. 'It must be interesting, living on a boat.'

'Erm, you could say that.'

We walked down the pontoon in silence. His hair was almost golden in the evening sunlight, trimmed and newly-washed. I felt conscious of the thin material over my bottom as I lead the way. Standing aside for him to climb on board, he gestured for me to go first.

'I've never been on a narrow boat before.'

'This one belongs to my Mum. She's been away for almost the whole year, so it's been a floating study while I've been at the uni.' I glanced at him, to see what he was making of the saloon.

'Do sit down.' I cleared the statistics books from the small armchair. He sat back arms behind his head, as if he relaxed anywhere he went. 'Would you like a drink … some tea or coffee, glass of wine? I've got some beer in the fridge.'

He checked his watch. 'Yeah, a beer would be nice.' I pulled out two bottles of Peroni. 'Don't bother about a glass for me,' he said, as I opened a locker door. 'OK, so what's the problem?'

'Err …' I sat down on the bunk. 'Err …' I raked my pile of papers for inspiration. 'Basically, I thought I was looking for significance levels at .01 or .05?'

'Yeah that's right. To disprove the null hypothesis, you need those sort of levels.' He was holding the beer as he spoke. He took a swig. 'Mmm, that's good. If you're getting anything up to 0.1, it does at least mean you're close, even if it's not significant.'

'Well, I'm coming in at .00001, or thereabouts.' Scott put his bottle carefully down on the floor next to him, before he started laughing.

'The participants certainly felt amazingly better after your drink! Oh, you've fed in some garbage. That's the usual, until you students learn to be meticulous entering your data. Have you printed everything out?' I nodded. 'Well that makes it easy for us to check. Where are the participants' test results?'

I scuffled through to find that pile of papers.

He glanced through them. 'At a quick look they seem all right. Did you run these data through parametric testing?'

I picked out that pile of papers.

'OK. And were you parametric or non-parametric? Did you choose chi-square or …'

I had the next pile of papers ready.

He looked down at the row of effect sizes. 'Well, that's a bit disappointing for you, to get virtually the same result from both groups. Don't worry. Just write it up and offer some reasons why that might be. You'll always get a Hawthorne effect, for a start. You're also stuck with a very small sample.'

'Hawthorne effect?'

'Yeah. A control group improves, just because someone's noticing what they do. In an industrial setting, productivity improves 15% with any interest at all.' He took another swig of beer. 'Now then, maybe you should exclude those couple of outliers who seemed to be as high as kites. They're a relatively large part of your result.'

'Oh no, I can't do that. I'd only have ten people left.'

'Well, we may be able to extrapolate some figures from Jonathan's main data sets by way of comparison. That might help. Tell you what, I'm in on Tuesday and Jono's back. Come and see me then.' He looked at his watch, picked up the beer bottle and drained it. He held up the green glass to the light and inspected it. 'Nice beer. Thanks. I must be off. Have a good weekend.'

'Yeah, thank you, Scott. He looked at me with a smidgeon of concern.

'Do some editing this weekend, and have a bit of time off.' He rested two finger pads lightly on my arm before he made for the saloon doors. 'I want you at your best for SHERPA.'

When I looked, it was twenty past eight. He must be going up to town to meet someone.

The boat still held Scott's smell when I went to bed that night. It was like ingrained denim I decided, too hot to sleep. I pictured Scott sitting in the saloon, laughing in the long summer light, a beer in his clean, competent hands and long fingers. I tried to imagine what he tasted like.

There was the clip-clop of water splatting at the hull, while the basin scoured. *Iris* tugged at her lines like an urgent dog.

When I got up tomorrow morning, the water level would have dropped by six inches or so.

When I shut my eyes, I conjured someone asleep, next to me in bed. It was easy, after thirty years' practice. Not Paul. I saw the lines on Scott's face in close-up; his up-ended shock of hair on the other pillow. His face, sagging down to the right side a little, as he turned to me. I put out an arm, as if he were there, to feel his left shoulder.

I wanted his body, whatever Midge thought of his character. There were parts of him that I was desperate to touch: the small upsurge of fat above his jeans; his buttocks, so that I could pull him against my hips; the bits of his chest covered by his shirt, where his open bomber jacket swung against his ribs as he walked. I imagined slipping off the jacket and unbuttoning his shirt, his mouth nuzzling down my neck.

A familiar feeling engulfed me. I sat up and put on the light, amazed at where I'd put myself. Between Me and my imagination, I was on a full charge.

I'd never faced this situation before. There'd always been Paul around and any hunk-driven erotica fed into our routinely adequate sex life. Before that? I cranked back in my memory to remember if I'd ever felt this physical surge for Paul, in the first flush of our attraction.

I'd been strong on romantic love and ignorant on the realities of sex. In those days, my corner of Chippenham wasn't nearly as swinging as the rest of England. I simply hadn't felt anticipatory arousal like this before. Even sitting up in bed made me conscious of *down there* preparing itself for action, like a holiday postcard arriving several months too late.

There was a remedy. Driven by passion, as they used to say in the car adverts, I switched off the light. Surreptitiously, I slipped out of bed. Using the street lights, I crept over to the clothes locker. On automatic pilot, I groped for Roger Rabbit, where I'd thrown him after Fenton's intimate search of his nether regions. Urrgh. I took RR out of his box, boiled the kettle and gave him a minute scrub at the galley sink in very hot water.

All the time, I could feel a miasma of excitement, welling up through last night's dinner. I peered cautiously out of the window to make sure nobody was spying. I closed the flowery curtains tightly, doubling them over, so there wasn't a single crack of night showing through. I wondered how much noise there'd be and put the radio on, just in case. The late night *Shipping Forecast* didn't seem quite right, so I spun the dial round until I found some soul.

Then I got back into bed, holding RR squeamishly between two fingers. I could feel my nose wrinkled, ready for a nasty smell. I looked at the rampant penis. I was pulsing to feel it. I flicked the switch experimentally, to see a vibrating penis in action. Nothing moved. Neither the rampant penis nor the little ovary bit sticking out from the handle. I was far too desperate to give up. I would have to consult the manual.

Ten minutes later, I'd taken out the soaked battery and fitted a new one. Now I could size up Roger's potential. I sat down on the bed again. I got him experimentally into position. Then I decided to lay back. That reminded me of Dr Stainton-Jones and my last smear test. Why was I doing this? How could I possibly feel revolted and rampant all at the same time?

Think of it as training, Nessie, I bolstered myself. Nobody else in the world is embarrassed by all this stuff. I made contact with the penis, and imagined Scott kissing my clitoris at the same time. The excited feeling moved up the sides of my chest and across to my nipples. Then I realised that, anatomically, my imagination had run away with me. I came back to earth and switched RR off.

A scooter buzzed along the road on the other side of the dock, then suddenly stopped. I leapt up, to check he wasn't peering in through the curtains.

Look, are you going to do this or not? If not, I need to get some sleep, said my Id. I thought about it. Sex, just for the hell of it? Give over. Sex is about procreation, isn't it?

I can do this.

Roger Rabbit astonished me with his brisk efficiency. While my mouth was still searching for a body to kiss, he delivered an electrically-charged orgasm in two minutes flat. Interval training, Nessie. Think of it as increasing the intensity and decreasing the time. While my brain still gasped at the sterility, I bundled hollow-inside Roger Rabbit guiltily back into his box, and stuffed him under a pile of jumpers in the back of the locker. Did people really fall for his unconditional love?

***

Next evening, Paul issued an ultimatum to my indecisive rabbit within.

'I don't know exactly what's going on, but I need you to make up your mind if you're coming back or not.' A whirl of emptiness spun me round and set me down further along, telling me I didn't want to make decisions.

'Oh. Well what do *you* want?'

He spoke stiffly, as if he'd rehearsed it several times. 'I don't think we should give up too easily. It doesn't make any sense financially ...'

'For goodness sake, Paul. What sort of reason is that?'

'I don't ... Look, I've got to go, now.'

I sat down, arms and legs out of control. Panic hot-wired my edges, now we'd come to the crunch moment. Thinking got me nowhere, just left a heavy weight of indecision to drag into bed. As Midge had said, Roger Rabbit caused none of the mess of a real relationship.

4.8

The *SHERPA* conference was held in the middle of Britain, that hot July. The host department was sidelined in a grey pre-fab, across the road from the red-brick conference centre. My accommodation was twenty minutes' walk away.

The Hall of Residence was miniscule. The toilets were so scaled-down, I had to reverse in, rather than turn round. My student study-bedroom was about the same size as Mum's cabin on *Iris*, which was designed to squeeze through canal tunnels. Fortunately, there weren't too many obese exercise scientists, or we might have had trouble squeezing them through the corridors.

I hung up my black trousers and sparkly vest, tidied my other clothes and kicked my zip bag under the bed so that everything was shipshape. My memory stick was safely stowed in my best leather handbag, now that I'd outgrown the rucksack. I'd remembered everything, except my HRT. Oh well, it wasn't exactly life-threatening.

***

Scott was about to pitch centre stage with his Monday morning presentation to fellow academics. I could see that he was nervous. He seemed to be joking with the other four speakers, up on the brick-framed podium. He was even wearing a suit with an architectural tie.

I'd put a message on his e-mail, before I joined the audience.

Good luck with your presentation!

The speakers sat down. I watched Scott pull out his BlackBerry and read it. While the chairman of the symposium made an introductory speech, Scott bent his neat haircut to key out an answer.

Scott spoke first. He stood up, tapping his notes against his leg, much the same as the first time I'd seen him. I hadn't a clue, then, how important he'd become to me. I listened, watching my fists clenching and my fingers fiddling on his behalf. His address sounded authoritative to me, though I was hardly an expert on children's activity levels. The Powerpoint slides vaulted high above the bar. If the presentation lacked the spicy edge it needed to make students sit up and listen, the expert audience clapped appreciatively enough for Scott to sit down with a modest grin.

In the coffee break, I nipped over to the IT centre to read the answer. There wasn't one. I left it at that. I didn't want to sabotage his concentration. In any case, I had plenty of juicy excitement in my brain, without adding new inputs for immediate processing. Like imagining what it would be like to live with a professor.

I didn't see Scott again, until after the Tuesday night dinner. Since the Christmas party, I wasn't looking forward to a disco in the student union bar. I thought I'd just call in as part of my conference experience.

I primed myself not to expect Scott. He'd probably joined a coven of professors by now, out to dinner somewhere posh. I'd waxed and polished to within an inch of my life, two days ago. Now I showered and dressed, as carefully as John Travolta in *Saturday Night Fever.* If only the end result could be dancing.

***

My surprise stopped me short at the entrance to the packed bar area. Every single delegate had succumbed to its unappealing dull wooden varnish. I faltered back.

'*Lively up yourself*,' Bob Marley would've said. I plucked up courage to worm through the crowd to the bar. I bought a bottle of wine to last.

Over in the far corner, a six piece band was setting up on stage: saxophone, trumpet, drums, two guitars and double bass.

'They're all academics,' said an American on my left. His BMI was so far over 40, you couldn't tell the difference. His prune coloured shirt had two thin strings at the neck, like a cowboy. The material stretched across his vast shoulders, then in spare folds under huge, inflated arms. His voluminous khaki chinos hitched up serendipitously with red braces.

My group from the university bunched on the far side of the room. Marooned, I offered the couple some wine. The Literature had told me that sport science students hold negative perceptions of obese people. I was keen to show I wasn't prejudiced.

'Do you know the band?'

'We've met all those guys, one way or another.'

'Have you enjoyed the conference, so far?' I asked, when they'd complimented me, in the American way, on the house white.

'Oh it's a great little conference. We enjoyed ourselves so much last year, we made the effort to come again this time.'

'Where do you come from?'

'Atlanta in Georgia.' His colleague was a tall, young Black African with a tiny miniskirt.

'Really? What do you do there?'

‘We’re researchers. I’m Gareth. This is Tabs.’

‘Hi, I’m Nessie. So do you know many other people here? I’m afraid I’m very new.’

‘Well yes, most of these people we know from their work. And we have friends in several of your universities. So what’s your area, Nessie?’

‘Um, well I’m a Masters’ student. My poster has been accepted, and it’s on display on Wednesday in the Conference Centre anteroom!’ At last, here was the payoff for all the time I’d spent on that bloody poster.

‘Wow! Is that so? What’s your subject?’

‘Err, mortality statistics.’

‘How about that! Well, I’ll be sure to come by and visit you on Wednesday. Is that the area for your doctoral research?’ That sounded good to my fast-mellowing ears.

‘Oh, I’ve no idea. The rest of my research group are over there.’ Gareth peered in the right direction, through the crowd. Scott and Jonathan were ensconced with the young Professor and his gang from up north. Vasulu’s head was nodding at two PhD students, designers of the other departmental posters.

We drank another glass of wine. Tabs wandered off in search of livelier society. By the time Gareth had confided why he hadn’t married and I’d told him all about Paul, the music started.

‘Would you like to dance, Nessie?’

‘Yeah. Thank you. In for a penny and all that.’

‘I beg your pardon?’

‘I’m trying to pretend I’m only about twenty-five tonight, Gareth.’

He laughed. ‘Can you jive?’

‘Oh, yes.’ The alcohol was cushioning me by this time.

'Those two guys over there love rock 'n' roll. They're going to do a session next, while Jeff takes a break.'

'You're on. I haven't jived for years!'

By the time we'd both run out of breath, Scott was nearby, talking to Tabs. To my amazement, Scott wore a pair of pristine expedition trousers with a new black shirt. There was a red hole in his ear instead of the ring. He looked respectably casual, as he shook hands with Gareth.

'I'm Scott Woodhouse. Very pleased to meet you again, Gareth. Do you remember, I was with Ron Rawlins last year when we met?'

'Oh yeah, I remember you, Scott. How are ya? Where's Ron tonight?'

'He's burning the midnight oil on a government report on children's physical activity. It's due next week, so my colleague, Jonathan Griffiths, is here with me. We've been working on activity and cognitive function with students. We'll have some very interesting results soon, Gareth.'

'I'd like to hear more about that, sometime. This is Nessie, who has a poster on mortality statistics.'

'Yes,' murmured Scott, smiling at me. 'I know Nessie already. She's one of my dissertation students. As a matter of fact, I'm lead author on the poster.'

Britain's two most distinguished professors appeared. Even I recognised them. Gareth introduced us, before he took off with them.

'Nessie, this is Charlie Keen and Chris Eiger.' The couple grinned at me. Chris stuck out her craggy hand.

'Very nice to meet you, Nessie. I'll come by on Wednesday.'

Scott watched them out of sight, before he turned back to me. He leant down to my ear, so I'd hear above the music.

'Did you know Gareth Anderson already?'

'Gareth Anderson? No, should I have done?'

'He's just published a landmark review of physical activity and the metabolic syndrome in the *New England Journal of Medicine.* Centre for Diseases Control, Atlanta. Visiting Professor of Public Health at Harvard. He's giving the conference keynote speech on obesity, tomorrow.'

'Ah. No idea, I'm afraid. I just felt sorry for him because he's so fat. No-one else was talking to him.'

'I need to network with him. There could be something in it for us.'

'For us? You and me?'

'For my new department. I've heard he's interested in working with transatlantic partners.' Scott crinkled up his eyes. His contact lenses glittered.

'Please stop doing that!'

'What?'

'Crinkling your eyes up, so it seems like you're laughing at me all the time.'

'Would I do that?' Music started.

I might never get another chance. 'Scott, are you going to dance with me tonight?'

'Sure.' I took his hand and led him onto the dance floor, just as Jeff the saxophonist took over with an incomprehensible jazz improvisation.

Scott held me in the loose grip of an unseasoned dancer. 'Are you enjoying yourself? At the conference, I mean.'

'Sure. It's been exciting. How about you? Have you had much feedback from your presentation?' I made a unilateral decision to abandon any particular dance style and Scott didn't seem any the wiser. At least the sax wasn't providing a regular beat for him to miss.

‘There’s been a lot of interest in the pilot study on children’s Type 2. ’

‘Oh yes.’ I ventured in a little closer. ‘And what about tonight?’

‘It’s very crowded.’ There was a space. Our footsteps shuffled awkwardly backwards and forwards in a random distribution curve.

‘So what’s with the trousers instead of the jeans?’

‘Oh, time for a change,’ he said vaguely, inching towards me.

‘Mmm,’ I said, sliding my hands round the back pockets. ‘But your bum looks nicer in jeans. Scott do you ever …?’ I tailed off. Was I really ready for Action?

‘Do I, what?’ He looked puzzled.

Last chance, Nessie. I switched on the afterburner, and crunched the sparkly bits from my tee-shirt against his body. ‘Do you ever … look at anyone else but your wife?’

I felt his body stiffen. I was pretty surprised, myself.

‘I didn’t think you were interested … after …’ There was a pause, when he didn’t seem to know which foot went where. My nipples pulsed against his chest in time to the music.

‘Your place or mine?’ he asked eventually.

***

‘It’s a bit small, isn’t it,’ I opined.

‘The choice is yours. Now we’re here, it’s this, or the long grass at the edge of the rugby pitch.’

‘Oh, er, I see.’ I sat down nervously on the edge of the single student bed. I didn’t really have too much current practice to call on.

'Here,' Scott turned round with a couple of plastic glasses full of wine and gave me one.

'Er … cheers,' I said, taking a sip from my third glass over par.

'Now, how can I help?'

'Erm, well I really wanted to talk to you about …' I leant back slightly, glass in hand. It took a bit more than that to touch the wall. I felt woozy. My abdominals didn't seem to be muscling in properly. Wine slopped over the edge of the glass, trickling down my hand. I was half recumbent on the well-used throw, before my back lodged safely against the wall. 'Oops, sorry.'

He frowned. 'Please tell me if I've got the wrong signals here, but I thought you wanted something else from me.'

'Erm, yes'

'Are you sure?' My vagina certainly felt sure, even if my brain and mouth weren't firing properly.

'Yes, of course I'm sure.'

Scott slipped off his desert-beige trousers and unclipped his pedometer. He sat down beside me, sliding a hand across the black material of my trousers to find exactly the right bit of my inner thigh. 'You're gorgeous, even when you're drunk, do you know that?' An amused look warmed the icy blue.

'How did you know that was the right place?' I whispered, purring like a cat.

'No idea,' he whispered back and nuzzled into my neck.

Now that I'd invested so much in a knicker-hole, I was keen to find out if it worked for real. That meant positioning myself so that Scott would discover the surprise. In the interests of science I scrambled aboard his lap, a little while later.

He looked startled. 'I had no idea you were like this, Nessie,' before excavating up the front of my sparkly tee-shirt and discovering the leopard-skin bra.

'I'm not, usually,' I said quite truthfully, since this was the first time my north-south orientation had ever mattered.

'Hang on.' He groped into his chinos, which were now on the floor. Finding the pocket, he fingered out a packet of condoms.

'Scott, you don't need to worry.' I felt blissfully recycled. 'I'm through the menopause.'

'It's more what you might pass on to me. Have you seen the most recent figures on chlamydia in the BMJ?' It seemed unlikely that I'd picked up chlamydia in training with a Rampant Rabbit, but that didn't seem an appropriate rejoinder.

I would like to say that he explored my body with his mouth, but unfortunately there wasn't time for that. Once he discovered the keyhole, there was no stopping him.

4.9

I'm impatient to see you again. Tonight?

Sure.

My texting was improving. I'd discovered full stops and capital letters.

A song erupted in my handbag. The people round me in the conference hall shot-putted grouchy glares at a second disturbance. A text message from a lover! Cleopatra on her barge, or what?

Ten o'clock, my place?

I'm looking forward to it already.

I replied eventually and fiddled for a bit. Then I switched my mobile off, since I just couldn't make it vibrate in silent ecstasy.

***

Tiny figures navigated the perimeter paths of baked-mud playing fields. I made it by the skin of my teeth, as the sun set into a grey mist of pollution. It was still sweltering and I was glad of my water bottle. In the foyer, the architecture of the hall was familiar. The marble chip tread on the stairs cooled my trailing hand, as I waited next to some climbing bolt-ons fixed to the Sixties brick wall.

Homecoming researchers appeared in laughing, glowing gangs, like adverts for a group holiday. Older men and women came in, jackets slung over their shoulders, shiny and relaxed after the humid walk from the conference centre. Two men bowled in, holding hands. A pretty girl in a 50's dress hobbled in with a broken high heel. I recognised one of the day's presenters, sweaty and emphatic as he harangued his mobile. A scruffy youngster arrived alone with a take-away. Curry, judging by the smell. Three couples slipped in furtively.

In my day, there was a curfew. Once in, you were imprisoned for the night. I could feel my excitement, beating in a thick layer, just inside my sweaty skin. From somewhere upstairs, a bass thumped 120 beats a minute. How many other rooms would host extra-mural activities in the cool, dark hours?

I took another swig of tepid water and tried the first two moves up the wall. The second handhold was too much of a stretch for my right hand. My sweaty fingers slipped as I reached out for the gritty pinch-hold.

Scott arrived from the car park, twenty minutes later.

'Hi.' He caught me in a quick pull against his chest. His eyes slouched down the inside of my white tee.

The lights in the foyer flickered, as my internal voltage surged. 'Hi. Have you had a good day?'

No answer. We started up the stairs into semi-darkness. At the first landing, Scott spat the lights on.

'Oh, don't do that!'

'Why ever not?'

'The dark's … nicer.'

'Not if you trip up.'

I smiled, caught out in my banality, as we turned down the narrow corridor.

'Here we are.' Scott unlocked the door and stood aside for me to go first. This time round, the room was hollow and stuffy, from being closed up all day, with a faint smell of new paint. I waited for an invitation to sit down. I stared at the brown noticeboard, battered from hundreds of empty pinpricks over years of student use. Not quite Cleopatra's barge.

Scott slung his jacket on the chair, opened the window and drew the thick curtains. He unclipped his pedometer. 'Only five thousand and thirteen. I need to do more steps than that, tomorrow.'

'Yeah, there's too much sitting around at the conference, isn't there?' I gabbled inconsequentially.

'I was in Cambridge, today … '

There was a pause. I waited for Scott to say something humorous about last night's rushed performance, so we could laugh about it and start over. That's what Paul would have done. Scott sat down on the bed and slowly took off his shoes and socks. His toes peeped out, dead-looking and clammy, indented where shoes had pressed his sock seams into white skin.

'Would you like a drink … coffee … glass of water?'

'No, er, thank you.' Out of the corner of my eye I looked to see if he was waiting for me to join him. He leant back, arms supporting his head, a typically-relaxed Scott pose that took up three-quarters of the bed.

'Can we talk a bit, first?'

'What do you want to talk about?' He sounded surprised.

'I guess, err, I'd like to know more about you.' I sat down anyway, trying to make it easier.

'Me? Like what?' He got up and went over to the washbasin, where he flipped out his contact lenses and binned them. He drank some water, then set the plastic cup carefully down on the bedside cabinet. A pile of journal articles stood next to the cup.

'Oh I dunno. Anything. Everything.'

'Really.' He looked at me with a ghost of embarrassment. 'Where shall I start?'

'You've accepted the new job, Scott?'

'I start first of September.'

I picked up his hand and stroked the delicate dark hairs on the back with my finger. I wanted to own them. 'And how does … your wife … feel about moving?'

He drew his hand away. 'What's that got to do with it?'

My voice came out squeaky, as I leapt in. 'Isn't she going with you, then?'

'Maybe … not.' I looked at him. Fierce little fizzes of hope sparked for a moment, like a faintly-lit marina pontoon stretching into the dark beyond.

He slid his hand round the back of my shoulders. I snuggled into the waiting arm. His chest smelled of sweat, denim and car. 'So you're going alone?'

He put his other hand on my belly and turned to me. His kiss tasted of strong beer. 'I don't know, yet.'

'I need a bit more time,' I warned him, as we undressed. 'Tell me about your childhood.' I folded up my black trousers, but there wasn't anywhere to put them, except on the stained carpet. 'Where did you grow up?'

He sighed and pulled me down onto the bed, so narrow we balanced like Pilates pencils in a tin. 'We moved around until I was thirteen. Scotland, Cyprus, North Wales, Singapore. My Dad was in the RAF.'

'That must've been difficult.'

'Maybe … sometimes.'

'And then where?'

'Oh, when Mum and Dad split up, near Reading, for a year or so. Dad worked at Aldermaston, as a civvie.'

'Really? Reading? I did my PE training there.' I propped on my elbow, facing him. 'So where did you live in Reading, Scott?'

'In a village outside, called Kingschase.'

'My goodness, I did a teaching practice near there. How old did you say you were at the time?'

'Oh, twelve or thirteen.' He squirmed uneasily.

'Let me think. Scott Woo… ' A stairwell popped up in my memory. 'Spotty little kid with glasses. Did they call you … Woodlouse?'

He flushed. 'I don't remember.'

I jerked upright, my smile jokey at the memory. 'You were a really undersized boy in those days, weren't you? All the rest of your class had growth-spurted, except grubby little Woodlouse.'

Scott grimaced.

I looked down at him, giggling in the relief of having found common ground. 'Don't you remember when they spat at you down the stairwell from the top floor? You were in a right old state. Tears, asthma attack, the lot, until I came along to rescue you. The boys got the cane for bullying. How amazing, to find it's you, after all these years.'

'Whatever do you mean?'

'Miss Reynolds, the PE student … you know, before I got married. You were in Year 8 … whatever did they call it? Err … the second year.'

He stared in horror. 'I had no idea you were that old. I thought you were about the same age as me.'

I attempted humour. 'I know. From my end it seems more like child molestation.'

'Whatever turns you on, Nessie.'

We lay back down. Scott slid his hand into position between my legs. I screwed up my face. What had happened to *infinite variety?* That place was so yesterday. 'What's the hurry?'

Scott gave me a myopic look. 'Big day tomorrow,' he said. 'We need to get our beauty sleep.' He groped with another hand. When he found a boob, he probed it like a doctor checking for lumps. Another hand slid briskly down my bottom. It was difficult to keep track of all the marauding hands at such close proximity. What was he looking for this time, piles?

Too late, I realised I was out of body, observing dispassionately from somewhere near the pinboard. My train was running some minutes behind Scott's rampant schedule. If I didn't get back on track, I was in for an arid ride.

A door slapped shut along the hollow corridor. Stiletto heels tap-tapped and passed by. I imagined one of the more sophisticated women delegates. Jealousy stabbed, unexpectedly close. A door at the other end opened … and clicked something in my brain.

Viagra! Why hadn't I realised before, that he had a problem? I remembered sneaking into The Literature only last week. The lived experience for Viagra patients' partners was frankly, demanding. It seemed like voyeurism at the time, but now I was grateful for a little understanding of Scott's predicament, once he'd taken a pill.

My hip protested at Scott's weight in its own graunchy way. 'Ow ... ouch.' I stretched my cramped leg to ease the agony. 'Sorry Scott. It's only a touch of arthritis.'

Scott hesitated, where Paul would have offered to start rubbing, and I lost it. I unstuck my damp right leg from Scott's sweaty left leg and the wall and sat up painfully.

'Maybe this isn't such a good idea,' he said tightly.

'I'm so sorry, I didn't realise it was a medical issue.'

'Whatever are you talking about?' Scott picked up the top journal article from the bedside and held it up near his face, disembodying himself from his penis, as it were.

'Lots of men have erectile dysfunction, these days. It's nothing to be ashamed of.'

A door opened at the far end of the corridor and flat feet padded along.

'Shh! Talk more quietly.'

'Look, it's so not a problem for me. Do you want me to gi …' I tailed off as I saw Scott's face.

'I haven't got erectile dysfunction, you intrusive old hag!' he bellowed. 'Look!' There was utter silence in the corridor outside, until a stealthy creaking betrayed a door opening discreetly at the far end.

Scott drank some water. I concentrated on fumbling my white netting bra back across my damp skin as quickly as possible. My knickers felt grubby from the floor; my best black trousers would need a wash, too. I was pulling on my tee-shirt by the time I realised the furious heat inside was already cooling into a swelling lump of miserable grey clay.

'Can we … talk about this?'

'Look, do you mind going? I need to get on with these journal articles tonight.'

There was an awkward silence, while I found my sandals.

'See you tomorrow, then.' I trailed downstairs and let myself out into a lovesick, warm night.

The air was sultry and still and smelled of city dust. Conurbation-candlepower polluted the asphalt path, backlighting the dark shapes of trees. Here and there, lit windows pinpointed halls, scattered round the site like

Monopoly hotels. A floodlit modern building thrust into the darkness, like the silver prow of a ship.

I turned right to skirt one side of the playing field, heading for the road to my accommodation. The empty playing field stretched out, waiting. I paused, feeling a vague need, difficult to isolate from the clutter of hormones, misery and fury.

After a dithering minute, I stepped over the rope staking out the circular cricket pitch. Even in the dim night light, I could pick out the mower's herringbone lines on the lush lawn in the centre. The feeling swelled until I kicked off my sandals and joined the white boundary line.

At first my feet landed on warm, soft stalks of grass, but out from the shade of the trees, the warm turned into hard-baked clay. I ran, a painful burst of raw sprinting, punching the ground, until my breaths became gasps. I had to slow down then, into a loping jog which would get me round the rest of the circumference without stopping.

Three-quarters of the way round, I headed for the green. I hurdled the low rope staking it off from the public, and searched for the centre, as if it were a hole without its flag on a golf course. When I got there, I stood for a moment, facing the hall, feeling the velvety grass with my toes and wondering if I really had the neck.

'Go on,' said my Supergo, generous for once. 'You're worth it.'

I felt for my Acme Thunderer, but of course it didn't live in my pocket any more. I planted my legs apart, stood up straight and expanded my chest with a deep breath. Then I hollered my humiliation, projecting across the playing field and out to the far corners of the conference, from deep down my roots as a PE teacher. It sounded like Eliza Doolittle's screech, by the time it had lost its consonants to the darkness.

'WOODLOUSE!'

By the time the noise faded into the shocked silence inside my brain, I was halfway back to the path. Did I really make that wolf-like wail?

Leaves rustled in the undergrowth and a cat pushed onto the path. Tail low-slung, he ignored me as he trotted by. In his mouth, a small rodent's head flickered. At least Manx killed his prey. This cat must play with his victims until they died.

A security guard appeared a couple of hundred metres up the path, containing a jerky Alsatian on a chain. I froze. The cat merged into bush. The Alsatian growled. The guard barked back. I put my shoulders down and back, pulled my belly to my spine and started walking. The opening notes of *I will survive* flooded my ears as I approached.

'Evening, Miss …' He had a jocular belly bulging out his navy uniform shirt.

'Good evening.'

'Did you notice where that noise came from, just now?' The Alsatian twitched round the guard's legs, his aggression caged for the time being.

I concentrated on Calm. 'No … what noise?'

'Sounded like a werewolf at the full moon …' he winked at me.

'Oh, that …. It came from back there somewhere.' I gesticulated towards Scott's Hall, lightly sprinkled with lit windows.

'I'd better go and have a look. Academics! They're worse than the students.'

I dragged back to a lumpen, restless night. A fountain bubbled acid into my body parts, as I peered into the abyss.

4.10

On the first tick next morning, everything was alright. On the second, I remembered.

I checked my mobile, just in case.

Missed call! I'd managed to silence songs of innocence and experience, just when I most wanted to hear them.

'Hello. You just rang?' Thunder rumbled outside.

'Oh, good morning Nessie.' An arcane voice. 'Sorry to bother you so early.' It wasn't Scott.

'Who's that?'

'Edward. Thank goodness you rang back so promptly. Did you get the message?' Adrenaline clipped through my system. 'Er, no.' I wouldn't know how to look.

'Ah. Well, Margaret's gone to hospital with Paul.'

I was already alert to every nuance. 'What's wrong?'

'They left about half an hour ago.'

A block of fear whammed in, nearly winding me. The study bedroom vanished, as I concentrated on hearing every word. 'Whatever's wrong?'

'Paul's had an accident.'

'My God. Is he ...?'

'He's alright, but he's fallen off his bicycle.'

'Is he hurt?'

'Not too bad. He cracked his head.' I saw the fall, a mess of legs and wheels. 'Nasty gash. It will need stitching. We don't know how long he lay there unconscious, before the postman found him on his morning round.'

'Anything else?'

'Er, his leg's injured.'

My panic eased a quarter-turn. Was that all? 'Oh Paul. He's always coming off that mountain bike of his.'

Edward slaked my optimism. 'He doesn't remember anything about the accident. He didn't recognise us at all; he didn't know where he was. We called an ambulance, of course, but it was quicker to take him by car.'

'Where to?'

'They've gone down to A and E.'

'I can be down in an hour. Thanks for letting me know, Edward. I didn't expect this.'

Within half an hour, I was on the motorway spur, with Smartie at full throttle, in thunder, lightning and torrential rain.

***

Something in the doctor's white pocket jingled as she padded past the cubicle yet again.

'What happened?'

'The first thing I remember is ... seeing the triage nurse.' Paul was so pallid, I avoided looking at his face. I followed the scuff marks around the wall, like a tally stick for all the trolleys in the hospital, coming and going.

'Oh yeah. What did she do?'

'She looked at me and asked me a few questions. She said I probably had a broken leg, and … I might have a head injury.'

'What did she ask you?'

'Well, my name and address, that sort of stuff.'

'And did you know them?'

'Oh yes. Then she asked me who the Prime Minister was.' He smiled a greenish smile. 'I said: *that's a tough one.* That was a couple of hours ago. I'm feeling a bit better now.'

I laughed down my nausea. 'Forget Tony Blair ... do you remember who I am?'

His eyes closed again and he felt for my hand. I watched our fingers intertwine the way they always did, his large, competent, familiar hand, startlingly limp on the paper sheeting. The back was almost hairless. The veins stood out, where they'd developed from all the labouring work of the past few months. His nails looked cleaner, now he'd finished. On the outside of the palm there was a raw graze. Below that, a deep cut would become yet another scar.

I lifted my little finger away, so it wouldn't press on the open wound. That hand was my marriage. It blurred as I made a cradle with both of mine. I didn't know where to start making sense of it all.

'Do the stitches in your face hurt?' I whispered, after a while.

'No, the anaesthetic hasn't worn off yet,' he murmured, eyes still closed.

My eyes felt sore and my body heavy, now we were just waiting. I saw moonlit stripes of grass and heard my desolate wail, before the anguished ache rushed back. I'd rejected a man who'd loved me for more than thirty years, for a man who rejected me after two nights. My fury fragmented into grey shards of guilt and fear, sliding down to fill my stomach like slate on a spoil heap.

His faded, grotty socks weren't thick enough to sit inside builder's boots. 'What were you going to do today?'

'No idea.' He mulled it over slowly. 'No. Sorry.'

'Were you going to work?'

'I don't know. What work?'

'Don't you work at the university?'

'I can't remember.' He sounded frightened.

There was silence. My body submerged in a congealed jelly of panic. Icy spits of fear impaled what was left of my stomach. Paul's survival became overwhelmingly, urgently important. Would he slump into a vegetative state … in the next few hours? A familiar limp foot with uneven, gnarled toes poked out of the alien cellular blanket. Oh God, he might *die.*

'Would you like me to try to contact them?' I asked, bright as a social worker covering up bad news.

'I suppose that would be a good idea.' He opened his eyes long enough to ghost a pale smile.

It wasn't that difficult. I drew a blank at the university. Then I thought of the agency.

'Paul Elliott? Yeah, he's gotta contract with the university. I think he's on late shift this afternoon.'

'Yes, that figures. He was out on his bike early this morning, when he had an accident.'

'Thanks for letting me know. I'll 'ave to find another white van man.'

'White van man?'

'Yeah, van driver, love. That's what Paul Elliott does for a living.'

Click. What a sensible solution to the cash-flow famine. Why on earth hadn't he admitted to it?

Paul, portaged in the corridor on a trolley, waited for a bed. 'It's alright. I found out that you were driving a van for Tony Harris from the agency. I've made your apologies and said we'll let them know how it goes.'

'Fine.' He looked surprised.

'Paul, why didn't you tell me you were a van driver?'

He looked at me and laughed. 'Oww, that hurts.' Gingerly, he fingered the large black knots of the stitches.

‘Am I? Sorry, I can’t remember. Perhaps you could tell me why I’m a van driver.’

‘Well, you were made redundant, then you didn’t have any work for about nine months. Maybe you were a bit ashamed of taking on that sort of job.’

‘Was I? What did I do before …?’

I couldn’t put up with this memory loss malarkey for long. ‘Look Paul, if you hadn’t been around to rescue me on race day, I’d probably still be in prison, now.’

‘Did I really?’ He looked pleased, his head propped on a white pillowcase stamped Edinburgh Royal Infirmary.

I thought my own thoughts for a bit, about the way being the principal provider was ingrained in the male psyche. How bringing less money back to the cave inevitably meant a damagingly inferior status to said psyche.

‘I don’t know why you thought that,’ I proffered, eventually. ‘Being a van driver’s important, isn’t it? Otherwise, no-one would pay you to do it.’ Paul didn’t answer. It was probably a bit too philosophical for the headache he was developing.

4.11

'Now, no cycling until the leg's out of plaster.' The sister eased off the wheelchair brake with flick of her foot.

I pushed him outside, as if he were a new baby. We propped his left leg on pillows, in the back seat of Edward's BMW. I sat in the front, checking at regular intervals he hadn't slipped into unconsciousness. When we arrived home, I cooked organic salmon and vegetables, which I'd left ready in the fridge, hygienically cling film-wrapped.

'How long's the honeymoon going to last?' enquired Paul, as he tucked in to his local strawberries and cream.

'Oh, at least a couple of days, I should think,' I replied, my panic easing its stranglehold a notch. 'It's good to see you safely back home again.'

'In that case, I might try the tuba, for half an hour, to see if I can get away with it.'

***

'Haven't replied? What invitation, Mum?'

'I'm sure I sent it nearly two weeks ago.' Mum was tweaking the creamy lilies she'd brought Paul.

'Have you seen an invitation, Paul?'

'I'm sorry. Everything around the time of the accident has disappeared out of my brain. I've turned into a vegetable.'

'No you haven't. You'll remember it again, in a while,' I put down the tea tray.

'Maybe,' he eyed the flowers. 'Those remind me of a funer …' I poked his good leg. 'Aah.' He squirmed his bottom on the sofa and lumped the plaster cast over a centimetre. 'I'm really peed off being out of commission. I hope it's not for ever.'

'How much longer for the plaster?' asked Mum.

'Four weeks.'

'I wanted to ask you …' She started coughing, the most lung-racking cough I'd ever heard from her.

'Mum! What … are you alright? Do you need a drink?' I leapt over to rub the thin knobbles of her stooped spine.

'Yeah … No, thanks.' Ten seconds later she came upright, her face boiled red and sweaty from the effort. 'Yeah!'

'Mum! Have you picked up TB or something?'

She breathed in cautiously. 'I don't think so … dear. It's the … pollution … in Bangalore. But … seventy-five per cent … of the children in Bangalore … ' She breathed out carefully. 'Phfaw, that's better are … asthmatic.'

'Really? That's terrible …'

'Haven't you noticed *any* news this year, Nessie?' Paul looked shocked.

'Never mind that now, Paul. We've … ' Mum weighed up Paul's plaster like a piece of evidence. ' … decided to go ahead and get married. We don't know how long any of us have got. We might as well enjoy life while we can.'

'That's wonderful news. Congratulations!' I put the teapot down to hug her. I needed something to cheer me up. 'It … it … it is Wolfgang you're marrying, isn't it?'

'Of course, you silly girl. You don't mind, do you?'

Yes, congratulations, Ella,' echoed Paul funereally. 'I hope you'll be very happy.'

'So I'd like you to give me away, dear.'

'Give away my mother-in-law? Delighted.'

'Stop it, Paul! He doesn't mean it, Mum, he's been saying some really peculiar things since the accident. When are you getting married?'

'Three weeks Tuesday, in the city Registry Office. We've booked for 4.30. It was the only slot they had left. Wolfgang's children are bringing their families. I've got photographs of them on my website. I'll show you later.'

'Can Benjie make it?'

'Yes, it's the day before he flies to Ibiza.'

'And of course Leah's home the night before.'

'Yes, there'll be fifteen of us. I've booked the *Duck on the Water* for afterwards, for six o'clock.'

'That's wonderful. However did I miss all this going on?'

'Well since I got back, you've never been in when I've phoned.'

'Oh ... er ... What are you going to wear?'

'I don't know yet. I was hoping you might help me choose. We could go down to Debenhams tomorrow.'

'Of course I will. Are you going somewhere exotic on honeymoon?'

'Better than that, Nessie.'

'Really?'

'We're taking *Iris* off on a summer cruise.'

I smiled. 'Romantic summer nights under a starry sky?'

'The Birmingham Ring, I thought. After we get the plumbing properly fixed at Fenny Compton on the way. Very romantic.' Paul grinned over his mug of tea. Mum and I cackled together, until Mum's coughing fit started again and she couldn't get her breath. 'Wolfgang's ever so keen. He wants to travel the waterways of Britain in our own barge. And I thought: *why not?* It's not as if it's much of a carbon footprint, chugging along a canal. And you always meet such interesting people along the way.'

'Well, why not, then?' I echoed.

***

I had little time over the next few days for my dissertation. While Paul dozed at home, Mum and I bought three alternative dresses, just in case. When I cleared out *Iris*, the HRT packet reminded me of my daily dose, forgotten since the conference. Well, what good had it done me, anyway?

I wondered if Gareth had been impressed with the poster. Only two weeks, but the conference seemed far away. Not real life, like cleaning the shower cubicle. I squeezed out the floor sponge, pondering the exact nature of my current relationship with Scott. The dearth of e-mails didn't seem like he'd forgiven me for humiliating him. As for me, the memory was still a third-degree burn.

I chucked out herbs with long-gone sell-by dates. I repacked the galley locker with Mum's Indian saffron, cumin and coriander. My face burned chilli-hot at my insensitivity. Viagra? Oh noooo. How could I have thought that? My internal RAM crashed to avoid sinking in the stormy waters of that part of my brain.

'*Malvolio,*' my Superego shouted in my ageing ear as I wafted round with the furniture spray. I told it not to be paranoid, but I couldn't polish away my self-doubts, after such a rejection. In a week the barge was ready. I returned home to dissertation writing, to distract me from the morass in my mind.

***

Midge phoned. I switched channels. 'So, tell me everything.'

I described the highly-strung atmosphere of the conference, and meeting three eminent American and British professors.

'And what about Scott?'

'What do you mean?' I hedged. She couldn't see my flame-grilled face. I decided to *deny any recollection of the past.*

'Oh, nothing. … How did the poster go?'

'I've … no idea. You see, I got the phone call about Paul that morning, dropped the tube off at the conference centre and rushed off to A and E, so I wasn't there.'

'Well, Scott was missing last week. The Department's keeping quiet, but there's a lot of subdued sniggering going on about something.'

After a couple of hours, I decided to e-mail.

> *Hi Scott*
> *I heard there was a problem on the last day of the conference. I hope you put the right poster the right way up!*
> *I really enjoyed the whole conference experience, especially Monday night. Thank you for spending so much time with me.*
> *I feel I should apologise for what happened on Tuesday night. Paul had a bike accident. He was concussed, but his brain is slowly returning to normal. His leg is in plaster for four more weeks, so I'm working at home again.*

That afternoon the university server jammed with a virus. Two days later, a brief e-mail from Ron Rawlins asked me to call in, the following Monday.

***

When I went into the Department, Scott's door was open. The room was stripped of furniture, with indentations on the carpet from the filing cabinet and bookcase. Hundreds of daily footfalls had shuffled a worn green pathway from the door to his office chair. The inaccessible wall under the desk revealed undisturbed cobwebs. Underneath, nine years' worth of silvery paper clips lay abandoned. Notes in Scott's untidy handwriting jammed the white-board. The emptiness of the rest was shocking.

Vasulu came up behind. He started to sidle by.

I smiled brightly at him. 'How are you? How's your diss going?'

'Hi, Nessie. Very well, thank you. I'm hoping to be finished by Friday.' He poked his right elbow down his back with his left hand, stretching his overworked triceps, presumably. 'Then holiday at home, before I start again.'

'Start again?'

He smiled modestly and jiggled his goatee at me. 'Starting my PhD in October.'

'Oh congratulations, Vasulu.' I indicated the empty room. 'Where's Scott?'

'Oh, didn't you know? He's gone.'

'Already? I thought he didn't leave until the beginning of September?'

'After the conference, he departed immediately.'

'What? Why was that, Vasulu?'

'The poster … backfired.' He looked at me guardedly with his melting brown eyes.

Like Anne Elliott, I felt *a confusion of varying, but very painful agitation.* 'Poster?'

'The poster on mortality statistics, you know, displayed on the last day.'

'Yes?'

'There was a misprint which made mockery of him at the conference.'

'What do you mean?'

'The title was incorrectly reproduced as decreases in morality in older age, you know. Someone had made a mistake in the reproduction of it.'

'Oh no.'

'Scott was furious. Nessie, are you alright?'

'That was me.'

'No, Nessie, how can that be? Scott was lead author.'

'W … what happened?'

'Scott stood by the poster. I think he tried to pretend to … that it was no mistake, when they all came round. You know, the big American professor Gareth Anderson, yes, and his friends? They all laughed very much, when Gareth pointed out what it should have been.'

'There were two posters there. I got Print Services to correct the mistake, when I spotted it. Why wasn't the right one put up?'

Vasulu shrugged. 'There were a lot of people round during the allocated time. Maybe Scott didn't have time to notice.'

'Oh God, it was all my fault.'

'How can it be your fault, Nessie? It was his responsibility.' His curly eyelashes crinkled up behind his low-slung glasses. 'Don't cry, Nessie. It was not your fault.'

***

'Good afternoon, Nessie. Do sit down.' There was a chair ready in front of Ron's desk. 'How are you?'

'I'm … very well, thank you.' Spurious pleasantries made me nervous. They presage bad interviews.

'I've asked you here this afternoon for a short chat. I've had a complaint from a member of staff.'

Panic nudged. I frowned at him. 'What do you mean?'

'A member of staff has complained about irregularities in the data for your study.'

'Scott.'

'Yes.' Shit. My sins were visiting with a vengeance. I stared at Ron's precisely knotted tie. 'He has further complained that you brought him and the department into disrepute, by negligent editing of a recent poster.' This was a hammer-throwing version of events. My eyes travelled up to Ron's pleasant face. In a month the world had changed from idyllic to awful.

'But … the right poster was there. I can't understand how the wrong one was displayed. You know, I wasn't there to sort it out. My husband had an accident. I was called away from the conference.'

'Yes, I understood that, from your email to me.'

'It was an emergency, so I just dumped the tube off at the conference hall.' I did a double take. 'I'm sorry, what e-mail, Professor?'

'I received a copy of your e-mail to Dr Woodhouse.'

Holy shit. What had I said? 'Did he send it to you?'

'No, you sent a group e-mail round to me and other lecturers in the department.' I'd only ever made up one group list, but it started with Scott's name. Surely I'd deleted it? I dropped my head, trying to hide under the concrete floor.

Ron voice stayed level. 'Dr Woodhouse felt the action might have been vindictive, since you evidently had some kind of personal squabble at the conference.'

'No … no, of course I wasn't being vindictive. Both posters were in the tube. Surely Scott should have seen the correct one?'

'Since I wasn't there, I must try to understand your disparate accounts.' Ron didn't seem inclined to explore the e-mail any further. I squirmed, in preparation for whatever bigger issue was logically to follow.

'Dr Woodhouse relinquished responsibility as your supervisor when he left for his new post, ah, rather precipitately. I understand he took the view that your research results could be explained by a number of modifiers. I've had a look at your data.' Ron looked at me over his gold half moons like a disappointed cherubim. 'In my view, they are insufficient for the level of significance you claim for your analysis. This can't be explained by psychological factors alone. Have you any other explanations?'

'Well ... yes ...' He had a big clock on his wall. The minutes hand suddenly jerked two forward. I forced myself back to eye contact. 'I'm afraid the carbohydrate solution wasn't exactly as … described in the method.'

'What do you mean?'

The full horror of what I'd done finally sank in.

'Well, in the stress of the moment, we … I … no-one else was involved … added some alcohol … to make the solution the right colour. I think that would pretty much explain why the participants' well-being improved … so dramatically.'

The tunnel of turbulence in the room slowed and stilled in a blizzard of silence. I looked down. My fingers were outspread, like Sir Walter Raleigh's hand beside the chopping block.

Ron frowned. 'I see. Thank you for volunteering that information.' He sat back in his chair and fingered a blue glass paperweight, while he considered. It must have been less than a minute before he spoke, because the clock's hand didn't move again.

'There are three options, in my opinion. One is to repeat the experiment, having recruited new participants, and analyse the new data within the permitted time span, which is just under four weeks, now. The other ethical alternative is for you to withdraw from the course with the award of a diploma, for the credits you have already accumulated. The third option is to retain the current results and hope that the inaccuracy isn't noted, and ignore the ethical considerations. Except of course, that now I'm the first marker.'

I dropped my answer into his silence. 'I would like to finish the MSc, if ...'

'Don't decide now. Assess the implications first. Unfortunately Dr Woodhouse escalated the situation by demanding that you be excluded, and sent the Dean of Faculty a copy of his email to me. You'll have to argue your case before the Dean and secure his agreement to continue.' He stood up and shook my hand. 'Let me know tomorrow. If you want to continue, I'll book an urgent appointment with the Dean for you, for Friday.'

'Err ... thank you ... for your understanding, Professor.'

I imagine I exited the room. Time to use the mobile phone to put a message on Cathy's answerphone and call Midge. This was a Full-blown Crisis.

PART FIVE
Conclusion
5.1

Midge and Cathy came up together, with Freya and Harry in the back of Midge's fraying Corsa. We left the kids inside with Paul, experimenting with the tuba and a box full of assorted percussion instruments left over from Benjie.

'So have I got this right? asked Midge. Her decrepit deck chair hid the brown grass covering the new soakaway. 'You and Scott had some kind of argument at the conference, which left him thinking you would retaliate. This lead to a reprisal when he fucked up the poster display, which left you fighting for your academic survival. In the meantime, he goes swanning off to his new job, getting off scot-free.'

'Well, not quite. I think he may have lost a little academic kudos along the way.'

'Why? I'm sure researchers examine morality as well as mortality.'

'It's not that, Midge.' Cathy wore a tropical print dress. She looked coolly wonderful, despite the heat. 'It's the fact that he didn't check the poster carefully at any stage before he put it up. Since he was the lead author, it was his responsibility. And then he tried to fudge it, when it went wrong.'

'Vasulu said it wasn't very scholarly.'

'But why should he suddenly fly off the handle? What was this argument about? Did he rumble about your research data?'

'Do I have to say?'

'No,' said Cathy.

'Yes,' said Midge, at the same time.

'He was offended when I told him not to go so fast.' My hot flushes had come back with a vengeance, now I was off the HRT.

Midge stared at me with giant marbles instead of eyes. 'Are you saying what I think you're saying?'

'... and I thought he was on Viagra, which didn't go down too well.'

'Look, Midge, this is up to Nessie.'

'But we're her friends. I bet she hasn't told Paul.'

I shook my head. 'Paul doesn't know about any of this.'

'Somebody's got to look after her.'

'OK. You're right, Midge. So how does that leave you with Scott?' asked Cathy.

'I would imagine it leaves me all washed up … well, about everything.' I could hear myself wobbling. I gripped the plastic arm of my chair, hard. 'As for my dissertation, Alan Rathbone will throw me out, for sure. Do you remember, I fell asleep in his lecture, in the autumn term. He's never liked me, since … oh, maybe I should just send in my resignation and call it a day …'

'Does that mean, you want to finish your dissertation, if you can?'

'Of course I do. To give up would be an admission of failure as a real person.'

'Whatever are you talking about? You're a real person already.'

'Midge, you must know what I mean. *Othered* … that's what The Literature calls us mums. Always there for somebody else, so in the end, you're a monochrome person, not technicolour like everyone else.' My voice went squeaky with emotion. 'I thought the course was something I could do.'

Cathy paused, in case there was any more self-pitying crap to puke up. 'Can you sort out your diss, in the time?'

'It's basically all written now, and SPSS is set up, ready to go. I'd have to do the tests again, re-analyse the data and re-write the results and conclusion.' I paused. There wasn't really any alternative. 'Do you think anyone will be prepared to help, when they hear …?'

'I'll help, I'm free until the end of September!' Midge glowed sweaty concern.

'Don't worry about it. Data collection has to be repeated for all sorts of reasons.'

'Well, I've done it all once. At least I understand the stats, now. The biggest problem is getting more participants.'

'Won't Nick help you out with some arm-twisting?'

'Yeah. I could try him tomorrow.'

'*Can we fix it?*' chanted Midge.

'*Yes we can!*' My shame loosened a notch.

Cathy shook her head as she sipped her spritzer. 'When will you two grow up?'

'Never,' I said, more firmly.

'Surely you must've wanted to disembowel him?' Midge still hadn't finished with Scott.

'Yeah, I was pretty angry, when I realised what he thought of me. Come to think of it, I'm still pretty angry with him now, Midge.'

'He was a bastard to Rosa, too. Do you feel like taking it any further?'

'I … I don't think I can, Cathy. I persuaded him into …, you know, to start with. It's not as if he …'

'So, now you feel it's your fault this has happened, like it's your just desserts or something?' translated Midge.

'Mmm …'

Cathy leaned forward and smoothed the knee of my jeans. It was the first time she'd ever made any physical contact.

'My hypothesis is that it's fifty-fifty. You know, half your fault, half mine, in any dyad situation. It makes more sense to me than blaming the other person. We're both responsible to some extent, so the negotiations should start from there.'

'Dyad ...?'

'A pair connected in some way. You and Scott. You and Paul.'

'Well maybe for you ... but it was obviously my fault ...'

'Well, Scott didn't wait to hear what you had to say. He just assumed you were being vindictive.'

'True, that's what made me so angry.'

'That says more about Scott's character, than yours.'

'Scott was never open with you, Nessie. The word on the street is that he and Sarah Rees are an item,' put in Midge.

'No! Sarah! How can ... Oh ...' Yep, it had the dull thunk of truth winging in, weighed down by the accompanying evidence. My breath gave way. 'He was never open about anything, really.'

'I told you so! He's not half the man Paul is,' Midge sounded triumphant.

'So how are you feeling about Paul, right now?' interpolated Cathy hastily.

'Oh ... Paul's accident has overtaken everything else. I can't ... well, of course, I wouldn't leave him on his own. He needs me to be here, looking after him. That's my first priority.'

'He's first priority?'

I felt the tears well over. Midge catapulted out of the deck chair to give me a hug.

'Paul's my history, isn't he? You know …' I took a breath, dithering whether to tell them.

Cathy sat back in her hardwood garden chair, sipping her drink solicitously, letting Midge mop my eyes and stroke my arm. It was funny. I hadn't spent that many hours in the company of these two, yet now we were blooded by inspiration and perspiration, just as Kirsty had predicted at the beginning of the year.

'You know, years ago, we had a still-birth. Fern would've been twenty-four … if she'd lived. We had a funeral and all that. People were very sympathetic, for a time, but y'know, for evermore … it's there, it stays with you, through whatever happens afterwards and for ever afterwards it's … right down to the stuff with Scott, it was always part of me. In the end, nobody asks any more … the world moves on and you've got no right to keep whingeing. But Paul's always been … I don't have to say anything, it's part of him, too.'

'Like a long shadow that leant over your lives?' suggested Midge, really paddling now.

'Yeah … especially over our sex life.'

'Sex life …?' mirrored Cathy empathically.

'It was very …' I couldn't begin to describe the barrier of normality I'd grown to protect me from Paul. 'Then Scott came along to fill the vacuum. It was all so extraordinary … to know what to do.'

'People have such different values these days.' Cathy remarked sentiently.

'So the decision's to stay with Paul, warts 'n all, is it?' exploded Midge.

There was a silence, which allowed us to hear an orchestra of tuba, triangle and jingle bells in the background, playing a staccato version of *Twinkle, twinkle, little star*. 'I think … I think … Oh, fuck and double fuck. Yes, I'm expecting the patient to make a full recovery, in time. Both of us.'

5.2

Paul was unimpressed by my plan to put the passenger seat down so his leg could drape sideways across the boot.

'Stop pushing,' yelled Paul. 'That hurts!' He wore his best grey suit jacket and tie. The ten year old baggy jeans underneath were the only trousers that fitted round his plaster. 'Wind the window down.' He wiggled over to the driver's seat and craned his plaster up with two hands. Then he wiggled back across to the passenger seat. 'What do you think?' Paul's left foot dangled out of the window, his unplastered toes lodged against the wing mirror.

'Can you manage like that?' I shuffled through the debris in the boot. 'There must be something in the car to use as padding.'

'Yeah, I think so. It'll be cooler in this heat. We need to get going, anyway.' I tugged my Gardener's World waterproof jacket round the plaster and padded the window rim with my empty rucksack. They were both pretty tatty, now.

I drove a sedate fifty down the motorway, not wanting to crack either the glass or Paul's plaster. 'Boy, it feels good to be out of the house.' Paul lolled back in his seat like Mr Big. 'Look at those clouds. It's going to rain any minute.' He paused. '… You're quiet.'

'Yeah … sorry. Concentrating on my driving.' I knew I'd skirted round engaging with Paul. Busy salvaging damaged fragments out of my pulverized emotions. Too confused to connect.

The mobile rang. Paul looked down. 'It's Benjie.' He flicked it up to his ear with a teenager's ease. 'Hi Ben. Did you find her?'

Paul raised his eyebrows. 'Oh?' He listened. 'Thanks for picking them up. There was no hope of us getting up in time.'

I glanced over. 'Leah's plane landed fifteen hours late. Then they were searched in Customs for two and a half hours,' he relayed to me.

'Really? Well, maybe not a complete surprise … yeah, yeah.' He mouthed at me, 'She's got a man with her. But no baggage.'

'Who is it?' I shouted back at Benjie, but Paul was talking again.

'What do you mean?' Paul was smiling. 'Congratulations! You're joking, Ben. How can you not …?' A long explanation ensued. 'OK, OK, yes, I'm sure your Gran were rather you were there than … oh, twenty minutes? Yeah, see you soon.'

'What was all that about?'

'Can you go a bit faster, Nessie? We don't want to be late.'

'Who's driving, Paul?' Steady at fifty.

'Benjie and Leah are nearly there. Ben must've been flying down the motorway. Who would you like to hear about first?'

'Leah's man, of course!' The speedometer had jumped to seventy.

'All I can tell you, is he's an Australian called Glen.'

'Is that all?' I calmed down to fifty again. 'How long is he staying?'

'Dunno, I'm afraid, but he's bound to be at home with us tonight. Do we have spare toothbrushes?'

'Is that all?'

'What did you want me to ask, his gene history and bank account details?'

I smiled. 'At least.'

'And ...' Paul paused for maximum effect.

'And ...?'

'The good news is, Ben was out last night celebrating. He's passed his first year.'

'Brilliant! What a relief!' Oops, I was up to sixty-five again.

'He said he didn't have time to go back to collect his stuff from Nicky's house, after you rang.'

'Yeah,' I said absently, searching for a gap to edge out into the middle lane, so I could overtake a grimy French container lorry. 'So what?'

'The bad news is, he's had to come in his party gear. You heard what I said. I'm sure Ella would rather have him there, irrespective of what he's wearing. It's just bad luck Leah's plane was so delayed.'

I didn't need to overtake the lorry in front any more. 'Urgh, I hope he's not smelly from too much beer and sweat. Whatever will the new relations think?'

'Well, it's not just him. Leah and Glen will have been in flight for nearly forty hours. Nessie ... you're only doing forty, now.'

***

The traffic ground to a standstill once more at the city junction. In the mirror, my hair looked windswept and in need of a good trim, like the rest of me. I wished I'd had several weeks to smarten myself up.

'Hurry up, Nessie, you're holding everyone up,' said my co-driver.

'The traffic's only just moving again.' Rain pelted down. Our little submersible groped its way into the city behind frenetic windscreen wipers.

'Is the traffic always as bad as this? There's only fifteen minutes til the ceremony starts.'

'It's always slow like this when it rains, Paul.'

'We're going to be late.'

'I'll go in the multi-storey down the end of Broad Street.'

A car hooted as I turned right. 'Nessie, I don't think you signalled. Oh God, look at the queue to get in.'

'Hang on, I'll drop you here outside the Registry Office and park up. Wow, look!'

A Silver Shadow swished wet tyres up to the entrance in front of us. Holding an umbrella, the chauffeur opened the back door. Mum jumped out, ignoring his helping hand. She smoothed her beige frock and jacket, looking uncharacteristically like the Queen.

'Mum!' I tooted Smartie's horn. She waved.

Edging into a large puddle at the kerb, I stopped. Wolfgang appeared bent double, straightening himself up with the chauffeur's help. I wondered if he was suffering from a stag night. The bride rushed over and tried to open Smartie's passenger door.

'Careful!' I leapt out to support the plaster before she dismembered Paul's leg. Next thing, Ella and Wolfgang propelled Paul, swaddled tenderly in my waterproof, up the marble steps of the Registry Office. I was despatched to find a parking spot in the downpour.

Twenty-five minutes later I arrived back, sundress flapping round my legs like a wet kipper and wind-blown hair water-pressured to my skull. The walk back had chafed my wet feet against the straps of my back-of-the-wardrobe high-heeled sandals. Weaving between the guests of the previous wedding's champagne reception, I climbed the grand staircase. Shivering with cold, I looked back. A stream of drips trailed me from the doorway.

I took a prophylactic, calming breath before I dived past the mahogany panelled door into white and gold splendour.

'The place in which you are now met …' A few minutes later and I'd have missed the ceremony.

Mum stood at the front with Wolfgang. Leah glanced round and beamed at me. She looked different: tanned, harder, with matted dreadlocks and a faded grey tee shirt over a thin body.

As I slipped into the empty place next to Paul, Wolfgang's family collectively leant away. Looking at my motley crew, I could see why. The other side fielded immaculate wedding finery and three neatly-dressed middle-class children.

Paul was in jeans and plaster. I could smell Leah and the Australian stranger's crumpled travelling gear from where I stood. My new frock clung wetly to my body and my legs looked as if I hadn't bathed in months. Benjie looked the worst in his fancy dress. Well, I presume he doesn't wear a basque and fishnet tights to medical school every day, even with a lab coat over the top.

Paul glanced at my face and whispered, 'Rocky Horror theme … Sorry you had to get wet.'

'…binding character of the vows you are about to make.' The Registrar darted an irritated, sidelong glance at us before facing the happy couple sternly.

I looked at Paul's tight face. 'Are you alright?' I hissed back.

'… according to the law …'

'Shh … yeah.' The Registrar paused and glared at me. Leah raised her eyebrows warningly. I shifted onto the other stiletto heel and crossed my arms, chilly, bolshie and apprehensive.

'… is the union on one man with one woman voluntarily entered into for life to the exclusion of all others.'

Two people brought together and bingo, no further problems, I thought sourly. What's so wrong with late-flowering passion in the dull world of the happy-ever-after? Who's hurt by it, once the birds have flown the nest?

'I do solemnly declare that I know not of any lawful impediment …' Wolfgang looked dapper in a light suit with a bow tie and crimson carnation.

Mum smiled steadily at him, her pink eye shadow glowing against beige swirls of chiffon round her hat, risking all in her new venture. '… matrimony to Ella Rosalind Reynolds…,' Wolfgang finished.

'I do solemnly declare …' Mum launched off. And I was all for frittering it away. Until yesterday's revelation, that is. The last dregs of fury trickled down my legs. However could I have mistaken Scott's egotistical lust for the real thing, standing beside me?

I glanced at Paul's contorted face. 'What's wrong?' He shook his head. Somewhere outside, a burglar alarm launched a shrill, steady warning. Yes, I do want to care for you when you're old, I thought.

'… do take you, Ella Rosalind Reynolds to be my lawful wedded wife.' Do you still want me with you? Imagine no rock of ages, no dry wit, no warm feet. I slipped my hand through his arm. Even my engagement ring had dulled, these days. However hard I tried, tears were seeping through my eyes.

Mum glanced at me and smiled happily as she took Wolfgang's hand. 'I do solemnly declare …' Now she was making her vows, great globules suddenly rose up my throat and behind my eyes, like a lava lamp spewing out voluptuous bubbles of raw emotion.

'I call upon these persons here present to witness that I, Ella Rosalind …' I stood straighter, sniffing an indrawn breath. Paul slipped his handkerchief across, his teeth clamped together, staring ahead. What decision had he made?

I stood, tense as a pillar of salt, fighting for control. Was I too late? If I couldn't put things right now, we'd never stand in that strong family line again.

'…to be my lawful wedded husband,' finished Mum. I blew my nose surreptitiously. When I came too, they were kissing in a very businesslike way.

'What's up?' I whispered, as soon as we sat down.

'My leg …'

'Your leg? What's wrong?' I panicked, as Paul screwed his face tight for second.

'Shh.'

'Do you want me to call an amb …'

'No. It's this itching. It's driving me crazy.'

By the time I'd retrieved Smartie and located a wire coat hanger that would fit down the inside of his plaster, I felt as small as a squashed bluebottle.

***

We sat in a queue of cars, only a couple of hundred metres from the Registry Office.

Paul tweaked the straightened coat hanger to reach his itch. I looked ahead, where a drain cover had lifted and grey sewer-water gushed down the kerbside. In slow motion, the cars forded the flood, showering badly-placed pedestrians with muddy spray. I braced and turned to face the passenger seat.

'Paul, I'm truly sorry that I've been so horrible to you these past few months.'

'Horrible …? Aaah, that's better.' The scratching stopped.

I rubbed my hands over my face, to cover my burning flesh and the in-car silence. 'I … I don't know what came over me. I seem to have messed up all sorts of things, recently.'

Paul looked at me as steadily as anyone can, when they've had a couple of glasses of champagne on top of painkillers. 'Do you know, I thought it was the HRT. All those hormones pumping in can't do you any good. I'm glad you've come off it, even if you do grow a beard and go bald in the next six months.'

I watched the rain dripping onto his bare toes. 'There's something I should tell …'

'You know, Nessie, when I looked into it, I thought we couldn't possible afford to live apart. I knew you'd realise that too, in the end.'

My world stopped spinning. 'Oh?'

'All I needed to do was to give you a bit of freedom and … wait until you came round.'

'Just a matter of degree, then?' I echoed, sprinting home over the golden bridge he'd built for me.

'Yep. And a bit of persuasion. You're far too sensible to go off course for long. Not like some fictional heroine.'

'Right …' A small girl struggled to close her umbrella, now the rain had stopped. Her dad stooped down to help her.

'And I'm sorry, too.'

'Uh?'

'I was taking you for granted, wasn't I?' Hunched-up daisy petals began to open into the warm sunshine.

'Well …'

'I do still love you, you know.' Just for a moment, he looked at me like Jester had looked at Scott, all those months ago.

'Thanks. I still love you, too.' I leant into the stillness to kiss him. The earth moved back into its normal orbit. The car behind hooted.

'Right, that's settled then. Let's go. Better impress these new relatives with our witty conversation, if nothing else.' Before I'd even registered that the windscreen was misty, Paul was fiddling with the blower control. 'I'm starving after all that hobbling round. I wonder what's cooking at the nuptial feast?'

5.3

'I've decided I'd feel a lot better if I repeated the results.'

Ron nodded, his voice expressionless. 'I'll contact the Dean. We have some latitude. Come to me with any problems, but please don't ask for an extension.'

The next day, I climbed stairs, all six floors, marble chip then carpet, to the Dean's office. I waited for ten minutes, with a sense of impending doom that didn't feel anything like a heart attack. Voices rose and fell inside. Ron came out, closing the ash door with an expensively quiet click.

'You may go in, now.' He gave me a wisp of a smile. His suited figure disappeared down the stairwell. I crossed my fingers that he'd been a good egg, despite the frost.

I took a breath, knocked at the door and tiptoed in. Alan sat behind a large desk, with the sweep of the city behind him. Over the far side of the long room was a large, glass-topped conference table. Behind me, an L-shaped sofa stretched round the corner of the room.

'Good morning Mrs Elliott.' He sounded scratchy and ascetic. 'I've asked you here today to discuss the irregularities in carbohydrate solution administered to athletes during the course of your research.' He looked at me over his half moons. I stood as tall as I could, ready for Judgement Day. 'This is a serious breach of … Hmmph!' His fingers drummed the blotter. 'It's … aren't you … somebody … Masters …' I waited, perplexed.

He came round the desk and grabbed my hand with his flaccid fingers. 'Thank you, my dear, for looking after me so well on the day I collapsed.'

'Oh, I'd forgotten all about that. It wasn't too serious, I gather?'

'It was only a touch of sunstroke.' He lead me over to the grey sofa.

'I hope you've recovered now.'

'Well,' he confided, patting the seat for me to sit down beside him. His neck crinkled in scrawny turkey folds. 'I've been put on all sorts of pills and potions. Statins, diuretics and suchlike. I suppose you have to expect that when you reach our age.' His eyebrows winged out at me.

'Yes indeed.' I omitted to mention that I'd ditched my own particular medication only last week. Breathing was all of enough for me, these days.

'I cannot thank you enough. But for your prompt action …'

'It was no problem, er, sir.' I felt like a twelve year old on *Blue Peter*.

'What a splendid result for the run! Ron and I … hmmph …have just been looking at the number of unexpected Firsts in the experimental group.'

'Really?' Now he was back on course, his chest pumped up again. The stain on his silk tie was greener and chunkier than any I'd seen previously.

'Oh yes. Ron tells me that the median mark in the experimental group shifted from 68% to 71%. The external examiners were astonished. Remarkable, really, what a bit of exercise can do. Next year I'll be encouraging everyone to join in.'

'I'm pleased the race did some good.'

Alan smiled, so the dark circles round his eyes almost disappeared in softness and hairy eyebrows. 'I hear from Rosa that you were so good as to take care of Bertie, that day.'

'How is Bertie? I er …'

'Bertie is *very* well. He is blossoming with Rosa, you know. She has really taken his language development to heart.'

'It's a lovely age, once their personalities start to develop.'

'Yes. Bertie is *almost* making proper words. He makes the sounds and Rosa converts them into a word. Bertie and I have long conversations together. He even took his first steps earlier this week and he is *only* eleven and a half months!'

'That's wonderful!' Now I was on to a winning diversionary tactic, I plunged in. 'And how is his mathematical development?'

Alan leant back. 'Oh, the little chap has a real talent for mathematics. He can already bang two tumblers together.'

'I've always understood that maths and music abilities run in parallel.'

'Yes. Rosa and I are discussing how soon Bertie can start Suzuki.' Violin, I presumed.

'How is Rosa?'

'Much better. This has been such an unfortunate time, for all of us.' For a moment, he looked regretful. 'I'm hoping she will stay on with me and Bertie and re-start her MSc next year.'

'Really?'

'I know her parents. In fact … hmmph … I suggested Rosa's MSc course to them. They were most concerned at the inappropriate lack of pastoral care from … that man. Have you … hmmph … would you care to make any comment from your own experience?'

'The rest of the department are very caring, in my experience,' I said gently.

'Hmmph, they are. We really can't have students falling by the wayside at the drop of a hat, after such cavalier treatment. Especially not our overseas friends.'

'Er … no, I … definitely not.'

'I do hope we can persuade you to stay on to complete your degree?'

'Yes, I'd like to do that … very much indeed.'

'Good. Well, I'll inform … hmmph … Professor Rawlins.' His telephone rang. 'So nice to meet you again and have the chance to thank you in person, for all you have done.'

By the time I'd dived down six flights of stairs, I was giddy with disorientation and relief. But at least I was still standing.

5.4

Nothing is so good it lasts eternally …

Softens the edges of the dark silence in my nearly-empty house. I smile. It's 2 a.m., an old faithful of a CD and apt, for my last week as a student. Oh, it's been so good, this year. In spite of everything that's happened it's been a pearl of a year, glowing into the future against the darkening velvet of invading old age.

Gerron, Nessie! Only eight hours, one final all-nighter, to finish and print out your dissertation. Focus!

The conclusion won't be long, which isn't a good sign. The rest is ready. Not brilliant, maybe, but good enough. At 10 a.m. tomorrow morning, Print Services will set to work, so that I can slip in with a bound book, before I turn back into a rabbit or something.

The handout from the Powerpoint presentation is in front of me. It's concise, but the elegant presentation marks it out. Scott was always concerned with appearances and I … well, I suppose I was deceived by them, like a Titania, briefly woken from her afternoon nap.

… Wanting far too much … For far too long …

breaks through, rich and reproachful. But why shouldn't we be life-long learners, we baby-boomers? Isn't life-long learning Government-speak for mental health for the ageing and redundant? People, really, just like me?

… Here we are. The constituent parts of a conclusion are:

1. Summary of main findings
2. Explanations to account for findings
3. Limitations of data

4. Suggestions for future research

... Wasn't it good? ... Wasn't he fine?

Elaine soars over Barbara.

***

I completed the data collection, thanks to my friends. Darren and Nick found me twelve victims. I sat in the gym for fifteen and a half days, until I'd persuaded each volunteer to be tested three times, on non-consecutive days. Once, they ran without a drink, once with the 6.5% carb drink (I promise) and once with a visually identical placebo. The youngest was sixteen, the oldest seventy-three, and the most surprising, Ron's partner, David. I ended up with a nicely homogenised sample, which made me feel like a milkman. Ben helped with data analysis, once he'd sobered up from Ibiza and before he went back for his second year in London. Manx looks up at me from his sleeping spot next to the radiator and on top of my pile of papers. He yawns, as if he's totally bored with the whole dissertation process.

The effect size for the difference between the drinks was too weak to count. Ron wasn't surprised. He said the exercise made everyone much chirpier, which basically sums up the syllabus of the MSc course, if you're interested in taking it. Then there was the Hawthorne effect of Nick, Midge or Darren (depending on the participant's age and sexual propensity) encouraging them on the treadmill. My research is unlikely to take the academic world by storm. I expect it will just get shoved up on the shelf in the Cupboard of academic dreams.

... Isn't it madness?

The Faculty have nine academic articles in review as a result of Run for Results. The link between physical activity and examination success was an academic coup that went down well with middle England and the BMJ. Jonathan sparkled on The World at One. Last time I saw her, Jenny was mincemeating Jeremy Paxman on Newsnight. Kirsty looked sensational fielding the preliminary findings on national news bulletins. She's fronting the next series of Healthwatch, with Hugh as co-presenter.

***

I must get on, now. Quite apart from tomorrow's deadline, my new job starts on the first of October. Cathy found it. She hasn't admitted it yet, but Cathy would like the lectureship in the Department that's being advertised shortly.

The PCT were thrilled to find someone who had published on morality in the ageing population. I was the first person in my year to get a job, even with (or perhaps because of my advancing years). I don't really know much about advising on sexual health for the elderly, but Wolfgang and Ella have been very helpful. And I'm a pretty cool researcher, these days.

... Looking back I could have played it differently,

whispers in my ear.

... Learned about the man before I fell.

I notice Scott has been writing, too, in the *BMJ*, so maybe we'll meet up again sometime, in a professional sense. The anguished ache died away in the end, though I still can't walk past a pair of expedition trousers in Marks and Spencer, without frisking them surreptitiously for condoms.

Glen, the cognitive psychologist from Queensland, went home to his post-doc primate research.

I'm afraid I can't reveal anything about the training Leah started today in London. Perhaps the family mantle of mothering will pass to her, eventually.

Paul's fast asleep. He managed to play the whole of *God Save the Queen* this evening, and went to bed a happy man. He returns to work next Monday. I never did quite get to the bottom of his van driving problem, but he's cheered up, now I'm back home. We're talking for Britain, these days.

... *I know him so well.*

It was quite tricky, with Benjie and Leah up 'til all hours while they were both at home. We had to bribe them to go out together, the evening Paul's plaster came off. Something had definitely clicked back in place, after all that time.

Manx stretches ready to disappear for his night's hunting. Freud was right about sex and work being the mainstays of human endeavour, wasn't he? Even frightened rabbits have a-place-in-the-world. Of course, further research is needed. They always say that, in the Literature.

References

Err, Acknowledgements

Thanks are due to Barbara Large, MBE, Faculty of Arts, The University of Winchester (I think the initials stand for Master of Belief and Encouragement), who picked me up, dusted me down, edited the first draft and nudged me along to publication. Experts from the Winchester Writers' Conference and Pit-Stop Refuelling Writers' Weekends provided enthusiastic guidance, particularly Paul Bavister, Lorella Belli, Julia Bryant, Teresa Chris, Veronica Heley, Jane Judd, Catherine King, Judith Murdoch, Jane Wenham-Jones and Lucy Whitehouse.

Jonathan Harry, Wendy Arnold and Cecil Smith at RPM Print and Design made the mad dash into print possible.

The real people mentioned in my story gave their ready consent in the cause of health promotion. Thank you for willing support to clear the final hurdles, especially Sir Tim Rice and Dr James Prochaska.

The Wessex Conference Centre at Sparsholt College **(www.thewessexconferencecentre.co.uk)** are supporting the charity book launch and the work of SOS Children's Villages **(www.soschildren'svillages.org.uk)** will benefit from the generosity of many donors. Thank you so much, everyone.

Eastleigh College Community Education classes, under Tony Cook's direction, are a hub of lifelong learning. Thursday morning Writing for Pleasure and Profit classes continue to inspire me, especially the example of my feisty friend, Wolfgang, who appears as himself in the story. He personifies Saga Magazine's ethos: *you don't have to be young to be cool.* Please note, I have already cast Wolfgang as himself in the film.

Core body strength means strong in body and mind: try it at a Leisure Centre near you. Body Pump instructors Lisa and Karen are great motivators. Pilates instructors Ann, Maria and Angie: you made me stand tall. **www.slm-leisure.co.uk** are making Everyone

Active.

A red letter day of sea-kayaking is a great stress-buster. Calshot Activities Centre, one of Britain's largest Outdoor Adventure Centres, is situated in a unique position on the shores of the Solent, adjacent to the New Forest. Calshot offers courses for all ages and abilities in dinghy sailing, windsurfing, canoeing, powerboating, rock climbing, skiing, snowboarding, track cycling and Field Studies. **www.calshot.com**

And then there's my local branch of Home-Start, the UK's leading family support charity, which provides a unique service for families, recruiting and training volunteers to support parents with young children at home … and we have a good time, too. Find out more from **www.home-start.org.uk/supporting us**, (which I will be doing with every copy of the book sold).

In pursuit of the story, I'm indebted to family and friends. My daughters provided real-life incidents and accepted the chaotic fictional consequences with grace and good humour. Thanks, Jill, Sandy, Rosie, Lucy, Wendy, Jacqui, Debs, Margaret, Jane, Ian, Kathleen, Tony, Shirley, Peter, Louise, Deb, Nic, Dee, Peter, Owen, Carol, Dianne and Robin for devil's advocacy, technical support, literary criticism, style counsel, hairdressing and environmentally-friendly gardening advice. Most importantly, my husband, always a *bricoleur extraordinaire,* turned heuristic co-researcher then backing angel to self-publish this book.

So many citations … so much help.

Long live do-it-yourself!

Zoe Simpson
February, 2008